RETURNING TO ROCKPORT

KELSEY CLAYTON

First Edition November 2019

Book design by Kelsey Clayton

ISBN 9781711766454

www.kelseyclayton.com

To my bonus mom, Weslie.
Thank you for saving me, for always believing in me, and for loving me unconditionally.
You're my saving grace and I love you.

WARNING

This book contains a love triangle, a tormented heroine,
cheating/infidelity, and a whole lot of angst. It may not be
suitable for all readers.

PREFACE

If I had known what would transpire, I never would have gone back to Rockport – or perhaps I wouldn't have left in the first place. From the moment that I stepped foot back in my hometown, a part of me knew it was going to be an unforgettable summer. Everything reminded me of him. I could still smell the salt in the air that used to cling to his skin and mix with his cologne; could still picture the places we went together, hidden away from the inquisitive onlookers of the small town. It was pure ecstasy. Unfortunately, most good things don't last forever, and the same was true for him and I. We ended in a fiery mess of hurtful words and teary eyes, and when I drove away from the house that final time, I never intended on going back – until I did. Only this time, I wasn't alone.

From Romeo and Juliet to Pride and Prejudice, I've always been one for romance novels. There's just something captivating by the way the characters feel so intensely for each other that they're willing to risk everything for it. Even as a kid, fairytales were always my favorite. The idea of someone loving me more than life itself has never lacked a certain appeal. Unfortunately, what you don't learn in the books is that happily ever after isn't guaranteed, and nothing can prepare you for how you'll feel if it doesn't work out.

The pain of living without the one I thought would last forever is all too fresh in my mind, despite the four years that have passed since the day *he* walked out of my life. I can practically still feel the way my chest ached from the void he left behind. The words from our last encounter replayed in my head for weeks as I tortured myself with wondering if I could've done something differently. The conclusion was always the same – he was gone from my life and I needed to come to terms with that. Since then, I've learned how to let people in just enough to satisfy them, but not give them the ability to hurt me.

"Hello? Earth to McKenna." Julia waves her hand in front of my face, pulling me back to reality.

"I'm sorry, what?"

"I said, I can't believe we're moving out."

My eyes glance down at the box I've been placing the last of my belongings into. It feels like the last four years have gone by so quickly, I've barely had enough time to enjoy them. Julia has been my roommate since freshman year. Needless to say, we have seen each other through some hard times and we've only become closer because of it. Now we're leaving this place and I won't have her right by my side by anymore.

"Can't we just stay? Convince the housing office that living here is essential to our mental health or something?"

A small giggle leaves her mouth. "I don't think your fiancé would appreciate that." She grabs my left hand and admires the ring on my finger before letting out a dramatic sigh. "I'm going to miss this beautiful rock."

"You could always come with us." The familiar British accent echoes into the room, causing both our heads to turn.

Parker is leaning against the doorway looking just as gorgeous as ever. His blonde hair is perfectly styled in a way that screams confidence. He's dressed in jeans and a button down, making for a well-rounded mix of casual yet sophisticated. I can't help but smile as I look at the man I've agreed to marry.

"You're early."

He crosses the empty space, placing his hand on my hip and pressing a kiss to my forehead. "I couldn't stay away any longer. Are you ready to go, love?"

Not even remotely close. The thought enters my mind but I don't dare to say it out loud. Instead, I look around the room at what was once perfectly decorated. Now, it's bleak and bland, lacking any sign of the happy times that have been spent here.

"Almost. Finishing up this last box, but the rest are done."

"These?" He gestures toward the stack at the end of my bed. Once I nod, he grabs one off the top and flashes us one of his dazzling smiles. "Okay. I'll bring them down to the truck while you say goodbye to our dearest Jules."

As soon as he leaves, I stick my bottom lip out at my roommate. "He's right. You could come with us."

She groans and throws herself onto my bed. "I wish. Are you sure he doesn't have a brother?"

"If he did, I think Ivy would have snatched him up by now."

"Yeah, you're probably right."

Julia was with me when I met Parker nearly two years ago. She had pulled me out to a party neither of us had any business being at. It was across town at Columbia University. I tried to talk her into going elsewhere, but she wasn't having it. She won by getting me to go, and I won by drinking my body weight in alcohol. By the time that I ended up next to the blue-eyed beauty, I was drunk enough to make fun of his pretentious looking outfit; just before I spilled my drink all down the front of him. It was an encounter that should've been caught on film, but I'm more than glad it wasn't. I sputtered hundreds of apologies while he just gazed at me like I placed the stars in the sky.

Having only the fact that I was wearing an NYU sweatshirt to go off of, he spent weeks trying to find me in the overly populated city. It wasn't until he ran into Julia at another party that he managed to get my phone number. After numerous attempts at asking me out and a long lecture from my best friend, Ivy, about the importance of giving someone else a chance, I finally agreed to a date – my first in almost two years at that point.

To say things have been smooth sailing from there would be a lie. With my trust issues and tendency to push people away for the sake of self-preservation, he's had to do more than his fair share to make our relationship work, but he's never faltered. At this point, I'm not sure anything could scare him away, and he proved as much when he got down on one knee after graduation. He had this look in his eyes that provided a sense of security when I needed it the most. That, paired with his promise to love me for the rest of our lives, had me saying yes without a second thought. After all, that's what I've been longing for isn't it – someone to love me with everything they have?

"I'm still shocked he convinced you into moving back home." Julia remarks, propped up on her elbow.

I place the box on the floor and sit beside her. "Well, what was I supposed to say? No, we can't because I've been avoiding my ex for close to half a decade?"

"No, but you could have suggested getting a place in Boston."

My head shakes rapidly. "I've lived in a city for far too long. I'm over it. I could use some small town living back in my life. And besides, his time is going to be consumed by med school. It'll be nice having friends and family around."

"And if you see C-"

"I don't want to think about it."

"McKenna." She says my name as a warning. "The likelihood of you running into him is almost a guarantee. You need to be prepared for it."

"I know and I am, sort of. I'm just going to wing it. It's been years and I'm engaged now. What's the worst that could happen?"

She gives me a look that tells me everything she wants to say, but thankfully keeps her comments to herself.

After saying goodbye to the people I've grown to depend on, Julia being the hardest to handle, I follow my fiancé down to the truck. The back is loaded up with boxes of our belongings, and the gas tank is filled in preparation for the five and a half hour drive we have ahead of us. Tears build in my eyes as we pull away from the building. I try to quickly wipe them way but Parker notices. He reaches over and places a comforting hand on my thigh. It's just the right amount to show me he's here if I need him, but gives me the space to make that decision on my own.

THE RIDE IS SPENT listening to music, making jokes about passing cars, and just enjoying our time together. One thing I've always admired about him is his ability to make me laugh, even if it takes making an utter fool of himself to do so. I'm leaning back with my feet on the dashboard when a familiar sign catches my eye.

Welcome to Rockport
A Seacoast Village on Cape Ann

My heart starts to race as I realized I'm back in my hometown for the first time in four years. Everything looks just like I remember it – the ice cream store I've walked to with my closest friends; the boats that fill the docks; the buildings that could almost be considered historic landmarks by now. I find comfort in the way everything hasn't been torn down and rebuilt to become something fancier. This is the town I've loved since I was young.

Pulling into my parents' driveway, I watch as my mother stands from her seat on the porch. Her eyes light up as we park the truck and climb out. I barely have a moment to admire the house I grew up in before she's tugging me into her arms.

"I've missed you so much."

"Mom." I chuckle. "You just saw me last week."

"Nonsense. You're my baby girl. Any time away from you is too much." She releases me from her tight hold, only to say hello to my fiancé. "Parker, it's nice to see you again."

"You as well, Mrs. Taylor."

"Please, we've gone over this. Call me Marissa."

"Right. My apologies."

He must be able to sense my hesitation because he takes my hand in his as we follow my mother inside. The house looks exactly the same, with the exception of the new couch that occupies the living room. Pictures of my older brother and I hang all over the walls, making it obvious that a family lives here to anyone that enters. I must admit, I've missed the feeling of being home.

"Hello Sweetheart." My father greets me as he walks down the hallway.

"Hi Dad."

A small frown graces my mom's face before she masks it with a smile. Instead of acknowledging the elephant in the room, I ask for a glass of her homemade iced tea and excuse myself to my room. Parker follows me up the stairs and through the familiar door. Everything is just as I left it. Even the hairbrush I forgot to pack lies perfectly in the middle of my dresser. Not a single thing has been moved.

"So, this is your childhood bedroom."

Crooked posters remain taped to the light gray walls. Photo booth strips of Ivy and I are still tucked into the sides of the mirror. The pale pink duvet still covers my queen size bed. Even the clothes I left behind are right where I left them, hanging in the closet.

"This is it."

He grins and pulls me toward him. "I like it. It's very, you." A feeling of warmth spreads through me as he kisses my cheek. "I'm going to go ask your dad where I can put the boxes."

With one last embrace, he disappears down the stairs. My eyes drift to the picture on my nightstand. I pick it up and use my sleeve to wipe the dust off. It was taken at the beach. I'm standing in the middle of two familiar guys; my brother and *him*. Both their arms are around me as we all smile brightly. My hair was a lighter brown than usual, the summer sun lightening it as it does every year. The jade in my eyes seemed to be especially bright that day. A dull ache in my chest builds as my eyes focus on the right side of the photo. His wet hair looks like he just ran his fingers through it to keep it out of his eyes - the oceanic pools that glisten in the sunlight. It's something I was glad got captured in the picture. I glide my finger over his hair and down the side of his face, remembering the feeling of him all too well.

"He asks about you all the time, you know."

At the sound of my mother's voice, I startle and drop the picture. It falls to the floor and the glass instantly cracks into pieces. Sighing in frustration, I pick up the damaged frame and put it back in its place.

"Don't." It's meant to sound strong but it comes out as more like a plea.

She gives me a sad smile and hands me the drink I requested. "Okay, okay. I won't mention him again. I just hope one day you'll tell me what happened between the two of you."

Despite our close relationship, the idea of telling my mom the events that lead to my heart being shattered, triggers a flight instinct in my brain. I do my best not to let it show and return to looking around the room.

"I can't believe you kept everything the way I left it."

"Why wouldn't we? As far as I'm concerned, this is *your* bedroom."

I give her a knowing look. "Is Maverick's still the same, too?"

"That's different." She waves dismissively. "His only became a guest room when he moved all of his stuff out and into his own house. You should see the place. He's really done well for himself."

The thought of my brother makes me smile. Being three years older than me, he was always my protector growing up. We fought like siblings usually do but loved each other all the same. I've missed him a lot. Only getting to see him over Christmas break hasn't been nearly enough time.

"Yeah, I'm meeting with Tatum tomorrow." Referring to his long-term girlfriend. "I spoke to Parker about hiring her to plan the wedding and he's completely onboard."

"That's great, honey. I'm sure she's thrilled." After the room goes silent, my mom exhales. "Could you do me a favor and go a little easier on your dad? I hate to see how distant you two have become."

"Mom." I whine. "I don't know if I can. Every time I look at him, I see that woman. He hurt you. I don't think I could ever forgive him for that."

"But I chose to stay with him. Don't let yourself believe I let him get away with it without repercussions. He's done a lot of work to earn my trust back. We're finally in a good place again."

"And I'm happy for you, I am." When I don't say anything else, she gives me a look that causes me to groan. "I'll try, but I make no promises."

"That's all I ask." She stands from my bed and walks to the door. "I'll be in the kitchen when you're ready to come down."

As soon as she's gone, I throw myself backwards onto my bed. The memory of the last time I slept here is in the front of my mind but I do my best to ignore it. I was eighteen and a completely different person then. I'm stronger now.

THE VOICE OF ONE of my favorite people booms through the house. My smile lights up when Ivy comes into the room, looking just as gorgeous as ever. Her blonde hair cascades over her shoulders and down just a few inches. The amount of poise that she possesses has always been something I admire. That girl can own a room like nothing I've ever seen.

"Missed me?" She smirks.

I jump out of my chair, running over and barreling into her. Her arms wrap around me as she chuckles softly. Every part of me that has been on edge since I got here, calms in an instant. I can't remember a time where she wasn't able to pull me from the verge of a mental break down. She's my better half and I'm so thankful for her.

"Hardly." I joke.

"I can tell."

My mother gets up from her seat and gives my best friend a hug. "Did you give your mother the cookies we baked last week?"

"I did. She loved them, as always."

My eyes narrow in slight confusion. "You bake cookies with my mom?"

Ivy grins widely and nods. "Every Saturday."

The look on my face must be enough to say it all because my mom starts to laugh. "Don't look so surprised, dear. You'd know all about it if you happened to come home during *any* of your school breaks."

I should have known this topic would come up eventually. My tendency to stay away wasn't because I didn't want to come home. There has never been a time where I didn't love this place. I just couldn't handle seeing *him*. So instead, I spent my spring breaks in various places with Julia and my summer vacations abroad with volunteer organizations. Thankfully, we spend Christmas every year at my

9

grandmothers in Vermont – a safe zone for me in some sense. Only seeing my family one week a year was never easy to deal with, but it was what I needed.

"Yeah Mac, don't look so surprised." My best friend playfully nudges me before focusing her attention on my fiancé. "Hey Parker. How are you?"

"I'm great, and you?"

"Still swooning over your British accent. When are you going to hook me up with one of your friends?"

"When you come to England with me."

She purses her lips and nods. "I really need to get on that."

The four of us sit around the kitchen table, talking about anything and everything - just enjoying each other's company. However, I can tell there is something on Ivy's mind. When my mom asks for Parker's help with something and they walk away, I raise my eyebrows at her.

"So, you going to tell me what's up or are you staying tight lipped?"

Her shoulders shrug and she gives me one of her caring smiles. "I'm just wondering how you're doing, being back here and all."

This is one of those things that makes her my best friend. No matter how convincing an act I put on, she can always see right through it. It's almost as if we're linked – whatever I feel, she does too.

"I'm okay. I've actually missed it here, believe it or not."

"Have you seen him yet?"

I don't need to ask to know who she's referring to, but just as I'm about to answer, Parker comes back into the room. His eyebrows furrow slightly.

"Seen who?"

"My brother." I lie, watching Ivy muffle a laugh at how quickly I covered that one.

"Ah. We're going there tomorrow, right?"

I nod. "Yeah, we have to discuss wedding plans with Tatum."

The look on Ivy's face tells me she wants to say something, but ultimately, she decides against it and masks her frown with a smile. I don't have time to question it before my mother comes in with stacks of embarrassing photo albums in her arms.

Whatever it is, it'll have to wait.

2

THE SUNLIGHT PEAKS THROUGH THE BLINDS AND lands softly on my face, waking me from my peaceful slumber. For a moment, I forget where I am until it all comes flooding back to me. The drive from New York City to Rockport, Massachusetts, seeing my bedroom again for the first time in years, laughing at memories with my mom and Ivy for hours; I'm home.

I open my eyes and lift my head to find Parker just beginning to stir. His hair is free of any product, which is rare for him. Using the moment to my advantage, I grab my phone and snap a quick picture. Just as I'm looking it over, he opens his eyes.

"What are you doing?"

I smile guilty. "Nothing."

"Did you just take my picture?"

"Maybe."

He rolls his eyes but pulls me down into a light kiss. "What am I going to do with you?"

"Love me forever?"

"That is what I promised, isn't it?" He takes my left hand into his and rubs his finger over my engagement ring.

"Having second thoughts?"

"Not even remotely close. I love you, McKenna."

"I love you, too."

It's true – I do love him, in the best way I know how. Parker's good to me. He holds me when I need it, yet still gives me enough space to feel in control. To be honest, had he not been so patient and persistent, I'd probably still be single to this day. I don't know where I would be if that were the case. Perhaps I'd be on another volunteer mission or convincing Ivy to move with me to Nashville; something we've talked about since we were younger. Regardless, I don't think I'd be back here. I wouldn't have the courage for it.

"I'm going downstairs. Are you coming?" I stand from my bed and run a brush through my long brown hair.

He stretches and yawns before answering. "I'll meet you down there."

I give him a bright smile and leave the room. The smell of bacon wafts into my nose as soon as I reach the bottom step. My favorite aroma of french toast comes immediately after. I can't help but feel that sense of comfort you get from being home. It's something I've really missed the last few years.

When I get into the kitchen, I find my mom standing in front of the hot stove, moving food around like some kind of professional chef. Ivy must be teaching her some things when they get together on the weekends. Having just graduated from culinary school, cooking is a passion of hers – and something she does incredibly well.

"Morning, Mom." I walk around her and reach into the third drawer, pleasantly surprised when I find my apron still perfectly folded inside. My mother smiles as I slip it over my neck and tie it behind my back. The second our eyes meet, I realize she's about to cry. "What?"

"Nothing. I'm just glad you're home. I've missed you around here."

I grin in return and bump my hip into hers. "Don't be

such a sap. It's too early for overwhelming emotions. At least let me have a cup of coffee first."

"Since when do you drink coffee?"

She looks genuinely surprised, though I'd be lying if I said she was the only one. Ever since the first time I tried coffee, I despised it. The bitter taste on my tongue was never pleasant for me. I've always been more for sweetness. It wasn't until Parker insisted on meeting at a small café in the city, that I actually started drinking it.

"Uh, since like a year or so ago, I think. When you have exams to cram for, doses of caffeine become lifelines."

"Fair enough." She goes back to flipping the french toast and making sure the scrambled eggs don't stick to the pan. "So, what are your plans for today?"

I take the freshly washed strawberries from the bowl and start to slice them. "We're going over to Maverick's. It'll be nice to see him again and I need to talk to Tatum about wedding stuff."

My mother stills and then exhales slowly. "Honey, there's something you should –"

"Good morning." Parker greets my mom as he walks into the room and whatever she was going to say goes right out the window.

She gives him a warm smile. "Hi darling. How did you sleep?"

He places a kiss on my cheek before taking a seat. "Like a baby. Your home has a cozy feel to it. It's very welcoming."

"You know, I've always said the same thing. It's the reason I chose this house in the first place."

"Speaking of houses," I interrupt. "We have a meeting with the realtor scheduled for Wednesday."

"You could always just live here." My mom suggests.

I sputter on my hot coffee. "Yeah, no. I actually *like* you and if I live here for too long, it could damage that."

"Nonsense. You're my baby."

That's exactly my point, I'm *not* a baby. Instead of arguing it further, I focus my attention back on my fiancé. "Anyway, please don't forget. The only other opening she has this week is Friday."

He nods. "Friday I have a meeting at Harvard and then we have our engagement party, so Wednesday it is."

Shit. I almost forgot about that. Will *he* be there? Who am I kidding? He's Maverick's best friend. I'd be stupid to think he won't be. *Ugh, focus McKenna.* "Okay. I'll confirm with Jessica."

Ignoring the pout on my mom's face and making a mental note to check who Tatum has on the guest list, I go back to helping make breakfast – though I'm not so hungry anymore.

WE PULL UP TO the two-story house and I'm blown away by it's beauty. The light gray cedar shakes mix well with the cliché white picket fence. The bay window that sits in front tells me it was designed with Maverick in mind. He's always said how he wanted a window he could sit in and watch as the rain poured down. The fence however – that must have been all Tatum.

Before I make it out of the truck, my brother is barreling through the door and down the steps, wrapping his arms around me as soon as he's close enough. I return the embrace and find my entire body relaxing. He's never lacked the ability to make me feel safe, even in the most chaotic of places.

His hair is a bit darker than mine but our eyes are identical. When I was a kid, people used to say we looked so much alike. Thankfully, as we grew, our differences became more apparent. There is no better ass-backwards compliment than someone telling you that you look like your brother.

"I've missed you, Squid."

Despite my initial reaction to cringe at the nickname, a part of me has missed it. It's something he's called me since I was a kid. I'm not even entirely sure of where it originated, but it's one of those things that just stuck. My parents went with it for a little while but stopped when I hit puberty. Maverick, however, rarely calls me by my real name.

"I've missed you, too." I turn to see Parker coming around the truck. "You remember my fiancé."

"Of course, the dude who's banging my baby sister, how could I forget?" Now *that* makes me cringe. Maverick notices the immediate tension and starts laughing hysterically. "I'm just fucking with you, man. Nice to see you again."

"You as well." He shakes my brother's hand in that professional way he does.

A part of me wonders if the two of them will ever become close, but I just don't see it happening. Parker comes from a very wealthy family in England, and with wealth comes rules. He's grown up believing that your image is everything and every action defines you. The only time I've seen him let loose is when it's just the two of us. Meanwhile, Maverick and I were taught to express ourselves and that we should enjoy life while we can. The difference in personalities works for Parker and I, but I think it's just too much for Maverick to handle.

"Come inside." He grabs my hand and pulls me toward the door as my fiancé follows dotingly. "You're going to love the place."

The second we step through the door, I can tell he's right. It's cozy yet modern. Down the hallway, the living room has vaulted ceilings that make it feel spacious. A white brick fireplace is stands perfectly in the middle of one wall, and in the back of the room is a floor to ceiling double door; displaying the oasis looking backyard.

I follow my brother through the house and into the kitchen. My jaw drops when I take in all the sleek looking

17

appliances and white marble countertops. There's a smoky glass door that leads out to the patio on one side, and an entrance to the dining room on the other. The main thing that catches my attention are the rose gold knobs on all the gray cabinetry. It adds enough to the room to keep it from being bleak without looking gaudy. Whoever added those is a genius.

When we enter the living room again, I take it in from another angle and notice a staircase we must have passed on the way in. It's discreetly hidden into one of the walls, leading up to the second floor that overlooks the large space. The child side of me wants to put a trampoline in the middle of the room and jump onto it from the balcony.

"Nothing special about the upstairs, just a few bedrooms, but yeah – this is it."

"It's amazing, Mav. I'm really proud of you."

My brother had a tough go of things for a while. He couldn't seem to figure out what he wanted to do with his life. One day he decided that what he *did* want, didn't exist yet. He decided to raise a startup company from the ground. For a while, I didn't think anything would become of it but he managed to make it work and became very successful. I couldn't be any prouder.

The three of us sit on the couch and catch up a bit. He asks if we're going to be staying with mom until Parker graduates from medical school – an idea I quickly knock down. It's not that I don't love my parents. I just know that if we continue to stay there longer than necessary, the closeness I have with my mom will start to become tainted. We're two very stubborn people and even before I went away to college, that caused us to clash.

Footsteps coming down the stairs pull my attention away and I smile when Tatum enters the room. I usually don't like red hair, but she manages to pull it off. It curls at the ends, the same way mine does, but hers is just a bit longer – going all the way down to her belly button. I don't think I could handle my hair being *that* long.

"McKenna! It's so good to see you."

I stand up to give her a hug. "You, too."

After she says hello to Parker, she grabs a large binder from underneath the coffee table and takes a seat across from Maverick. The two of them have been dating since their senior year of high school. We've had our fair share of differences. I was only fourteen when they met, and while my brother liked when I was around, she didn't. It took until I was older before I understood her possessiveness. Since then, we've gotten along great.

"What is *that* monster?" I ask, referring to the book.

"Your wedding." Maverick deadpans.

My eyes widen as I quickly become overwhelmed. She can't possibly expect me to look through all of that. I think she senses my hesitation because she snorts.

"Relax, hun. It's mainly just a bunch of choices and color swatches."

"Oh." I release a breath I didn't know I was holding.

She gets right down to the details, getting them out of the way as soon as possible. "So, what date were you looking at again?"

"September 21st"

"Of next year?"

"No, this one."

Tatum chokes on air and coughs. "And that's not negotiable?"

I shake my head but Parker answers her with his typical professionalism. "My nan is not doing well, and I'd very much like for her to be in attendance at the wedding."

Her eyes soften in understanding. "Okay, September 21st it is. It won't be easy, but we can make it work." She opens her phone up to the calendar. "Mac, I'm going to need to get you into a dress boutique within the next two weeks to make sure we have time for alterations."

"That's fine. Whatever you need, I'll make myself available."

She smiles, then turns back to Parker. "I assume you already have a tuxedo?"

"That's correct."

We go over a few more minor things, such as when we can go looking at venues. It needs to be soon in order to find somewhere that isn't already booked for that weekend. In the end, we decide it'll be best for Tatum and I to go on Tuesday. Parker will be at Harvard to handle some things with his enrollment, but he trusts my judgement.

Just as she slips the binder back where it was, the sound of the front door opening and closing has her looking at me like a deer in the headlights. It isn't until I hear it that I understand why.

"Mav?"

My whole body tenses instantly. I'd recognize that voice anywhere. After all, I've spent enough time listening to it whisper sweet nothings into my ear.

"In here!" He yells back.

I'm not even sure if I'm breathing. Tatum is watching me carefully, being only one of few who knew about the two of us. Maverick, however, still has no idea. I try to play it cool but I'm dying inside.

Before I even have a chance to compose myself, he walks into the room looking every bit as gorgeous as I remember, yet still slightly different. His light brown hair is just a little longer. He's put on some muscle in his arms, but not too much. Stubble coats his cheeks, making him appear older. I guess technically he is. He's *four years* older than the last time I saw him.

He smiles at Maverick and Tatum, but when his eyes land on me, they widen. "McKenna."

"Colton, hey." My voice comes out squeakier than I intended.

Crossing the room with ease, he pulls me up and into a hug. As if it's a natural reflex, I breathe in the smell of him. He's essentially the same guy I fell in love with so many years ago. His chest feels exactly like it used to as my head rests against it.

He hurt you. He hurt you. He hurt you. No matter how many times I repeat those words in my head, my heart is doing summersaults while his hand rubs my back. Being in his arms always was my favorite place.

"When did you get back?"

I remove myself from his hold and run my fingers through my hair. "Yesterday."

"Oh wow. It's really great to see you." His attention turns to my fiancé. "I'm sorry, she's rude." He quips and puts out his hand. "Colton Brooks."

"Parker Hall." They shake in a way that looks like a contest of 'who's manlier' but I can't determine the winner. "McKenna's fiancé."

Tatum trying to conceal a laugh pulls my attention from the pissing war taking place in front of me. Colton shoots her a glare then looks back at me.

"Oh, right. You got engaged. Congratulations."

"Thank you." I smile shyly.

I can see the confusion of who he is in Parker's eyes, so I clarify. "Colton has been Maverick's best friend since they were ten."

"Ah, ok. It's nice to meet you."

"Yeah, you too." He mumbles but it doesn't sound sincere.

Colton's expression appears completely neutral, but I know him better than that. There's something brooding in those topaz eyes of his. Maverick would probably be able to see it too if he was paying any attention. Thankfully, he's messing around with his phone, oblivious to the way his best friend is plotting a murder in his head. *What the hell is his deal?*

In perfect timing, a ringing in my ex's pocket breaks through the silence. He pulls out the device and glances at it to see who's calling.

"I'm sorry. I have to take this." Walking backwards toward the hallway, his eyes look me up and down once more. "It was great seeing you."

He's gone just as fast as he came, and like usual, I'm left a flustered mess by the brief encounter. Tatum's gaze is on me in a wordless question of asking if I'm okay. I plaster the best fake smile I can manage on my face and focus back on Maverick.

"I see you two are still close."

His phone falls onto his lap and a small crease appears in his forehead. "Who, me and Colton?" I nod. "Yeah, of course."

"Does he always show up unannounced?" I need to figure out if being at my brother's house is a safe place, or somewhere I need to avoid.

A small chuckle bubbles out. "Well, being as he lives here…"

"He's what?!" I screech. My brother's face is enough to tell me I need to get my emotions in check. "Sorry, that just surprises me. Why is he living with you?"

"He wanted to get out of the city, and his house is being built. He didn't want to buy a place just to sell it a year later."

I didn't know he lived in the city in the first place, but then again, I've been avoiding knowing about him at all. It would make sense given his career. Since graduating college, he's thrived at his job - becoming very well recognized and in high demand. The only reason I found that out was because my mom boasted for weeks about a magazine article he was in about people to look out for in the business world.

"I'm guessing he designed it himself?" I glance over at Parker. "Colton's an architect."

"An architect god." Maverick corrects me. "He helped Tatum and I design this place."

Looking around, I should've known. He's always had a knack for beautiful creations. His taste mixed with his ability to be creative yet realistic, he was meant for the job he's in. His specialty is houses but he's also been hired by large companies to draw up renovations to make their buildings more modernized and appealing.

"The place he's having built is probably incredible." I breathe, once again taking in all the intricate details of Maverick's home.

Tatum snorts. "We wouldn't know. He won't let anyone see it."

"Seriously?" That's unlike him. Colton has always been one to get other people's opinions and bounce ideas off them. It's one of the things that makes him so talented.

"Yeah. We've tried for months. He won't even show us the blueprints."

Maverick and Parker stray off into a conversation about business while my mind is still stuck on my ex. I thought he was exactly the same, but clearly, I was wrong. Something is different about him, and even though I shouldn't care what it is – I can't let it go.

Since the two men are distracted, I excuse myself and go into the kitchen, watching the door swing closed behind me. I lean forward and grip the edge of the edge of the sink. The cool ceramic feels good against my skin.

"Breathe, McKenna. Just breathe." I whisper softly.

"Still talking to yourself, I see."

My body jolts upright and spins around to see Colton standing in the doorway that leads to the dining room. I place my hand over my chest and mentally beg for my heartbeat to slow.

"Christ. You scared me."

He grins apologetically, leaning his back against the fridge and messing with something on his thumb nail. It should be awkward and uncomfortable, being as neither of us are saying anything, but it's not. It feels just as natural as it always has and I hate that.

Just when I'm about to walk out the door, he opens his mouth once again.

"You didn't tell him about me."

I stop dead in my tracks. I hadn't expected him to bring up anything about our past. After all, he was the one who wanted to end it and I was left to deal with the aftermath. Memories of the times we shared together start to play through my head.

"What are you doing?!" I ask as he sneaks into my bedroom. "Maverick is going to wonder where you went."

He chuckles. "He's out cold. If he wakes up at all before 10 AM, I'll be shocked."

I'm about to argue it further but he doesn't give me a chance. Before I can say another word, his mouth is on mine – wiping every thought on my mind clean so the only thing I can focus on is the soft feel of his lips.

"I missed you." He places his forehead against mine.

There they are again, the butterflies that come anytime he acts like what we have is more than a secret love affair; something that doesn't only exist in our own little world. I melt in his arms and allow myself to believe every word he says.

"I missed you, too. How was the party?"

"It was like any other party. There was drinking and loud music. Your brother got wasted and I had to call a taxi to bring us home."

"Did you hook up with anyone?" The words slip out before I even

have a chance to stop them. I know I've made a mistake the second I feel his body tense.

He sighs and takes a step back. "You know what, I'm actually really tired. I think I'm just going to crash."

"Colton, wait. I shouldn't have asked that. I'm sorry."

Unfortunately, my words do nothing. He gives me a sad smile and places one last kiss to the top of my head. "Goodnight, McKenna."

Like so many times before, he slips out the door and down the hallway – and like every other time, I beat myself up for thinking this will ever be anything but a good time to him.

Looking at him now, he's a little less confident than I remember, but he's still the same Colton. He's still the guy I spilt more tears over than I'd like to admit; the one who would get my hopes up only to make them come crashing back down. It would do me a lot of good to remember that.

"There was nothing to tell." I lie, leaving before I can see his reaction to my words.

3

THE PAVEMENT RUSHES BY BENEATH MY FEET AS I try to control my labored breathing. Crisp morning air blows softly against my skin. While I was at NYU, running was essentially limited to treadmills. In a city that's crowded with people, it's difficult to keep a good pace without trampling over someone. Here, however, it's perfect. The breeze that's coming off the shore does just enough to keep me from becoming overheated, and the sight of the sun glistening on the water is striking.

I come to a stop right in front of the docks. It's a place I remember well. My dad used to have a boat in one of these slips, which meant every night of the summer was spent down here. I can still picture Maverick and I pulling up the crab traps we left. We never caught much but that didn't dull our excitement to check them every time we arrived.

My phone vibrating in my hand pulls me from my nostalgia. The number that flashes across the screen is local, yet not one I recognize. Curiously, I swipe to answer and put it to my ear.

"Hello?"

"So, you *are* avoiding me." My best friend accuses.

Groaning, I find the nearest bench and sit down. I should have expected Ivy to call me from another number after dodging her for a few days.

"If I am, do you really think tricking me into answering the phone is the way to fix that?"

She sighs. "Well, that depends. I don't know what you're mad about."

"Oh? And why's that?"

"Because you haven't told me and I can't think of anything I've done wrong."

A dry laugh leaves my mouth. "Nothing?"

"Not a thing."

"So, you *didn't* let me go to Maverick's without giving me a heads up about Colton living there?"

I can picture the way she cringes at the realization. "Oh, that."

"Yeah, *that*."

It's quiet for another second before she exhales. "I'm sorry. I know I should've told you, but then you wouldn't have gone."

"You're right. I wouldn't have."

"And then what? Spend the rest of your life avoiding him? It's a small town. You were bound to run into each other sooner or later."

"Maybe, but that doesn't matter. You should've given me the heads up." I run my hand over my face. "My reaction to finding out he's my brother's *roommate* almost spilled everything I've worked so hard to hide."

"Shit. I didn't think about that."

As much as I want to be mad at her, I know she meant no harm. She may not make the best choices all the time but she's been my best friend since we were eight. If she made a conscious effort not to tell me, it's because she thought it was in my best interest - wrong, but innocent all the same.

"I know you didn't." I cave. "But next time, warn a girl. Jeez."

She chuckles in relief. "Noted. So, was it a total disaster?"

I give her a rundown of Saturday and by the time I'm done, my head is spinning. A part of me wishes I'd never have to see Colton again, but another part longs for the next time we're in the same room.

"Ugh. Why does he still have this effect on me?! I'm engaged!"

"Probably because you spent your entire adolescence in love with him."

Her brutal honesty almost knocks the wind out of me. It's not like she's wrong. This thing I've had for Colton has existed for as long as I can remember. I hoped that four years at college would rid me of my feelings for him, but apparently they hadn't. However, none of it matters. The reality is I'm getting married in four months to an incredible guy. I'd be stupid to risk messing that up.

TATUM OPENS THE DOOR looking nowhere near as ready as I expected her to. Her hair isn't done and she's sporting a pair of sweatpants with one of Maverick's old t-shirts. If I had to guess, I'd say she just woke up.

"You okay?" I ask carefully, not wanting to seem judgmental.

She squints at me before pulling out her phone. When she notices the time, her eyes widen.

"Shit. I must have fallen back asleep and lost track of time." Running her fingers through her hair, she turns and heads for the stairs. "Give me five minutes and we can go."

I let myself in and close the door behind me. The house seems empty enough but the two-car garage makes it so I can't be sure of who's home. I shake my head and rid my mind of everything Colton. Using the extra couple minutes to my advantage, I make my way into the kitchen to get something to drink.

The second I reach the doorway, all the air in my lungs comes rushing out. Colton is standing in front of the coffee maker. His torso is complete bare and the way his sweatpants hang low on his hips, it leaves very little to the imagination. As if he can feel me staring at him, he turns his head and our eyes meet.

"Oh, hey." He greets me as if the sight of him right now isn't making me nearly combust. "What are you doing here?"

"I h-have plans with T-Tatum." *Smooth, McKenna. Way to play it cool.*

He nods but I don't miss the way his eyes sweep over my body. While I hadn't planned on seeing him today, I'm glad I picked one of my favorite outfits. The black skinny jeans rest perfectly on my hips and the white crop-top hangs low enough to still be tasteful. When he looks back up at my face, he smirks.

"What?"

Something familiar flashes in his eyes but it's so short that I wonder if I imagined it. He raises his eyebrows and shakes his head.

"Nothing."

I roll my eyes. "Whatever."

Deciding to get what I was looking for and get out of here, I march towards the coffee maker and grab two of the disposable travel cups next to it. As I go to grab the handle of the pot, Colton's voice startles me.

"Careful, it's hot."

I hear his warning but it's a second too late. My hand meets the scorching metal and I release it with a hiss. In my haste to pull away, I stumble backwards until I land against the firm feeling of Colton's chest. His hands instinctively grip my sides to stabilize me. As soon as his skin meets mine, the spark that I once fed off of like a drug shoots my mind into four years ago.

The long day at the beach was exactly what I needed. However, I won't deny that this outdoor shower is what truly feels like heaven. The mixture of sunscreen and salt washes clean from my body. The fresh water is cold but contrasts nicely against the humid air.

"Do you know how hard today was?" His voice echos in the small space as he steps behind me and places his hands on my hips. "To have to look at you in that bikini and not be able to touch you? It was absolute torture."

I spin in his arms, pressing myself to the front of him and allowing my hands to skate over his impeccably sculpted abs. "No one said you couldn't touch me."

"Right." He lets out a bellowing laugh - my favorite of many. "Because I'm sure your brother wouldn't kick my ass for laying a finger on you."

To be honest, whenever he brings up reasons why we're not together, it sparks a bit of anger inside of me. If he wasn't such a coward, he would go to Maverick and tell him about us. Nothing would stop him if he really wanted to be with me the way that I want to be with him. But that's the thing, isn't it? He doesn't want to be with me at all; at least not when we're in public.

He gently grazes his knuckles down my cheek and I'm right back under his spell.

"Colton." I breathe, lulling my head back against him.

His grip on my waist tightens and I don't miss the way he gasps just slightly. After everything we've been through and all the pain he's caused me, he still has the ability to light my nerve endings like wildfire. My subconscious is screaming at me to move but I can't. I'm frozen in place, milking this moment for everything it's worth. It's been four years without his touch - four *very long* years.

"I-"

"Mac?" Tatum's voice echoes through the house. "Are you ready to go?"

Whatever he was going to say is effectively cut off by the sound of my brother's girlfriend. Within seconds, his touch is gone and he's at least three steps away. I don't get a moment to question anything before Tatum is standing in the doorway, looking at us like a judgmental parent.

"Everything okay in here?" She asks suspiciously.

I'm stunned into silence but Colton handles everything with a practiced ease. "Yup. We're all good."

He makes his way out of the room and pats her on the shoulder as he passes by. However, just before he's out of sight, he spares one last glance at me. The way the corner of his mouth raises in an involuntary motion has my stomach doing backflips. *Fuck. This isn't good.*

"What was *that*?"

"What was what?" I play dumb. If I'm being completely honest, I really don't know the answer.

She looks like she wants to question it, but instead shakes her head. "Ready to go?"

I nod and follow her out of the house, hoping to leave Colton and the moment we just had completely behind me.

I SHOULD BE EXCITED to look at wedding venues. The only thing that should be on my mind is my fiancé and the fact that I'm planning the most important day of my life. Unfortunately, that hasn't been the case at all. Every place we've looked at has been gorgeous but I can't get my brain to focus.

The feeling of Colton's touch lingers, staying there like he permanently branded me. No matter how many ballrooms I walk through and the amount of times people congratulate me on my engagement, nothing can wipe the memory from the very front and center place in my mind.

"I personally like option two. The chandelier in the ballroom is gorgeous." Tatum voices her opinion.

"Yeah, gorgeous."

Her eyes narrow from across the table, but I'm not really paying attention enough to notice. "And the bright purple walls really made the room pop don't you think?"

"Definitely. Great color."

The next thing I know, a flying mozzarella stick hits me smack in the forehead. It shakes me from of my dazed state and I find Tatum giving me a knowing look with her eyebrows raised.

"What was what for?!" I balk.

"There wasn't a single place we went today with purple walls, Mac." I open and close my mouth to speak, but nothing comes out. I'm busted. "You've been out of it all day. What's up with you?"

"Nothing. It's nothing. I'm just in my own head."

"Does this have anything to do with me finding you and Colton in the kitchen this morning?"

"No."

"McKenna." She says my name like a warning.

"Okay, yes." I groan, rubbing my hands over my face.

"I knew it! Spill."

Taking a sip of water, I try to figure out how to even put this morning into words. "I went to grab the coffee pot and didn't realize it was basically on fire. Why the hell does your coffee pot get so damn hot?!"

"It's broken." She waves me off dismissively. "Not the point. What happened with Colton?"

"Well, I almost burned my hand and in the process of

pulling away, I slipped and ended up in his arms." I stop to take a breath but I can tell she's waiting for me to continue. "Neither of us moved for a couple minutes and I started to remember how things used to be between us. I can't explain it and I sure as hell can't get it out of my head."

Letting out a long sigh, she runs her fingers through her hair. "Do you need me to tell you all the reasons this is a horrible idea?"

"I don't know what *idea* you're referring to."

"Don't play coy with me. It's not cute." I pout but she doesn't let me say anything before she's speaking again. "You and Colton ended horribly. Do you remember that? Because *I* remember you showing up at my door at one in the morning. You were a mess - sobbing so hard I thought you were going to have brain damage from lack of oxygen."

The memory of that night is all too clear. After Colton had left, I was a wreck. I wanted to run to Ivy but she had already left earlier that day for college; a one semester stunt she did at Pepperdine University before deciding she couldn't handle being so far away. Thankfully, Tatum was home. I spent most of the night soaking her lap with my tears.

"Trust me, I remember."

"Do you? Because I'm not sure you do. If you did, you wouldn't entertain the thought of you and him for a single second - not when you have someone like Parker wanting to spend the rest of his life with you."

The mention of my fiancé is like being doused with a bucket of ice water. What kind of horrible person am I? I'm supposed to be planning my wedding, the day Parker and I vow to spend forever together, and here I am, hung up on an ex. Hell, I don't even know if I could call him an ex. He was never my boyfriend to begin with.

"I'm such a bitch."

She snorts but shrugs her shoulders. "I mean, I won't tell you you're wrong. You have a great guy who only wants to give you the world. I really don't want to see you mess that up for someone who treated you like a summer fling and tossed you away when it was over."

I won't lie, the way she describes what Colton and I had together burns, but I think that was her intention. Tatum has always been the kind of person who tells it like it is. It's something I admire about her. Besides, she has a point. Colton shattered me into pieces, and Parker managed to at least somewhat put me back together without even realizing he was doing it.

"You're right. I'd be an idiot to let myself get wrapped up in all things Colton Brooks again. I have Parker and our wedding coming up." Taking another sip of my water, I nod with a newfound determination. "Him and I will just have to stay away from each other."

I WAKE IN THE morning to my alarm blaring into my ear. I slam my hand down on the snooze button and groan tiredly. When I roll over, I'm happy to find Parker asleep next to me. He had gotten tied up in Boston with something and didn't end up getting home until after I was asleep. I smile as I see his eyes flutter open and lean over to kiss his cheek.

"Mmm. Good morning." He greets me.

"Morning."

"What's got you looking so chipper? Are you that excited for house shopping?"

Honestly, I had forgotten about our plans for the day, but I won't tell him that. "Of course. Who wouldn't be excited to go buy a house?"

He chuckles and stretches before sitting up. "Well, try not to get your hopes too high. It's only our first time looking and I don't want you to settle on something you don't absolutely love. I want you to have everything you have ever imagined."

My heart swells in my chest and I realize everything Tatum said was right. This man would hand me anything I asked for on a silver platter. I smile brightly and move to wrap my arms around his shoulders from behind.

"I already do. I have you."

The memory of Colton's hands on my waist still lingers in the back of my mind, but I do my best to push it away. I'm marrying Parker and he loves me. That should be enough, right?

4

I PULL DOWN THE MIRROR TO MESS WITH MY makeup for what's probably the 100th time in an hour. Ivy chuckles from the driver's seat, causing me to roll my eyes at her. I don't wear much of this stuff often, so when I do, I never think it looks right.

"Will you stop? You're going to end up resembling a raccoon if you keep fucking with it." My best friend chastises me as she switches her focus between me and the road.

"I just need to look as good as possible."

She hums. "Why? A certain brunette you need to impress?"

My blood runs cold at the mention of Colton. I never did check with Tatum to see if he was invited, but judging by our talk on Tuesday, I doubt she would allow him to attend.

"No. Some of Parker's close family friends are going to be there and I've never met them before. I want to look my best."

If she doesn't buy my excuse, she doesn't mention it. That's one thing I can say about Ivy. If I need to lie to make myself feel better about something, she usually doesn't call me out on it. She only voices her opinion if she knows I'm going to regret whatever it is I'm about to do. She's the total opposite of Tatum.

Pulling up to the outdoor venue, I'm blown away. The sun is just barely beginning to set. Twinkling lights hang all around while other soft lanterns help illuminate the place. There are pink and white lace accents that work well with the ivory decorations. Teagan and the staff she's hired did an amazing job.

I'm in awe as I climb out of the car and grab onto Ivy's arm, using her as support while I take in the scene in front of me. Even she seems to be a little shocked by it all. As soon as we get close enough, someone comes to hand us each a glass of champagne. We thank them and both take a sip.

"This is incredible." I mumble, slightly unable to speak. I can't believe this party is for *me*.

"Well, this is what happens when you get engaged to one of England's elite."

I snort. "You make it sound like he's part of the monarchy or something. He's not."

"Mhm, and how many vacation homes did you say his family owns again?"

"Twenty-three."

Her eyebrows raise. "Oh, that's all? I take it back then. He's a total peasant. You could do better."

I can't help but laugh and shake my head. There are two things about Parker that make Ivy absolutely swoon whenever he's near. The first is his accent. I never knew the girl had such a thing for British men. The second is his family's wealth. She knows I'm not using him for his money, but she does envy the fact that I'll never have to worry about finances.

"Now, if only I could find him."

The two of us look around the venue which is already starting to fill with people, but none of them are my fiancé. He's been at Harvard all day dealing with stuff for his

38

upcoming semester, but he promised he would be here. I can't exactly celebrate an engagement without the man I'm engaged *to*.

"Tatum!" I shout, getting her attention. She glances over at me for a second to wave, then excuses herself from the cater waiter to come our way.

"Hey, you're here. What do you think? Do you like it?"

I nod enthusiastically. "It's gorgeous! You've really outdone yourself."

"Well, it was easy with the endless budget your fiancé was kind enough to give me."

"Speaking of, have you seen him yet?"

She shakes her head, confirming what I was afraid of. "I thought he was coming with you."

"Nope." I pop the p for emphasis. "He had some things to do in Boston for school. He's supposed to meet me here."

"Hmm. Well, don't worry too much. I'm sure he'll be here soon." Her words are meant to soothe me but she's clearly distracted with everything she needs to do. "Excuse me, the bakery just arrived to deliver the cake."

As Tatum walks away, Ivy watches me carefully. I take my phone out of my clutch and open my texts with Parker. I haven't heard anything from him since this morning when he let me know he arrived at Harvard safely. My fingers compose a quick message asking where he is. I watch as the bubble pops up shortly after, indicating he's typing. Sure enough, his response comes quickly.

Parker: I'm so sorry love. Things ran late. I'm on my way but there's traffic.

Dread washes over me as I realize I'll be spending part of our engagement party without him. There are already people I don't know walking around. I don't want to be rude, but I don't know what to say to them without Parker to do the introductions. Ugh, I hate that he put me in this uncomfortable situation after promising me he wouldn't.

I don't bother answering him as I click the screen to my phone off and toss it back into my bag. Ivy must notice the change in my attitude because she sighs and hooks her arm with my own.

"Come on, let's go get something a little stronger than this champagne."

A COUPLE SHOTS OF tequila later, I'm standing at a high-top table with Ivy and Tatum. The party is going well, sans the fact that Parker is still MIA. The more time that passes without him here, the angrier I become. No amount of alcohol in the world can dull the irritation coursing through my veins.

"I'm telling you, he is *by far* the hottest man I've ever seen in my life." Ivy gushes about one of the waiters she works with.

"I'm pretty sure that's how you describe every new guy that catches your attention."

She makes a face at me and goes to continue, but Tatum's voice cuts her off.

"Crap. McKenna, I'm *so* sorry. I completely forgot to un-invite him."

"What?" I ask, turning around to find who she's referring to.

My sights land directly on Colton. He's standing next to Maverick while they say hello to my parents. The way he looks in that suit is enough to bring any girl to her knees.

Every feeling I had geared towards Parker's absence vanishes as soon as Colton's eyes meet my own.

I haven't seen him since I fell into his arms on Tuesday morning. I've done everything I can to avoid him, but apparently, my luck has worn out. I don't know how I feel about that exactly.

The way his stare bores into me, I'm finding it hard to remember why I didn't want him here in the first place. Neither one of us look away as him and my brother make their way over to us. Maverick gives Tatum a kiss hello then focuses on me. Colton is the first to break the eye contact before smiling subtly at the ground.

"You look beautiful, Squid."

I wince in embarrassment. "Shh, people can hear you."

"What?" He chuckles. "I can't compliment my baby sister?"

"I think she was referring to the nickname." Tatum explains.

"Ah. Okay then, you look beautiful, *McKenna*."

A shy smile stretches across my face. "Thank you."

"Where's your fiancé?" Colton finally chimes in.

"He's... uh, he's running late." His eyebrows raise. I'm not sure if it's Parker's absence that surprises him or the way I don't seem to mind it right now. Regardless, it makes me feel like I need to explain. "He had a meeting at Harvard for medical school, and you know how Boston traffic is."

"Harvard Med School? Well damn, Mac. You really hit the jackpot."

I don't respond. Even if I wanted to, I don't think I'd have any idea what to say to that. I thought him and I had shared a moment a few days ago. Did I imagine the way he shuddered when I whispered his name, or the way his fingers dug into my waist? I could have sworn he was just as affected as I was but looking at him now, he seems completely indifferent.

"It's that British accent. Right, McKenna?" Ivy nudges me playfully.

I giggle, knowing exactly what she's doing. "Definitely"

"And here I was thinking it was my charming personality." A familiar voice catches my attention.

We all turn our heads to see Parker only a few steps away, wearing a light gray tuxedo and looking like sex on legs. Ivy gapes while my smile grows. He walks directly to me and wraps his arms around my body, placing his lips against my ear.

"I'm sorry, love. The bloody traffic was horrible."

I hug him back half-heartedly before taking a step back. "You knew it would be. You should've left earlier."

His eyebrows furrow. "I apologized. What more do you want from me?"

"I *want* you to keep your promises. You said you would be here on time, not a half hour late."

"McKenna." He says my name like a parent warning their child. "Do you really want to do this here?"

After a short internal debate with myself, I realize he's right - I don't want to ruin our engagement party. He's here now and that's all that matters. I sigh and arch onto the tips of my toes to kiss him innocently.

"I missed you today." He whispers.

If you missed me, you wouldn't have been late. "I missed you, too."

Parker turns his attention to the rest of the group and greets each one of them. Ivy, like usual, melts in the palm of his hand. If she wasn't my best friend, I'd wonder if I had something to worry about. As his attention reaches Colton, I hold my breath and watch the exchange.

"Nice to see you again, mate." Parker extends his hand.

After looking at it like it's diseased, he takes it. "You, too."

"If you lot don't mind, I'm going to steal McKenna for a bit. There are a few people I'd like for her to meet."

When none of them protest, Parker leads me over to a group of men who look old enough to be my parents. I spare a glance at my friends only to see Colton scowling at where Parker's hand rests on the small of my back. I don't get a chance to try to analyze the meaning of his reaction before Parker speaks.

"Gentleman, let me introduce you to my fiancée, McKenna Taylor."

I'M NOT SURE WHERE Tatum managed to find this DJ, but he's really good. After spending an obnoxious amount of time listening to Parker talk to his friends from Columbia University about the growing stock market, I excused myself and found Ivy and Tatum on the dance floor. The three of us move to the music, losing ourselves in the beat of the song. As the tempo slows, Maverick spins Tatum around to slow dance.

"Want to go get a drink?" Ivy questions.

I nod and go to follow her until a hand wraps around my wrist. With a subtle tug, I'm pulled directly into Colton's arms. My breath gets caught in my throat as I look up at him.

"Dance with me."

I think it's meant to be a question, but it comes out more like a demand. I try to find Ivy but she's no help as she smiles, walking away with a smug look on her face. As I turn my head back to Colton, he's already starting to sway to the music. I take a deep breath before resting my arms on his shoulders.

"We never got a chance to talk the other day." He murmurs.

"Oh? What did you want to talk about?"

We both glance around the party, looking anywhere but at each other. "How've you been?"

Really? That's what he wants to know? "Good. How about you?"

"Can't complain too much."

"My mom showed me an article about you a couple years ago. Seems like you've really made something of yourself."

"I guess you could say that."

"I bet your mother is proud." She always was his biggest supporter.

He laughs softly, and God, I've missed that sound. "She tells anyone that will listen that her son is the biggest architect in Massachusetts."

"Is she wrong?"

His shoulders move in a subtle shrug. "It's a bit of a stretch." When I don't say anything else, the two of us fall into a comfortable silence, just letting our bodies sway with the song. After a minute or so, he sighs. "You look gorgeous, McKenna."

For the first time since we started dancing, my eyes meet his. The way he's looking at me is so familiar and no matter how much my mind is screaming at me to turn away, I can't. Just like Tuesday, I'm frozen in place. His eyes glance down at my lips then back up. *Don't do it.*

"Mind if I cut in?"

Ivy's voice breaks the spell he had me under. I nod and step out of his arms, giving her a thankful smile as I walk away. *I really need a drink.*

AN HOUR LATER, THE party is almost over and Parker has barely paid any attention to me all night. I get that he doesn't see these people often, but if it wasn't for us cutting the cake and the massively oversized photo, no one would know we're together - let alone engaged. Since the dance, I've done my best to avoid Colton. I can't say for certain that we wouldn't have kissed if Ivy hadn't interrupted, and even the idea of that is trouble.

I excuse myself from a conversation with my parents and some of their friends and make my way over to Parker. However, as soon as I'm within earshot, his words stop me in my tracks.

"I know it'll be a bit difficult to juggle settling into a new house with summer courses, but it's best for me to get a jump on things."

"S-summer courses?" I choke out.

Parker turns around, looking guilty. "McKenna."

Suddenly, nothing he has to say is anything I want to hear. I shake my head and walk away, but he catches up to me quickly.

"McKenna, wait." He grabs my hand.

I stop and spin to face him, quickly pulling myself from his grasp. "Don't!"

"I can explain."

"Explain?! Explain what? How you promised this summer would be all about the two of us? How you were so excited to spend time with me?"

"I'm still going to spend time with you."

"When? You're going to be at class all day and studying all night. When did you even decide to do this?"

"Can we talk about this later?"

I cross my arms. "*When* Parker?"

"Last night."

Nodding as everything starts to make sense, I roll my eyes. "So that's why you were late. You were signing up for courses." His silence confirms that I'm right. "That's just great."

A familiar song flows from the speakers and straight to

my ears; a song I haven't let myself listen to in years. It's a bittersweet memory.

What kind of eighteen-year-old doesn't know how to slow dance? It has to be the easiest kind of dancing and yet I can't do it without stepping on the guy's toes. Maybe I should just skip prom all together instead of risking embarrassing myself.

"Ugh." I groan, tossing my iPod onto my dresser. "It's hopeless."

"Well don't you look happy." A voice startles me.

My head whips towards the sound to see Colton, my brother's best friend, standing in the doorway. He looks so soft in a T-shirt and sweatpants with his hair messy as if he just ran a towel over it. God, he's gorgeous.

"How long have you been standing there?"

He chuckles and takes a step inside my room. "Long enough to watch you freak out. What's wrong?"

"It's nothing."

"It's not nothing if you're this upset about it."

I shake my head. "It's embarrassing."

"McKenna." He gives me a knowing look. "I've known you since you played pretty, pretty, princess."

"Oh god, don't remind me."

What he doesn't know is that I've had a crush on him since the day he first came over to hang out with Maverick. I was seven and they were ten. I can still remember the way he rode his skateboard without a helmet. He looked so dangerous and carefree. I was mesmerized.

"I don't know how to slow dance." I confess.

His eyebrows raise. "Is that all?" I nod and he picks up my iPod from my dresser. "I can teach you."

Teach me?! Just the idea of Colton's hands on me causes me to feel something so intense I can barely handle it. "Y-you don't have to do that."

"Nonsense." He presses play. From the Ground Up by Dan and

46

Shay fills the room. "Come here." I step closer. He lightly takes my wrists and places them on his shoulders before putting his hands on my hips. "Now just follow my lead."

The two of us sway back and forth. Every time I've tried this with anyone else, I've messed it up. I've stepped on the guy or moved too fast. With Colton, though, it's different. I let him control my movements as I get lost in the lyrics. Every word they sing is everything I wish would happen between us. Is there a reason he chose this song? Yeah, right. What would a twenty-one-year-old Adonis want with a high school senior?

The feeling of being this close to him is better than anything I've ever imagined. I mentally will the song to never end and wonder if maybe I should mess up on purpose so I can say I need more help. Unfortunately, the last note plays before I have a chance to try it.

"See? You're a natural."

I look up and my eyes lock with his. The room is so quiet I can hear the pounding of my own heart. The music is gone but neither one of us moves. Then, as if we don't any control over it, we both start to lean in. My eyes close and I can feel his lips ghosting across my own but not touching.

"Colton." I whisper, afraid I'll ruin the moment if I speak any louder.

"I just…"

He cuts himself off my pressing his mouth against mine. My stomach is taken over by butterflies as I get exactly what I've wanted for the past decade. He tightens his hold and pulls me closer, using my gasp to slip his tongue into my mouth. He tastes like mint toothpaste and heaven. My fingers lace into his hair as I try to find something to ground me. Lifting me up by my waist, he sits me on my dresser and slots himself between my legs. Our lips don't separate for a second as the kiss turns heated.

"Colton?"

In the worst timing ever, Maverick's voice echoes down the hallway. Colton breaks the kiss, placing his hands on either side of my body and taking a deep breath with his eyes still closed. When they

47

finally open, his pupils are so blown that I can barely see any of the turquoise blue that surrounds them.

"Colton? Where'd you go?" Maverick calls out again.

"Coming." He answers before backing away.

Just as he reaches the door, he spares one last glance at me and smiles. In another second, he's gone. I raise my hand and touch my bottom lip with the tips of my fingers. The feeling of his kiss still lingers.

"McKenna, are you even listening to me?!" Parker goes on but I'm not paying attention.

Colton looks away from his conversation with Tatum and directly at me. The smile that appears tells me he knows exactly what song this is, and then he winks. I can't handle anything anymore. With being angry at Parker and all these feelings for Colton flooding back, I just need a minute to breathe.

I turn to leave but don't get very far before Parker is stopping me again.

"Where are you going?"

Again, I pull myself from him and take another step back. "I just need some time to myself. *Don't* follow me."

Without giving him a chance to say another word, I walk away. I go down the back steps and onto the lower patio, far enough from prying eyes and people who want to make small talk with the 'bride to be'. I sit on the ledge and take a deep breath, rubbing my hands over my face. Only a few seconds later, I can hear someone coming up behind me.

"I thought I told you not to follow me!" I shout, but as I turn around, it's not Parker behind me. "Oh, sorry. I thought you were someone else."

"Are you okay?" Colton asks carefully.

I shrug. "Define okay."

48

He comes closer and stands in front of me, placing his hands in his pockets. "Trouble in paradise?"

"You could say that." It's probably not something I should talk to him about, but this is Colton. Word vomit comes naturally with him. "He promised me the whole summer just the two of us, then today he goes and enrolls in summer courses without telling me."

"Well, that's messed up."

"You're telling me." I look at the starry night sky as my eyes tear up. "Is there something wrong with me? Is that why he'd rather take classes than spend time together?"

Within seconds, Colton steps closer and pulls me into his chest, rubbing my back soothingly. "No, McKenna. You're perfect."

"If I was perfect, he would want to spend time with me."

"Well, he's an idiot then. Anyone would be lucky to spend time with you."

I give myself a moment to breathe in his cologne. He's always worn the same kind and I've missed it. I remember the way the scent used to coat my pillow long after he left my bed. *Shit. What am I doing?*

Using as much force as I can manage, I push him away from me. "We can't do this."

"Do what, exactly?"

"This." I motion between him and I. "It's dangerous."

"Mac." He moves to come closer again.

"No, stop. It's way too easy to fall back into old habits with you and I can't risk that. I'm engaged." I swallow before allowing the words to leave my mouth. "We need to stay away from each other."

His eyes widen at the idea and he lets out a choked laugh. "That's not possible."

"Yes, it is. I'll try to stay away from Maverick's while you live there. I'm moving out of my parent's house on Sunday. We don't have to be around each other."

He opens his mouth to argue but stops as Tatum cuts him off.

"McKenna, people are leaving. You have to come say goodbye and thank them for coming."

Sparing one last glance at Colton, I give him an 'I mean it' look, then walk up the stairs to join Tatum. The two of us leave him standing there alone and head back to the party.

"Do I even want to ask what that was about?" She asks.

I shake my head. "I've got it under control." *Or at least I hope I do.*

5

In the past couple weeks, I've learned one very important thing about myself - I *hate* packing. First it was my dorm room, which was hard but tolerable. My childhood bedroom, however, is a totally different story. All the memories that fill every inch of this place make leaving it so hard. I'm about to move into a house with my fiancé; the man I promised to spend the rest of my life with. I should be less scared and more excited, but I'm not.

"Knock, knock." My mom interrupts my mental freak out. "Can I come in?"

"Of course."

She comes beside me and helps fold the clothes I have in a pile and place them in the box. "Where's Parker? Shouldn't he be helping you?"

"He went to pick up the keys."

"Ah. Those would be useful, wouldn't they?"

I chuckle. "Just a bit."

After folding a couple more shirts in silence, she sighs and sits down on my bed. "Are you sure this is what you want?"

"What? Why wouldn't it be?"

"Because I saw you two at the engagement party. Aunt Rachel didn't even know which one was your fiancé." Worry is evident in the tone of her voice, but I don't dare to look at her. "What were you two fighting about?"

I shake my head. "It was stupid."

"It didn't *look* stupid. It clearly upset you."

She's right. It *did* upset me. It still does if I'm honest, but there isn't much I can do about it now. He starts classes on Wednesday because that's what *he* wants to do. My opinion didn't matter when he made the choice to enroll, and it doesn't matter now. That's just something I need to accept.

"He signed up for summer courses without talking to me about it first."

"You don't want him to get a head start?"

"It's not that." I will myself not to get emotional. My mom will go all protective mama bear and I don't need that right now. "Since we met, one of us has always had some kind of obligation. We both promised to spend this summer *together*."

"That's not very considerate of him. If you two are going to get married, he needs to know that he can't make all these decisions on his own anymore. You're supposed to be equals."

"Yeah, well." I toss the shirt into the box with a little more force than necessary. "It's a problem but it's not going to make me leave him. I'll get over it."

"And what about Colton? Will you get over *that*, too?" My whole body tenses and my eyes fly up to see my mom staring right back at me - not judging, just the soft gaze I'm used to. "I saw the way you looked at him when you were dancing."

"That-"

She holds up one finger. "I also saw the way he chased after you when you ran off. So, I'm going to ask you again. Are you sure this is what you want?"

Running my hands over my face, I take a deep breath.

"Yes, I'm sure. I love Parker. Colton was just being a good friend."

"Honey, I've known that boy since he was ten years old. If you think the way he looks at you is like a *friend*, you're not as bright as I thought you were."

"Mom!" I laugh in disbelief. "We're not talking about this. There's nothing going on between *me* and *Colton*. I'm moving in with Parker and in four months, I'll be marrying him. That's all there is to it."

"I just-"

I shake my head. "That's *all* there is to it."

"Okay, I get it." She stands from my bed. "Let me know if you need any help."

Without another word, she leaves me alone to process my thoughts. After I walked away from Colton on Friday night, he didn't try to talk to me again. I caught him looking at me a couple times but he left with Maverick shortly after.

My eyes move to the picture on my nightstand. I walk over and take it into my hands, looking at it for the millionth time since I got home. Like a habit, my finger rubs right over Colton's hair and down his face as I remember what he feels like. It's been two days since I saw him and while I know it was my idea to stay away from each other, I'd be lying if I said I like it.

"Hello love." Parker greets me as he comes into the room. I startle but it's too late. "What are you looking at?"

I shrug to seem apathetic and hand it to him. "Just a picture from a few years ago."

"Is that Maverick and Colton with you?"

"Mhm."

He looks up at me and smiles. "You all look happy."

I take the picture as he passes it back to me and glance over it one more time. "Yeah, we were."

The sun beams down on me, warming my body as I relax on the beach. Waves crash against the shore and just barely kiss the dry sand before retreating. The sound of seagulls and the ocean provide a feeling of calmness that can't be beat.

"If you stare any harder, your eyes are going to dry out. At least blink, jeez."

I chuckle as Colton jumps off his surfboard and into the water. "Shut up, Ivy."

"I'm just saying, with the way you look at him, I'm surprised Maverick hasn't caught on yet."

"How do you know he hasn't?"

"Because Colton's still in one piece."

My eyes roll instinctively. "Oh, please. He wouldn't hurt his best friend."

"No, he wouldn't hurt him. He would kill him." She looks around to make sure the coast is clear before turning back to me. "You're his baby sister. His best friend is boinking his baby sister."

"Okay one, don't ever use the word 'boinking' again. And two, I'm not anyone's baby anything." Glancing back at the water, I see Colton and Maverick coming toward us. "Now zip it before you accidentally let something slip."

The guys drop their boards onto the sand and grab towels to dry their faces. Colton smirks when he notices me staring at him. He reaches back and pulls the zipper on his wetsuit down, peeling the top half from his wet body. I need to stop myself from moaning at the sight of his perfectly sculpted abs.

"I'm going to rinse off. You coming?" Maverick asks him.

"Nah, I think I'll stay here."

Not thinking anything of it, my brother nods and heads for the showers. Once he's out of sight, Colton plops himself down next to me. He puts one hand on my cheek and pulls me in, pressing our lips together. It's not long, but enough to make my knees weak and my body tingle. Ivy mocks disgust but the two of us ignore her. When he breaks the kiss, he rests his forehead on mine.

"I have wanted to do that all morning." He whispers.

I don't stand a chance in fighting the smile that comes from his words. "Me too."

Ivy grabs a bottle of water from the small cooler and hands it to him. He thanks her, then pours the liquid into his mouth. I watch his Adam's apple bob as he swallows. When he's done, he flings it toward me. I gasp as the cold water splashes against my heated skin. He smiles guiltily and winks at me.

"Seriously?"

His grin widens. "Seriously."

Knowing how much he hates when the sand clings to his body, I grab a handful and press it against his chest. He bites his lip and closes his eyes. When he reopens them, my breath hitches.

"You really just did that?"

"Yup." I reply, popping the p.

He hums and then nods. "I'll give you five seconds to run." At first I think he's kidding, but then he raises his eyebrows and starts to count. "One, two…"

"Shit."

I get up to run but within half a second, he catches me - wrapping his arms around my waist and digging his fingers into my sides. A squeal leaves my mouth as he tickles me and no matter how much I beg, he doesn't let go. Ivy laughs until a voice makes us all freeze.

"What are you doing?"

Colton releases me instantly and the two of us turn to see Maverick looking at us like he's trying to solve the worlds hardest puzzle. He glances from his best friend, to me, and back again - waiting for an answer. Thankfully, Colton snickers and runs his fingers through his hair.

"Just messing around. She threw sand on me."

My jaw drops as I turn to him. "You splashed me with cold water!"

"I would've thrown you into the ocean if big brother hadn't come to your rescue."

I roll my eyes, but nothing can stop me from giggling. Maverick's eyes narrow at my reaction and he turns his attention back to Colton.

"Is there something going on between you two?"

55

"Between me and Mac?" He asks, as if the idea is absurd. "Dude, are you really asking me that?"

Ivy, being the godsend that she is, grabs her phone and stands up. "Maverick, go stand next to McKenna. I want to take a picture of you three."

Her idea to distract him works and Maverick shakes himself out of whatever internal debate he was having. He comes over and stands next to me. Him and Colton both place an arm around me and the three of us smile brightly for the picture. In that moment, with the two most important men in my life, I feel content.

I SHOW IVY AROUND my new house. It's empty but still beautiful. Parker and I had only looked at three before seeing this one. I instantly loved it. It's two stories, with all the bedrooms upstairs. The kitchen has all top of the line appliances and looks out into the living room. It's the perfect home for a family.

"McKenna, your brother is here!" Parker calls from the front yard.

Ivy and I quit pondering what the point is of fans on a vaulted ceiling, and head to the door. As soon as we step outside, I stop. My best friend bumps into the back of me from my sudden halt but I barely notice - too stuck on the sight in front of me.

Colton is leaning up against the side of Maverick's SUV, laughing at something Parker said. His arms are crossed against his chest and his smile makes my heart skip. This is exactly why I told him to stay away. I can't handle the way my body comes alive when he's around, especially when my fiancé is in the same place.

"Well, well, well. If it isn't little McKenna Taylor." Another voice pulls my attention away from my ex.

I turn my head to see Roman, my brother and Colton's

friend since freshman year. He's grown since I saw him last. He has probably gained somewhere near thirty pounds of pure muscle. His shirt clings to his body, the white fabric contrasting with the dark tone of his skin. The smile on his face reminds me of why it's so nice to be home.

"Rome!" I greet him excitedly, wrapping my arms around him. He lifts me up and squeezes. When he puts me down, I run my fingers through my hair. "How are you? It's been forever."

"I know. I'm sorry I couldn't make it to your engagement party. There was something at work I had to tend to."

"Don't you work for Colton?" My eyes narrow. When he glances at him with a nervous look on his face, it becomes clear. He dealt with the work issue so Colton didn't miss the party. *Was going really that important to him?* I don't have time to question it further because Maverick speaks up.

"What am I, chopped liver?" His tone is playful so I flip him off. "Oooh. I'm going to tell mom."

All of us laugh at his shenanigans and my eyes meet Colton's for the first time in two days. I don't allow it to linger for longer than a second before I look away. Suddenly finding the ground very interesting, I can faintly hear Maverick talking to Parker.

"This place is nice."

"McKenna picked it. She has much better taste than I do."

My brother chuckles. "I feel you there. How'd you get the keys so quickly though? Buying a house usually takes months."

"The power of paying with cash, mate."

"Ah." He nods in realization. "I keep forgetting you're loaded."

"Maverick!" I chastise him.

He puts his hands up in surrender. "What? He is."

Rolling my eyes, I focus on my fiancé. "The furniture will

be here in a couple hours, so we should probably get a move on things."

The four guys follow me over to the moving truck while Ivy goes to sit with Tatum. I explain to them how each box is marked with where it needs to go. One by one, they grab a box and start carrying it into the house. Thankfully, Colton is last. When he turns around to walk off the truck, I step in front of him.

"What do you think you're doing?"

His eyebrows furrow. "Huh?"

"I thought I told you we had to stay away from each other. Does this *look* like staying away from each other to you?" He chuckles and goes to walk around me but I stop him again. "I'm serious, Colton. What are you doing here?"

"Maverick asked me to come help you move. What was I supposed to tell him? *No sorry, I can't because we fucked four years ago so she doesn't want to be around me?*"

My eyes widen and I look around quickly before shushing him. "You could've made an excuse or something. You shouldn't be here. We agreed."

Dropping the box on the ground, he cages me in with his arms on either side of my body. "No, you gave an order and then walked away like I had no say in the matter. I told you this idea of yours wouldn't work."

"I-It has to." I struggle to maintain my composure with him so close. "It has to work. I'm engaged, and I can't be dealing with you invading my personal space all the time."

He smirks. "You may not be able to control yourself around me, but that doesn't mean I can't." I try to push him away but he doesn't budge. "It's not my fault you still quiver when I say your name." His lips move to the shell of my ear. "*Princess*."

My eyes close as I take a deep breath. *This can't happen.* I place my hands against his chest and push as hard as I can. It works, but he quickly moves to come closer again. I put my finger up to stop him.

"No." I say firmly. "You don't get to do this. *You* ended things between us, remember?! *I* wanted to make it work and *you* said no. You were fine, while I had to put myself back together all on my own. So, you don't get to act like you didn't break me." He doesn't say anything as I wipe a stray tear from my eye. "If I say we're staying away from each other, then that's what we're doing."

Slipping past him, I go to leave the truck but stop when he calls my name. I turn around with a defeated look on my face, only to find the same expression looking back at me.

"I'm sorry."

I give him a sad smile and shrug my shoulders, before continuing to walk away.

I DIDN'T THINK WE had a lot of stuff, but watching the guys move everything in, I'm starting to dread unpacking. However, I don't want to get in their way, so I need to wait til they're done to start. Instead, I'm sitting on Parker's tailgate with Ivy and Tatum, talking about how much fun we're going to have this summer.

"I'm telling you." Ivy presses. "Myrtle Beach would be perfect for your bachelorette party."

I shake my head. "No. No trips. I just want to stay he-"

My words get stuck in my throat as Colton comes walking out the front door, devoid of a shirt, with sweat glistening on his torso. His jeans hang low on his hips giving me the perfect view of the v that heads to places I shouldn't be thinking about. He looks like something out of a magazine. His abs must have been sculpted by the gods and his skin is sun-kissed in a way that tells me he walks around shirtless often.

As I take in the sight of him, my eyes land on a tattoo that rests right beneath his collarbone. It's a set of Roman numerals in a format that looks like a date, but I have no idea what it means. *How did I miss that the other day?*

"Close your mouth before you drool all over yourself." Ivy teases, making Tatum snicker.

"I was *not* drooling." My words lack confidence as I reach up and check my mouth anyway.

"What happened to your shirt?" Tatum shouts at Colton.

He looks up at us and smirks in a way that makes my heart skip and my stomach twist. When his eyes land on me, my cheeks flush. All the resistance I had earlier is gone and I'm left with way his stare can make my blood run hot.

Just as I'm about to open my mouth with whatever sassy comment I can think of, Parker walks out the door. His upper half is also bare. He's not as toned as Colton, but still just as hot. The way he carries himself shows the level of confidence he possesses. It's a quality that greatly increases his sex appeal.

My mouth opens and closes like a fish out of water while I try to figure out when my life became a PG-13 version of Magic Mike. When I can't think of what to say, I bite my lip and divert my eyes to the ground.

Once they're out of sight, Ivy groans. "Seriously, Mac, the way they both look at you - you're such a lucky bitch."

All I can do is laugh.

AFTER FIVE HOURS AND countless trips to the truck and back, all the boxes and furniture are finally inside. We're drinking beer to celebrate as I look around at everything I need to unpack. A part of me considers Parker's offer of hiring someone to do it, but then I would have to learn where everything is.

Maverick is looking at his phone when suddenly, he lights up. "It's supposed to be 80 degrees tomorrow."

"Thank you, Mr. Weatherman." I tease.

He rolls his eyes. "No, Squid. I'm saying we should go swimming at my house."

"Maverick, just because the air is warm doesn't mean your pool won't be freezing. It's only May."

Colton snorts. "It's heated."

"What?"

"The pool." He clarifies. "It's heated."

"Oh, that changes things then."

"Well, I'm up for it." Ivy volunteers. "What do you say, Mac?"

"Yeah *Mac*, what do you say?" Colton pushes.

I narrow my eyes at him, wondering what in the hell he's doing. I've told him more than once we can't be around each other and he doesn't seem to want to accept that. It's like he's taunting me right now, mentally rubbing in my face that my plan isn't going to work. However, everyone is looking at me expectantly and I can't think of a reason to say no.

"Sure, why not."

Tatum and Ivy high-five while Colton's grin widens. I can't help but smile back until my fiancé's words break our stare.

"Well, you lot have fun. I have a meeting tomorrow in Boston with my advisor."

My expression falters as I realize I'm going to be around Colton without Parker's presence to keep me from doing something I'll regret. *Lovely.*

6

Spending our first night in the new house was nothing short of amazing. Granted, there are still tons of boxes scattered around. Tatum and Ivy helped me unpack a few yesterday, but we somehow ended up drinking wine and laughing on my kitchen floor while the guys watched the football game in the living room. It wasn't productive in any way, but it *was* fun.

I step out of the shower and can already smell breakfast cooking downstairs. A smile spreads across my face as I pull on my robe and tie it around my waist. Sure enough, when I get into the kitchen, I find Parker standing in front of the stove, flipping pancakes in a way that tells me he has no idea what he's doing. Giggling softly, I sneak up and hug him from behind. He flinches for a second, then relaxes in my arms.

"I didn't know you could make pancakes."

He hums. "I can't. They probably won't taste very good."

Glancing into the bowl, I can still see clumps of dry mix. "Maybe you should let me take over?"

"I was hoping you'd say that."

My fiancé steps aside and hands me the spatula.

Immediately, I dump the burnt food in the pan, into the garbage can. Parker scoffs playfully.

"Oi, I worked hard on that!"

Pulling my wet hair into a ponytail, I raise my eyebrows at him. "Oh? So, your goal is to give us food poisoning?"

He steps closer and places his lips on my forehead. "You, my love, are a pain in the arse."

"I know." I wink.

I make quick work of salvaging the breakfast that he almost botched and the two of us sit down to eat. He takes a bite of the pancakes and moans at the taste.

"I'm a very talented chef." He boasts.

A humored laugh leaves my mouth and I shake my head. "Sure honey, you're the best." Looking around, I feel warm inside at the fact that this is our house. "I can't get over how nice this place is."

He hums in approval as he chews and swallows then washes it down with a sip of coffee. "Mr. Brooks does great work."

I nearly choke at the mention of Colton. "I'm sorry, what?"

"Colton Brooks. This house is one of his designs."

"How do you know that?"

"It was in the paperwork from the builder. He was listed as the architect. He didn't tell you?"

I should've known with the way everything is so perfectly blended together. Still, he said nothing yesterday as all of us were talking about how nice it is. I'm surprised he didn't at least mention it to Maverick or Tatum. Neither of them had any idea either – they would've told me.

"No, I had no clue."

"Hmm. Well, that'll give you something to talk about today. You're still going to Maverick's, aren't you?"

To be honest, the thought of being around my ex without Parker there is scary to me. It's not that I would jump at the chance to cheat on him, but with how Colton acted when we were alone in the truck yesterday, I'm not sure it's a good idea.

"I don't know. I think I might stay here. We still have a lot to unpack."

He stands up and takes both our empty plates from the table. "Nonsense, go have fun. You and I can unpack tonight after I get home."

"Are you sure? Because I can stay and get a lot done. I don't mind."

"I'm positive, McKenna. We just got back a week ago. You should be spending time with your friends."

Friends, right. The fact that all I can focus on is Colton being there is *every* reason why I shouldn't go. No part of my brain acknowledges that Maverick, Tatum, Ivy, and Roman will all be there, too. However, I'm not ready to tell Parker about my history with Colton so instead, I nod and get up to go get ready.

———

AFTER SAYING GOODBYE TO my fiancé, I put on my helmet and climb onto my tiffany blue Vespa. It was a gift from my parents when I turned seventeen. I didn't take it with me to NYU because the traffic there scares me more than clowns do, but my dad took care of it while I was gone. I've missed being able to ride this thing.

I make the drive over to Maverick's place. It's short, maybe only five minutes, which barely gives me any time to prepare myself for the situation I'm about to be in. As I pull up in front of the house, I shut off the Vespa and take my helmet off. Running my fingers through my hair, I take a deep breath – telling myself that my brother will be there. There is comfort in knowing he won't come onto me in front of Maverick.

When I finally feel like I at least have *somewhat* of a handle on things, I walk up to the front door and step inside.

"Hello?" I call out.

"Squid!" Mav yells back.

I walk through the dining room and into the kitchen. My brother is leaning with his elbows on the island while Colton rests his ass against the counter. I can feel my heart start to race at the sight of my ex but I will myself to calm down and focus on Maverick.

"Drinking a beer already? It's eleven in the morning."

He smirks and shrugs his shoulders. "Are you saying I can't?"

"I'm saying it's a little early."

Picking up the can from the counter, he chugs the rest of it in one shot. I roll my eyes as I nudge him playfully. He laughs and crumples the can in his hand before tossing it into the can.

"It's nice to have you home. We've missed you around here."

With a quick ruffle of my hair, he disappears out the back door – leaving Colton and I alone together. I do my best to fix the damage to the top of my head. It's a good distraction, until he speaks.

"I'm drinking coffee. Do I get out of being lectured, *squid*?"

My eyes narrow on him. "Okay, you don't get to call me that. You lost *the right* to call me that."

"Oh yeah? When did that happen?" He brings the cup up to his mouth to take a sip, but his eyes stay focused on me.

With a level of confidence that I didn't know I had, I cross my arms and pop my hip to the side. "The first time you fucked me senseless."

Colton sprays the coffee from his mouth all over the counter, coughing to clear his throat. He looks shocked by my words but that was the point. I smirk triumphantly and turn to go to the pool.

"You may want to clean that up." I call out as I close the door behind me – not missing the faint laugh he lets out.

I MUST ADMIT, TODAY is perfect for lounging outside. It's warm but there isn't enough humidity to make it uncomfortable. Maverick splurged on the expensive chairs, and honestly, I could lie here all day.

"Can I just tell you how much I've missed that Vespa?" Ivy's voice echoes through the backyard, signifying her arrival.

"You still can't have it."

She sighs and plops down into the seat next to me. "Fine, then you can't have this." The notebook she waves in front of me is so familiar that my eyebrows furrow.

"Is that…"

"The notebook we passed back and forth the end of senior year? Yes."

I sit up and grab the book from her hands. "I can't believe you kept this."

"Are you kidding?! It's like the holy grail of our friendship." She gets comfortable and puts her feet up. "I have the rest of them too but I only brought that one."

Opening it to the first page, I notice it starts in April. We wrote so many notes back and forth that we would fill one of these up within just a couple of months. From complaints about teachers to gushing about boys, there wasn't a single thing we didn't write down. It's fun to look back at them.

April 7, 2015
Mac,

I swear, if the boy next to me continues to smell like fish, I'm going to end up dropping out of school. I don't care if I only have two months until graduation. Nothing is worth not being able to breathe during pre-calc. I can't wait to go to college. I'm going to meet some cute California boy and we're going to have gorgeous tan babies together. Okay, maybe not. I don't know if I could handle kids. But I will meet a tanned hottie who will sweep me off my feet. Can you believe prom is only a month and a half away? I think I'm more excited for the trip after than I am for the dance, but whatever. It's all exciting. Okay, time to switch classes now. See you in a minute.

Love you loser,
Ivy

I laugh at the pointlessness of the entire thing, but that's what they were – just pages and pages of useless information. Well, at least most of it is, until I reach a page I remember writing quite well.

April 20, 2015
Ivy,
So, I may have already chewed your ear out about this all last night and this morning, but seriously - I cannot stop thinking about it. I can't believe Colton kissed me. Colton Brooks fucking kissed me! What does this even mean? I didn't see him before he left my house this morning, so I have no idea what is going to happen from here. Do I try to talk to him about it? Do I play it off like nothing happened? Did he even mean to do it or does he regret it now? Seriously, Ivy. I'm losing my damn mind. I can still feel the way his lips felt on mine. It was amazing. By far the best kiss of my life. Okay so it was the only kiss of my life, but still. Maybe I won't end up going to college a virgin after all.

Help me before I go crazy,
McKenna

I remember the way I drove myself insane thinking about it. Looking at what I scribbled in the corner, I pause.

McKenna
+
Colton
04/19/2015

Why does that look so familiar? I wrack my brain trying to figure out why I can't look away from that date. *Four, nineteen, two thousand fifteen. Four, nineteen, two thousand fifteen.* The minute it hits me, my entire body tenses up. Suddenly, there isn't enough air in my lungs. My eyes search frantically for Colton and when I find him, he's standing next to Roman near the tiki bar Maverick has outside. I look at his tattoo and it confirms everything.

IV.XIX.MMXV

"Oh my god." I gasp.

"What?" Ivy asks, but I can't look away. "Mac? Are you alright?"

"Oh. My. God."

"McKenna, what is it?!"

Colton's head turns at the sound of Ivy's concern. He gives me a confused look as I stare at the tattoo. When he glances down at the book in my hands and then at ink on his own skin, his eyes widen. He puts his beer down on the bar and rushes over to me. In one quick motion, he grabs my wrist and pulls me inside. I follow behind him willingly, too shocked to fight it.

We go straight up the stairs and into his bedroom. He grabs a shirt and throws it on, but it's too late. I've already seen it. My eyes stay fixated on where the tattoo is, even though it's now covered by fabric.

"Y-you…you…" I try to speak but the words just won't come out.

Colton sits down on the edge of his bed and puts his head in his hands. "Spit it out, McKenna."

"Your tattoo…"

He looks up and his eyes meet mine. "What about it?"

"It's the date of our first kiss." The words sound foreign on my tongue so I say it again. "You got the date you first kissed me tattooed on you."

"I did."

"W-why?"

He runs his hand through his hair, messing it up in a sexy, distracting kind of way. "What do you mean, why?"

None of this makes any sense. The man sitting in front of me is the one who spent the whole summer making me feel like nothing in the world could drag me down – then broke it off like it was the easiest thing in the world. Now, I come to find out he has a very sentimental date permanently inked into his skin.

"Why, Colton? Why did you get that? We broke up, and that was *your* choice. I wanted to be with you. I wanted you to tell Maverick, and I wanted us to spend the weekends and holidays together. I even considered transferring to Boston

University for you! So why in the world do you have *that date* tattooed on your body?!"

He opens and closes his mouth a couple of times before he exhales. "It's not a big deal."

"Not a big deal?! *Henna* is not a big deal. *Pen* is not a big deal. Is that either of those?"

"No."

"Then how in the world is it *not* a big deal?!" When he doesn't answer, and starts to pace around the room, I grow impatient. "Colton!"

"I was drunk, okay?" He stops and turns to look at me. "It was shortly after you left and I missed you. I got drunk and it seemed like a good idea at the time."

I'm not sure if his words make me feel better or worse. Hearing that he missed me enough to get drunk over it makes me realize that maybe he wasn't as okay as I assumed. That shouldn't matter though. He knew where I was. If he was *that* upset, he could have done something about it.

"So, four years ago, you missed me, got drunk, and somehow wound up at a tattoo parlor?"

"Pretty much."

An involuntary giggle bubbles out of me. I cover my mouth to try and stop it but it's no use. The next thing I know, I'm tearing up from laughing so hard. Colton looks at me like I'm crazy before he joins me.

"Y-you got a drunk tattoo about m-me."

"I'm glad you find this so funny."

I take a few minutes to calm myself down and catch my breath. "I'm sorry. I'm good now."

"Mhm." He smiles.

"Why didn't you just get it removed?"

His eyebrows raise. "Do you know how much that shit hurts?! And you need to go like seven times before it's gone. I'd rather just leave it."

"Okay, understandable." I lean against his dresser and let

it all sink in. My childhood crush has something about me permanently on his body. Then, a thought pops into my mind. "What do you tell people?"

"Huh?"

"Like when you're with women. I'm sure some have asked you about it; what it signifies."

He looks as if he's about to say one thing, but then shakes his head and settles on something else. "I make shit up, like the date I decided on architecture or something."

"Probably smart. It wouldn't be much of a turn on if you told them the truth."

One second the mood is light, but in another it changes to something serious. The two of us stare at each other from across the room. The tension is so thick it's overwhelming. Out of habit, I take my bottom lip between my teeth. He stalks toward me and doesn't stop until our bodies are only centimeters apart. His fingers lightly touch my face and pull my lip free before he glides his knuckles down the side of my neck.

"Colton." I whisper. "We can't."

"Tell me you don't want me. Look me in the eyes and say it. Say the words and I'll walk away right now."

"You should walk away regardless."

"Say it."

I try to. I try forcing the lie out of my mouth but I can't get my brain to cooperate. Instead, I sigh. "Colton."

"You can't say it because you feel it, too." He places his hands on my hips and rests his forehead against mine. "The pull that was between us all those years ago, it's still there. You know it as well as I do."

Closing my eyes, I try to find some balance – convince myself of all the reasons this is a bad idea. I can't let myself do this, no matter how bad I may want it.

"Whether I do or not is irrelevant. I'm getting married in a few months."

"I know." He pauses then groans before stepping away and running his hands over his face. "I know. I just, I miss you, Mac. I miss having you in my life, and this whole avoiding each other thing you want to do is my worst nightmare. I can't know you're this close and not be able to be around you. I've known you for more than half my life."

"I-"

His finger raises to stop me. "Just let me finish." I swallow what I was about to say and nod. "I don't like it, but if it's what you really want, I'll do my best. I'll try not to be here when you have plans with Maverick or Tatum. I'll make an excuse not to go places where I know you'll be. Hell, I'll even figure out a way to not be at your wedding if it comes to that. You deserve to be happy, McKenna, and if that's what you need – I'll do it."

I don't know what to say, so I choose to not say anything at all. I think he knows that because instead of expecting me to speak, he places a soft kiss to my forehead, then leaves me alone in his bedroom. Giving myself a minute to breath and compose myself, I fix my hair and head back downstairs.

Through the glass doors I can see Colton sitting with his guitar on one of the lounge chairs while Roman and Maverick are playing a game of corn hole. Just as I'm trying to see where Ivy and Tatum are, I hear their voices coming from the kitchen. The last thing I want is to be alone with Colton right now, especially not when I have no idea what to say to him. So, I follow the voices of my two closest friends.

"There you are." Ivy sounds relieved to see me. "What the hell was that about?"

"Please tell me you two didn't just fuck." Tatum chimes in.

I ignore them both and head straight for the fridge. Thankfully, the bottle of wine is right in front. I grab it, pop cork out, and bring it straight to my lips. It's a little dry for my taste, but I don't care. All I need is for the alcohol to course through my bloodstream so I can process what the hell just happened.

"They did. They totally just fucked." Ivy murmurs.

"Damn it, McKenna. I told you not to go there." Tatum rubs her temple frustratedly as I pull the bottle away from my mouth.

"Will you two just shut up for a minute?!" I shout, causing them both to freeze. I focus my attention on Tatum. "Did you know?"

"Know what?"

"About his tattoo. Did you know?"

"What tattoo? The roman numerals on his collar bone?" I nod. "No. He never told me what it's about. Why?"

I turn to Ivy. "It stands for April 19th, 2015."

Her jaw drops. "That's the…"

"The night we first kissed. Yeah, I know." Neither of them seem to know what to say as I take another swig of wine. "He said he was drunk and basically made it seem like a mistake."

"Do you believe him?" Ivy questions.

I shrug. "I have no reason not to, I guess."

"How did I not catch that?" Tatum whispers to herself. "He's…"

My eyebrows furrow. "He's what?"

"Nothing. It's nothing. So, what now?"

"Well, he said that he wants me in his life but that if I really think we should have nothing to do with each other, he'll do it. He'll stay away."

"That's good, right? That's what you want."

Ivy snorts beside her. "If you honestly think that's what she wants, you don't know McKenna."

I rest my elbows on the counter and put my head in my hands. When did everything become so complicated? Why couldn't I have come back home to find him in a serious relationship with someone else? Ugh, even the thought of that makes me feel sick to my stomach.

"This is stupid." I tell them. "Isn't it? I mean, it's Colton. He was my friend long before he was something more."

Tatum makes a face of uncertainty. "I don't think he was ever just a *friend* to you."

I look to Ivy but she just smiles sympathetically. "I have to agree with Tate on this one. You were in love with him for years. He may have thought you were just friends, but you always wanted more."

They're not wrong. All little girls have one epic crush. It's the one person they picture marrying when they're older and starting a family with. When they think of their dream wedding, it always has that crush standing at the end of the aisle. Colton was that person for me. I was only seven when we met, but I'd never looked at a boy the way I looked at him.

Still, can I really do this? Can I live in this town and not have him in my life? He's Maverick's best friend and my parents have watched him grow up. To avoid each other, it would take a constant effort on both our parts. Is it really worth the hassle when I don't want to stay away either?

Not giving myself another second to overthink it, I go into the fridge and grab two beers, then head for the door. It isn't until I'm about to open it that Tatum tries to stop me.

"You're playing with fire."

I look back at her and shrug. "I'm not afraid of getting burned."

As soon as I step outside, I can hear Colton playing his guitar from across the patio. It's something he taught himself to do when he was thirteen. He said he needed to occupy his mind and playing music is the perfect outlet for him. I recognize the tune – Happier by Ed Sheeran. My brain starts to dwell on the significance, but I shake myself out of it. *Not the time.*

When I step in front of him, he looks up at me. His tropical blue eyes meet mine and I can see the vulnerability in them. It almost breaks my heart, *almost*. I hand him the beer, making him stop playing to take it, then I sit down on the chair beside his. The sound of both cans popping open fills the silence.

"Does this mean…"

I take a sip of my beer before laying back in the chair and pulling my sunglasses back over my eyes. "Friends. Just friends."

He doesn't say anything else, but I don't miss the way the corners of his mouth raise and how the song he was playing changes to something a lot more upbeat. I can handle this. We're mature adults. Just because we have a history together doesn't mean that we can't have be friends. Nothing has to happen between us. We can stay… Okay, maybe this *is* dangerous.

7

I'VE NEVER UNDERSTOOD THE CONCEPT OF mimosas. How does mixing champagne with orange juice make it an acceptable morning drink? If that's true, wouldn't screwdrivers be the same? They just switch out the bubbly for vodka. The same thing goes for a Bloody Mary – just because it's vegetable juice doesn't mean it goes with your oatmeal.

My phone vibrates on the table. I glance around to make sure no one else is paying any attention as I grab it and open the new message.

Colton: Hey Short Stack. What are you up to?

The beat of my heart intensifies, though I do my best to ignore it.

McKenna: Day drinking, apparently. What about you?

"McKenna, what do you think?" My mom asks, causing Tatum and Ivy to turn to me.

"About what?"

"The floral arrangements. Weren't you listening?"

Shit, no. I really should have been.

"Oh, uh, I was."

Ivy chuckles beside me. "No, you weren't."

"Whose side are you on here?"

"Yours, babe. Always yours."

My brows raise as I take a sip of my mimosa, but my best friend just smiles innocently. Today, I'm going wedding dress shopping. However, according to Tatum, it's a big deal and requires at least half a day of festivities – which is why I'm currently at brunch with her, Ivy, and my mom. Tatum recommended I invite Parker's mother as well, but I didn't see a point. It's not like she would fly over from England just to see me try on a few dresses.

Another text comes through, making my phone vibrate in my hand.

Colton: Working like a normal person on a weekday.

Then another.

Colton: Day drinking? Should I be looking up AA meetings in the area? Have you become the next good girl gone bad?

I can't help but grin at his antics.

McKenna: Definitely. Alert the press.

Colton: I can see the headlines now. "McKenna Taylor – How She Went From Pretty, Pretty, Princess to Drunken, Drunken, Slob."

Laughter bubbles out of my mouth before I can stop it, causing everyone to look my way. Mom doesn't seem too concerned, but Tatum and Ivy share a suspicious look. It's like they're communicating without words before Ivy sighs and turns to me.

"What's got you all giggly?"

Can I tell them? Are they capable of understanding? If they knew I was texting Colton, would they really think it's a good idea? Ivy might not try to stop me, but Tatum would give me the lecture of all lectures. I can practically hear her voice in my head, reminding me of how much he hurt me and how stupid I am for even giving him the time of day. I mean, it's not like they're enemies – she likes Colton. She just doesn't like Colton *for me*. To be honest, I don't blame her. She saw the damage he caused that night. Maverick was confused for the seven weeks Tatum refused to be anywhere near him when he was around his best friend. There was no way she could explain why though. If my brother found out the reason why I stayed away from home the past four years, he would kill him with his bare hands, then sit down at the dinner table like nothing happened.

"Just something Parker said." I lie, hoping to hell they can't see through it.

Tatum and my mom coo, breaking off into their own conversation about how cute we are together. Ivy, however, gives me a knowing look. I smile apologetically and glance over towards Tatum, hoping she gets the point – she does. It's like an unspoken bond between my best friend and me. She knows that I'll tell her everything when I figure it out for myself, and I know she'll have my back no matter what it is.

THE FOUR OF US finish our meals and alcoholic beverages, then climb into the ridiculously unnecessary limo that Tatum *insisted* on reserving. I told her repeatedly that we didn't need one. The boutique is so close to the restaurant that we could walk there and then each take an Uber home if we were too intoxicated to drive, but she didn't listen. Every time I suggest doing things in a way that's less than spectacular, she gives me this long speech about how you only plan a wedding once and it should be the best time of your life. Well, I don't know about her, but the best time of *my life* would be sitting on the beach and drinking a beer.

The bridal boutique is filled with extravagant dresses. They have everything from short and cocktail-like, to ones with a poof large enough to fit the whole wedding party underneath it. I was instructed to look up some styles before coming, but then Colton and I had gotten into a debate about whether longboards are better than shortboards and all thoughts of my upcoming nuptials went flying out the window.

"Welcome to Atelier Cape Ann. Do you have an appointment?"

The woman standing in front of us is older, maybe mid-sixties. Her gray hair goes down to just above her shoulders. She gives off the same compassionate vibes my mom does. It's comforting.

"We do." Tatum answers. "It's under McKenna Taylor."

"Ah, I see. And are you the bride?"

I don't miss the way she winces at the question. She's been waiting for my brother to propose to her for years now. I'm sure he heard an earful when Parker and I got engaged. To be honest, I don't know what he's waiting for. They've been together for almost eight years. If he doesn't pop the question soon, she's going to leave him behind and find someone who's willing to commit.

"I'm not. This-" She gestures toward me. "-is McKenna."

The woman puts out her fragile hand. "It's very nice to meet you, Miss Taylor. Congratulations on your engagement."

"Thank you, and you can just call me McKenna."

"Well, then you can just call me Sophie." She smiles. "I have a room in the back set up for you and your guests. There's champagne and water bottles for your enjoyment. Is there any kind of dress style you had in mind?"

Tatum gives me a look, making me immediately feel guilty for not doing the research I was supposed to. An idea comes to mind and I jump on it.

"Honestly, I couldn't really decide. I was hoping my friends could help me out with that. They know what looks best on me."

"Correction, *I* know what looks best on you." Ivy pipes up. "Miss Limousines and Mimosas over there will have you looking like something out of candy land."

"Hey!"

I put my hand up to stop the argument I know is coming. "Nope, she has a point. Okay, it has to be ivory or white, and can't fit more than one person underneath it."

"Oh, it's *so* on." Tatum challenges.

Her and Ivy disappear into the many racks of dresses, making playfully snide comments to each other about who knows me more. I chuckle to myself and walk with my mom to our reserved room. It has a platform in the middle that faces a wall full of mirrors, some flat and some angled to provide all different views of the dress at once. There are tiaras and veils showcased on the wall right above an elegant looking dresser. Sitting in a bucket of ice is a bottle of champagne. There are flutes next to it and waters beside them. My mom takes a seat on the couch while I open the champagne and pour us each a glass. We already started drinking; no point in stopping now.

I sit down next to my mom and hand her one of the glasses. She thanks me quietly and takes a sip, looking around the room in awe. I watch her for a second before placing my hand on her knee.

"Are you okay?"

She smiles as tears build in her eyes. "I just can't believe this is happening. My baby is getting married."

"Oh God, don't start the waterworks yet. I'll have mascara running down my face before I even get into a dress."

A wet laugh leaves her mouth. "I just always thought I'd be watching Maverick and Tatum plan their wedding first. You were always so closed off from boys that I wasn't sure you'd ever let someone in enough to get engaged, let alone married."

"Oh, thanks." I chuckle.

What she doesn't know is that the only reason I seemed 'closed off' is because I was too focused on one boy in particular. My entire world revolved around Colton. The way his hair stuck to his forehead from sweating in the summer heat. How his eyebrows furrowed as he tried to land a skateboard trick. The definition of his abs when his shirt would raise while stretching. I had every part of him memorized like the lyrics to my favorite song. There was no time for anyone else, nor did I want there to be. He was all I wanted, all I *needed*.

"I'm so glad you found Parker." She interrupts my thoughts.

I don't answer. It's not that I don't love my fiancé, I do – but I'd be lying if I said I hadn't thought of what all this planning would be like if the groom was different. Would the idea of dress shopping have me researching the style I would look best in for all hours of the night? Would I be excited to pick out floral arrangements instead of dreading it? Parker has pretty much left all the decision making up to me, and I've left it all to Tatum. Maybe wedding planning just isn't my thing.

Yeah, that's bullshit. I was excited until my ex walked back into my life like a hurricane, destroying the walls I've spent the last four years building.

The thought of him reminds me that I never answered his

last text during brunch. I take out my phone, snap a picture of my drink, and send it over with nothing more than a few heart emojis. Just as I'm slipping it back into my pocket, Ivy and Tatum come barreling into the room with their arms full of dresses.

"Wow, okay." My eyes widen. "I said to help me pick a dress, not bring the whole store into the dressing room."

"Ha ha. Very funny." Ivy quips. "We each picked three, so you have six to try on, unless Mom wants to go choose three more – then you'll have nine."

"I think I'll just see what you've found so far." My mom answers and I let out a breath I didn't know I was holding.

After a short debate between who's choices go first, I follow Tatum into the dressing room. She's got one of her's and one of Ivy's dresses hanging on the wall. In true competitive nature, they won't tell me who picked what so that I don't choose based off who I like more. If I know, I'll be inclined to pick Ivy – hands down, always.

"Okay, you're not going to like this, but I have to put a corset on you." I turn around and look at the item Tatum has in her hands and raise my eyebrows at her. "It will make the dresses look better. Don't be difficult."

Reluctantly, I raise my arms and let her squeeze me into the tight garment. It practically forces the air out of my lungs with how much it constricts my body. If I need to wear this, I can guarantee I won't be able to sit down at my wedding.

"Jesus Christ. Could this thing be any tighter?!"

"Oh, relax."

"*You* relax. My ribs are going to be bruised by the time I get out of this."

She rolls her eyes and chuckles as she grabs the first dress. "Alright Drama Queen, come on. Let's get this dress on you."

BY THE TIME I'M trying on the fourth option, I'm exhausted. All of them are nice but none make butterflies erupt in my stomach. Sophie told me to try to picture saying my vows in each one. That didn't work either. I make my way back into the dressing room and grab my phone as I wait for Tatum to come in to untie me. Finding two messages from Colton, I smile and open them.

Colton: Wow. You weren't kidding about the day drinking.

Colton: Don't get too wasted. It's only noon on a Wednesday. You don't want all the old ladies in town talking about what an alcoholic you've turned into.

I chuckle. He's right but I know I'm nothing close to drunk.

Me: What if that's exactly what I want? 🙂

Tatum coming in causes me to throw my phone down onto the bench. She narrows her eyes but when I don't say anything, she shakes it off and steps behind me. Just as she's finished unlacing the back of the dress, there's a loud vibration against the wood and my phone lights up – Colton's name on full display. I close my eyes and wince; I'm caught.

"*Why* is Colton texting you?"

"I don't know. I'll just check it later."

The two of us stare at each other for a second and then both move at once. I get to my phone first but she snatches it out of my hand before I can get a good grip on it. *Fuck. Why didn't I set passcode when Julia told me to?!*

"Tatum, give me my phone."

She laughs. "Yeah, that's not going to happen." Her finger

swipes up and the phone opens right to the texts between him and I. I read the newest one over her shoulder.

Colton: Just be careful, Princess.

"*Princess?*"

"It's a joke. He calls me that because I used to play pretty, pretty, princess when I was seven."

Ignoring me completely, she scrolls up and sees the never-ending texts from the last four days. On Sunday, after I left Maverick's, Colton had messaged me to make sure I still had his number. Since then, we've been in almost constant contact. We've talked pretty much all day, every day, so I know how bad it looks as Tatum flicks her finger through the message thread.

"McKenna, these go on for fucking ever."

I grab my phone from her hand but this time she doesn't put up a fight. Instead, she turns to me and puts one hand on her hip, looking at me expectantly. I put it back on the bench and run my fingers through my hair.

"We're friends."

"Really? That's what you're going with? *Friends?*"

"I'm not *going with* anything. It's the truth."

"Okay, so I take it Parker knows about all those texts in your phone?" I hesitate and that's all the answer she needs. "Mac. Come on, you know better."

"We're not doing anything."

"Maybe not physically, but you haven't told your fiancé about you two being *friends*." She puts air quotes around the word like the idea of it is outlandish. "If you honestly believed there's nothing wrong with what you're doing, you'd have nothing to hide."

I peel the dress down my body and step out of it, leaving me in nothing but the corset and my underwear. "I'm not hiding it. There just hasn't been anything to tell."

"You lied earlier. You said that you were laughing at something Parker said, but he hadn't said anything, had he? You were laughing at a message from Colton."

"And your point?"

"My *point* is that you're hiding it. How would you feel if you found out Parker was spending multiple hours a day texting someone he used to hook up with? Someone who he was over the moon *in love* with." I cringe, genuinely feeling sick to my stomach at the thought. Tatum sighs and the two of us sit on the bench. "Trust me, babe. I get it. He's Colton Brooks. He's funny, and successful, and has a smile that could light up the room – but he's never going to be the type to settle down. He's always going to be the guy who took your virginity and broke your heart a few months later. It sucks, I know, but do you really want to risk your future with a man who loves you to death, for a guy who hurt you like that? I've seen the way Parker looks at you. He'll go to any lengths to make you happy. Don't give that up."

With that, she stands and leaves me alone to think about what she said. I let my head lull back against the wall, wondering if I'm even capable of giving Colton up completely. Now that I've had him back in my life, I don't know that I can.

———

WE END UP FINDING the perfect dress after spending a total of six hours in the boutique. I lose count of the gowns I try on. Finally, my mother goes to look through the selection and comes back with a gorgeous dress. It has lace on top and no poof at the bottom, allowing the silky material to flow down my body and show off my figure. Once Sophie puts a veil on my head and I turn to look at myself in the mirror, I see exactly why my mother and Ivy started to cry the second I stepped out. It's beautiful. *I* look beautiful.

Tatum pays for the dress with the credit card that Parker gave her for wedding expenses and all of us climb into waiting limo. I won't lie, I'm a little tipsy. After getting caught texting Colton, I started to drink more champagne than I probably should have. Still, no amount of alcohol has helped me figure out what I'm going to do.

We drop Ivy off first, since her house is closest to the boutique. She gives me a 'we'll talk' look before climbing out and heading inside. For a minute, I think Tatum is going to bring the subject up again, but thankfully the fact that my mom is with us makes her decide against it. The limo pulls up to my house next and I smile when I see that Parker is back from his first day of classes. I hug my mom and Tatum goodbye, thanking them for their help today.

As soon as I step inside, I'm greeted by the smell of delicious food. My stomach growls, being empty since brunch. Soft music is coming from the living room and I can faintly hear my fiancé humming along.

I walk through the house and into the kitchen. Parker is standing at the counter, chopping up vegetables. He looks up from what he's doing and sends a breathtaking grin my way. I couldn't stop myself from smiling back if I tried. My feet carry me over to him and he immediately places the knife down and wraps his arms around me.

"How was dress shopping?"

"Long." I extend onto my tippy-toes and place a soft kiss on his lips. "How was your first day of med school?"

"Long." He jokes. "No, it was great. It's going to be a lot of work, but I'm excited."

"I'm really proud of you."

"Thank you, love." Returning to what he was doing, he gestures towards the fridge. "I picked up a bottle of your favorite wine on my way home."

"Best. Fiancé. Ever."

I pour myself a glass and sit on the island, watching

Parker cook the only dish his mother taught him how to make. He said it's the only thing she cooks herself, but she taught him one day when the power was out and there was nothing better to do. We talk about how much he likes Harvard and how even though his professors seem tough, they're geniuses and he's excited to learn from them.

When dinner is done, I move to go to the dining room but he stops me and heads for the couch. I look at him like he's gone crazy. Since we've been together, he's always said that meals should be eaten at a table and that a couch is for relaxing. When he notices my expression, he shrugs and continues into the living room.

He puts the plates on the coffee table and goes back into the kitchen to get more wine. I thank him while he refills my glass and then sits down next to me. The two of us eat in silence, too wrapped up in the mouthwatering meal to speak. However, when we finish, he turns his entire body to face me and takes my hand into his.

"I owe you an apology."

"You do?"

He nods. "I didn't talk to you before signing up for courses. I'd made you a promise about this summer and then I went and changed it without speaking to you first. You don't deserve that and I'm sorry."

Pulling me into his arms, I go willingly – letting him hold me. He brings my hand up to his mouth and kisses across my knuckles. I smile and relax against his chest. Despite the rocky start we've had to the summer, there have also been great things happening. We bought a house, chose a date for the wedding, and today, I found my dress. So yeah, maybe him starting school a little early throws a wrench in my plans, but it's not the end of the world.

The two of us spend the next couple of hours drinking wine, cuddling on the couch, and talking about everything under the sun. He tells me about a guy who thought he was smarter than the professor, only to be wrong and embarrass himself in front of the entire class. I tell him about how Ivy and Tatum spent hours trying to find me the perfect dress, and my mom managed to find it in ten minutes. We laugh together, reminding me of all the reasons I agreed to marry him in the first place.

When nine o'clock hits, Parker stands up and stretches, telling me he needs to get to sleep. Harvard is over an hour away and his first class starts at eight, meaning he needs to be awake really early. Just as he gets to the doorway, my phone vibrates – a text from Colton.

"McKenna?" My fiancé questions. I look up at him and he gives me a soft smile. "Are you coming?"

My sight moves back and forth between my phone and the man I promised to spend forever with. This is it. Do I stay awake and talk to Colton, or do I go with Parker upstairs? *Colton or Parker, McKenna? Colton or Parker?*

"Yeah."

I get up and walk towards the door – leaving my phone on the couch and the text unanswered.

8

PARKER'S CONTAGIOUS LAUGH BELLOWS THROUGH the car. I can't help but giggle along with him. It's Sunday, and we're currently on our way to my parents' house for family dinner. Somehow, we ended up talking about embarrassing stories from when we were younger. I told him about how, when I was a kid, I thought tentacles and testicles were the same thing. When we came back from a vacation in Florida, the teacher asked me what the coolest thing I saw was. I told her I saw a jellyfish with really long testicles and the whole class broke out in hysterics.

"How old were you?"

"I don't know, I think eight."

"That's ace."

He chuckles a little more as he pulls into the driveway. I notice my brother is already here. He must have gotten off work early, because I didn't expect him to show up until later. My dad steps out of the garage and smiles warmly at us. I do my best to mask my distaste but judging by the way his expression falls, I fail.

"Hi sweetheart." He greets me as I climb out of the car,

then turns his attention to my fiancé. "Parker, nice to see you again."

"You as well, Mr. Taylor."

"Son, we're going to be family soon. You can call me John."

I snort, causing both men to focus on me. When I get a disapproving look from Parker, I roll my eyes.

"Oh please. We haven't been a family in *years*. Our wedding isn't about to be the magic cure for that."

"McKenna." Parker glares at me like I'm being unreasonable.

"Whatever. I'll meet you inside."

I walk away from the two of them, hearing him quietly apologize to my dad for my behavior. A part of me wants to stop and tell him not to speak for me, but that would only cause an argument I'm not in the mood to have right now – especially not before all of us sit down to dinner.

As soon as I walk in the door, I can hear my mom and Maverick talking in the kitchen. I follow the sound of their voices and the second he notices me, my brother engulfs me in a bear hug. He picks me up and spins me around. I playfully smack his arm, telling him to put me down. When he does, I go to my mom and give her a hug.

"I've missed you." She confesses. "And don't give me the excuse that I saw you on Wednesday. You haven't been by the house since you moved out."

"I know." I frown. "I'm sorry. There's been a lot of unpacking to get done."

While that isn't a total lie, it's also not the whole truth either. I haven't come here because seeing my dad isn't something I particularly *want* to do. No matter how much she may want us to repair our relationship, I just don't think it's going to happen – at least not any time soon anyway. The damage his actions caused is too severe.

"Are you sure this is a good idea?" I ask Colton as he pulls into the parking lot.

Don't get me wrong, it's not that I don't want to be on a date with him. Hell, that's all I've ever wanted for as long as I can remember. What I don't want is for someone to find out and tell my brother. I don't think I'd be able to handle knowing that I ruined their friendship, and believe me – it would be ruined.

He climbs out of the car and comes over to open my door, holding his hand out for me to take. "Do you trust me?"

With my life. Instead of getting overwhelmingly real about my feelings, I choose not to answer and place my hand in his. He closes the door behind me and leads us into the restaurant. To be honest, I hadn't even noticed the place until he pulled into the hidden lot. It took about a half hour to get here, meaning it's not one of the typical places someone from our small town would go.

When he opens the door for me, I step in and take a look around. It's very discreet. The lights stay low and each booth has high backs for privacy. A deep red color coats the upper half of the walls while the bottom half is a black wood. Each table has a chandelier-type light over it, dimmed as much as possible. It takes my eyes a minute to adjust to the darkness.

"Reservation for Brooks." Colton tells the hostess.

After looking in her book, she grabs two menus and leads us to a table close by. I slip into one side while he takes the other. I thank the woman as she tells us to enjoy our meal and walks away.

"How did you find this place?"

"A friend suggested it."

"A friend? Isn't the reason we're here because no one can see us together?!" My eyes widen as I frantically look around the place for anyone I may recognize.

Colton chuckles and reaches across the table to grab my hand. "Relax, babe. No one will see us."

Hearing the pet name come from his mouth, my body instantly

93

calms. His ability to make me go from frantic to zen in seconds flat has always been like magic to me. He knows exactly what to say and just how to say it. It should scare me, the way he can get me to do anything, but it doesn't.

The server comes and takes our orders. I choose the baked ziti while he goes with the filet mignon. Before she leaves, I ask her where the bathroom is. She gives me the directions and then she's gone.

"Alright. I'll be right back."

Just as I'm about to slide out of the booth, Colton's eyes grow bigger than I've ever seen them. My brows furrow as I try to figure out what's going on. If it wasn't for the fact that there's no food at our table, I'd think he's choking. He's looking at the door but when I go to see what has his attention, he lunges across the table and kisses me. Our mouths move together like they were made to do exactly this. By the time he pulls away, I've lost the ability to think of anything but him.

I shake off my dazed state and excuse myself to the bathroom. Thankfully, it's rather easy to find in the back corner of the restaurant. Splashing some cold water on my face, I need a reminder on how to breathe. My reflection stares back at me through the mirror as I try to talk some sense into myself.

"It's not a big deal, Mac. You're just on a date with the guy you've wanted forever. It's really not a big deal."

Who am I kidding? It's a huge deal.

After a couple more minutes, I manage to compose myself before leaving the bathroom. I'm halfway back to my table when the sound of someone's voice has me stopping dead in my tracks. I spin quickly to find my father, only he's not alone – he's sitting at a table ten feet away with a woman from his office. The way his hand rests on top of hers, I can tell this is anything but a business dinner.

"Dad?!"

He whips his head towards me, looking like a deer caught in the headlights.

"McKenna? What are you doing here?" When I raise my eyebrows *at his dinner guest instead of answering, he tries to talk his way out of it. "No, this isn't what it looks like."*

"Seriously?! You're going to lie to my face about it?! Are you fucking kidding me?!" With every word I say, my voice gets louder until I feel a pair of arms wrap around my waist. I don't have to look to know who they belong to. "Get the fuck off me, Colton."

"No. We're leaving. Come on."

He pulls me out of the restaurant, tossing some cash on our table as we pass by. I try thrashing around to get free but it's no use. He's stronger than I am and the hold he has on me is tighter than he's ever held me before. It isn't until he puts me in the car that the reality of the situation causes my world to crash down around me.

My dad is cheating on my mom. My poor mother, who has done everything for him the last twenty-three years, is sitting at home believing whatever excuse he gave her while he's out to dinner with some mistress whore. I can't believe him.

"Are you okay?" Colton's voice is low, which tells me he's afraid of saying anything at all.

"You knew."

"Huh?"

"You saw them when they came in. That's why you started to freak out and kissed me so I wouldn't look at the door. You fucking knew and you said nothing."

He reaches over to put his hand on my knee but I immediately push it off. Instead of trying again, he sighs and places it back on the steering wheel. We ride the half hour home in complete silence while I wonder what my life is going to be like now.

That night was the first time we ever fought. I wouldn't talk to Colton for a week after that, and I've barely spoken more than ten words to my dad since. When he got home from the restaurant, I told him that either he tells my mom or I will.

I'll never forget how hard she cried, or how Maverick punched our father in the face when he found out.

"Honey, do you mind helping your brother set the table?" My mom asks, handing me a stack of plates.

I take them from her and walk into the dining room. Maverick is already placing down the napkins and tablecloths when I get in there. I follow behind him and put a plate at each chair. However, when I'm done I realize something looks off.

One. Two. Three. Four. Five. Six. Six? Why are there six?

"Mom, I think you gave us one extra." I call out.

Counting once again, I still come up with the same number. When I look confused, Maverick starts to count as well, but with names.

"Mom. Dad. You. Parker. Colton. Me. No, it's right."

The sound of his name has goosebumps rising across my skin. "Wait. Colton's here?!"

"Yes?"

"Why?!"

A chuckle comes from behind me and all the air seems to leave the room. "Well damn, Mac. Try not to make me feel too wanted."

Fuck. Fuck. Fuck. I didn't expect to see him today, and the last thing I want is to sit at dinner with him, Parker, and my family. It's bad enough I need to pretend to like my dad. Adding more awkwardness to an already tense situation is making me feel sick.

In the worst possible timing, my mom calls for Maverick and asks for his help. He walks out of the room, leaving Colton and I alone together. I stay completely still. Maybe if I don't move, he won't say anything.

"McKenna." *Okay, maybe not.* "McKenna, look at me."

I take a deep breath, willing myself to stay calm before turning around. The second my eyes land on him, I begin to salivate at the mouth. He's wearing the shirt I got him for his

21st birthday – a turquoise, plaid button down that brings out the color in his eyes. The jeans he has on hug his hips perfectly, and his hair is messy in the way I've always loved on him. *Why does he have to be so good looking?*

"You've been avoiding me." He's not asking; he's telling me that he knows.

"Yes."

"Why?"

I mess with the bottom of my shirt, giving myself anything other than him to focus on. "Because, it's not right. I'm engaged."

A dry laugh leaves his mouth. "It's a friendship, McKenna, not a damn offer to run away together."

"I'm sorry."

"Seriously? That's *all* you have to say? You're sorry?" My eyes meet his but I don't say anything, so he continues. "You can't do this. You told me we could be friends. You can't expect me to have you back in my life for four days and then not care when you take it away again. You can't do that!"

I motion for him to quiet down, not wanting anyone else to hear us. "What are you so hell bent on being my friend for? Why is it so important to you?"

He looks as if he wants to scream, but instead, he clenches his jaw for a second then rolls his eyes. "It's not. Screw it, okay? It's fucking not."

With that, he storms away – leaving me standing in the dining room, as confused as ever.

THE SIX OF US sit around the table, eating my mom's famous lasagna. I can't remember exactly what she does differently, but I've never had anything that comes close to hers. All throughout dinner, I can feel eyes on me, and I know they're not Parker's. Staring at me the way he has been is dangerous. If Maverick notices, if he even gets the slightest idea of Colton and I ever being anything more than friends, we'll all see a side of him that puts the hulk to shame. No one will be able to stop him from leaving nothing but destruction in his wake.

"So, where's Tatum?" I ask, noticing the absence of my brother's girlfriend.

"Her sister needed her for something tonight, otherwise she'd be here."

"Oh good, so I can safely ask you when you're going to propose."

Maverick chokes a little on his drink and starts coughing profusely. "I'm sorry, what?"

"You heard me. You two have been together for nearly a decade. What are you waiting for?!"

My mom looks shocked while my dad smirks at my straight-forwardness. Neither one of them come to his rescue. They probably want the answer just as much as I do. When my brother realizes I'm still expecting a response, his eyes narrow.

"So, what? You get engaged and suddenly you're the expert on the proper timeframe now?"

A little taken back by his defensiveness, I recoil. "No, I was just wondering-"

"Cause I'm pretty sure before Parker came into the picture, you spent half your life swooning over Colton."

My jaw drops. For one, I had no idea he knew anything about my feelings for his best friend. I mean, I guess I wasn't the greatest at hiding things as a child, but I didn't think he could tell. He never said anything.

"Maverick." My mom tries to get him to stop, but he's too focused on his snickering best friend.

"What the hell are you laughing at? You can't talk either. You haven't hooked up with anyone since that mystery chick from four years ago. I mean really, that's a long time to stay hung up on a summer fling."

His words are a sudden blow to my chest. *Four years ago.* That's what Maverick said – that Colton hasn't hooked up with anyone in the last four years. Either there was someone else while he was with me, which is what I've always assumed, or the mystery woman my brother is referring to, is me.

Colton's laughter stops immediately and he looks down at his plate. His sudden discomfort is obvious. A part of me would like to believe it's because it just came out what he was, in fact, seeing someone else on the side, but I know it's not. The man who spent the past hour sneaking glances at me, now won't look at me at all.

"I-I'm sorry. I need a minute." I get up and head for the door when a hand wraps around my wrist. I turn to see Parker looking at me, mentally asking if I'm okay. "I'm fine. I'll be right back."

As I rush up the stairs, I can hear my mother reprimanding Maverick for his behavior, though I don't care to listen. My mind is racing with so many thoughts I shouldn't be having. The second I get into what was once my bedroom, my lungs search desperately for air.

Inhale, exhale. Inhale, exhale.

The sound of someone walking down the hall causes me to freeze. I know there's only one person who would dare to follow me, and it *isn't* my fiancé. Sure enough, when I turn around, I find Colton leaning against the doorway, his arms crossed over his chest and his gaze focused on the ground.

"You didn't get that tattoo when you were drunk."

He looks up and smirks but I can see it in his eyes – the pain and vulnerability he's been doing his best to hide. Suddenly, I'm right back to how I was before I left for NYU, staring at him and feeling a million things all at once.

No. This can't happen.

I do the only thing I can think of to try to push him away – lie.

"There is *nothing* between us."

"I don't believe you." He replies, taking a step towards me.

"I love Parker."

His feet move another small stride in my direction. "I don't believe you."

"You should."

"Should I?"

With one last step, he's so close that I can feel his breath on my skin. The smell of his cologne infiltrates my senses while my heart pounds rapidly against my chest. His stare bores into me with an intense level of hunger and need, reminding me of the times he's explored my body with his hands – as if he was committing it all to memory. I can feel it; that electric buzz in the air that makes my blood run scorching hot and keeps my attention solely focused on him. There isn't anything in existence that could keep the honesty from slipping off my tongue.

"No."

That's all he needs to hear. He wraps his arms around my waist and pulls me into him, pressing his lips to mine. Sparks zing through my body, a feeling only he's ever been able to cause. He's breathing life into me and sucking it out all at the same time. His tongue slips inside my mouth, letting me taste him for the first time in entirely way too long. *God, I missed it.*

My hands move to his head and my fingers lace into his hair. A groan emits from the back of his throat as I tug. The sound causes my sex to spasm, craving something to clench around. In this moment, there is nothing I want more than to rip his clothes off and dive right back into everything Colton Brooks.

"McKenna? Are you alright?"

Parker's voice from the bottom of the stairs has me pushing Colton away in an instant. My hand flies to my mouth as I realize what just happened. *I cheated on my fiancé.* My eyes tear up at the thought. Colton must realize what I'm thinking because he takes a step back, careful not to say anything. To be honest, I don't think there is anything either one of us could say right now. All I know is that I need to get out of here. I slip past him and hurry towards the door.

"Mac." He tries to stop me but I don't listen.

My feet fly down the stairs so fast that I think I might fall. When I reach the bottom, Parker places his hands on my arms to stop me. I rip myself from his grasp as the first tear slips down my face.

"I want to go home."

"What's wrong? Are you alright?"

"No. I want to go home. Just take me home or give me the keys and I'll take myself."

Thankfully, he doesn't question it. He pulls the keys out of his pocket and gives them to me, telling me to wait for him in the truck. I take them from his hand and head for the front door. Judging by the way I can feel someone staring at the back of my head, I know Colton is watching me from the top of the stairs. I can't handle seeing him again – not right now, not after that kiss. So, I do exactly what he did four years ago; I leave.

9

I LIE IN MY BED, STARING AT THE CEILING AND watching the fan blades spin. There are a million and one things I should be doing, but I can't seem to focus on any of it. The only thing I can think about is the intoxicating feeling of Colton's kiss and his body pressed against mine. However, every time I let my mind go there, it always travels back to four years ago...

"I'm telling you Ivy, today is the day."

She chuckles into the phone. "You said that yesterday, and the day before that, and the day before that and the day-"

"Okay. I get it, but there was never the right time. The fact is, I can't wait any longer. I leave tomorrow morning so it has to be tonight."

"If you say so."

I roll from my back to my stomach. "I do say so. Tonight, I'm going to tell him."

Her and I spend the next hour going over exactly what I'm going to say. When I finally feel like I've got it down, she wishes me luck and hangs up. To say I'm nervous would be an understatement of epic proportions. Before this past April, I never thought Colton would look at me as anything other than Maverick's little sister. Now, well, now I just hope to hell I'm not thinking too far into this.

This summer has been amazing. Every chance we've had, we've spent time together. He sneaks into my room after Maverick passes out. We sneak away on dates that only the two of us know about. He even slips in brief touches when no one is looking. All of it has only made my feelings for him go from puppy love to the head over heels, I'd marry you tomorrow, can't imagine my life without you, kind of love.

I'm leaving in 12 hours for NYU and the idea of ending things between us scares me half to death. Four months of finally having him is not long enough. Hell, I'm not even sure if forever is enough, but it's a hell of a lot better than one summer.

I shower quickly, making sure to shave everywhere. If I know Colton as well as I think I do, we'll be all over each other tonight. It sucks to think it might be the last time for a while, but if everything goes according to plan, it won't be too long until I see him again. Thanksgiving break is only a few months away and that's assuming he doesn't come to visit me at some point beforehand.

After blow drying my hair, I throw on a pair of gray shorts and a white camisole with lace on the bottom. I don't bother straightening my light brown locks, knowing they're going to end up in a ponytail by the end of the night anyway. Just when I finish spraying some perfume, I can hear Colton's Shelby Mustang pull in the driveway. The engine is so loud, I'd be able to recognize it anywhere.

I run down the stairs and to the front door, opening it just as he's walking up the steps. Before he gets inside, I jump on him. My arms wrap around his neck, my legs around his waist. He chuckles while he carries me inside and closes the door behind us. Usually we would be careful about any PDA, but no one's home.

"You seem happy." *He places a kiss on my neck.* "I half expected you to be all mopey today."

"Mopey?"

"Well, yeah. You leave tomorrow. I know I'm not happy about it."

I pull myself back to look at his face. "I don't want to think about that right now."

"Oh? What do you want to think about, Princess?"

My teeth bite down on my lower lip. "I can think of a few things."

"Hmm. Maybe you should show me."

Colton presses me up against the wall as I pull him into a deep kiss. Our tongues tangle in a heated battle over dominance. Like always, he wins and conquers my mouth. As the taste of him takes over my senses, he grinds himself into me. I moan at the contact. The sound only motivates him further.

He pushes us off the wall and carries me up the stairs. Blindly walking towards my bedroom, he kicks the door with enough force to make it slam shut. It's so sexy the way he takes completely control. He lays me down onto the bed and climbs on top of me. I can feel his hardened length straining against his jeans.

One hand grips my side while the other slides up my shirt to cup my breast. He takes my nipple between his fingers, tweaking it in just the right way. I arch my hips up in search of some friction. Anything to rub against would be fine but I'm happily satisfied when he pushes his pelvis down onto mine.

After he rids me of my shirt, he pulls his off as well – giving me the mouthwatering sight of his perfectly toned abs. The gym has been so good to this man. I run my fingertips down the front of him, committing it all to memory. When I finally reach the bottom, I undo the button and zipper of his jeans. He slips them off with his boxers in one swift motion.

Seeing Colton naked is something I've done so many times now, but it never gets old. It's as if his entire body was sculpted by the gods. His muscles are defined in all the right places. Even when he doesn't try, he's perfect.

He pulls the rest of my clothing down my legs and tosses it onto the floor. Once he's done, I tug him back on top of me and connect our lips again. It doesn't take long before I can feel him at my entrance. He teases me for a minute, causing me to whimper. A seductive laugh bubbles out of his mouth but before I can say anything, he's pushing inside of me.

Building up a pace that manages to hit all the right places, he drives me wild in the way he moves. The room is filled with breathy moans and the sounds of our bodies moving together. When he can hear that I'm getting close, he smirks and slips his thumb between us – pressing it against my clit. My whole body contracts as my orgasm rips through me. The way I squeeze his cock causes him to explode. He pulses as he empties everything he has inside of me. We haven't gone without a condom often, since I've only been on birth control for a few weeks, but the rawness of it makes me feel so much closer to him.

He collapses on top of me and tries to calm his labored breathing. I wince as he pulls out and rolls over onto the bed. His cum leaks from my sex and drips down. It's every reminder to me that he has claimed me completely – mind, body, and soul.

After getting cleaned up and dressed, I run my fingers through my knotted hair, cringing when they get stuck. Colton pulls me until I'm lying with my head on his lap. My stomach churns as nerves get the better of me. My face does nothing to hide my emotions because his brows furrow as he runs his knuckles down my cheek.

"What's wrong?"

"Nothing." *I shake my head and look away.*

"McKenna." *With a light touch on my chin, he turns me to face him again.* "Talk to me."

"I-I just…ugh." *I sit up and face the window, too afraid to see his reaction.* "I don't want to end this."

"End what?"

"This. You and me. I don't want things to change."

He moves to sit up next to me and places a hand on my back. "Babe, you're leaving for college. Things are going to change. There isn't anything we can do about that."

"We could make it work."

"Make what work? What are you saying?"

"I'm saying I want you. I want to be with you, like in a relationship – a real one. I want to be able to walk down the streets of*

New York City holding your hand. I want to talk on the phone at night while we're apart. I want your arms wrapped around me even when my family is around. I want you."

The way he takes his hand off me, as if I burned him, is instantly enough to make me regret everything that just came out of my mouth. I don't have to look at him to know he doesn't have the bright smile I imagined when I planned this out. He stands from my bed and I can already feel everything beginning to crumble as he paces in front of me.

"You can't honestly think your family knowing about us, your brother especially, is a good idea."

"Why not?"

"Why not?! Because he would kick my ass from here to Kenya! That's why not!"

I flinch from his tone. "Please don't yell."

Thankfully, he calms and moves to sit next to me, brushing my hair out of my face. It should be comforting, but I can tell by his expression I'm not going to like what he's about to say. I brace myself for the impact, though I don't think it'll do much good.

"I'm sorry. I didn't know that's what this was. I thought we were just having some fun for the summer."

"Fun?! You're saying all this – all the late nights in my room, the secret trips out of town, the hidden touches – all of that was nothing more than a casual fuck?!"

"McKenna."

"Don't!" Now it's my turn to shout. I scoot away from him and lean against my headboard with my arms crossed over my chest. "Don't say my name like that."

"Like what?"

"Like you're trying not to break me. There's no way to avoid that at this point."

He runs his hands over his face then turns to look at me. "I don't want to hurt you."

"Then don't."

"What else can I do?! Tell my best friend that I went behind his back and screwed his little sister for four months?! That I lied to his

face all damn summer? I'll lose him. He'll beat the shit out of me and cut me out of his life."

My eyes narrow. "That's not true. Yeah, he might be pissed but he could never hate you."

"I'm sorry, I can't. In a choice between you and him, I have to pick Maverick."

"I'm not asking you to choose between anyone! I just want you to give us an actual chance."

He stands from the bed and shakes his head. "I can't. We can't." Running his fingers through his hair, he looks at me as I start to break. "I'm sorry." He bends down and places a kiss to my forehead as the first tear slips out of my eye. "Good luck at NYU. I hope you find someone who makes you happy."

"You're what makes me happy." I sob.

He shakes his head and frowns. "I can't be."

With that, he turns and heads toward the door. The pain in my chest is more than I can bare. Just as he pulls it open, I jump up and run over – slamming it closed again.

"Don't do this. Don't go."

"I have to."

"You don't. We can try to figure it out. There has to be a way."

"There isn't." With his hands on my shoulders, he moves me out of his way. I crumble to the floor. "Bye McKenna."

I don't even see him leave, my eyes too watery to see anything. All I hear is the sound of his car pulling away from the house. I know they say that heartbreak is painful, but I can't imagine anything feeling worse than this. It's like my entire world is crashing down around me. All the plans I had for my future are now tainted by visions of the boy who will never truly be mine.

I TAKE A GLASS from the cabinet and place it down before grabbing the orange juice from the fridge. As I pour it into the cup, my phone vibrates on the counter and Colton's name appears on the screen. *Call number six*.

"You're not going to answer that?" Ivy's voice startles me and I almost spill the juice.

"Christ, you can't sneak up on me like that."

"Sorry. Your mom told me to come check on you. She said your brother managed to piss you off last night and today you've been radio silent."

I hit ignore on my phone and slip it into my pocket, then grab my drink. "That's half true."

"Well, judging by the way you just ignored Colton's call, I'm guessing it's not the radio silence part that's false."

I'd be stupid to think I could lie to my best friend, and honestly, I don't want to. I need to talk to someone about this and I sure as hell don't trust anyone else with it. Walking over to the couch, Ivy follows behind me. Once we sit down, I sigh as the events of last night become all too real.

"Colton kissed me."

"He what?!" She shrieks. "When?! Why?! Did Parker hit him? Please tell me Parker didn't hit him. Wait, a fight between those two might be fun to watch."

"Ivy, focus!"

"Right, sorry. What the fuck happened?"

I take a deep breath then explain everything to her – the tattoo being something he did intentionally, my brother's comment about how Colton hasn't hooked up with anyone since a 'mystery chick' four years ago, how he followed me up to my bedroom when I needed some space. She listens intently and waits for me to finish before speaking.

"Damn. I mean, the tattoo doesn't surprise me. I never believed you meant nothing to him. Anyone with eyes can see the way he looks at you. Well, everyone except your brother, apparently."

"Not helping."

"Okay, think of it this way then. Maybe it was just something he needed to get out of his system. Now it is."

I groan frustratedly. "That's the problem. I don't *want it* to be out of his system."

It takes a minute to click in her head, but when it does, her eyes widen. "Oh fuck. You're still in love with him."

"Okay, let's not make this bigger than it is. I didn't say that."

"You didn't have to. It's all over your face. That kiss meant something to you."

The butterflies in my stomach flutter as I replay it in my head. I can still feel the tight hold he had on me, pulling my body against his. He kissed me in a way that told me he needed it like he needs air to breathe. When I felt his dick harden in his jeans, I wanted nothing more than to fall back into bed with him. Meanwhile, my fiancé was right downstairs – worrying about my mental wellbeing.

"Of course, it did. This is Colton we're talking about. I don't think he'll ever be able to kiss me and it *not* mean anything, but it doesn't matter."

She looks at me as if I've grown a second head. "Uh, how *exactly* does it not matter?"

"Because it doesn't change anything. It doesn't make it so I'm not marrying Parker."

"Well, no, but *you* could make it so you're not. If Colton is who you want, you don't *have* to go through with the wedding."

She's right, but I'm not willing to let myself even consider that. "He broke my heart once. I won't give him the opportunity to do it again. I can't."

She looks as if she wants to say something but ultimately decides against it and nods once. Just like that, we leave the conversation about Colton and what that kiss could have meant in the past – right where it belongs. The two of us spend the day watching movies and eating junk food. It's everything I needed to distract my mind and relax.

QUARTER PAST FIVE, THE sound of the front door opening lets us know that Parker's home. He places his keys on the table by the door and comes into the living room less than a minute later. When he sees Ivy and I cuddled under every blanket we own, his eyebrows furrow.

"You're not ready?"

I rack my brain to try to figure out what he's talking about, but I come up empty. "Ready for what?"

"Maverick's birthday dinner. We have to be at the restaurant in an hour."

"Shit! I completely forgot."

I remove myself from the little cocoon I made with my best friend and head for the stairs. I'm halfway up them when I hear Ivy saying goodbye to Parker. As soon as she gets to the front door and I realize she's leaving, panic ensues.

"Y-you're not coming?"

"I can't. I have a date, remember?"

"Ugh!" I drop my voice down to a whisper. "How am I supposed make it through seeing him tonight without you?"

"You'll be fine. Tatum will be there, *and* your brother. He won't do anything in front of them."

I give her a knowing look that silently tells her how wrong she is. After spending an entire summer together, he learned how to get away with so many things in front of Maverick. She chuckles before giving me a hug and heading out.

WE GET TO THE restaurant a couple minutes late, mainly

because I took as long as I possibly could to get ready. Even still, I need a moment before facing Colton again, so I tell Parker I'll meet him at the table and head to the bathroom.

The room is freezing, but thankfully empty. I have the urge to splash some water on my face, but unless I want to look like a raccoon, I better not. I do, however, touch up my makeup. The bright lights in these places always make it easier to see.

After giving myself a rather motivating pep talk, I head out and over to where everyone is seated. As soon as I see them, I immediately regret not getting here earlier. The table is completely filled with my brother and everyone who loves him, and there's only one seat left for me – between Colton and Parker.

THERE ARE CERTAIN THINGS YOU'RE OBLIGATED TO
do in life. To be a good student, I had to do all my work and
study hard. To be a good daughter, I had to stay away from
drugs and not break the law. And to be a good sister, I have
to sit at this dinner with Colton on my left and Parker to my
right.

The feeling of eyes being burned into the side of my head
could be coming from one of two places – either Colton
himself, or Tatum as she watches him and I like a hawk. It's
not like I wanted to be in this position. I would have
preferred to sit in Parker's seat, next to Roman. At least *he*
didn't kiss me last night and throw me into complete mental
turmoil. Unfortunately, my fiancé took the seat next to Rome
and it would gain way too much attention if I asked him to
switch.

The hibachi restaurant is rather busy for a Monday night.
Chefs at different tables flip their spatulas and move food
around the grill like they're putting on the show of their
lives. It's mesmerizing to see how they've perfected their
craft. From cracking the egg without their hands to creating a

volcano out of onion slices – the whole thing is something no one wants to look away from.

A waitress comes to take mine and Parker's orders. While usually I would go with a water, my ex being this close makes me feel like I need something alcoholic. Once she walks away to put our choices in, Maverick leans behind Colton and closer to me.

"McKenna, I'm really sorry about dinner yesterday. I was out of line."

I can always tell when he's being sincere because he uses my name instead of the nickname I have such a love/hate relationship with. Still, at the mention of the events that lead to the moment in my bedroom, my whole body goes tense. I take a deep breath and remind myself he doesn't know anything other than I got upset and left.

"It's fine. I overreacted. Don't worry about it."

"Are you sure? You seemed pretty worked up."

"Mav, it was nothing, really. There was *nothing* significant about last night."

The double meaning is obvious and I can tell Colton hears it. He always listening, even if he makes it look like he's not. Avoiding the shift in his body, I smile at my brother and turn my attention back to Parker, though he's fully immersed in a conversation with Roman – something about why Americans call a sport football when they rarely touch the ball with their feet. Leave it to Rome to bring up one of few topics that gets his blood pumping.

The feeling of a hand on my thigh causes me to freeze. Colton squeezes just enough to get my attention. I smile at the waitress as she hands me my drink. Bringing it to my mouth, I speak in hushed tones.

"What the hell are you doing?"

He pulls my leg towards him and leans in closer. "You know as well as I do that last night was *anything* but insignificant."

"I have no idea what you're talking about."

He snickers darkly and shakes his head. "We're going to have to talk about it sooner or later."

"We don't." I rid myself of his touch and turn my whole body away from him.

This would be a lot easier had I been sitting anywhere near Tatum. She would keep me distracted and make sure Colton kept his hands where they belong – in his own damn lap. Instead, both Maverick and Colton are between us. I know better than to believe the empty seat being next to my ex was a coincidence.

The chef arrives at our table. All conversation stops as he goes over our orders and starts the show. He lights a fire that covers the majority of the grill. The heat makes all of us recoil back a little. Just as I take a sip of my drink, Colton pretends to scratch his calf as an excuse to get closer to me.

"I've always found it so sexy that you'd rather drink a beer than some fruity cocktail."

I roll my eyes but the corners of my mouth raise involuntarily. Judging by the way he smiles, I can tell he noticed.

The food is delicious, as usual. Maverick picking this place wasn't a surprise to me at all. It's been our favorite restaurant for years.

Halfway through eating my meal, Colton reaches over and takes one of my pieces of filet mignon.

"Do you mind?"

"Nope." He stares into my eyes and grins, shoving the piece of steak into his mouth. "Wow. That's really good. I should have gotten that."

His fork comes closer to grab another but I smack it away. "Stick to your chicken, Brooks."

"Oh, come on. Didn't your mother teach you sharing is caring?"

"Yes, but you're assuming I care."

He mocks offense and places a hand over his heart. "Ouch. You really know how to hit a guy where it hurts."

Is he for real? He's *actually* flirting with me, while we're sitting between my brother and my fiancé. I glance to my right and see that Parker is too focused on an email to be paying any attention. Even if he wasn't, would he think anything of it? Before I can overthink too much, Tatum leans forward and raises her eyebrows.

"Colton, switch seats with me?"

He doesn't look away from me for a second as he answers. "Nah, I'm good here."

I'm too absorbed in the intensity of his gaze that I don't notice him taking another piece of my food until he's bringing it to his mouth. I can't help but chuckle and look away. Still, I rotate my plate so that the steak is closer to him and easier to share. He grins triumphantly.

When we're all done eating, Maverick claps his hands together.

"Alright. Who's ready to go to the club?"

Uh, what? Everyone looks around the table, confused. The only two people who aren't surprised by his plans are Tatum and Maverick himself. When no one says anything, Colton shakes his head.

"Yeah, sorry man. It's a Monday night. I have work in the morning."

"Don't give me that shit. You can do whatever you damn well please."

"It's called responsibilities."

"*It's called* your best friend's birthday."

Colton's face lights up in amusement. "Do you want a Birthday Girl sash to go along with that narcissism?"

"Depends. Will it make you come out tonight?"

Before he can answer, Roman pipes up from beside Parker. "Well, not all of us own the company we work for, so I'm gonna have to pass."

Maverick scoffs. "Just call out. Your boss is a douche bag anyway."

We all laugh while Parker's brows furrow. "Isn't Colton his boss?"

"Yeah. Yeah, I am." Colton takes another sip of his beer and smiles at his best friend's antics.

He nods. "Well, while I'd love to continue celebrating your birthday, Maverick, I have a class in the morning and I'm afraid it's one I mustn't miss."

"You're the only one with a reasonable excuse, man. I get it. Thanks for coming to dinner though."

"It was my pleasure."

To be honest, I'm not quite sure my brother cares that Parker isn't joining them at the club. It's not like they're the closest of friends. I, however, know it's going to be difficult to get out of going.

"I think I'm just going to go home with Parker. I'm exhausted."

Sure enough, Maverick gives me a dead stare that tells me I don't stand a chance. "I don't think so, Squid. You missed my last *three* birthdays. You don't get to miss this one, too. You're coming."

I look to my fiancé for some support but he only shrugs. "He's right. You should go and have fun."

"I knew I liked you." Mav grins at Parker.

"Fine." I sigh, not missing the way Colton perks up at my submission.

After an intense debate between who's paying the bill, which Parker somehow managed to win, he says goodbye to everyone and I tell them I'll be right back. I walk him out to the car. He gives me a kiss and tells me to have fun tonight. When he drives away, I head back inside and straight to the bathroom.

The door is locked, telling me that it's currently occupied, so I lean against the wall and wait. In the meantime, I take out my phone and frantically dial Ivy. It only rings twice before she answers.

"Hey. Everything ok?"

"No." I reply without hesitation. "I need you to come to Mixx 360."

I can hear her shuffle around and the background noise fade. "Does this have something to do with Colton?"

"It has *everything* to do with Colton. Parker went home because he has class in the morning, but Maverick won't let anyone else out of going. I can't be alone with him, Ivy. I can't."

"Okay, okay. Calm down. I'll meet you there."

"Thank you."

We hang up the phone and I let out a long exhale. I have no idea how Colton's flirting went unnoticed by just about everyone tonight, but if I know Colton, it means that he'll only get more ballsy at the club. At least with Ivy there I'll have someone in my corner.

"Calling for back up?"

I startle and turn to see the devil himself standing unnecessarily close. "How long have you been there?"

"Long enough to hear you tell Ivy that you can't be alone with me."

Great. That's just great. I swallow down the lump in my throat and try to appear strong. "What are you doing here, Colton?"

He gestures back to the restaurant with a confused look on his face. "It's Maverick's birthday."

"No, what are you doing *here*, in this hallway? Why'd you follow me?"

"I told you, we need to talk."

Shaking my head, I look away from him and down at the ground. "No, we don't. It was nothing."

"It wasn't nothing. I kissed you, and unless I was imagining things, you kissed me back."

"I'm sorry. It was a mistake."

He takes a step closer to me, the same way he did last night, and I'm forced to look up. "A mistake? Is that right?" I nod, not trusting my voice enough to speak. "So, if I did it now…"

His voice trails off as he runs his fingertips up my side. His presence alone is enough to throw me off completely. Everything in me is screaming to move but I can't. I stay frozen, waiting for him to do something, *anything*.

"McKenna."

Tatum's voice makes Colton's head drop in defeat and he takes a step away. He gives me a look that tells me this is far from over, and turns to leave. When he passes Tatum, she smacks him upside the back of the head.

"What was that for?!" He rubs where her hand connected.

"You know what."

Colton chuckles and goes back to the table, but Tatum comes right toward me. I brace myself for the words of disappointment I know are about to come out of her mouth.

"What the fuck, Mac? What are you doing?!"

"I don't know."

"Well, you may want to figure it out real fucking quick. You're lucky it was me that found you two and not your brother. Do I even need to ask or are you still going with the 'we're just friends' excuse?" She shakes her head and takes a deep breath. "He destroyed you."

I run my fingers through my hair and push myself from the wall. "Okay, stop. Stop reminding me of what happened between us. Stop lecturing me on how wrong it is to have him in my life. And stop telling me what I should and shouldn't be doing." Her eyes widen at my outburst but I'm not finished yet. "Do you realize that every time you try to push me away from him, it only makes me want it more? It's like sticking a big red button in front of someone and telling them *not* to push it. Making him off limits isn't going to suddenly make all of this easy. I get it, he broke my heart and that should make me hate him – but I don't. He's still Colton."

Her once hard expression softens and she frowns. "I was afraid this would happen."

"What?"

"That you would come back and he would have you falling in love with him again at the snap of his fingers. I just don't want to see you give up a good thing, only for him to hurt you again. You're the closest thing I have to a sister. I worry about you."

I nod in understanding. "I get it, I do. But this is one of those things I need to learn for myself. As of right now, I'm not doing anything, so there's nothing to worry about. If there is, I'll let you know."

THE LOUD MUSIC BOUNCES around the walls of the club. The floor vibrates to the beat of the song, making you feel it in your bones. It's been a long time since I was in a place like this. Julia had brought me to someplace in the city for my 21st birthday. It was fun, but way too overcrowded. Thankfully, since it's a Monday night, it's not bad in here.

We step up to the bar and while Colton orders everyone a round of drinks, I look around for Ivy. I find her just as she's walking in. Her long blonde hair is a contrast against the black dress she's wearing. A part of me feels bad for interrupting her date, but she could've brought him along.

She comes over, greeting everyone and wishing Maverick a happy birthday. Colton gives me a look as if he's teasing me for the reason she's here in the first place. I discreetly flip him off, to which he mouths 'yes please' in response. *Ugh.*

After taking a sip of his beer, Maverick places it down on the table and drags Tatum onto the dance floor. I brace myself because I know without the worry of my brother seeing, there's nothing holding Colton back. Ivy must sense my nerves because she pulls me into a conversation about her date.

"It was nice. We went to Seaport Grille. He was a gentleman and pulled my seat out for me."

"Ooh. You don't come by those very often anymore."

She smiles but it doesn't reach her eyes. "I know. He's really sweet."

"So, what's the problem?"

"I don't know." She takes a swig of her drink. "There just wasn't that really strong connection, you know?"

"Ouch. Yeah, I could see why that would be an issue."

Ivy looks behind me and raises her eyebrows, but I don't need to turn around to figure out why. A familiar body plasters itself against my back. I try to stay calm as the burn sets in.

"We don't have that problem, do we Princess?" His tone is sulky with his lips against the shell of my ear.

I tilt my head to the side. "What do you want, Colton?"

"Dance with me."

"No."

"Please?"

"No."

His hand slips under my shirt. The feeling of his skin against mine sends shockwaves through my body. *Fuck, this is so wrong.* He pulls me closer and I bite my lip to suppress a moan.

"Dance with me, or I'll find someone who will."

It's a tempting threat, really, I won't deny that. But still, giving into him is not something I'm willing to do. I glance down at the ring on my finger, watching as it glistens in the light. No matter how much I may want him, I can't.

I turn in his hold to face him, momentarily taken back by how close we are. He smirks and glances down at my lips then back up. With all the self-control I have, I put my hand on his chest and lightly push him away.

"Then go do it."

His eyes glisten with something I can't put my finger on but it makes a chill run down my spine.

"You asked for it."

———

IT ONLY TAKES COLTON ten minutes before he has some perfect Barbie-lookalike all over him. Ivy tries to distract me, but I can't seem to stop myself from watching them. The way she giggles and puts her hand on his arm makes me feel sick to my stomach. I always knew I was possessive over him, but this is out of control. The sight of him with someone else shouldn't affect me this much.

I down my drinks like their water, needing the buzz to relax me. If I don't manage to calm down, I'm afraid I'll end up going off on him in front of my brother, and that wouldn't do anything good for anyone. *Talk about ruining his birthday.*

When Colton leads the girl to the dance floor, I head straight for the bar. Ivy watches as I down three shots in a row. By the time the fourth one gets put in front of me, I've got enough alcohol coursing through my blood to make my speech slur. I swallow the next shot, embracing the way it burns my throat.

"Can you fucking believe him?" I spit. "The nerve of that guy, I swear."

"The nerve." Ivy mocks me.

I glare at her but before I can respond, Rome steps up next to us.

"What's up with her?" He asks Ivy.

She says nothing but nods her head over to where Colton has that bimbo grinding into him on the dance floor. When he sees what she's referring to, his mouth makes the shape of an O. I scoff and wave the bartender down for another shot.

"Aw, is someone jealous?" Roman teases.

"No. I just think he could do better."

"You mean, with you?"

The logical side of me knows I should keep my mouth shut, but the drunk side just doesn't give a shit. I flip my hair over my shoulder and stand up a little straighter.

"Please. If I wanted Colton, I could have him. That girl is nothing but a petty attempt at getting a reaction out of me."

"Oh yeah?" He leans his back against the bar and crosses his arms over his chest. "Prove it."

I narrow my eyes at him. The challenge is laid on the table and I can do one of two things. I can stick to my morals and tell Roman to fuck off, or I can throw caution to the wind. The bartender places the shot in front of me and I take it in one fluid motion. I slam the glass down onto the counter and turn to Ivy.

"Go find Tatum and tell her to keep Maverick distracted."

Before she can even try to stop me, I turn and march my way towards my ex – pushing through the crowd until I'm standing directly in front of him and his flavor of the night. They're moving to the music and I almost vomit when I see the way she's humping his leg like a dog.

"Get your hands off her." I tell him.

His eyes meet mine and just like that, his hands are in the air. The girl is confused as she looks from me to him. He shrugs and gives her a cocky smile.

"Sorry babe, she's the boss."

She gives me a dirty look before pushing her way past me, shoving me with her shoulder. I'm about to return to Roman and Ivy, knowing I made my point, but Colton grabs my hand and spins me around – tugging me into his arms.

"You can't scare away my dancing partner with your jealousy and then leave me alone."

"Fine, then shut up and dance."

He holds my waist and starts to grind against my ass. I move with him to the beat of the music, losing myself in the way his body meshes with my own. My hand reaches up to wrap around his neck, pulling him impossibly closer. I really hope Ivy got to Tatum in time, because if Maverick sees the two of us this way, he's guaranteed to lose his shit.

"Did I mention how sinful you look tonight?"

All it would take is the slightest turn of my head and his lips would be on mine. I'm walking a dangerous line between frowned upon and downright wrong. Yet, as horrible as it is, while I'm dancing with the devil, my engagement isn't even a blip on my radar.

He pulls my hair to one side then places his mouth on my neck. My head lulls back against his shoulder. The moan I release is barely loud enough for him to hear but I can feel the way his dick twitches in his jeans.

"Colton." I murmur, unable to think clearly while he's *this* close. He hums in response. "Take me somewhere."

Not needing to be told twice, he wraps his fingers around my wrist and leads me off the dance floor. We walk down a darkened hallway before reaching a door. He pushes it open and pulls me inside. It's your typical stingy club bathroom, but no part of me cares at the moment. I lean against the counter and watch as he locks the door then checks to make sure no one else is in here. Once he's done, he stalks towards me like a lion with his prey.

"Do you know how long I've waited for this?" He runs his hand up my side. "How many times I've dreamt of this body." Nuzzling his face into my neck, he sucks lightly on my skin. "It's damn near impossible for me to be in a room with you and *not* be able to have you." He pulls away and places his forehead against mine. "I tried to resist you, McKenna. I tried so goddamn hard, but the need that burns inside me when I see you is so strong. I can't do it."

"Then don't."

It's the same two words I told him when he said he didn't want to hurt me, but this time the meaning is *so* different. He moves his hand to my face, rubbing his thumb over my cheek before pressing his lips to my own. For the second time in a little over 24 hours, my blood runs hot as sparks fly between us.

He grabs my hips and lifts me up, sitting me on the counter and stepping between my legs. I wrap them around his waist and my arms around his neck. When I nibble on his lower lip, a groan emits from the back of his throat. I smile into the kiss, pleased with his reaction.

His hands slide up my back as his tongue licks into my mouth. I moan at the taste of him – beer, and spearmint, and Colton. Arching my back, I do my best to grind myself into him. My intense need to have him is overwhelming.

"Colton." I breathe, saying his name like a prayer.

"Yeah Princess?"

"Fuck me."

He kisses me again, only harder this time. He grips my thighs so tight I think he may leave bruises. It doesn't hurt, but it's enough to remind me he's there. When my hands move to his belt buckle, he stops me.

"Not here."

"What?"

Letting out a long exhale, he braces himself on the counter and bows his head down – trying to calm himself. "I haven't had you in four years. I'll be damned if the first time I get to be with you again is in a dirty bathroom while we're both too drunk to think clearly."

His words cause me to suddenly feel stone cold sober. The reality of the situation hits me like a ton of bricks. We're somewhere that looks like it could give me hepatitis if I touch the wrong thing. My diamond engagement ring is so out of place in the filthy room. When my mind finally goes to Parker, a pain shoots through my chest.

"Get out." I all but whisper.

"McKenna, don't do this."

"Get! Out!"

He takes a step back as I shout in his face. The internal debate he's going through is obvious as he tries to decide if he should leave the room or try to come closer again. When his eyes meet mine, he must realize there's nothing he can say to change my mind.

"Fuck!" He screams, at no one in particular, and swings his closed fist right into the paper towel dispenser. Then, he storms out of the room, leaving me alone to process what the hell just happened.

COLTON

I STARE DOWN AT THE DOZENS OF TEXT MESSAGES I've sent McKenna. Each one has gone unanswered. Judging by the way she is when it comes to her phone, there's only one logical reason – she's avoiding me, *again*.

After we shared that kiss at her parents' house, I knew I'd fucked up. It didn't surprise me when she wouldn't answer my calls the next day. But Monday night, that was something else. Going into that bathroom was entirely her idea. Yet still, she's gone radio silent.

I get it, or at least I think I do. She's getting married. In what I assume is only a few months away, judging by the way Tatum is frantically throwing everything together, she'll be vowing to devote her life to someone else. I won't lie – the thought sucks. Parker seems like a decent guy, despite being some British trust fund brat, but the thought of his hands on her body sends me into a jealous rage. The only person that should be able to touch her like that is me, and for a while, I was the only one who could.

The summer we spent together before she left for college was everything from my wildest dreams. We had a chemistry between us that burned hotter than the sun. Whenever her eyes met mine, she had this look in them that made me feel like I was invincible. I was ready to give her everything she wanted in life, but when the time came to make it real, I panicked.

Maverick has been my best friend since I was ten years old. He's my brother for all intents and purposes. When I tried to imagine the look on his face after finding out I'd been screwing his sister behind his back, it was enough to send me running for the hills. I did the one thing I never thought I would – I walked away from McKenna and left her crying on her bedroom floor.

By the time that I realized what a monumental mistake I'd made, it was too late. She had already left for NYU. My calls and texts wouldn't go through. Her social media was no longer visible to me. The message was clear; she was moving on with her life, and I was no longer welcome in it.

I'd waited for her to reappear but as holidays and summers came and went, she never showed. Maverick would mention something in passing about how she was in some foreign country on a relief program. Her actions were noble, there's no denying that, but I knew her reasoning for not coming home. The only thing I could do was respect her decision and stay away.

Despite how much I told myself it would never happen, that I had lost her, I still couldn't seem to move on. There was always a part of me that held other women in comparison to McKenna, and let's be real here, there is no comparing to her. They all lacked the ability to make me smile just by being in the room. They didn't have the jade green eyes she had, and even if they did, their's didn't shine as bright. So, after a few pitiful attempts at finding someone else, I gave up.

The day Maverick told me McKenna got engaged was the day my chest cracked wide open. He mentioned it like it was just another day, but his words knocked the wind out of me.

Don't get me wrong, I always knew it was a possibility. I guess a part of me just still held out hope that her and I would end up together.

I spent a few days avoiding everyone whenever I could and it didn't go unnoticed. I was an asshole at work, barking orders at my employees like they were all incompetent fucks that couldn't do their jobs correctly. After one particularly rough day where I put my fist through a newly built wall, Roman shoved me into his truck and drove us to the bar. For the first time ever, I told someone about the four months I spent with my best friend's sister.

Being as Rome has been Maverick's friend just as long as he's been mine, I half expected him to punch me in the face and ask me how I could do something so stupid. So, imagine my surprise when he just smiled at me and chuckled like he already knew. He didn't – or at least he didn't know I acted on it – but he had his suspicions.

When I walked into the living room to find McKenna sitting there, looking as gorgeous as ever, it was like everything came to life again. Colors that had gone so dull became so vibrant. Without even realizing it, she was thawing out my frozen heart. Then, I met her fiancé.

I tried to keep my composure but I failed, miserably. The moment I realized that McKenna had never mentioned me to him, it felt as if someone doused me with a bucket of ice water. Did what we have mean so little to her that she didn't even think to say anything about it? No, that couldn't be it. She wanted a relationship with me. The only reason that didn't happen was because of my own fear and stupidity.

The morning she almost burned herself on the broken coffee pot, I knew. My name slipped from her tongue the same way it always did. The connection her and I shared hadn't gone anywhere. If anything, it was stronger. All the time we spent away from each other did nothing to extinguish the flame that burned between us. Yet still, she was engaged.

I couldn't keep going without her in my life, not when she was so close. The only reason I made it the four years I did was because I wasn't able to contact her even if I tried. Now, with her being dangled in front of me like a treat I'm not allowed to have, I needed at least part of her. I told myself I would shove my feelings down into the deepest corner of my chest and settle for being friends. Was it going to suck? Of course. Would it hurt to see her with Lord Douchebag? Like a bitch. But, in the battle of being her friend or not having her at all, the choice was clear.

During the few days that she didn't push me away, I learned she hadn't changed nearly as much as I thought. She was still the sassy, headstrong girl I remembered. There wasn't a single day we talked that I didn't have a smile on my face, until it abruptly ended. All of a sudden, most of my messages went unanswered and the ones that didn't, lacked the enthusiasm her responses once held.

A part of me knew I should leave it alone. I was too invested. I felt too strongly towards her to resist the temptation, but I didn't listen. The need to be around her was so intense that it made every logical part of me cease to exist. Reasonability never stood a chance.

When we stood in her parents' dining room and she repeated for the third time how wrong it was for us to be talking, I nearly went off. Here I was, trying to be a good guy and settle for being her friend – instead of telling her exactly what I thought about her upcoming nuptials and the wrong guy being at the end of that aisle – and it still wasn't okay in her eyes. With the exception of calling her Princess, which will stop over my dead body, I had done well with keeping everything strictly platonic between us. It wasn't easy, but I managed. So, to hear her say that even *that* was wrong, made me see red.

I was going to walk away. I was going to respect the request she made at her engagement party, regardless of how ridiculous and impossible I thought it was. My eyes couldn't seem to look away from her that whole dinner, no matter how risky I knew it was. In my mind, it was going to be the last time I saw her for a while. I planned to go stay in Boston for a bit, to give her some distance. I had enough work there to last a few months at least. However, that isn't what ended up happening.

Maverick proposing to Tatum has always been a touchy subject, and everyone would understand that if he told them that he tried. Five years ago, while we were all still in college, he bought a ring, got down on one knee, and asked her to marry him – she said no. In her defense, it was more of a 'not yet' but rejection is all the same. Being one of few people who know this, it was no surprise to me when he practically bit McKenna's head off for bringing up the topic. What I didn't expect, was to get caught in the crossfire.

No part of me had ever planned on McKenna finding out that I never moved on from what she and I had. It's not exactly the kind of thing that makes you look manly and strong. So, the second Maverick spit those words at me intending to cause harm, I knew he hit his target. I instantly felt McKenna's gaze shooting daggers into my head. A little voice in my head told me to look up – to hold her stare and play it off like he was talking about someone else, but I couldn't. She meant more to me than that.

When I got to her bedroom, the first thing out of her mouth was calling me out on the lie I told her – that I had been drunk when I got the date of our first kiss tattooed close to my heart. There was no denying it at that point. I could hear in the tone of her voice, she had it all figured out. My eyes met hers and finally, for the first time in years, I saw it. Just like that, I was rendered completely defenseless.

Once I gave in, I knew walking away was no longer an

option. Stealing another man's fiancé was never something I aspired to do, but if we're being honest, McKenna was never his to begin with. How could she be when every part of her heart was left here with me? Still, she's the most stubborn woman I've ever met and I knew that the only way I stood a chance was to get her to come to me.

Making her jealous at the bar was Roman's idea, and I must admit, it was brilliant. I'd purposely chosen someone I knew would be all over me. I turned on the charm and let the situation play out. I could feel McKenna watching me for over an hour before she ended up at the bar, downing shots like they were going to give her the answers to life. By the third one, I started to worry. And by the fourth, I texted Rome and told him that if he didn't stop her, I was going end this game and do it myself. Next thing I knew, I had a very angry looking ex standing in front of me, demanding I remove my hands from the girl grinding on my leg – I listened without hesitation.

The way her body moved against mine on that dance floor made me feel things that could send me straight to hell. In that moment, I didn't care that people could see us, or that her brother was most likely within eyesight. All that mattered was the way my arms wrapped around her and the moan that left her mouth when I kissed her neck.

When we got into the bathroom, I had to refrain from attacking her mouth with my own. Like I said, if I stood a chance at all, I needed her to come to me. I needed her permission, and the second I got it I didn't hold back. But when I heard her asking me to fuck her, I knew we needed to stop. God, turning down that offer was one of the hardest things I've ever done, but she deserves so much more than drunk sex in the back of some club. *We* deserve more than that.

As soon as I told her it wasn't going to happen, I saw the look in her eyes. All the walls she had built to keep me out had gone right back up in a millisecond. I could've stood there all night and begged her to talk to me, but it wouldn't have gotten us anywhere. The liquid courage she had was gone and all that was left was the girl who only remembered how I hurt her.

I LOOK DOWN AT my hand, seeing the fading bruises on my knuckles from the way I took out my anger that night. Roman tried insisting I go get x-rays, but I didn't listen. I knew it wasn't broken, and I was right.

Leaning against the counter while I wait for the coffee to finish brewing, I pull out my phone. It's been three days since the night at the club and McKenna is yet to answer a single one of my texts. How is it so easy for her to go without talking to me, while I can't go longer than a few hours? Ugh, I wish I had her self control.

As much as it hurts to think about, perhaps her actions that night made her realize I'm not the one she wants. Maybe she really does love her fiancé and wants to spend the rest of her life with him. If that's the case, if he's what makes her happy, I'll back off. All I know is that every time I get her within my reach only for her to slip away again, I break a little more.

I type out the only thing I can think to say at this point.

I'm sorry if you're hurting and if I had something to do with that pain. I never meant to make things difficult for you. I understand you don't want to speak to me. I'm walking away.

I stay still for a few minutes, waiting for the three dots to appear and show she's responding, but they never come.

SUNDAY ARRIVES QUICKER THAN expected, and while I'm not thrilled about the idea of going on a date with someone who isn't McKenna, I'm trying to remain optimistic. I meant it when I told her I was walking away. If that isn't what she wants, she can tell me. Otherwise, life goes on.

I'm sitting on the couch with Maverick going over the financials of his business. When he told me his idea a couple years ago, I immediately offered to invest. Being his silent partner, he runs everything the way he wants and I get 15% of net profits. The only thing he ever needs to come to me for are big decisions, such as the expansion he's currently considering. It comes with a bit of a risk, so I know that part of him is looking at me as less as his partner and more as his friend.

"Do you think you can pull it off?"

He nods. "I think it'll take a decent amount of work at first, but yeah, I do."

"Then go for it."

"Really?"

"Yeah. The data looks good and you're ready and willing to make it happen. If this is what you want to do, I trust you're making the right call."

He smiles gratefully and slips the documents back into their folder. Just as he finishes closing his briefcase, the doorbell rings. Tatum calls down to us from the balcony.

"Can one of you get that? It's McKenna."

Goosebumps rise across my skin at the mention of her name. I don't move as Maverick cups his hands over his mouth and yells across the house.

"It's open!"

Tatum scoffs. "I could have done that."

"So, why didn't you?"

Their banter is usually something I find amusing, but all I

134

can focus on is the sound of the front door closing and footsteps coming down the hall. As soon as she comes into view, my lungs forget how to breathe. She's in a pair of black leggings and an oversized, gray sweater that goes down just past her ass. Her eyes meet mine for only a second before Maverick pulls her attention to him.

"I didn't expect to see you. Are you coming to dinner with us?"

She shakes her head. "Tatum has some paperwork I need to sign."

"Paperwork? For what?"

I don't miss the way she nervously plays with her sleeve and glances quickly at me. "The venue."

It doesn't take a rocket scientist to figure out she's talking about her wedding. Every thought in my mind disappears and I can only think one thing – she's still marrying him. Even after kissing me, not once but twice, he's still the one she wants.

I stand up and head for the stairs, mumbling something about needing to get ready and for Maverick to have fun at dinner. As I slip past McKenna, she looks down at the ground and steps out of my way. It isn't until I get to the top of the stairs that I hear her even acknowledge my existence.

"Is he okay?" *Not even in the slightest.*

"Yeah, don't mind him. He has a date tonight. I think he's just nervous."

Not waiting to hear her answer, I go into my room and try to figure out what I'm going to wear. We're not going anywhere fancy. Hell, this wasn't even my idea. Roman set it up. Apparently, Layla is a friend of a friend. She saw a picture on his facebook a while ago and has asked him about me a few times since. After turning down the proposition twice, I decided to let him play matchmaker. We're meeting for dinner at 7th Wave, a restaurant down on the ocean front.

I hear Maverick and Tatum call out that they're leaving

and then the door shuts behind them. Relived to finally be alone, I let out a breath. A guy can only pretend he isn't emotionally wounded for so long.

I pull on a black button down and stand in front of my floor length mirror. I'm about to start buttoning it when something catches my eye. McKenna leans against my doorway, looking as if she wants to say everything and nothing all at the same time. Her gaze meets mine through the mirror before I force myself to look away and focus on the task at hand.

"So, you have a date?"

"Yup."

"That's, uhm, that's good."

I turn to face her. "Is it?"

"Yes." She sighs and shakes her head. "No. I don't know." I don't really know what to say to that, so I don't say anything. I grab my cologne and spray it across my chest. She hums. "I've missed that smell."

"Don't do that. Don't play innocent like you're not the reason this date tonight isn't with you."

Her eyes narrow. "Excuse me?"

"What? You can't tell me I'm wrong. Twice now you've kissed me and then went fucking AWOL. Not once, *twice*."

"Well I'm sorry this isn't all black and white, but you can't blame everything on me. Besides, you moved on pretty quick. I can't be that important to you."

Did she just…?

I run my fingers through my hair frustratedly. "What the hell do you want me to do, McKenna? You've made it crystal fucking clear that you don't want to be with me. Christ, you're *engaged* to someone else! Am I supposed to just wait around for you while you go spend your life with him?!"

She rolls her eyes and shakes her head, starting to walk away. "This was a bad idea."

"So, what, you're just going to leave?"

136

Her body stops and when she turns to face me, the look in her eyes makes me wish I had just kept my mouth shut. Gone is the warmth that radiated off her and all that's left is nothing but hurt and anger.

"You taught me how."

<hr />

I'M SITTING AT THE table across from my date while we both pick at the appetizer - coconut shrimp with a sweet Thai chili sauce. Her mouth is moving, signifying she's talking, but I'm not paying any attention. She's a nice girl and if I weren't all hung up on someone else, I may even be interested, but I can't get how broken McKenna looked out of my head.

"So, Colt, tell me about you." Layla picks up her drink and plays with her straw in a way that I'm guessing is supposed to look seductive.

"Not much to know."

"Oh, come on. Give me something. Roman said you're an architect?" I nod half heartedly. "So, what? You build houses?"

"I *design* houses." I correct. "Amongst other things."

"So, you're not a construction worker?"

"No."

I can tell what she's doing. She's trying to use conversation to gauge my income. If this girl saw the amount in my bank account, she'd become even more obnoxious than she already is. I'd be lying if I said she was the first gold digger I've met. After being published in a magazine, women would approach me on the street to make small talk and pretend they love my work. The dollar signs in their eyes weren't fooling anyone.

Layla excuses herself to the bathroom and I pull out my phone. Unable to help myself, I go straight to McKenna's facebook. She had unblocked me when we agreed to being friends, and thankfully, hasn't shut me out of it again since. To be honest, she probably forgot about it. I don't do anything on the site very often, so the chances of me coming up on her news feed are slim.

I scroll down her page and notice her most recent post was only a half hour ago.

Take me back to that summer, when we hid from everyone in our own precious space. Wrapped in a little world where all that mattered was you and I – take me back there.

I read it over; once, twice, three times. Each word sticks out like it's ready to jump off the page at me. *Our own precious space.* I look out at the water and remember the secret place shared. It was somewhere I'd found for when I needed some time to think. I kept it to myself for the longest time, until I didn't. I brought McKenna there for the first time on the Fourth of July. It's hidden away enough but provided an amazing view of the ocean. We spent that night with her wrapped in my arms, watching the fireworks – it was pure bliss.

The likelihood of it being a coincidence are high. It could be song lyrics or a poem she saw that she liked, but the small possibility that it's a message meant for me has me standing up and pulling out my wallet. Layla returns to the table just as I'm tossing down a couple $20 bills.

"What's going on?"

I put on my best fake smile. "I'm sorry, something came up so I need to go."

"Oh, okay. Well, call me and we'll plan for another night."

"Will do."

I head out of the restaurant, not caring at all that I don't even have her number. I'm sure she'll realize it and try to get my contact info from Roman. I make a mental note to tell him not to give it to her as I climb in my car.

THE WOODS I HAVE to walk through are dark. Usually, I'd be able to navigate this area like the back of my hand, but I haven't been here since McKenna left for college. I couldn't bring myself to come back to this place where we spent so many moments. It was too hard.

When I get to the point where everything opens up, I notice I'm not alone. The moon is bright, shining just the right amount of light over the giant rock and providing her with the perfect silhouette. I stand there for a minute, just letting myself admire her beauty and remember all the times we spent here. We were always happiest when we were away from prying eyes – free to just enjoy each other.

"I was hoping I'd find you here." I say, making myself known.

My voice startles her but she recovers well. "What happened to your date?"

"I left early."

"Why?"

I walk over to the rock and lean against it, right next to where she's sitting. "Well, for starters, she kept calling me Colt."

"Like, a baby horse?" I nod and bask in the giggle that leaves her mouth. "Oh god, that's horrible. What was the other reason?"

"She wasn't my type."

"Oh." The gears turn in her head until finally she speaks again. "What *is* your type then?"

I turn my attention away from the water and over to her. "I'm looking at it."

For the first time since I got here, she looks directly at

me. It's then that I notice her eyes are wet. *She's been crying?* I reach out and place my hand on her face, using my thumb to wipe a tear from her cheek. She brings her hand up and rests it on my own as she leans into my touch.

"Why is it that no matter how hard I try to not want you, it only makes me want you more?"

Her words make me laugh. "I know what you mean."

"Do you?"

"More than you might think."

Mossy green eyes stare into mine, searching them as if they hold the key to everything she's trying to uncover. Her gaze drops down to my lips and a shiver runs down her spine. I don't move an inch, too afraid to ruin the moment. If I've learned anything lately, it's that any wrong move can send her running in under five seconds flat.

She slides her hands up my chest, to my neck, then onto my face. Her thumb rubs over my bottom lip and I have to resist the urge to playfully nip at it. Clearly, she's looking for something, and I'll be damned if I get in the way of her finding it.

When her fingers settle in my hair, I can't help the way my eyes flutter closed and I whimper slightly. She massages my scalp and pulls me just a little bit closer. It's so sensual, so *intimate,* and *so* right. I force my eyes to open again and they meet hers instantly.

"Fuck it."

McKenna pulls me toward her and presses her lips to mine in a heated kiss. It's the first time she's initiated it on her own, and hell if I'm not loving it. I place one hand on the back of her head as I lay her down slowly. As soon as I climb on top of her, she drags her fingernails across my back and arches her hips up. The club may not have been the right place for this, but here – here is perfect. Here is *ours.*

Still, I need to be sure she isn't going to shut me out again. I don't think I could handle it if I got to have her tonight, only for her to be gone again tomorrow. I break the kiss and rest my forehead on hers, rubbing soothing circles into her hip so she knows I'm not stopping anything just yet.

"I need you to promise me something."

Her brows furrow as she sees the seriousness on my face. "What?"

"That you're not going to run. That I won't wake up tomorrow morning to find out that you're avoiding me again. I know things are complicated, and I know it won't be easy, but I want the chance to fight for this – for *us*. I have a lot to make up for, and I don't expect you to trust me right away or leave Parker tomorrow, but I'm willing to do the work. So, tell me you're not going to disappear again, because there are a lot of things I can handle, but I'm damn sure that's not one of them."

She smiles in a way that makes my knees weak and puts one hand on each side of my face. "I'm not going anywhere, I promise."

The relief that runs through my body feels like the weight of the world has been lifted. That was all I needed to hear. I reconnect our kiss, pouring all my emotions into it – all the fear and want and need. It's raw and it's overwhelming, but it's real and I'm done pretending with her.

She kisses me harder, as if I'm everything she needs to survive. Her hands slip under my shirt to grab at my back. The feeling of her cold hands against me is a reminder that this is actually happening. I pull my shirt over my head and toss it to the side. Her movements pause momentarily and for a second I think I did something wrong, until I see where she's looking.

I follow her eyesight to my collar bone and the dark ink that's permanently embedded in my skin. She brushes over it with her finger, almost like she's expecting it to wipe away with her touch. When she presses her lips against it, my breath hitches. I've never regretted getting that tattoo, and because of *that*, I never will.

I slide my hands up her sweater, relishing the way my touch makes her shiver. My fingers trace the bottom of her bra before I reach behind and unclip it. She lifts herself up just enough for me to pull the articles of clothing over her head. When she lies back down, she's naked from the waist up and panting hard.

"Please." She begs.

I smirk. There's nothing that makes me happier right now than knowing I still have the same effect on her. "Please what? What do you want, Princess?"

"You. All of you, *everywhere*."

Rolling her nipple between my thumb and index finger, I skim my touch down over her stomach until I reach the top of her leggings. I hook into both sides of them and slowly pull them down her legs. Seeing the black lace panties she's wearing is enough to make me cum on the spot. I bite my lip in an attempt to control myself.

I spread her legs a little more and kiss the inside of her thigh. She whimpers, which only motivates me more. My mouth grazes over her skin, leaving a trail of light kisses in my path. When I get to the place she wants the most, I breathe over it before moving to the other leg and repeating the same motions.

Using the smallest amount of pressure, my fingers press lightly over the only clothed part of her body. Her panties are already soaked. I slide my palms to her hips and grip the underwear before slipping them down her legs – finally exposing the most intimate part of her. Being the only one to see her like this was something I prided myself on for the longest time. Vulnerability looks so damn sexy on her.

The second my tongue connects with her clit, she screams out. Her hand moves to the top of my head and she laces her fingers into my hair. I repeat the action, loving the way her grip tightens. It may have been years since I've gotten my hands on her, but I'll never forgot the things she loves.

I slip two fingers inside her and bend them to find the little bundle of nerves. As soon as I find it, she arches her hips up, pushing harder against my mouth. She tastes so good and I would be completely content if the only sounds I heard for the rest of my life, were the breathy moans she's letting out.

My hand turns, using my thumb to apply pressure right where she needs it while I fuck her with my tongue. She uses her hold on my head to pull me closer. My name comes out in incoherent mumbles until she tenses. An orgasm rocks through her body as she cums. I don't stop until she releases my hair and lets out a sigh.

Standing up, I undo my belt buckle and release my cock from my pants. I'm harder than I've been in the longest time, the angry red color looking like it could explode from the simplest touch. I look up at McKenna to see her watching me, nibbling on her bottom lip the same way she did when I took her virginity. Her eyes meet mine and she nods, silently giving me the permission I was looking for.

I push inside her and groan out as her warm, wet heat encases me. She's so tight that I have to stop myself from blowing my load right then and there. As I bottom out, she moans loudly – exactly like she used to. I lean down to kiss her, not caring one bit that she can taste herself on my tongue. I pull out before thrusting back in, slow but deep. Her nails run down my chest and over my abs.

"Fuck, you feel so good." I murmur as I start to speed up my pace.

Seeing the way her hair is messily spread across the rock, and how she wraps her legs around my waist to try to fuck herself on my dick – there can't be anything better than this. I'm holding her hips so tight I'm afraid I might leave bruises, but she doesn't seem to care so I don't either. As my pace quickens even more, I know I'm getting close.

"Mac, I don't have a condom."

She doesn't stop for a second, grabbing my wrists and putting my hands on her breasts. "I'm still on the pill."

With that, I fuck into her – hard. My body rocks in a messy, chaotic motion as I chase my own release. I roll her nipple between my fingers while I slide my other hand down to press my thumb onto her clit. She lets go for the second time, clenching around me and sending me into oblivion. I explode inside of her, claiming every inch of her body for my own.

Maybe, one day she really will be.

I WAKE IN THE morning to the sound of Maverick accidentally setting off the alarm as he leaves the house. While usually I would be irritated, the memories of last night playing in my head cause a smile to spread across my face. I didn't end up getting in until almost two in the morning, after making sure McKenna made it home safe. It sucked to watch her walk into a house I know she shares with someone else, but baby steps.

I grab my phone from my nightstand and compose a quick text to her.

Good Morning Beautiful.

My morning picks up quickly as I make some coffee and get a call from my contractor. He has some questions about the house I'm having built for myself, and he knows better than to make his own judgement calls on any of them. I designed that house with very specific views in mind and I won't settle for it being anything less than perfect.

After I get out of the shower, I throw on a pair of jeans and a t-shirt. I run my towel over my hair then toss it into the laundry basket in the corner of my room. My phone lights up on my bed but when I grab it, my excitement dissipates.

It's not McKenna. It's 11 AM, and she still hasn't answered. An uncomfortable feeling sits like a rock in the pit of my stomach.

So much for promises.

12

MCKENNA

I THROW THE CUSHIONS ONTO THE FLOOR, frantically searching the couch. *Nothing.* I grab my purse for the third time this morning and scour through it. *Again, nothing.* My hands go into my hair, pulling on it frustratedly.

"Where the fuck *is it*?!"

When I woke up this morning, Parker had already left for Boston. While normally I'd be a little disappointed that I wasn't able to see him, this time I was relieved. I know that the minute I have to face him, I'm going to feel guilty.

I had reached to grab my phone off my nightstand, but it wasn't there. I looked for it in the bed, on the floor, in the pockets of the sweater I wore yesterday, but it's nowhere to be found. If I'm going to talk to Ivy about what happened last night, which I desperately need to do, I need to find my phone.

The feeling of Colton's hands on my body are burned into my mind. Every time I move, the soreness from him stretching me open reminds me of the ecstasy of having him inside of me again. I can't remember the last time I orgasmed that hard, not just once, but *twice*. I'm not saying Parker is bad in bed – he's not. He's just repetitive. He sticks to the same movements and the same pace, which feels good, but it's nothing like sex with Colton.

Colton doesn't just put my pleasure before his own, he gets off on it. The louder I get and the better I feel, the more he loses control. He knows exactly what my body likes because he took the time to learn it. Even after spending so much time apart, he still manages to make my whole body tingle.

When I realize that my phone is nowhere to be found, I decide to go for a run. I slip into workout gear and lace up my sneakers before fishing my old iPod out of a drawer in the entertainment center. It hasn't been updated in over a year, but it'll do.

I lock the door behind me with the hideaway key and take off down the street. The songs blasting into my ears are a straight shot of nostalgia. As I focus on pacing my breathing, I think about what Colton said last night.

"I want the chance to fight for this – for us."

While it was exactly what I've wanted to hear come out of his mouth for years, I don't know what it means. Our past has been so rocky and chaotic that I don't know which way is up with him. He used to have moments like this during the summer we spent together - moments where he would make me feel like I was the only girl he had eyes for. But despite how strongly he made me believe he felt, he still walked away like it was the easiest thing in the world.

A couple miles into my run, I stop to take a breather. It takes me a second to realize where I am but when I spot the familiar gray house, I can't help but laugh. Colton's car sitting in the driveway tells me he didn't go to work today. Before giving myself a chance to overthink it, I walk up the steps and ring the bell.

The door opens less than a minute later and the breath is sucked out of my lungs when I see Colton standing there in only a pair of gray sweatpants. His perfectly defined torso is on full display and the way the pants hang loosely on his hips gives me just the right view of the V on his lower abdomen. Normally when I check him out so blantantly, he makes some sarcastic comment, but when my eyes meet his he's looking at me like my presence is completely unexpected.

Great. Here we go again. The only thing that attracted him to me again was knowing he couldn't have me. Now that he's had me again, he's no longer interested.

My thoughts are completely cut off as Colton grabs my wrist and pulls me inside. As soon as he shuts the door, my back is pressed against it and his mouth covers my own. The kiss is heated, and desperate, and makes it hard to concentrate on anything but him. I don't think I could ever get tired of this feeling.

Everything starts to go a bit hazy as I run low on oxygen. Colton must feel it too because he breaks the kiss and rests his forehead against my own. The feeling of his breath on my lips is dizzying as we're both left panting.

"I thought you were gone again." He whispers.

Oh crap. I hadn't even thought about if he would try to get in touch with me. He's never been someone who's had to worry about me not coming back to them, until now. Now I've given him a reason to get scared when I don't answer. Though, in a twisted way it makes me happy. The way he got scared that I was going to avoid him again only shows me that he cares.

"I can't find my phone."

All the tension leaves his body and he presses his lips back to mine. This kiss isn't like the one when I got here – it's slower and more calculated. He runs one hand up my side while the other goes to my face, brushing over my cheek with his thumb. Unlike all the one's before this, there's no intentions behind it. Him and I both know that nothing is going to happen in the foyer of Maverick's house, nor would either of us want it to. We're kissing for the sole reason being that any distance between us is too much.

The sound of someone clearing their voice has Colton groaning before forcing himself to pull away. Neither of us need to look to know who's standing there. He gives me one of his heart-stopping smiles and I have to remind myself to breathe.

"I'll meet you in my room."

With one more chaste kiss, he turns around and heads toward Tatum – who's standing there with her arms crossed.

"Cock-block." He teases, earning a playful elbow from her.

Just before he goes up the stairs, he glances at me once more and grins. I bite my lip as I watch him until he's out of sight. When he's gone, I turn my attention to Tatum. She gives me a knowing look and I sigh. There is no getting out of the talk I know is coming.

"Walk me to my car." It's not a question, it's an order. I follow her out the door and as soon as it shuts she scoffs. "So much for nothing to worry about."

"I know."

"Do you though? Do you know how dangerous this is? How messy it could get?" She's not even looking at me as she fishes her keys from her purse and heads toward her convertible.

"Yes, but what do you want me to do? Any time I'm around him, it's like I can't control myself."

"Well, for starters you could stay away from him."

I roll my eyes. "I tried that, remember? It didn't work. Our lives are too intertwined."

"Oh please." She opens her driver's side door and tosses her purse onto the passenger seat before leaning against the car. "You told him to go away like twice, and with as much conviction as a homeless man saying he's not hungry." I look down at the ground and focus on kicking the nearest stone.

"So what, you two are together now? Should I start notifying people that the wedding is off?"

It's a question I've been asking myself for the last twelve hours. I know none of this is fair to Parker. He's a good guy and he deserves someone who is going to love him the way he deserves. I wish the debate in my mind was as simple as love versus like, but it's not. The feelings I have for Parker may not be as strong as the ones for Colton, but they *are* there. All I'm sure of right now is that I need to talk to Ivy.

"Not yet. Give me a few days to figure all of this out."

She doesn't look happy about it but she nods and gets in the driver's seat. "I really hope you know what you're doing."

I don't answer as she closes the door and backs out of the driveway. As soon as she's gone, I contemplate my options. I could leave and go find Ivy, or I can go back inside where Colton is waiting for me. Even the thought of there being a choice to make at all is comical. When it comes to Colton Brooks, I'm powerless.

I get to his bedroom door to find him sitting on the bed with his back against the headboard. I could never understand why he didn't get into modeling. It's no secret that Colton has always been one of the most attractive men in our small town, which is part of the reason why I always thought I'd never have a chance. Every girl who knew him wanted to be with him, except for Tatum. Maverick has always been the only one she wants.

He must feel me watching him because he looks up from his phone and smirks in a way that makes my insides melt. I grin in return and walk over to his bed. The second I'm close enough, he pulls me in closer to him and wraps his arm around my waist. I lean against him, feeling the heat of his body against my own.

"Did Tatum give you a hard time?"

I shrug. "I've heard worse."

He scoots us both down until we're laying flat and I roll

over to rest my head on his chest. The sound of his heartbeat echos into my ear – it's soothing. His hand gently rubs up and down my back and I feel him press a kiss to the top of my head.

"So, you don't regret it?"

It doesn't take a rocket scientist to know what he's talking about and I *should* regret it. I know I should. Tatum was right when she warned me about how this could get messy. Maverick could find out and Colton could lose his best friend, Parker could get his heart broken, I could end up in just as many pieces as I was when I left for college – or maybe even more. But when it comes down to if I regret what happened last night, the choice is easy.

"No, I don't."

He sighs in relief and places his hand over mine. We've been in this position so many times before, but this time doesn't feel the same. This time feels like we have the potential to be something so much more, like there isn't an end date lurking closer and closer. It feels like he's mine.

AFTER LOUNGING AROUND, AND talking about nothing and everything all at the same time, we finally get up and head to our spot. It's the last place I remember having my phone and the only other place I can think to look. If it isn't there, then maybe Parker took it with him for some reason. The thought makes me nervous because I'm naïve enough to never put a password on it.

As we pull up, I can see my Vespa still sitting where I parked it. After we had sex last night, Colton lectured me for the millionth time on why I shouldn't be riding it up here. The street winds too much and there are too many people who fly down the road. He insisted on driving me home and told me I could come pick it up in the morning, when it's light enough for other drivers to see a small scooter.

Walking through the woods, Colton holds branches out of my way and it reminds me of the first time he brought me here. It was the first time I actually felt like I had a piece of him that no one else had. I'd complained about not being able to watch the fireworks together. We couldn't risk someone seeing us and it getting back to my parents or Maverick. So, on the evening of the Fourth of July, Colton told me to meet him behind the library and he came to pick me up. He had a blanket laid out and a bottle of champagne. The way he was with me that night only made me fall even more in love with him.

Once we step into the clearing, I walk over to the rock where I was sitting and look around. Sure enough, my phone is laying face down on the ground.

"Found it."

I pick it up and press the power button. I had shut it off after making a post on facebook. I didn't need Ivy calling me and asking what it meant or Parker texting to see when I was coming home. All I wanted was some time to think, and I ended up with *so* much more.

The phone comes to life and within a few seconds texts come in. There are three from Ivy talking about her hot assistant chef that she wont make a move on, one from my mom reminding me of my interview this week, and one from Colton. The time stamp on it is from eight in the morning, which means he must have texted me as soon as he woke up. What it says makes my heart flutter.

Colton: Good Morning Beautiful.

I don't know how something so simple can make me feel so much, but he's never been that sweet with me. His pet names stayed in the range of babe and baby, and the compliments he gave were either that I was adorable, which made me want to shoot myself, or that I was sexy. While I clung to those like I needed them to survive, they were never words that made me feel like I was anything more than his latest fuck.

"So, you think I'm beautiful, huh?" I tease.

"No, I don't." His straightforwardness makes the cocky smirk fall right off my face but he just smiles. "I think you're so much more than that, but beautiful was the closest word to describe it."

Just like that, every thought of the way he was four years ago leaves and is replaced with the way he's looking at me. I step closer to him and rest my head on his chest as he wraps his arms around me. This all may be chaotic and could end up backfiring in my face, but right now I can't find it in me to care.

"Come on." He hands me his keys and I look up at him, confused. "I'm riding your Vespa down the hill and then I'm taking you to lunch."

THE DINER WE DECIDE on is closer than I would have preferred, but Colton keeps reminding me that it's not against the rules for us to get lunch together. If anything gets back to Maverick, all we have to say is that we ran into each other both happened to be hungry. I had no argument left after he pointed out that he deliberately flirted with me at Maverick's birthday dinner and only Tatum batted an eye.

"So, what do you have planned for the rest of the day?"

I smile at him from across the table. "Well, first I need to go talk to Ivy, and then I need to go shopping for my interview."

"Oh, you got an interview?" I nod. "Where at?"

"The elementary school. They're looking for a new

kindergarten teacher and an old friend of mine recommended me for the job."

He takes a sip of his drink and then grins. "That's great, Mac. You'll make an amazing teacher."

"Well, let's not jump the gun. It's only an interview. I haven't gotten the job."

"But you will. They would be crazy not to hire you."

This is one of the things that I've always loved about Colton. He's great at making me feel like I can do anything. When we were younger, I had fallen off my bike and was too afraid to get back on it. No matter how much my parents and Maverick promised me I wouldn't get hurt, I didn't budge. It wasn't until Colton came and talked to me that I actually got back on. He told me that they were all liars, and that chances are I *will* fall off again, but that it won't be the worst thing ever. I'll be okay.

Now, maybe it was because my world revolved around him and at the time I probably would have followed him into a lion's den, but he's always known the right things to say. The way he always has so much confidence in me is heartwarming. A part of me wonders what college would have been like with him in my corner. All the times I was freaking out over an upcoming test or worrying about starting a new class – he would have talked me down so easily. If only things hadn't gotten so messed up.

After we're done eating, Colton pays the bill and the two of us get in his car. It's the same Shelby mustang he's had for years. The horsepower in this thing is intense, and only increases his sex appeal – not that he needs it. This man could make a Prius look hot.

He pulls up to where he parked my Vespa and reaches in the back seat to hand me my helmet. I take the keys from his center console and thank him quietly. I'm just about to get out of the car when he grabs my wrist to stop me. When I turn back to face him, he puts one hand on my cheek and presses a soft kiss to my lips.

"Text me?"

I nod. "I will."

As I watch him drive away, I wonder how we went from not speaking for four years to *this*. He's treating me exactly the way I wanted to be treated back then, and I'm loving every second of it. I just hope it's not a phase. I'm not sure I can handle having my heart broken by him again.

MCKENNA

CALLING IVY WASN'T EVEN SOMETHING I THOUGHT to do. I just started driving straight to her mom's house. Thankfully, as I pull in the driveway, I see her car. I need to talk to her so bad I probably would've ended up going to the restaurant if I had to.

I take off my helmet and rest it on the seat before stepping onto the porch. It feels weird to knock but I haven't been here in so long that I probably shouldn't let myself in. Her mom answers the door looking like she hasn't aged a single day. When she realizes it's me, she lights up.

"McKenna Taylor! What are you doing knocking? Get in here."

She pulls me in for a tight hug and I bask in the comfort of it. This woman was always like a second mom to me. When the incident with my dad happened, she let me stay here for a week until I was willing to go back home. A part of me feels bad for not staying in touch with her while I was gone, but she doesn't seem to be holding a grudge for it.

"I didn't want to just walk in. It's been a while since I was last here."

"Oh, that's nonsense. You're always welcome in this house."

I smile warmly. "Thank you."

The house is just as I remember it, the only difference being the picture of Ivy's graduation from culinary school on the mantle. I've spent so much time here over the years that I could probably navigate this entire place with my eyes closed. I can still remember Ivy breaking her arm when we tried to be like Maverick and Colton and slide down the banister. Apparently, it only works if you have good balance and don't lean too far back. Ivy didn't get the memo.

"Mom? Who's here?" My best friend makes her way down the stairs. "Oh, hey Mac."

"Hey."

The look on my face must convey everything going through my mind right now because she instantly catches on. "Let's go to my room. I need to start getting ready for work."

She's lying, but if she made it obvious that there was something we needed to talk about, her mom would try to eavesdrop. It's something she's done so many times before. Any time we had something secretive, my mom would always manage to find out. It took years before we finally figured out how.

As soon as I spot the familiar bed, I throw myself on top of it and scream into her pillow. She watches me with amusement and sits at the end. I glare at her when she chuckles at my small outburst.

"I'm so glad you find humor in my misfortune."

Her eyebrows raise. "I would hardly call having to choose between two hot guys a misfortune."

"How do you know this is about two guys?"

"Because I've known you since I was four." She says pointedly. "So, what happened?"

"IhadsexwithColtonlastnight." It all comes out as one word.

"Uh, a little slower please."

"I had sex with Colton last night."

Her eyes widen drastically and I can tell she's holding back a laugh. "I'm sorry, you did what now?"

I groan. "We got into an argument because he was going on a date with someone and apparently, I'm a jealous bitch."

"And that ended up with his dick inside you *how*?"

"I went to our secret spot and he found me."

Her expression changes to one of realization. "So *that's* what your cryptic facebook post was about. I mean you could have just texted him and told him to meet you there."

"I didn't know I wanted him to until he was there. I just needed a place to think, and that's the one place where I know people won't bother me."

"Except Colton."

She doesn't have to elaborate for me to know what she's insinuating. I'm not exactly sure what made me go to that spot. I hadn't been there since things between Colton and I ended and to be honest, I had planned on avoiding it at all costs. It holds too many memories. Regardless of the breathtaking view, I wasn't sure I could handle it. But when I left the house after the spat we had, I knew going home wasn't an option. I mean, how do you tell your fiancé you're upset over your ex going on a date with someone else? It's simple – you don't.

So, I drove around for a while before ending up at the secret rock. It was strange, being there alone, but it made me feel closer to him. For a minute, I was able to pretend that things hadn't gone to such crap – that we hadn't broken up and stopped talking for nearly half a decade. I watched the moonlight glisten off the water and tried to remember the last time I felt whole.

When Colton showed up, for a moment I wondered if maybe I had wished myself back in time, like a reverse '13 Going On 30' kind of thing. But the engagement ring still sat heavily on my finger and he was still wearing the button down he had on when I left. Realizing he dipped out on his date early made me feel better than it should have. At least for the time being, I didn't have to come to terms with him dating someone else. And when he stood in front of me, looking at me like I held his heart in my hands, I couldn't hold back anymore.

"Tell me what to do, Iv."

She gives me a sad smile. "I don't know what to tell you. I wouldn't know what to do in your situation either."

"I don't want to hurt Parker. He doesn't deserve it."

"Maybe not, but does he deserve to be married to someone who only stayed with him out of obligation?"

I sigh. "That's not the *only* reason I'd stay with him. I love him."

"And that's where the problem lies. You love Parker, but you've always been *in love* with Colton."

Groaning, I throw my face back into her pillow. I wish I could tell her she's wrong. That I fell out of love with Colton during the four years I spent trying to forget his existence, and maybe I had. But the second he walked into Maverick's living room looking like he came straight from my every fantasy, all the progress I'd made was instantly undone. In just a few words, I was right back to crushing hard on my brother's best friend, only this time he was off limits for other reasons.

My mind has been a ping pong game lately between forgiving him for the past and holding it against him for the rest of our lives. The image of him walking away as I broke into pieces is still burned into my brain and I'm not sure it'll ever fully go away. It took a year before I could handle hearing his name without becoming an emotional train wreck; two before I would even *consider* dating someone else. If I let him in again, if I give him that part of me and it happens again, I won't have somewhere to run this time. I'll be stuck living in a world where he's a constant fixture.

"How do I know he won't hurt me again?"

Ivy wraps her arms around me and holds me close. "You don't. You just have to ask yourself if it's worth the risk."

As I'm thinking it over, my phone vibrates in my pocket. I pull it out and see a text from Colton. I'd be lying if I said I don't get excited by the simple sight of his name. I swipe it open immediately.

Colton: I know this may seem a little backwards considering the last 24 hours, but can I take you out tonight?

The corners of my mouth raise and Ivy coos from behind me, showing she's reading over my shoulder.

McKenna: Like, on a date?

Colton: Yes Mac. On a date.

I don't answer right away. Instead, I toss my phone down on the bed and put my head in my hands. When did my life become so messy? A few weeks ago, I expected to move home and spend the summer planning my wedding. I knew I'd see Colton at one point or another, but I genuinely believed he had moved on. None of this is anything close to what I imagined.

"Go." Ivy nudges me.

"What? How? Parker is going to wonder where I am."

"So, tell him you're with me."

My eyebrows furrow. "You think I should have a secret affair with Colton?"

"Well, from where I'm standing, what other option do you have? You're too afraid to leave Parker for Colton because he has the track record of a convicted criminal. So, you can either play it safe and avoid Colton as best you can – since lord knows you two can't be in a room together without wanting to rip each other's clothes off – or you can sneak around for a bit and figure out what it is you want."

I run my fingers through my hair. "I don't know. It doesn't feel right."

"Maybe not, but do you really want to spend the rest of your life wondering what if?"

I CAN HEAR THE engine of Colton's car as he pulls into the driveway. He had told me not to wear anything fancy, but the workout clothes I was sporting from earlier didn't seem like proper date attire. I borrowed a pair of jeans and a crop top from Ivy, and took a shower at her place. As far as Parker is concerned, I'm having a girls' night.

When I walk out to the car, Colton goes around to the passenger side, opening the door like a total gentleman. He greets me with a kiss on the cheek.

"I missed you."

I chuckle. "I saw you like six hours ago."

"Five hours and 59 minutes too long."

After I get in, he shuts the door and goes back around to the driver's side. He pulls out of the driveway and starts heading away from town. I had expected him to go towards Boston, but instead, we're going North.

"Where are we going?"

He smiles and reaches over to place one hand on my leg. "Now, what fun would it be if I just told you?"

"Plenty. I hate surprises."

"Some things never change, but you've always loved *my* surprises."

I roll my eyes because he's right. No matter how much I

162

used to beg him to tell me where we were going or what it was that he had for me, he never gave in and I always loved it anyway. I kick off my flip-flops and put my feet up on the dashboard, knowing he'll hate it but getting under his skin is one of my favorite pastimes.

"Ay." He lightly taps my leg. "Feet down."

"Nope." I pop the p just to dig it in a little more. He turns his head to glare at me. "Eyes on the road, Brooks."

His amusement is all over his face. "I'll remember this."

FORTY-FIVE MINUTES LATER, we pull up to a beach that's only illuminated by streetlights and the moon. Completely bewildered, I climb out of the car and meet him at the trunk. He opens it, pulling out a blanket, lantern, and a picnic basket – like something out of a damn movie.

"A picnic? Seriously?"

He smirks. "Do you have something against picnics, Princess?"

I shake my head. "Not at all. I just never took you for a picnic planning kind of guy."

"What can I say? You bring out the best in me."

"Wow. You're laying it on thick tonight."

His head falls back as laughter bellows out of his mouth. "Alright, brat. That's enough out of you. Let's go."

I follow him onto the beach and towards the water. He lays the blanket down on the sand, then turns on the lantern and places it in the middle. We sit across from each other and he takes two subs from my favorite deli out of the basket, along with a bottle of my favorite wine and two glasses.

"You really put some thought into all this."

He looks up from what he was doing and tilts his head to the side. "That surprises you?"

"Honestly? Yeah. I've never seen this side of you. Well, at least not when there wasn't a bed involved."

"Okay, fair enough." He finishes pouring a glass of wine and hands it to me before filling his own. "I just wanted to show you how serious about this I am."

My heart pounds inside my chest as I ask the question I've been thinking all day. "And what is *this* exactly?"

"Dinner?"

"Colton." I say his name as a warning. "You know what I'm talking about."

He leans back on his elbows as he finishes chewing the bite of his sub. "It can be anything you want it to be."

"So, if I wanted you and I to get married tomorrow?"

I expect him to panic as I call his bluff, but he remains indifferent. "I designed a house for a pastor once. I'm sure he'd do it if I asked him to."

Good god, it's all too much. The way he's looking at me, the picture-perfect date he set up, the things he's saying – it's everything I've always wanted and it's four years too late.

"Why couldn't you have been like this before I left?"

My words aren't meant to ruin the mood, but I watch the playfulness fall from his face. He looks up at the stars and takes a sip of his wine as he figures out how to answer my question. When he finally looks back at me, all I see is sincerity.

"I was a stupid, naïve, little boy who was too scared of what his best friend would think to realize what was standing right in front of my face."

It's brutal, and honest, and real. He's not saying it as an excuse or to justify his actions. He simply wants me to know that he understands the mistake he made. I can't help myself as I lean over the lantern and give him a quick kiss, but then I sit back because I need to lay this out.

"I'm not leaving Parker." He opens his mouth to speak but I put one finger up. "Not yet, anyway. I meant what I said about not going anywhere. You want the chance to fight for us, and I'm giving it to you. But I'm not going to leave him until I'm sure."

Colton breaks our eye contact and looks over at the ocean but nods. "Understandable. You need to learn to trust me again."

"So, you're okay with it?"

"Well, I'm not saying I *like it*. I don't think I'll ever be able to see someone else's hands on you and not want to rip them to shreds. But, I want you and if dealing with that for now gives me the chance at that, then I guess I'm going to have to be."

AN HOUR AND A half into our date, the food is long gone and we're just lying on the blanket – listening to the waves and talking. I tell him stories about Julia and me in college, and he tells me all the things I've missed since being home. That's one thing I've never forgotten about him. Anything I talk about, he listens with 100% of his attention, not to be polite but because he's genuinely interested.

As the conversation starts to die down, there's one thing on my mind I've been dying to know.

"Can I ask you something?"

He looks over at me and his eyebrows furrow. "Anything. What do you want to know?"

"Why won't you let anyone see the plans for the house you're building?"

"Ah, going straight for the jugular."

I giggle and turn my head back to the stars. "I know it's not because you're self-conscious about it. You run all your ideas by those closest to you. Why is this one different?"

"Because this one didn't need anyone else's opinion. It's perfect just the way I designed it."

"Can I see it?"

He chuckles and shakes his head. "Maybe one day, but not any time soon. And besides, what if I *am* self-conscious about it?"

"Oh please. I've seen the houses you've designed. Hell, I *live* in one of them."

"Caught onto that, did you?"

I smile. "Parker saw your name in the paperwork. Why didn't you say anything?"

"You were still in that 'stay the fuck away from me or I'll kill you' phase. I was afraid if I told you, it would ruin the place for you."

My arm covers my eyes as I laugh. "You make me sound so violent."

"Hey, I watched you punch a girl in the face once."

"Oh my god. That was eight years ago and she cut off my hair!"

"Still happened." He teases and chuckles when I smack his side.

There are a million things that should be going through my mind as I lie here with him - one of which being my fiancé - but as I listen to the waves crash against the shore and cuddle closer into Colton's side, I can't be bothered with any of it. Tonight, I'm giving myself what I've wanted for as long as I can remember. Tonight, is perfect.

14

MCKENNA

I GO THROUGH MY CLOSET, TOSSING EVERYTHING that won't suffice onto the bed. My room is starting to look like an absolute wreck but I don't care. Instead of going shopping for my interview like I was supposed to, I went on a date with Colton. And instead of going the next day like I planned, I met up with Colton on his lunch break. Needless to say, as much as I love spending so much time with him – it's distracting. Now, I'm stuck finding something to wear out of the things I already own.

"Bloody hell, what happened in here?" Parker asks as I toss another sheer shirt across the room. You can't wear sheer to an interview. Especially not one at an elementary school.

"I can't find a single thing to wear and I forgot to go shopping."

"Ah." He walks over next to me and holds up a tight fitting black dress. "What about this one?"

I narrow my eyes at him. "I'm trying to get a job as a kindergarten teacher Parker, not a damn prostitute."

Placing the dress back where he got it, he raises his hands in surrender. "I'll just stay out of your way then."

"Probably a good idea."

I take out my phone and send an SOS text to Ivy, telling her I need something to wear for my interview, stat. My mouth is dry and I realize that in the midst of my freak out, I forgot to have anything to drink this morning. I go downstairs just as the doorbell rings. My eyebrows furrow as I pull it open to reveal a flower delivery man.

"I have a delivery for Miss McKenna Taylor."

"That's me." I tell him and take the paper to sign for the beautiful arrangement. Once I'm done, I hand it back to him and he hands me the vase.

"Have a nice day, ma'am."

"You too."

I bring the flowers into the kitchen and place them down on the island. When I spot the card sticking out of them, I pull it off so I can read it.

Good luck at your interview, Princess. They're going to love you. –
Colton

"McKenna? Was there someone at the door?" Parker ask as he walks into the kitchen and spots the flowers. I quickly shove the card into the waistband of my yoga pants. "Oh, someone got you flowers?"

I nod. "Ivy wanted to wish me luck on my interview."

"That was very kind of her. She's a good friend."

"The best." I murmur, trying to calm myself from that close call.

God forbid I had decided to get in the shower before getting a drink. Parker would have been the one to sign for the flowers and *he* would have seen the card. Either Colton is just downright stupid, or he did it on purpose. Regardless, I'm pissed.

I grab my phone from the counter and open mine and his text thread.

McKenna: Are you out of your fucking mind?!

While I wait for his response, I take a few sips of water and try to calm myself down but it's no use. Between my nerves about this interview and the way Colton almost just blew our cover, I can barely handle anything this morning.

Colton: Uh, what?

McKenna: The flowers. Are you insane?

Colton: You don't like them? They're your favorite.

Leave it to him to play dumb in this situation. He's a multi-million-dollar architect. He's anything but idiotic.

McKenna: I see that, and they're beautiful, but Parker almost saw the card. Why on earth would you think delivering flowers to my house is a good idea?!

Colton: I just wanted to wish you luck.

McKenna: No, what you WANTED was for Parker to find the card and see that they came from you.

Colton: …

I scoff.

McKenna: Unbelievable. YOU are unbelievable.

The three dots show he's typing for an excessive amount of time before his text comes through.

Colton: What do you want me to say? Do you want me to

tell you that you're wrong? Ok, you're wrong. I didn't send them with the intention of Parker seeing the card, but if he had I wouldn't be upset. He doesn't deserve you.

My fingers move violently across the screen as I type my response.

McKenna: Oh, and you do?! Save it, Colton. I don't want to hear it.

I throw my phone onto the couch with more force than necessary and it ricochets onto the floor. *Great. That's exactly my luck.* I pray it's not broken as I walk over to where it landed. Just as I go to pick it up, I hear the front door open.

"Interview outfit crisis team!" Ivy jokingly yells through the house.

I walk towards her and throw myself into her arms. "You are my lifesaver."

"I know. Now come on, you need to get ready."

THE ELEMENTARY SCHOOL LOOKS exactly like I remember it. The walls are still painted the same powder blue. The lockers are still a dark yellow that looks like a failed attempt at gold. You can see where they renovated certain things like the floors and crappy ceiling tiles, but for the most part, it's still the same place I spent six years of my life.

I walk up to the front door and hit the button for the intercom.

"How can I help you?" A voice echoes through the device.

"My name is McKenna Taylor. I'm here for an interview with Principal Jackson."

"Okay, great. Please come to the office. Through the door and to your right."

As soon as she stops talking, a buzzer sounds, signifying the door is unlocked. I walk inside and straight to the office as directed. The woman behind the desk is older with ash blonde hair that goes down to just below her ears. She looks sweet enough as she smiles at me and tells me to have a seat.

After a few minutes, a man comes out of an office in the back. He's taller, probably around mid-forties, with black hair that's styled into a military cut. He looks like someone who doesn't just ask for respect, he demands it.

"Miss Taylor?"

He extends his hand towards me and I stand to shake it. "It's nice to meet you, Principal Jackson."

"You as well. Why don't you follow me back to my office?"

The two of us walk through the swinging half door that blocks off the administration side. He gestures for me to enter the smaller room and he follows behind, shutting the door after we're both inside. There is a football jersey hanging up on the wall with his last name and the number 14 on it.

"You played for Ohio State?"

He nods. "All four years. I was on a scholarship. Almost went pro."

"How did you end up becoming a principal?"

"I tore my ACL during my senior year of college. By the time I was healed, the season was over and I had missed my chance."

I can't help but frown at the loss of his dream. "That's terrible. I'm so sorry."

Walking around to his desk, he takes one last look at his jersey and then sits down. I take the seat in front of him and fold my hands over my lap. It feels like my stomach is in my throat as I wait for him to begin.

"So, Pamela has nothing but great things to say about you."

The corners of my lips turn upward. "That's very nice of her. We've known each other since we were younger."

"I take it you're close then."

"We used to be. Our schedules haven't been in our favor for us to get together since I've been back, but I'm hoping to see her soon."

He grabs a folder from the side of his desk and opens it to pull out my resume. "I see you're a recent graduate of New York University. Magna Cum Laude, that's impressive."

"Thank you. My studies were always very important to me."

"As they should be. Do you plan on working toward your Master's Degree?"

A part of me wonders if that's a trick question. If I say no, I look like I'm not someone who's content with only a Bachelor's, but if I say yes, he might question if I'll be able to juggle both a full time teaching job and schooling.

"Right now, I'm primarily focused on starting my career, but it's not something I'm opposed to doing in the future."

He looks pleased with my answer as he grins broadly. "And what are your plans for upcoming years? Do you intend on staying in Rockport?"

"Yes, sir. My fiancé and I just recently purchased a house over on Seagull Street."

"That's a great area."

"It is." I confirm.

"Well." He claps his hands together and leans back in his chair. "You seem like a great fit and I have a feeling you'll do very well with the kindergarteners we have coming in this fall. So, if you're interested, I'd like to offer you the teaching position."

My head nods vigorously as my smile widens. "I graciously accept. Thank you so much for the opportunity."

He grins in return. "I'm looking forward to having you join us. How about we go see your new classroom, shall we?"

COLTON

I toss my phone onto the island as I enter the kitchen. McKenna is probably halfway through her interview right now, but I wouldn't know because she hasn't been speaking to me since her outburst this morning. I knew it was risky to send her those flowers, but I genuinely believed Parker would be at class. Grabbing a beer from the fridge, I pop off the cap and flick it across the room, into the garbage.

"You know, your accuracy with that should be alarming." Tatum says from where she's seated at the table in the corner.

I chuckle. "Sorry, I didn't see you there."

"How could you when you're on a war path?" She eyes the beer in my hand. "It's two o'clock on a Thursday and you're already drinking?"

"It's been one hell of a morning."

She shuts her computer and gets up, motioning for me to follow her into the living room. I leave my phone on the counter and exit the room. I fall back onto the couch as I hold my beer steady to prevent it from spilling. Tatum rolls her eyes and joins me on the other side.

"So, what's got you all out of sorts?"

"It's complicated."

She smiles. "Oh, so it's a McKenna thing." My eyes widen as I quickly look around for Maverick but she giggles and shakes her head. "Don't worry. He's not here. He took my car to get an oil change."

Realizing we're alone makes me feel a lot better. The last thing any of us needs, is for Mav to hear me talking about hooking up with his sister – especially being as I currently live in his house. I sit up and place my elbows on my knees, leaning forward.

"I sent her flowers this morning, wishing her luck for her interview."

"That was sweet of you."

I snort. "See, that's what I thought, but she flipped out. She said that I was trying to sabotage things with Parker by signing my name on the card."

"Oh shit! Did he see it?!"

"No." Something I'm rather annoyed by. At least if he *had* seen it, she would have a reason to be mad, but instead she's pissed at me over a hypothetical situation that never happened.

I never expected when I woke up this morning, that McKenna and I would be fighting. Over the past couple days, we've been spending so much time together that I thought I'd died and gone to heaven. She's been meeting me on my lunch breaks and we've even figured out how to get together after. As long as she's not home too late, Parker hasn't thought much about it. I guess I have Ivy to thank for it all. She's been the cover for Mac and me. If anyone asks her where she is, she tells them she's with Ivy. It's not hard to believe, being as the two of them used to be inseparable.

A throw pillow flies across the couch and hits me square in the face, pulling me from my thoughts. I glare over at Tatum but she only smirks.

"The fuck, Tate?"

"That's for being an idiot. You're lucky she's even giving you the time of day after the shit you pulled. Don't mess it up by pushing for too much. You won't win by playing dirty."

I run my hands over my face. "I'm not sure I'll win at all."

"Please. That girl has been crazy about you for as long as I've known her. You being a douchebag hasn't changed that."

"I really hope not. I need her, Tatum. I've never needed anyone but *fuck*, I need her."

She smiles knowingly and nods. "I know you do, and you'll have her – in her own time. I mean really, Parker Hall doesn't stand a chance if he's up against you."

Maverick walks in the door just as I finish thanking Tatum for the pep talk. He finds us both in the living room and smiles when his eyes land on his girlfriend. His hand reaches in his pocket and pulls out her keys, tossing them to her from across the room.

"It's all good to go."

She gets up and walks over to give him a kiss. "Thank you, baby."

"You do know I could've changed the oil, right?" I chime in.

Maverick laughs. "Yeah, with all the free time you've had lately. I feel like I haven't seen you in days and we live in the same house."

Okay so maybe he's right, but I can't exactly tell him where all my time has been spent. First, he would slaughter me, and then McKenna would bring me back to life just to kill me all over again. Instead, I just smile and nod.

"Fair enough. Works had me on a pretty tight schedule."

Tatum snorts but covers it with a cough. I narrow my eyes at her which only makes it harder for her to not laugh. Knowing she's about to risk blowing my cover, she grabs the large binder from under the table and turns back to Maverick.

"I'll be back in a bit." She presses a kiss to his cheek and heads out the door.

As soon as she's gone, Maverick groans and flops onto the couch. "I really wish my sister would just cancel this damn wedding."

His words have me perking up in an instant. "You don't like Parker?"

"Of course not. He's banging my little sister and I think he's a complete tool, but I was referring to how I get practically no time with Tatum because she's too busy planning their rush-down-the-aisle wedding."

I'm not sure what makes me feel sicker to my stomach – knowing that *I'm* banging his little sister too or that Tatum is still planning their wedding. Clearly McKenna didn't tell her to stop. I hadn't expected her to cancel it entirely, not yet anyway, but I at least hoped some of the planning would slow down. I mean, at this point they're wasting time and money on something that won't even happen. Well, at least it won't if I get my way. After this morning, I can't be too sure, regardless of what Tatum said.

"He doesn't seem all that bad."

It's a total lie. I hate him more than I hated the kid that stole my Game Boy in third grade, but it's enough to make it look like I'm not hopelessly obsessing over McKenna like some raging hormone, teenage boy.

Maverick steals the beer from my hands and takes a swig. "Don't give me that shit. I saw how relieved you were when he said he wasn't coming to the club last week. You would've rather cut your own dick off than hang out with him any longer than you already had to."

Okay, so maybe Maverick wasn't as clueless that night as I thought, but if he wants to believe Parker's absence was the reason for my mood change that night, I'm not going to correct him.

———

AN HOUR LATER, MAV and I are playing Call of Duty, yelling obscenities at what I can only assume is some thirteen-year-old kid who won't stop talking shit. It's been a while since him and I have been able to hang out like this. We may live together but with both our schedules lately, it feels like we only ever see each other in passing.

Just as the results pop up showing we won the game, the front door opens. At first I think it's Tatum, but when I hear McKenna's voice, my heart starts to race. I don't know if she's tried calling or texting me because my phone is still in the kitchen, but she's here. My car is in the driveway, so I know she's not surprised by my presence.

"You will never believe what happened!" She says excitedly as she walks down the hallway.

As soon as she comes into view, I'm stuck in a trance. She's wearing a pair of gray business type pants and a white blouse, looking like a sexy school teacher from every one of my teenage fantasies. Her hair is up in a bun with only a few strands hanging down to shape her face.

She smiles as she sees me but when she spots Maverick, it falters. It's enough for me to notice, but thankfully Mav is too into his victory to catch on. He steals my beer, again, and focuses his attention on his little sister.

"Well? Are you going to tell us or are you just going to stand there?"

As if she remembers what she came her for in the first place, her grin returns. "They offered me the job! You're looking at the new kindergarten teacher for Rockport Elementary."

My chest fills with pride as I look at how happy she is. I had no doubt in my mind that they would hire her. They'd be crazy not to. She's sweet, caring, and brilliantly smart. Anyone who spends more than five minutes with her can see she will make an amazing teacher.

"Congratulations, Squid! That's great!" Maverick gets up to give her a hug, one she accepts graciously. "What did Parker say when you told him? He doesn't expect you to be a trophy wife, does he?"

I snort, hearing the defensive brother persona in his tone. It wouldn't surprise me in the slightest if that was exactly what Parker wants. He seems like the kind of guy who needs to trap someone into staying with him. Yeah, he might appear all perfect and princely now, but once he knows he has her, he'll turn into someone totally different.

"O-oh." She stutters. "I… I didn't tell him yet. He's at class."

Uh, what? I look up at McKenna and smirk as she side-eyes me, mentally begging me not to say anything. It's unnecessary. I wouldn't call her out on lying, at least not in front of Maverick. That would just open everything up to questions I'm not ready to answer yet. So instead, I smile down at my lap.

"Well, I'm sure he'll be happy for you, too." Maverick says dismissively as his phone rings on the coffee table. He picks it up and looks at who's calling. "I have to take this. Congrats again."

He walks down the hallway and out the front door, leaving McKenna and I alone in the living room. She pulls her hair from the bun and shakes it out before running her fingers through it. I watch as it cascades over her shoulders and down her back. She doesn't even realize how gorgeous she is.

"You know, you're getting pretty good at that."

Her eyebrows furrow as she looks as me. "Good at what?"

"Lying."

She chuckles, falling back onto the couch beside me. "Yeah, well, I've had a lot of practice."

I'm not sure if it's a dig at me or if she's just being funny, but I can't find it in me to care. She just admitted to lying to Maverick, which means Parker is home and yet she came here first to share the big news. Judging by the surprised look on her face when she noticed her brother, she didn't come to tell him. *She came for me.*

I cautiously reach my hand over and place it on hers. "I'm really proud of you, McKenna. I knew you'd rock that interview."

Her head falls to the side so she's looking right at me. "How do you do that?"

"Do what?"

"Always have so much confidence in me."

I tighten my grip just slightly. "It's not confidence. It's just a matter of knowing the truth. The only one who can't see how amazing you are, is you."

Her eyes soften and she looks at me in that familiar way she always has. The look that makes my heart beat faster and time slow down. The look that tells me everything I need to hear every single second of my life. I've never seen it on anyone else, and I never want to.

"I'm sorry I snapped at you this morning." Her voice is so low it's almost a whisper, as if she's embarrassed to admit she did something wrong.

"It's okay. You were right – it was reckless."

"No." She shakes her head. "It was thoughtful, and generous, and really sweet of you. They're beautiful."

I use the hold I have on her hand to pull her into my arms. She goes willingly and I place a soft kiss to her forehead. "*You* are beautiful, but they'll do."

15

MCKENNA

My head hangs over the toilet as I empty the contents of my stomach into it. Between the dizziness and the discomfort in my abdomen, the tile floor feels good against my heated skin. Parker wets a washcloth and hands it to me to rub over my face.

"Are you okay?"

In an attempt to nod, I only make myself more nauseous. "I'll be fine. I just need to rest."

"So much for seeing my nan today." He mumbles disappointedly as he leaves the bathroom.

I don't know what I managed to come down with, but it's not fun. I spent the whole night vomiting, which means I'm completely exhausted. The idea of making the three-hour drive to Connecticut just to throw up in his grandmother's house is just a whole lot of no thank you. Still, that doesn't mean he shouldn't go.

I brush my teeth and gargle some mouth wash before drying my face and heading downstairs. I'm sure that I look like death, with my baggy shirt and sweatpants. My hair is tied up in a messy bun that looks like it was done by a blind person. The paleness of my skin and bags under my eyes make my lack of sleep obvious to anyone that glances my direction. If his grandmother saw me this way, she would think her precious grandson is marrying a hobo.

When I get into the kitchen, I find Parker rummaging through the fridge for something to drink. He pulls out two bottles of water and hands one to me. As soon as the cool liquid slides down my throat, I sigh in relief. It feels so good to wash the acidic feeling away.

"I'm sorry I'm sick, but you should still go."

He turns to me, frowning. "I can't leave you here by yourself, not when you're like this."

"Babe, I'm a big girl. I can handle being sick on my own. And besides, she's been really looking forward to this visit. You haven't been there since Christmas."

"Speaking of..." He starts and I already know what he's going to say. "You still haven't told me if you're going to come to England with me this year."

I roll my eyes. "Parker, it's like six months away. Is an answer right now *really* that necessary?"

"Yes. I'd like to book our tickets in advance. Flying over the holidays can be expensive, especially international flights."

This, this right here, is one of the things that drives me insane about him. The man standing in front of me is the same man who bought a new truck simply because he liked the color better than the one he had for only three months before that. Money has never been, and will never be, an issue for him. He's simply being impatient and wants my answer now rather than later.

"Well, if the price of the flight is that important to you, maybe you should save the money on my ticket all together."

He scoffs but doesn't say anything before grabbing his wallet and keys off the counter. I watch him carefully as he walks towards me and kisses my cheek.

"Feel better and call me if you need anything."

I nod. "Tell Nan I said hello."

His grandmother is a wonderful person, and even though Parker may be pissing me off at the moment, I hold no resentment towards her. She's a sweet old lady who would rather horde teabags she found on sale than take the money her daughter offers her. Parker's mother met his father during a year of studying abroad in London. She was completely enchanted with him and never ended up leaving. He comes from a wealthy family and his mother knew she wouldn't have to work a day in her life, so she dropped out of college and they were married the following summer. Nan, however, absolutely refused to leave America, and while she's always been happy for her daughter, she doesn't hide her disappointment at the way she gave everything up for a man.

As soon as I hear the garage door close, signifying that he's gone, I grab the softest blanket I can find and wrap myself in it on the couch. When you're sick, there's nothing better than feeling as comfortable as possible. I turn on the investigation discovery channel – my guilty pleasure – and immerse myself into the world of criminally insane.

Halfway through the second episode of Stalked, my phone dings with a Snapchat from Colton. I open it to find a picture of him, standing in the middle of a half-built house and looking as sexy as he always does in a tight fitted t-shit. There are no words, just a picture of him staring into the camera. I swipe to respond and take a picture of myself, wrapped in my blanket with my lip puffed out in a pout.

The last few weeks, Colton and I have been spending every possible moment together. With Parker constantly being in Boston for school, it hasn't taken much sneaking around. Don't get me wrong, I feel guilty about going behind his back, but there's just something about the way Colton makes me feel. I don't think I could stay away if I tried.

Things with Colton are perfect. He's been acting the way I'd always wished he would. There hasn't been a single day where I haven't gotten a good morning text from him. He always asks how my day has been and when I'm in a bad mood, he tries to make it better. I'd be lying if I said I'm not completely wrapped back up in all things him and now I don't know what to do.

Parker is everything I *should* want. He's kind, and sweet, and makes sure I know he loves me every single day even if we're mad at each other – which isn't often. He is the epitome of the perfect guy... for girls who *want* the perfect guy. Personally, I want someone who is going to challenge me. Someone who won't deal with my bullshit simply because he's too afraid to piss me off. I'm not asking for my house to be a constant war zone, but when everything is flawless 100% of the time, you start to get a little bored.

Colton sends back a picture, mimicking my face with text this time. *What's wrong?* I take a photo of the couch in front of me to answer. It's bad enough I let him see me looking like a hot-mess-express once today. He doesn't need more.

Sick 😩

He reads it immediately but doesn't respond. I don't think too much of it. Judging by his pictures, he's at work and probably got caught up with something. I put my phone down on the couch next to me, letting the stories of people being stalked lull me to sleep.

I WAKE TO THE sound of the doorbell before my phone starts ringing next to me. Colton's name flashes on the screen. I sit up, rubbing my eyes with the back of my hands before answering.

"Hello?"

He chuckles. "Are you going to let me in?"

Shit, the doorbell. "Oh. That's you?"

"Yeah. Unlock the door."

The two of us hang up the phone and I let my bare feet pad across the hardwood floor. As soon as I open the front door, I find Colton standing there, holding a bag from the pharmacy. He smiles warmly at me and steps inside.

"I brought the necessities."

My eyebrows furrow as I follow him into the kitchen. "Necessities?"

"Yeah. Tylenol, Gatorade, Crackers, the whole deal. I wasn't sure what you already had so I just grabbed it all."

Seriously, any time I feel like he can't possibly be any cuter, he proves me wrong. Everything he's been doing lately has made me swoon like a teenager with her first crush. Well, let's be real for a minute – he *was* my first crush.

I watch him unload everything from the bag and put it all away before turning to me. The way he's standing so close almost has me stepping back. Parker is always too afraid to get sick himself, so whenever I come down with something he tries to stay as far from me as possible. He glances me over, frowning when he sees how tired I look.

"Crap. I woke you up, didn't I?"

"No." I lie. He gives me a knowing look. "Okay, yes, but I'm glad you did."

"I'm not. You need your rest." He raises his hand and places the back of it against my forehead. "Have you had a fever?"

"I don't think so. Just nausea."

"So, kissing you then…"

I cringe. "Probably a bad idea."

He presses his lips to my forehead. "Thanks for the heads up. Now, back to bed for you."

"I wasn't in bed. I was on the couch."

"Okay, smart ass. Back to *the couch* then."

I murmur a string of playful obscenities as I make my way

into the living room. Colton stays behind to pour me a glass of Gatorade and then comes to join me. I thank him and take a sip of the drink. It's so much better than water when you feel so drained. An involuntary moan leaves my mouth at the taste of it and I notice the way Colton squirms in the seat next to me.

"Don't get any ideas, Casanova."

"Ideas? What ideas?" He mocks.

"I'm sick. There is no way in hell I'm going to get you sick too. You should probably move over a seat."

He gets up to move but only ends up closer. I glare at him even though it has no affect. "McKenna Rae, if you think something like a stomach bug is going to keep me away from you, you're sadly mistaken."

His arm wraps around my shoulder as he rearranges me to lay with my head in his lap. Then, he takes my blanket from earlier and drapes it over me before running his fingers through my hair. It's everything I didn't know I needed. The soothing feeling of his touch on my scalp almost makes me forget how gross I feel.

"What time is it? Shouldn't you be at work?"

He grins. "Eh, my boss firmly believes in ditching all responsibilities to go take care of your sick girlfriend."

Girlfriend. That's a new thing he's been saying lately and I must admit, I love the way it rolls off his tongue. The first time he did it, I choked on my drink and sputtered water everywhere. It was unexpected and caught me completely off guard. Judging by the way he smirked at my reaction, he knew exactly what he was doing and did it on purpose.

Calling Colton my boyfriend feels wrong, and not only because I'm engaged to someone else. It feels unnatural, like he's meant to be so much more than that. The term boyfriend just isn't enough. It lacks significance.

"If you *had* a boss, he would hate you."

He laughs. "Okay, enough from you, Princess. Go back to sleep. You need your rest."

I want to fight it, but the urge to doze off again is hard to resist with he way he's massaging my head. The smell of his cologne relaxes me in a way nothing else does. I nuzzle my face into his shirt and let the need to sleep take over once again.

I run down the street, as fast as I can. After watching Parker's heart shatter right in front of my eyes when I told him I no longer wanted to marry him, I need to get to Colton. I never meant for things to get so messy, or for anyone to get hurt, but when push came to shove, the choice was obvious. It's always been obvious.

When I get to the familiar house, the door is already unlocked. I let myself in and go straight up the stairs, finding Colton laying with his hands behind his head. His abs are full on display and almost make me forget what I came here for in the first place. He narrows his eyes at me when he notices I'm standing there.

"What are you doing here?"

I pant and try to catch my breath. "I did it. I ended things with Parker."

"What the hell did you do that for?"

"So that we can be together. So that we don't have to hide anymore."

He sits up and tilts his head to the side before breaking into a fit of hysterics. My chest starts to hurt when I realize what's happening. He doesn't even need to open his mouth for me to know what he's going to say. Finally, when his laughter subsides, he looks at me with an expression full of pity.

"Mac, I've told you this before and I'll say it again. In a choice between you and Maverick, I'm going to pick him. You're great in bed but you're not worth losing my best friend over."

I shake my head as I listen to him repeat the same words he said to me the day my heart broke. "B-but you said... You said you wanted to fight for us."

"I said whatever I had to." He stands up and walks toward me, running his knuckle over my cheek once he's close enough. "You and I are never going to be more than a good time. Haven't you learned that by now?"

My body turns to leave his room, only to find Tatum standing there with a knowing look on her face. "You can't say I didn't warn you."

Their laughter bellows through the house as I run down the stairs and out the front door. The tears in my eyes make it hard to see anything at all. By the grace of God, I manage to make it back to my place. I rush through the door and into the living room.

"Parker?! Parker!" I call out through the house. "I'm so sorry. I think I made a huge mistake."

When I don't find him anywhere downstairs, I go up to our bedroom only to find that everything of his is missing. His clothes are no longer hanging in the closet. His dresser is completely empty. The picture of him and I from the nightstand lies shattered on the floor. He's gone and I'm left broken and alone, again.

I jolt awake, gasping for air. The pain in my chest is excruciating as I take in my surroundings. *It was just a dream. It wasn't real.* I hear Colton's voice in the kitchen, and right after, I hear Parker respond. *Shit. He's home?!* As soon as I sit up, the two of them look over at me.

"Hey, you're awake." Colton smiles. "I was just telling Parker about how Mav asked me to come take care of you."

Everything I felt in that dream is still rushing through me. It seemed so real. Hell, it *could* end up being real for all I know. Parker eyes me carefully as if he's trying to read what I'm thinking and I know I need to play along.

"Yeah. Can you please tell him to stop being so overprotective?"

Colton snorts. "You know that's never going to happen."

That's what I'm afraid of.

When Parker comes over to hug me hello, Colton shifts uncomfortably. "Well, now that he's home, I'm going to get going."

"Are you sure?" Parker responds for me. "You're welcome to stay for dinner."

If I didn't know Colton as well as I do, I'd miss the pain in his eyes. "No, that's okay. I've got some work to catch up on, but thank you anyway."

"I'll walk you out." I offer.

The two men say goodbye and Colton follows me over to the door. We both step outside and I close it behind me, making sure Parker can't hear us.

"Thank you for coming over. You really didn't have to do that."

He grins and all of the emotions I can see on his face are so overwhelming they almost knock the wind out of me. "There isn't anything I wouldn't do for you, McKenna. Never think otherwise."

With a soft kiss on my forehead, he walks down the steps and gets in his car. I watch as he drives away, trying to rid my mind of the nightmare I just had. It only took a few weeks, and now I'm right back to where I was four years ago – hopelessly in love with Colton Brooks.

I really hope this time is different.

COLTON

THE SUN BEAMS DOWN AND HEATS MY SKIN WHILE music echoes through Maverick's backyard. McKenna and I stand on opposite sides of a ping-pong table, shooting balls into the plastic cups. Ivy is beside her giving Roman what I'm guessing is supposed to be an intimidating look. We've been at this all afternoon. Rome and I are yet to lose one game, but they're giving us a run for our money.

"Had I known you were this good at beer pong, I may have reconsidered my partner." I tell McKenna as she sinks another shot.

She shrugs. "There's plenty you don't know about me, Brooks. I'm full of surprises."

"I'm sure you are, Princess." I chuckle.

As if she knows my every weakness, she pulls off her tank top and tosses it onto the chair behind her, leaving her in shorts and a bikini top. I swallow hard and try to focus but it's no use. The shot goes wide, missing the table entirely and causing Roman to laugh.

"You don't play fair."

She smirks. "I don't know what you're talking about."

I don't miss the way she glances at Rome and back at me

in a silent warning to play it cool. A part of me acknowledges I should tell her that he already knows, but I don't want to scare her away. To her, it's bad enough that Ivy and Tatum know what's going on between us. The way she sees it is the fewer, the better.

As McKenna goes to take her shot, I pull my own shirt over my head. My bathing suit hangs low on my hips but I don't bother fixing it. She chokes on her own saliva as her eyes gaze over my torso. *Two can play this game.*

"Take your shot, Princess."

A low groan escapes from the back of her throat and she tries to focus. Just as she's aiming the ball, I raise my arms above my head and stretch, making sure to flex in the process. She throws the ball so hard it hits Roman in the stomach. She glares at me, causing me to flash her a cocky grin in response.

McKenna may be completely distracted by me, but Ivy isn't. She tosses the ball straight into the cup, tying the game up with one left for both sides. Roman goes first for our team. The ball bounces off the rim and onto the ground. I do my best to ignore McKenna as I focus on lining up my shot. I can see her moving in my peripheral vision so I close my eyes and let the ball leave my fingertips.

"Shit." Ivy whines and I know I made it.

It's McKenna's turn. As she's dunking the ball in the water cup to clean it off, I walk towards her. She puts her hands up and takes a step back.

"Stay on your side of the table, cheater."

Laughter bubbles out of my mouth as I slip past her and go to the cooler to grab another beer. Just as I'm coming back, I slide myself against her backside and place my lips near her ear – careful to watch for Maverick.

"If you win, I'll let you tie me up."

She whimpers loud enough for only me to hear and her teeth sink into her bottom lip. I skate my hand against her lower back as I return to my spot. Her eyes meet mine. She raises one brow and doesn't look away while she shoots the ball. It's a perfect shot and I'd be a damn liar if I said I wasn't impressed as hell. She's so fucking sexy, it's intoxicating.

The game goes into overtime and it's the worst thing that could have happened for Roman and I. After we each miss our first shot, McKenna and Ivy both make theirs, sending the balls back to them. McKenna licks her lips as flicks the ball across the table and straight into the cup. My jaw drops and she winks. I don't have to be a rocket scientist to know exactly what's going through her mind. Still, this isn't over.

Roman and I each make our shot, leaving only one cup left to send the game into double overtime. Rome goes first but misses by a hair. Just as I'm about to go, McKenna takes her sunglasses off her head and puts one of the temples into her mouth, sucking on it just enough to make my cock twitch. Before the ball even leaves my fingers, I know I'm completely screwed. She has me right where she wants me.

Sure enough, I miss the shot and they take the win. McKenna and Ivy hug in celebration. Roman turns to me and chuckles. He places his hand on my shoulder as he goes to walk past me.

"You're so whipped. You know that, right?"

My eyes don't leave McKenna, seeing the bright smile on her face as she laughs with Ivy. "I think I'm okay with that."

Maverick comes back from getting more beer and calls for my help bringing it in from the car, effectively pulling my attention away from his sister. I give her one last look before disappearing into the house.

I'M STANDING WITH MAVERICK and Roman, listening to them discuss the new renovations Mav is planning at his office. I toss my opinion out there every few minutes, but I'm focused on McKenna. She seemed fine up until about twenty minutes ago when she started to look pale. Ivy is next to her but it's driving me insane that I can't be. All I want right now is to take her into my arms and make sure she's okay.

After she came down with that stomach bug, she seemed fine no more than 24 hours later. Still, the way she's looking right now makes me wonder if she got better at all. McKenna is a very stubborn person. If she doesn't want to be sick, she will convince herself she's not and make everyone else believe it too.

"What do you think, Colton?" Maverick asks.

"Huh?"

"Floor to ceiling windows or a more secluded looking office?"

Just like that, I'm wrapped back up in work as I explain to Maverick that while yes, a wall of windows makes him look like a big shot, it doesn't do much when his view is of the building next door and he's only three stories off the ground. He nods along as if he's listening, but I know better. When he his mind is made up about something, there's no changing it – opinion of a top notch architect be damned.

"Holy shit! Are you pregnant?!"

The sound of Ivy's voice causes every one of us to freeze. My eyes meet McKenna's and widen drastically as she slaps a hand over her best friend's mouth. The entire world seems to stop spinning and I'm floating in an inescapable limbo. *Pregnant? Is she pregnant?!*

"Well damn, who knew Parker had it in him to knock her up *before* the wedding." Roman quips, causing Maverick to punch him in the arm. "Ow, bro."

"*Bro*, that's my baby sister."

The small spat between them made me look away from McKenna, and when I look back, she's gone. Maverick and Roman are going back and forth about how Mac is only three years younger than us and engaged. Obviously, Maverick doesn't care to hear it. McKenna could be eight or eighty-two – she'll always be a little girl in his eyes.

I stand in complete agony for a few minutes, knowing I can't walk away from Maverick right now without looking suspicious. Finally, I see Tatum come out from the house and walk towards me. The expression on her face tells me this isn't a drill, and Mac being pregnant is a *serious* possibility.

"What the hell is going on?" She whispers, careful not to let Maverick hear us.

I shake my head. "I don't know, but keep him distracted while I go find out, please."

She nods and I waste no time before heading inside. As soon as I step into the kitchen, McKenna and Ivy look up at me from the other side of the island. Ivy has a hand on McKenna's back, rubbing it soothingly as Mac looks like she's about to have a mental break down.

"How much have you had to drink?" I ask Ivy, making sure to keep my expression neutral for McKenna's sake.

"Just what I drank during beer pong, but that was a couple of hours ago."

Grabbing my keys and wallet off the counter, I walk over and hand them to her. "Good. Go to the store and get a test. Come straight back here and don't let Maverick see you when you do."

She nods and after McKenna silently tells her it's okay to go, she heads out the front door.

My head is reeling as I grip the edge of the island for support. Being as she's on birth control, I know this isn't something that either of us planned. Sure, we could've been more careful but I didn't think we needed to be. Apparently, I was wrong. *So very fucking wrong*.

It's not that I'm mad at the possibility that McKenna could be pregnant. Hell, the thought of my baby growing inside of her makes me feel even more possessive than I already do. It's the idea that it might not be *my* baby that has me on the brink of insanity. I just got her back. Being pregnant with Parker's kid would send her running right into his arms and I wouldn't stand a chance.

"I'm sorry." A very faint whisper comes from next to me.

I look over to find tears streaming down McKenna's face. Every feeling I have about the current situation dissipates and the only thing I can focus on is her. I walk around the counter and pull her into my arms. All the emotions she was trying to hold back come pouring out at once.

"It's okay." I murmur into her hair, placing a kiss on her head.

"It's not." She sobs. "What are we going to do?"

"Well, have you taken a test yet?" She shakes her head. "Then we wait for Ivy to get back and we go from there."

"You're not mad?"

I back up just slightly and look down at her. "Mad? Why would I be mad?"

"Because we just got started and we're still trying to figure this out. Being pregnant would throw a major wrench in things."

"I know, but it's not like you planned this. Accidents happen."

She snorts. "Pretty big accident."

"Hey, an accident is what brought me to *you*."

I'm sitting on my couch, watching cartoons on TV while I drown out the sound of my baby sister, Avery, crying. She's only one and when she's sick, she screams – a lot. My parents are frustrated and as much I want to help, there isn't really anything I can do. I'm only ten.

A loud bang sounds from upstairs and is very quickly followed by an ear-piercing scream. My mom starts to panic and I can hear my dad rushing into the room to find out what happened.

"Sh-She fell." My mother cries. "I dozed off for a second and she fell off the changing table. I think she hit her head."

"Oh god. Okay, we need to take her to the emergency room."

I can hear them coming down the stairs and I stand up to see what all the commotion is about. My dad gives me a sad smile, trying to assure me everything is okay, but I can see the worry in his eyes. When my mom sees me, she cringes.

"We can't bring Colton to the hospital. He just got over the flu."

My dad sighs. "Well, what else are we going to do? My parents are at least an hour away and yours are on a cruise."

Trying to help, I offer to stay home alone but they both shake their heads. Then I get an idea. "I can go to Maverick's house."

Maverick Taylor is a kid in my class. We met a couple months ago when I moved here and if I had to choose someone as my best friend, it would be him. We've hung out a couple times after school but only at the park.

I go over to my backpack and pull out the piece of paper where he wrote down his phone number. It's smudged and crumpled but you can still read it. I walk over to my dad and hand it to him. He smiles and pats me on the shoulder before walking away to make the call.

The four of us get in the car. Avery is strapped into her car seat and while she looks fine, I'm still worried. I make faces at her that normally make her smile, but this time she doesn't. I look up at my dad through the rear-view mirror.

"Is Avery going to be okay?"

His expression softens as he glances back at me. "Well son, she hit her head but she should be okay. We just need to take her to get checked out by a doctor."

I turn back to my sister and hug her as best I can with the restrictions of being in the car. She may be a pain in the butt sometimes, but she's my sister and I love her.

The rest of the drive is short. It's a small town and I probably could have ridden my bike but it's starting to get dark. We pull up to the Taylor's house and my mom gets out of the car and walks me up onto the porch. A woman answers the door who looks like an older, *female version of Maverick. She smiles warmly at me and then turns to my mother.*

"Thank you so much for taking him."

She waves her off dismissively. "Oh, of course. Your husband explained the situation over the phone. Please let me know how your daughter is doing as soon as you know. And don't worry about Colton. I'm sure him and Maverick will have a great time."

My mom gives me a hug goodbye before running to the car. I watch them drive away, clearly in a hurry to get to the hospital. I think Maverick's mom can tell I'm scared because she puts a hand on my shoulder and whispers that everything will be okay. I nod my head before following her into the house.

It's cozy inside. There's a staircase directly in front of me with a living room to the left and a dining room to the right. Maverick's mom points out where to find everything, telling me that Mav's room is upstairs, the kitchen at the end of the hallway in front of me, and there is a bathroom to the right of it. She mentions that Maverick is in the shower and I should make myself at home while I wait for him.

"Marissa, can you come help me in here?" A man's voice comes from the end of the hall.

She calls back that she'll be right there and ruffles her hand through my hair. Then, she disappears, leaving me standing alone at the door. I hear laughter in the living room and my curiosity gets the better of me. Tiptoeing closer, I see a little girl sitting on the floor playing a game by herself. She has plastic necklace around her neck and her fingers are covered in fake rings. Her giggle is the first thing that makes me smile since I heard Avery get hurt.

"What are you playing?" I ask.

The girl looks up at me and gives me a wide grin. Dimples accent her cheeks and her green eyes remind me of freshly cut grass in the spring. She's definitely younger than me and I remember Maverick telling me he has a little sister. This must be her.

"Pretty, pretty, princess. Want to play?"

I walk around the couch and sit on the floor in front of her. "I don't know how."

"I can teach you. My mom was playing with me but now she's helping my dad, so you can take her spot." She hands me a spinner. *"I'm McKenna."*

"I'm-"

"Colton. I know." She cuts me off. *"You're Maverick's friend."*

The two of us take turns passing the spinner back and forth and moving our pieces. Every time I land on a piece of jewelry, she helps me find it and puts it in a pile in front of me. I know the rules of the game are that you wear it, but I'm a boy and if Maverick saw me wearing fake jewelry with his sister, he might not think I'm cool anymore.

McKenna looks adorable as she puts the fake earrings on and hands me the spinner to take my turn. I move my piece and land on the crown.

"No fair! You got the crown!" She gapes jealously and grabs the fake silver headpiece to hand it to me.

I look down at it and then back at her. *"You can have it."*

"Really?"

"Yeah." I reach over and put it on top of her head, resting it on her light brown hair.

Her face lights up and I can't help but smile back. *"How do I look?"*

"Perfect. It looks much better on you."

The two of us laugh until the sound of someone coming down the stairs makes McKenna roll her eyes. I turn my head towards the doorway and Maverick comes up behind the couch.

"Hey Colton. What are you doing with Squid?"

"Squid?"

McKenna groans loudly. *"Stop calling me that! It's embarrassing."*

"Whatever, twerp. Leave my friend alone."

I shake my head. *"No, it's fine. I asked if I could play."*

He looks at me like I've lost my mind but then nods towards the stairs. *"Come on. Let's go to my room and play video games."*

I get up and walk around the couch to follow him, but just before I *leave the room, I turn back to McKenna. "Thanks for letting me play with you, Princess."*

The blush that coats her cheeks and the way my words make her smile is something that will stay burned in my mind for the rest of my life.

"So, *that's* why you call me Princess?" She asks, like it's something she's always wondered.

I nod. "You were adorable, and I knew *then* that you were something special."

Her tears have long since dried up and all that's left is the way she's looking at me like I'm everything she's ever wanted in her life. My heart pounds inside of my chest, threatening to break through my rib cage and throw itself at her feet. Roman was right – she has me wrapped around her pretty little finger. If this doesn't go my way, I'll never make it out alive.

17

MCKENNA

HOW DID I GET HERE? HOW WAS I SO INCREDIBLY irresponsible that I ended up in this situation? I mean, it's one thing to be cheating on my fiancé while I try to figure out what in the world is going on between Colton and I, but to end up pregnant with a secret love child? Well, let's just say my mother raised me better than that.

When I started feeling nauseous, I honestly believed it was just a stomach bug. My immune system never has been the best so it wouldn't surprise me. The thought of being pregnant hadn't even entered my mind until Ivy asked when my last period was. She's always been the voice of reason to my madness. The moment I could tell where she was going with her million and six questions, I planned to freak out in private. I was going to make an excuse to leave, go get a pregnancy test, and take it alone in my empty house. However, all that changed when Ivy lost the ability to control her volume.

The shocked look on Colton's face as he stared back at me made me want to crawl in a hole and never come out. I was almost positive he was going to be sent running for the hills. I mean, we aren't even in a legitimate relationship. The amount of people who know about us can be counted on one hand alone. We're still in that phase where it's new and exciting, and sneaking around has had a sort of sex appeal to it. Throwing a baby into the mix would cause so much chaos, just thinking about it makes my stomach churn.

I hold my head in my hands as Colton paces around the kitchen. He's trying to maintain his composure but I can tell he's freaking out. He grabs a beer from the fridge and pops the cap off before chugging more than half of it. Once he's done, he places it down and leans on the counter.

"Okay." He breathes. "Okay, this is fine. We can do this."

His words peak my interest. "We can?"

"Yeah. It doesn't change anything, at least not yet anyway. I mean, we can still keep us a secret until you figure out what you want to do." I'm about to question what he means, but he continues. "You can get a paternity test during the pregnancy, right?"

"A-a paternity test?" I choke.

"Yeah. I think I read once about them doing it using amniotic fluid or something. That way we don't have to wait until you have the baby to find out."

"Find out *what* exactly?" My blood starts to boil as I realize what he's insinuating. "You don't think this baby is yours?!"

His brows furrow and his eyes narrow. "Well, it could go either way, couldn't it?" I look at him as if he's crazy and he clarifies. "The baby could be mine or Parker's."

Wow, okay. A part of me wonders if I should correct him. Would he lose the thrill of the chase if he knew the truth? Hell, for all I know, he could only want me because he doesn't fully have me. Once he knows, he might not be interested anymore. Still, I can't put everyone through a shit show of madness for something I already know.

"No, Colton, it couldn't." His eyes widen before I even say the words. "It couldn't be Parker's because I haven't *slept* with Parker, not since you and I..." My words fade out because I know I don't need to explain further.

He looks shocked, opening and closing his mouth like a fish out of water. Just when he seems like he's finally going to say something, Ivy comes bursting into the room.

"Okay, I got it." She tosses Colton's keys and wallet onto the counter and nods towards the stairs. "Let's go find out if *you* have a bun in the oven."

Glancing over at Colton, he swallows down his words and shakes himself out of whatever mental debate he was just having. The three of us go through the living room and up the stairs. Colton goes straight into his bedroom while Ivy follows me to the toilet. She shuts the door behind her and pulls the box out of her purse.

"So, there are two. I figure you can take one now and take the other first thing tomorrow morning." She tells me as she rips open the wrapping and pulls one of the tests out. "I'd read you the directions but it's pretty self-explanatory. Pee on the stick, wait three minutes, ya-de-ya-de-ya."

I roll my eyes as I take it from her, personally finding it ridiculous that I even need to do this. I know birth control pills aren't 100% effective and a lot can make them fail, but a missed period and a little bit of nausea doesn't automatically mean I'm knocked up. Still, I guess it would be better to know than to wonder – especially because if I am, I'll need to make an appointment for prenatal care.

After I finish peeing on the test, I put the cap back on it and wipe it off before washing my hands. The two of us leave the bathroom and find Colton sitting on the side of his bed. I put the test on his dresser while Ivy sets a timer on her phone.

When Colton's eyes meet mine, there is a glint of something in them that I don't recognize but it causes a shiver to run down my spine. He pats the space next to him and I go willingly, letting him wrap his arm around me and pull me close. The soft kiss he presses to my forehead relaxes me a little until Ivy plops down beside me.

"If it's a girl, can you name it after me?" My jaw drops as Colton snorts. "What? Ivy is a great name!"

I shake my head and chuckle slightly. Leave it to my best friend to make light of the situation in a time like this. The ugly truth of the matter is that if I am pregnant, if Colton's baby is growing inside of me, everything is going to come out. Parker will learn about the affair I've been having for the past month. Maverick will learn that his best friend and his little sister have been sneaking around behind his back. My failed engagement and adulterous tendencies will be the talk of the town.

"My mom is going to kill me." I murmur before looking at Colton. "And probably you, too."

He gives me one of those boyish grins that make him look like an innocent little cupcake. "Who me?" I nod. "No way. Marissa *loves* me. She'd probably be thrilled and throw a party in my honor."

"In *your* honor?"

"Absolutely. You, well, you're right. She'll probably kill you, but she'll at least wait until the baby is born safely first."

Ivy sniggers as I roll my eyes playfully. "You really know how to make me feel better."

He laughs and pulls me closer, searing his lips over my own. The kiss isn't anything close to heated, but it takes my breath away. The way he holds my cheek like I'm the most delicate things, and how he uses the arm wrapped around my waist to keep me pressed against him – it's mind blowing. Every thought I had, every stressful thing on my mind, is all replaced by tingles running through my body and the feeling of his mouth on mine.

When he breaks the kiss, I blink my eyes open to find him smirking at me. "Better?"

I nod. "Thank you."

Staring at the test from across the room, I know it has to be getting close to time. In a matter of minutes, my entire world could be flipped on its axis. When I was growing up, I always imagined finding out I was pregnant with my first child and how I would tell the father. Sometimes it was this big announcement with balloons and a onesie wrapped in a present. Others, it was a small private moment where I whispered the news just before we fell asleep, cuddled up together in bed. Regardless, it was never like this.

The timer sounds and my whole body tenses. I know I should get up, but I can't seem to move. My feet are planted to the floor and my hand grips Colton's thigh. He looks up at Ivy and something unspoken passes between them. She nods and stands, taking a deep breath before walking towards the dresser.

Everything plays in slow motion as I watch my best friend take the test into her hands. She looks up at the ceiling then turns to me with relief all over her face. I don't need to ask to know what it says. I throw myself back on the bed and release a breath I didn't know I was holding.

"It's negative?" Colton asks like he needs to be sure.

"It's negative. She's not pregnant."

A small laugh bubbles out of my mouth, then another, then another. Before I know it, I'm breaking out in full hysterics. Colton holds himself up with one arm as he hovers slightly over me. Tears are brimming in my eyes from laughing harder than I have in a while. The amusement that graces his face as he watches me is evident.

"You find this funny?" He asks with one eyebrow raised and a sexy as hell smirk.

"A little."

Ivy murmurs something about giving us a minute before walking out and closing the door behind her. Once we're completely alone, the tension between us grows until I'm clenching my thighs together to try to control myself. The humor vanishes as we stare into each other's eyes. Colton's hand rests gently on my cheek.

"You really haven't slept with Parker?"

I shake my head. "Were you hoping I had?"

He looks at me like I've lost my ever-loving mind. "Of course not! Why in the world would you think that?"

"I don't know." I shrug. "I thought maybe you were counting on the baby being his."

Realization crosses over his face and he quickly turns his body so I have his undivided attention. I sit up and allow him to take my hands in his own. He looks at me with such admiration that I'm completely awestruck.

"Babe, that wasn't at all what I was thinking."

"It wasn't?"

He smiles. "Not even a little. If you were pregnant, I would have spent the next however many weeks praying to God that it *was* mine. The only reason I was freaking out was because I thought that if the baby was Parker's, that I would lose you for good."

My heart is beating so hard and fast that I feel like it might combust. I'm surprised he can't hear it from where he sits. My smile stretches until it hurts while I stare back at him, unable to speak. There are no words for what I want to say, so instead, I lunge across the small space between us and press my lips to his.

He hums and kisses me back instantly while his hands grip my hips. As soon as he lays back, I straddle his waist and grind down on him. The moan that leaves my mouth mixes with the groan that comes from his. Being with him like this, with everyone just downstairs, is risky and dangerous but I can't find it in me to care.

"Fuck, McKenna." Colton murmurs as his lips move down to my neck.

I continue to move against him, feeling the way he grows harder in his bathing suit. Only two thin pieces of clothing separate us and all I wish is that they would just fall away. I need him inside of me, stretching me open and filling me up.

His hand skates down my body and cups my sex. I throw my head back and moan loudly. He chuckles at my reaction and covers my mouth with his.

"Shh, baby." He whispers against my lips. "You need to be quiet or someone will hear us."

I don't know if it's the thrill of sneaking around or the fact that we haven't had sex in a week, but I want him so fucking bad that I may consider screwing him on the living room couch right now if that's what it takes. Having to stare at him all damn day with his shirt off and his perfectly sculpted abs glistening with a light coat of sweat – it's been absolute torture.

"Colton." I pant.

"What do you need, Princess?"

"You. I need you."

He uses his hold on me to flip us around so I'm lying on the bed and he's hovering over me. "You have me. Any way you want, I'm yours."

My hands move to his head and my fingers lace into his hair as I pull him into a bruising kiss. It's messy and heated and passionate as sin. Colton makes an animalistic noise as he grinds himself down onto me, hard. Just as he hooks his thumbs under my bikini bottoms, the door swings open.

"Yo, Brooks. Do you have a charger? My phone is-WOAH!" Roman's eyes widen before he very quickly turns back around and leaves the room without another word.

"Oh my God." I breathe, pushing Colton off me and starting to panic. "Oh my God!"

"McKenna, relax."

"Relax?! Are you kidding me right now?! Roman just caught us!" He isn't freaking out nearly as much as I assumed he would, and that alone confuses me. "Why are you acting like this is no big deal?"

He shrugs. "Because it *isn't* a big deal. Rome knows. He's known for a while now."

Suddenly, it all makes sense. The way Colton doesn't care about openly flirting with me in front of him. How Roman pushed for me to get in-between Colton and the chick he was dancing with at the bar. Hell, even Roman keeping Parker wrapped up in conversation for most of Maverick's birthday dinner. He's been helping him. He's known about us this whole damn time. I don't know if that makes me feel better or worse.

"Still, we shouldn't be doing this. What if that was Maverick?"

Hearing my own words, everything changes. The nightmare I had the other day replays in my mind in a way that feels alarmingly real and absolutely terrifying. What if that *had* been Maverick? Would Colton have ended everything with me to please my brother? I mean, he's done it before and without Maverick even knowing about us. Who's to say he wouldn't do it again when the stakes are so much higher?

"Mac, relax. Rome isn't going to say anything." He reaches to grab my hand but I yank it away.

"That's not the point!" I take a deep breath and lower my voice. "At any moment, my brother could walk through that door. We shouldn't have risked it. It's too reckless."

Before he can stop me, I back away and walk out his bedroom door. The sound of him calling my name faintly echoes through the house as I make my way down the stairs and outside. No matter how bad I want him to hold me after the potentially life changing scare we just had, I can't let him. We've gotten too close lately and I've let my guard down way too much. If I don't protect myself and things go wrong, there's only one way this could end – with me broken and in pieces on my bedroom floor. I can't let that happen again.

I step up next to Ivy and Tatum and plaster on the best

smile I can manage. If either of them realize it's fake, they thankfully don't mention it. A few minutes later, I hear the door open and glance over to see Colton stepping outside. Our eyes meet and we hold the gaze for a minute before he looks away and shakes his head. I do my best to ignore the pang in my chest. *I need to be more careful.*

18

MCKENNA

It's been a week since the party at Maverick's and I can't get the thought of Roman walking in on us out of my head. If Colton didn't trust him so much, I'd be terrified he's going to say something to Maverick. They've all been friends for the same amount of time, so it's not like he holds any more loyalty to Colton than he does Mav, other than maybe the fact that Colton is his boss. Ugh, it's just all so frustrating.

I'm sitting at the nail salon with Ivy on one side of me and Tatum on the other. The foot bath feels amazing as the chair massages into my back. A day out with two of my favorite girls is exactly what I need.

"Oh Mac, before I forget, the bakery called to confirm your appointment for next Saturday. Parker *is* going with you, correct?"

My brows furrow as I try to figure out what she's talking about, then it hits me. "The cake tasting! Right, yeah he'll be there."

Ivy snorts and rolls her eyes. "You're going through a lot of trouble for a wedding that won't end up happening anyway." Mine and Tatum's jaws drop as we both turn to look at her and all she does is shrug. "What? I'm just saying what no one else will. It's *Colton*."

"Exactly. It's Colton. It's my brother's *best* friend. It's the guy who made it so I felt like physically ripping my heart out of my chest would hurt less than the pain I was in. It's dangerous, and reckless, and almost guaranteed to ruin me."

"Mac…" Ivy sighs.

"Don't." I cut her off. "I don't want to talk about it. I'm just trying to keep my distance for a bit. I let my guard down too much, and I need to make sure I'm protected. I can't afford not to be."

"Oh because avoiding him has done *so well* for you in the past."

I glare at my best friend until I can't help but smile. "I'm not avoiding him, per se. I still answer his texts. I just make excuses as to why I can't hang out. I don't even think he realizes anything is wrong."

Tatum chuckles, not looking up from her phone. "I live with the guy. Trust me, he realizes."

Okay, maybe a girls' day wasn't such a great idea after all. I grab the earbuds from my bag and slip them in place. The best way to not listen to their opinions on my hot mess of a love life, is to drown them out. As the beat blasts into my ears, I close my eyes and lay my head back. Now *this* is what I needed.

MY LEGS BURN AS they move at a faster pace than usual. I do my best to control my breathing but it's hard. Running has always been an outlet for me. It's a way to clear my head and allow me to focus on what's important. The harder I push myself, the better I feel.

I arrive at the docks a full three minutes quicker than I usually do, making me smile at the accomplishment. If I keep this up, I'll reach a five minute mile in no time. I pull the earbuds out and walk over to take a drink from the water fountain. Being in the end of June, it's really starting to heat up outside. The breeze coming off the bay feels good against my skin. I walk over to the railing and lean against it to take in the view.

"Beautiful, isn't it?" A familiar voice says from behind me. I don't need to turn around to know who's standing there.

"Gorgeous."

As Colton steps up next to me, I can feel the way my heart yearns for him. After spending a week and a half apart, I don't know how I've made it this long. Every inch of my body craves him all of the time. There hasn't been one day that's passed where I didn't consider throwing caution to the wind and risk getting hurt to be with him.

"How'd you find me?" I ask, still focused on the water in front of me.

"I was already down here. I just happened to see you when I was about to leave."

I turn to face him and lean against the railing while I cross my arms over my chest. "Do you ever go to work?"

He smirks and points to himself with one finger. "Boss."

"Mhm. That excuse can only get you so far, ya know."

The urge to be closer to him is strong. I can practically feel his strong arms wrapped around my body, holding me tightly as he presses light kisses to my neck. My sexual frustration has reached an all time high, and I'm almost positive being near him when I'm like this is really dangerous.

He looks away from the view and catches me staring. I watch as he inhales a deep breath then lets it out. "I've missed you."

"I didn't go anywhere."

"Mmm, but you did." He tilts his head slightly to the side.

"We spent just about every day together and then all of a sudden you're too busy to see me? You can't tell me you didn't spend half this past week watching Netflix on your couch."

I chuckle at how well he knows me. "Fair enough. So why didn't you come over and force me to see you?"

He shrugs. "Because I figured if you were avoiding me, it was for a reason and something you had to work out on your own. I was just giving you the time and space to do that." I go to speak but he puts one finger up to stop me. "But, it's been a week and a half and I'm losing my mind, so I need to know. Are things over between us? Do you not want to be with me anymore?"

The thought alone of losing Colton has me shaking my head before he's even done asking the question. "No. That's not at all what I want." I gesture over to a bench and he follows me, sitting closer than necessary before I continue. "When Roman walked in on us, it freaked me out. If that had been Maverick, everything would've gone from calm to chaos in under a minute. To be honest, I got scared."

"Scared of what though?" He reaches over to hold my hand.

"Of this, of us. You've picked Maverick over me before when there wasn't even a choice to be made yet. Even the idea of that happening again makes my chest physically hurt."

Colton gets off the bench and kneels in front of me, forcing me to look at him. "McKenna, you have to believe that isn't going to happen again. It shouldn't have happened the first time, but it sure as hell won't happen now. I've spent the last four years away from you, and I'll be damned if I let Maverick cause me to go through that again."

His words overwhelm me. He's been saying every single thing I've wanted to hear, and he's doing it again now. Without another thought, I lunge forward and press our lips together. He sighs into the kiss, showing just how relieved he is. His hands are on my back, pulling me impossibly closer as my tongue dances with his. It's probably way too racy for such a public place, but his mouth on my own makes everything else disappear.

"I want to show you something." He murmurs, pulling his head back to look into my eyes.

I'm a little confused, but I nod anyway. He stands up and interlaces our fingers as he leads me down onto the docks. I let him pull me along until we reach one boat in particular. It's a massive sailboat – the kind my dad would have killed for while I was growing up. Hell, it's one *I* would have killed for. It's breathtaking, with a wood finish and looking like it's in mint condition.

Colton wraps his arms around me from behind as I admire the vessel. The places I would go in that thing are endless. I can just picture sunbathing on it as it soars across the water. I hadn't realized how much I missed being on a boat until being placed in front of this one.

"It's really pretty." I whisper, afraid I'll ruin it with too loud of a tone.

"And?"

"And what?"

He chuckles and moves my chin so I'm looking at the back of the boat. *McKenna.* I gasp and cover my mouth.

"Why is my name on there?!" My voice is muffled by my hand but I know he can hear me.

"Because it's mine." He says as if it's obvious. "Well, *ours,* if you'll have it with me. I bought it."

"I'm sorry, you did *what*?"

He turns me in his arms to face him and gives me one of his panty-dropping smiles. "I bought it for us. You're afraid of getting caught. Well…" He gestures to the boat. "No one knows about this. Just you and I."

"Colton, this boat costs a small fortune! You can't spend

that much money just so we have a place to be alone together."

He presses a soft kiss to my forehead and holds me close. "I can, and I did."

It's an obnoxiously sweet gesture and shows me how much he cares, no matter how extreme I think it may be. He took a problem I had and he found a way to solve it. I mean, a hotel room every now and then would have sufficed but I'm not about to complain. I'm completely enamored by the way he's trying so hard to make us work. To earn my trust back. To make me happy.

"I don't know what to say."

He grins. "Say you'll spend the day with me."

Making a face and pretending to consider it, I squeal when Colton starts tickling my sides. "Okay, okay. You win, but only because the boat is just *so* pretty."

"Is that the only reason?"

I smirk. "If it's not, I'll never admit it."

AFTER COLTON DRIVES ME home so I can change, we head back down to the boat and climb on board. It's gorgeous. I take in the whole thing, from the sails to the antique looking ship wheel. Stepping down into the cabin, it has a kitchenette on one side and a small couch with table on the other. The door to the bathroom is right before a door leading to a small bedroom, where a queen size bed is perfect fit into the shape of the bow of the boat. The closeness of it all provides a cozy feeling.

"Do you like it?" Colton whispers with his lips against the shell of my ear.

"Mmm, it'll do." I tease.

Messing with him is definitely one of my favorite things. He wraps his arms around me and pulls me into him. Within seconds, my entire body is practically on fire. Want and need course through me at an uncontrollable rate. My head lulls back as his lips press light kisses against my neck.

"Colton." I moan his name like it's the only thing I can think of right now. Truthfully, it is. He's infiltrated my every thought with just a simple touch.

I can feel him grin where his mouth is on my skin. "What is it, baby? What do you need?"

An involuntary whimper slips out and I can almost picture what this is all doing to his ego. He's already cocky. Seeing how he can get me all worked up with such minimal effort on his part is only going to make that worse. Despite the huge part of me that doesn't seem to care at the moment, an even bigger part wants to knock him down a few pegs.

"I want…"

"Yeah?"

"To feel…"

"Mhm?"

I can't help but smile as the next words come out. "The way this thing can glide across the water."

He releases me with a pout and I instantly miss his warmth. The burning desire in his eyes almost has me dropping this façade, but I hold my ground and plaster a sickeningly sweet grin across my face. As if he can read me like an open book, he narrows his eyes.

"You're fucking with me."

Chuckling softly, I slip past him. "I don't know what you're talking about."

Once I reach the stairs to climb back out, I turn around and wink at him. He groans, showing his disapproval, but follows behind anyway. Just as I lean against the railing to look over the side of the boat, he presses himself up against the back of me. I can feel his hardened length pushing against my lower back. *Fuck.*

"I can play if that's what you want, but just know – you're going to lose."

Biting my lip to suppress my moan, I take a deep breath before answering. "So you think, but I can hold my own. I'm not the same virgin you once knew."

"No, baby." He slides his hand from my shoulder, down my side to my hip. "You most definitely are not."

Seconds later, Colton releases me and steps back, going over to the console and starting up the boat. I follow as I wonder what exactly the plan is for today. When I see him starting to untie everything, I'm sure I have a pretty good guess. Still, I ask anyway.

"What are you doing?"

He looks up at me and smiles brightly. "You said you want to feel the way this thing can glide across the water."

My eyes widen. "We're taking it out? Now?"

He nods, then his expression turns to one that has me swallowing hard. "Out in the ocean where there is no where for you to run."

The rest of the morning and half of the afternoon passes by quickly. Colton and I spend the day on the boat as he teaches me how to sail. The little game we started when we first got on continues, and it's hard to say who's winning. I drive him wild by bending over in front of him, under the pretenses of needing to grab something or wanting to look down at the water. However, he gets me back by faking sea legs and falling into me, causing my body to be pinned up against the nearest wall. Every time he touches me, my drive to beat him at this becomes a little weaker.

BY THE TIME THE sun sets, neither one of us are yet to cave. It hasn't been easy, believe me. Once the sun was at its peak, Colton took his shirt off – leaving me to gawk at his perfectly toned body. I instantly cursed myself for not wearing a bikini under my clothes.

My phone dings with a message from Parker. I know I should feel guilty, being with Colton behind his back, but to be honest – today has been the best day I've had in a while. I mean, Colton bought a boat simply so that we could be alone together. That has to be the sweetest thing anyone has ever done for me.

I grab my phone and swipe it open to read the text.

Parker: Going to be late, love. My study group moved to tonight. Don't wait up.

The second I read the words, I grin. Getting wrapped up in studying isn't something new for Parker. He used to do it all the time while he was at Columbia. Academics are very important, not only to him, but to his parents. Their very strict rules were that if he got anything under a B while at university, they would force him to transfer back to a school in England. Needless to say, he constantly thrives for the A. So, while he stays and studies at med school, I'll stay with Colton and learn a much different version of anatomy.

"What are you all smiley about?" He asks as he comes out from the cabin with two beers for him and I.

"Parker is going to be in Boston until late tonight."

His one eyebrow raises. "So, I don't just get you for the day, I get you for tonight, too?"

I tilt my head to the side. "I don't know. I was thinking I should go see my other boyfriend."

He puts the bottles in the cup holders before lunging at me, tickling my sides and causing me to thrash around in his arms. No matter how much I move, I can't seem to get out of his grasp. It isn't until I arch my hips up to grind into him that his demeanor changes. He growls lowly before lunging, covering my mouth with his own. It's hot, and passionate, and makes me feel like my heart is going to burst right out of my chest.

"I want you so bad." He pants, licking over my bottom lip. "You've been such a fucking tease, all day."

I smile into the kiss, knowing I succeeded in my plan to drive him wild. It was fun to spend hours rubbing up against him and then playing it off as innocence. I could see how much he was struggling to teach me as I wriggled my ass into his crotch. The way he kept tensing up told me everything I needed to know. Now, our every move has lead to this, neither one of us being able to control ourselves any longer.

A moan flows from my mouth as he grinds down into me. His lips attach to my neck and suck, hard. A part of me wants to chastise him for potentially leaving a mark, but it feels too good to make him stop. With very little effort, he picks me up and carries me down into the cabin. He slams the bedroom door shut with his foot and tosses me down onto the bed.

"You are something else, McKenna." His eyes rake down my entire body before going back up to my eyes. "Something else entirely."

I'M LAYING ON THE floor of the boat, staring up at the stars, while Colton sits in the chair beside me. The glass of wine in my hand rests on my stomach. The two of us take turns asking each other questions – each one ranging anywhere from meaningful to stupid.

"Okay, my turn." He smiles. "What's your favorite memory from NYU?"

I take a minute to think it over. There are tons that flow through my mind, and deciding on one is difficult. Finally, I figure it out.

"Okay, so there was one night after Julia's boyfriend

cheated on her. After consuming so much wine and ice cream that we thought we were going to be sick, we got our RA to let us use his printer. We printed out a ton of pictures of the guy with cheater written really big across it. Then, we went up to the roof and tossed them it." I giggle at the memory. "I swear it took *weeks* for him to get rid of them all."

His eyes widen as he chuckles. "Whose idea was that?!"

"Mine."

He looks me over and takes a sip of his beer. "You're not as innocent as you make yourself seem."

I laugh. "Oh please. After the summer you and I spent together, I couldn't have looked innocent if I tried."

"Touché." He smirks. "Okay, your turn."

"Hmm." I sit up just a bit to drink some of my wine then lay back down. I know what I *want* to ask, but I don't think I have the balls to ask it. Instead, I go with something safer. "Out of all the houses you've designed, which one is your favorite?"

"The one I'm having built right now." He answers without any hesitation.

"The one you won't let me see?"

He grins and rolls his eyes. "You'll see it eventually. Just not yet."

"Yeah, yeah. So you keep saying. Okay, next."

With one more swig of his beer, he places the empty bottle down next to him. "What's your biggest regret?"

My eyebrows furrow. "Honestly, I don't think I have one."

"Come on. Everyone has something they wish they could have done differently."

Oh I do, but I've had way too much wine to get *that* real. So, I shrug. "I cheated on a test once."

"Did you get caught?"

"No, but I felt horrible about it for weeks."

His head falls back as laughter flows out with ease. "Okay, I take back what I said earlier. You're *definitely* still innocent."

"I think your dick would say otherwise." I slur, watching his expression go serious in a millisecond.

"Fuck, McKenna. You can't just say things like that."

I could push it further, tease him a little like I was doing earlier, but I'm actually enjoying this little game we're playing so I don't. "If everyone has one, what's yours?"

"My what?"

"Biggest regret."

He smiles down at me and puts out his hand. When I take it, he pulls me up and sits me on his lap. His hand brushes a strand of hair out of my face and then rubs against my cheek. The way he's looking at me makes me feel like he can see straight into my soul.

"Letting you leave for New York without telling you how I really felt."

And in that moment, I fall a little more.

19

MCKENNA

THE BAKERY IS A CUTE LITTLE PLACE WITH AN assortment of delicious things on display. I want to try them all. A girl behind the counter with pink hair greets us as soon as we enter, asking if there is anything she can help us with. When I tell her who we are and that we have an appointment for our cake tasting, she directs us to a table and tell us she will go get the owner. I thank her before Parker and I sit down.

"This place is adorable." I remark, looking around at all the different décor.

Parker smiles and nods. "Tatum chooses the best of everything, I've noticed."

"Yeah. She's really good at her job."

The owner comes out and introduces herself. Her name is Elizabeth. She's an older lady, probably mid sixties, with short black hair. You can tell by the way she talks about her cakes, that she loves what she does.

"You two are a beautiful couple." She compliments.

Parker thanks her while I smile down at my lap. His arm goes around my shoulder and I swallow down the lump in my throat. Would he still be like this if he knew about all the time I've been spending with Colton lately? Who am I kidding? He wouldn't even be *here* if he knew.

Elizabeth goes to retrieve the samples from the back. Once she's gone, Parker leans over and kisses my cheek. "I feel like this is one of the few things we've done for our own wedding."

I shrug. "That's what happens when you hire a wedding planner. They do it all for you. It's what we're paying her for."

"Well, I still want to be the one to pick out your wedding band."

As I think about how quickly the summer is starting to go by, I can't help but feel uneasy. I'm supposed to be using this time with Colton to figure out what I want, but if anything, it's only confused me more. On the one hand, Parker is amazing. He's everything I always knew I *should* want. On the other, Colton was the first person to hold my heart in his hands and I'm not sure I ever got it back.

"Okay." Elizabeth returns, placing two plates in front of Parker and I. The tiny cakes on each one make my mouth water. "We're going to go one at a time and I'll write down your thoughts and a score from 1 to 10. Don't be afraid of offending me. Everyone has their likes and dislikes."

The first piece we try is a white cake with a hazelnut filling. I let the taste settle in my mouth, really thinking over how I feel about it. The cake itself is perfectly moist, but I'm not sure many people like hazelnut. Overall, I rate this one a six. I'm sure it won't be my favorite, but I can't bring myself to give it a lower score.

The second is a red velvet cake with a sweet cream cheese filling. It's absolutely mouthwatering and if it were for something less formal, I would probably go with this one. However, my mother has always insisted there is something taboo about a dark wedding cake. And trust me, this wedding has enough bad karma already.

By the third piece, my phone vibrates in my pocket. I discreetly slip it out to find a new text.

Colton: Can you sneak away for a bit? I miss you.

I smile around my fork and type my response.

McKenna: I miss you too, but I'm stuck at a bakery for at least the next hour and a half. 😅

Within seconds, my phone starts to go wild with incoming texts. My brows furrow as they come in faster than I can read.

Colton: Wow.

Colton: You're at the cake tasting?

Colton: With him?

Colton: So, what am I? Just someone you're filling your time with while you wait for your wedding day?

Colton: I can't even believe I'm surprised. Of course you're still planning on marrying him.

Colton: Forget it. Have a GREAT time, McKenna.

Okay, so maybe his reaction isn't a total surprise. If the situation was reversed, I'd probably be even angrier than he is. But, at the same time, I *told* him I wasn't going to leave Parker right away. Sure, maybe I don't need to continue planning a wedding that might not even happen, but if I put a pause on things, he'll know something is up. It's better to just go along with it and make up my mind before the end of September.

McKenna: Can you relax? The appointment was made. All I did was come to it.

"Miss Taylor?" Elizabeth pulls my attention away from my phone. "What do you think about that one?"

Ugh, to be honest, I didn't even allow myself to taste it. I was too wrapped up in Colton blowing up my phone. I make an unsure face and take another small bite. It's a yellow cake with a lemon filling. It's delicious, but I don't think it would go over too well with all the guests.

"A 7.5." I plaster on the best fake smile I can manage.

Content with my answer, Elizabeth writes it down on her pad and directs us toward the next piece. Meanwhile, my phone vibrates again.

Colton: Oh, sure. Play innocent like you're not planning your wedding to someone else right now. If you want him, then fucking be with him, but don't string me along in the process.

Is that what I'm doing, stringing them both along? Fuck, of course it is. It's not like I'm doing it on purpose. If the choice was clear, I'd make it – but it's not. My brain tells me to choose Parker. That he will always do whatever it takes to make me happy and would never dream of hurting me. But my heart, well that's 100% team Colton. Despite all the pain he's caused in the past, it still yearns for him. I love Parker, but it's not the same and that's where I struggle.

Maybe I've just never let myself feel for Parker like I do Colton. I'd be lying if I said I haven't always been a bit closed off. How could I not be? I've never experienced a heartbreak like that, and to be honest, I'll do whatever it takes to make sure I don't go through that again. The way my whole world crashed down around me – it was like no matter how deeply I breathed, I couldn't get enough air.

I sigh as I focus solely on my phone.

McKenna: Can we talk about this later?

Colton: No. What's the point? Seriously, don't even bother.

The idea of him running away has me on the verge of tears, but I can't let my emotions show.

McKenna: I told you I wasn't going to leave him right away.

The three little dots to indicate he's typing come up and then go away again. When I hear my name called, I barely manage to taste the cake and let Elizabeth know what I think about it. Just as another message finally comes through, Parker places his hand on my wrist. I look up at him.

"Love, can you please put your phone down?" His words are too soft for how I feel right now. "This is important and we need to be sure on which one we choose."

An anger bubbles inside of me at the idea of him telling me to stop texting Colton. Can't he see I'm having a mental crisis here?! But how can I expect him to know that? As far as he's aware, I'm hopelessly devoted to him and excited to get married in the fall. Unless I'm sure I want all of that to go away, I know I need to put this argument on the back burner.

"Right, sorry." I click it off and slip it back into my pocket, hoping I didn't make things so much worse.

BY THE END OF the tasting, we happily decided on a white cake with a strawberry amaretto filling. The design for it that Tatum already picked out is impeccable. It's a five tier cake with white icing and a geode design on the side in pale pink and gold. Even just seeing the sketches Elizabeth drew up, I know it's going to be incredible.

Parker drives us to a nearby restaurant for lunch, although I'm stuffed from all the cake we just tried. It's a little diner I've never been to before, but it seems cozy enough. As soon as we're seated, he excuses himself to the bathroom and I take the opportunity to pull out my phone. The only text I find is the one from earlier.

Colton: Don't play coy. It doesn't look good on you. Not leaving him and still planning your wedding with him are two totally different things.

He's mad, that much is clear, and for the most part I get it. If the tables were turned, I'd never be able to handle knowing he goes home to some other woman. Then again, if the tables were turned, I never would've walked out on him all those years ago, so I guess the point is moot.

To text him back right now would be pointless. I already know that. There is no talking to him and getting him to listen unless we're face to face. He needs to be able to look me in the eyes and hear what I'm saying. Otherwise, we will just continue to fight. I know him well enough to know that.

Just as I put my phone away and take a deep breath, Parker returns and sits in the booth across from me. He gives me a warm smile, making my insides flip. There was a time where I used to enjoy spending every minute I could with him. If I'm being totally honest, a part of me still feels that way. I'm just not sure that part is big enough.

"Is everything alright?" He questions softly, reaching over to grab my hand. I let him. "You seem bothered by something."

I should deny it, but clearly that would do no good. I may not have let him know me as well as other people, but he *has* learned things over the couple of years we've been together. So, instead of making matters worse, I shrug.

"I just feel a little off today. That's all."

He frowns. "Well, I was planning on studying tonight for an exam I have next week, but if you'd rather, we can snuggle up on the couch and watch a movie."

The idea sounds enticing, but the argument with Colton is still in the forefront of my mind. I need to get to him so we can talk. The longer I let him stew, the worse it could get.

"No, that's okay. I already told Ivy I would meet her for dinner." I lie. "And besides, you need to study. Med school is nothing to mess around with."

"Okay love. As long as you're sure."

I nod, and just like that, he lets the matter go completely. If he had pressed on, would I have ended up telling him everything? I almost feel as if it's right there, ready to boil over at any minute. Ugh, I can only imagine the mess that would turn into – sitting in this diner trying to rationally explain to my fiancé that I've been cheating on him for the last month and a half with my brother's best friend. I mentally roll my eyes at the idiocy of it all.

I WALK DOWN ONTO the docks with my phone clenched in my hand. As soon as I left the house, I tried calling Colton. He didn't answer, though I'm not sure I expected him to. He very well may not be here, but it's my best shot. I know that if he *is* on the boat, he wanted me to come and find him. If he's here, there's hope for us yet.

The lights are on across the entire boat and the cabin door is wide open. A part of me starts to panic. What if he's in there with another woman? He wouldn't bring her back to Maverick's because Tatum would either kick his ass, or tell me about it. Okay, maybe this was a bad idea.

As soon as I go to turn around, Colton emerges from the cabin – alone.

"McKenna?"

I stop, knowing I can't leave now. He's already seen me and if I walk away, he'll think I don't want to talk about this, which I do.

"What are you doing here?"

Running my fingers through my hair, I try to conceal the way my heart is pounding inside of my chest. "I was looking for you. I wanted to talk, about earlier."

He looks as if he's having some intense mental debate before he finally relaxes and puts his hand out to help me step onto the boat. It's obvious that neither one of us want to let go, but we do anyway. We sit down across from each other. As he looks into my eyes, I can see all the pain he's trying to hide. The thought alone of him hurting makes me feel sick to my stomach.

"I'm sorry." I start. "I know we discussed me staying with Parker while we figured out whatever this is, but we never talked about the wedding. I didn't realize continuing to plan it would be such a big deal."

He snorts. "How could it not be? God Mac, every time I even *think* about you walking down the aisle to him, my blood runs ice cold. If it were up to me, you would've cancelled the whole ordeal months ago."

The options weigh heavily in my mind. In my heart, I know I can't cancel everything. To do that would require me to tell Parker that marrying him is no longer what I want, and I'm not sure that's true. Cancelling the wedding would hurt

Parker, but continuing to plan it hurts Colton. Overall, I can't win. So instead, I settle on a happy medium and hope it's enough for him.

I take out my phone, press speed dial five, and put it on speaker. Colton watches me carefully as it rings. Finally, his eyes widen when he hears the person answer.

"Hey. How was the cake tasting?" Tatum asks.

"It was good, but I needed to talk to you about something."

"Okay." She says hesitantly. "Is everything alright?"

My eyes lock with Colton's as I say the next words. "Yeah, but I need you to slow down on the planning."

"D-did you make a decision?!"

Colton raises one brow, as if silently asking me the same thing. I chuckle softly. "Not yet, but just go at a more lax speed."

She groans, clearly not happy with me. "McKenna, this wedding is two months away. If it's going to happen, I need time to get everything done. It's already on a crammed schedule as it is."

"I get that, I do, but for now, I just need the planning to slow down."

Tatum sighs but ultimately agrees. After all, when it comes to this, she works for me. As soon as I hang up the phone, Colton stands up and takes a step toward me. I narrow my eyes at him and lean back in the seat as he hovers over my body.

"What are you doing?"

"Well," He murmurs, pressing his lips against my neck and causing me to shiver. "All day, I've had this anger pent up inside of me, just begging to get out. So now, I'm going to fuck it out of me and absolutely ruin you for anyone else. By the time I'm done, you won't even remember who *he* is."

Without giving me a moment to respond, he covers my

mouth with his own and sucks the words right out of me. I gasp at the contact, giving him the perfect opportunity to slip his tongue inside and tangle it with mine. My nails drag down his back as he grinds himself into me. I can already feel how rock hard he is beneath his shorts.

"Colton." I moan.

He smirks against my lips. "That's right, baby. That's the only name I want to hear come out of that pretty little mouth of yours."

I whimper at his words, loving the way he takes control. His body radiates a level of seduction and domination that makes every part of me his for the taking. It's so sexy that it's dizzying. I'd follow him blindly if it meant he continues to touch me like he is right now.

My hips arch up to rub against him and I love how he groans into my mouth. He grips my waist with such need that I quiver. He starts to kiss down the side of my neck, nibbling and sucking softly.

"Please." I beg, not even sure what I'm begging for.

He snickers. "Please what, babe? Tell me what you want."

"You."

"You have me. I'm right here."

I whimper as he pulls away slightly to tease me. "Ugh. You know what I mean."

"Do I?" He taunts, moving his hands to the hem of my shirt and slowly lifting it up my torso. "I'm not sure I do. Maybe you need to tell me."

As I manage to gain back some of my mental balance, I glare at him. "Or maybe you should do what you said you were going to, before I get someone else to do it for me."

"You wouldn't dare."

"I don't think you want to test me on what I will or won't do right now."

He shakes his head before pressing his lips against mine

in a bruising kiss. It's rough, and heated, and everything I want from him right now. He sucks my bottom lip into his mouth, then growls.

"You are an infuriating woman, and I know exactly what I want to do to that smart mouth of yours."

I'm lifted up and into Colton's arms as he carries us down the stairs and into the bedroom. He tosses me onto the bed, staring at me like he's starving and I'm his next meal. I pull my shirt over my head and dispose of it onto the floor, using my body to entice him further. He calls my bluff and stands back, taking off his own and allowing me to gawk at his toned chest. The smirk on his face isn't even enough to make me stop. He's gorgeous, and there isn't anyone who would say otherwise.

I slide my hands down my stomach to the waistband of my shorts, popping the button and zipper before slipping them down my legs. Colton swallows harshly as he watches me. Just like the first time I was on this boat, we're wrapped up in a game of who will cave first – and I'm not willing to lose.

Closing my eyes, I imagine that I'm alone and let my hand rub over my clothed sex. The slightest bit of pressure causes me to moan and squirm on the bed. I bite my lip as I continue to move my fingers in a circular motion. The feeling of his gaze burns into me.

After a couple minutes of convincing myself to keep going, to push him some more, I move to slip my hand under my panties when a strong grip on my wrist stops me from going any further. My eyes snap open to find him staring down at me, daring me to fight against him. His pants are long gone and his hard cock is straining against the fabric of his boxers.

"Are you going to do something with that?" I taunt.

He grins deviously and nods. "You better believe it, but

first, you are." His hand reaches inside and pulls out his length, hard as a rock and an angry red. Using his hold on my wrist, he tugs me closer to him and lines himself up with my mouth. "Why don't you show me better uses for that tongue than sassy comments?"

My hand wraps around him and he lets out a sigh at the contact. I know I could continue to push back, make him fight a little harder, but I don't want to. I'm so wet that I can feel it dripping down my thigh. Something about him like this turns me on to unprecedented levels. I don't think I'll ever be able to explain it.

As soon as I kitten lick the tip, Colton throws his head back and lets out an animalistic moan. The sound only motivates me further as I take him into my mouth. My tongue circles the tip before I slide him in as deep as can go. The second he hits the back of my throat, I gag around him.

"Fuck, that feels so good." His voice is practically a whisper but I hear it loud and clear.

I hum as my hand slips lower to cup his balls. Between the vibration and my touch, I have him exactly where I want. His legs are shaking as he starts to thrust into my mouth. I press my tongue to the underside of his cock as he pushes himself as far back as he can. Just when I feel like he's about to let go, I slide him out of my mouth with a pop and lay back on the bed. His eyes narrow on me as I smile sweetly back at him.

"You know," He starts, letting his boxers pool at his ankles and stepping out of them. "I was going to return the favor. Maybe let you cum a couple times before I completely had my way with you." He kneels on the bed and grabs my hips. "But after that, I think someone just needs to fuck some sense into you."

He flips me onto my stomach and pulls me up so my ass is arched off the bed. My face is pressed into the mattress as he rubs himself against my sex, gathering some of my juices on the head of his cock.

"You're so wet, baby. Is that because of me, or *him*?" I can't seem to respond, so I just let out a small whine. Suddenly, his hand comes down hard on my ass cheek, the sound of the slap radiating through the small room. "Answer me, McKenna."

"You." I cry out in bliss. "Fuck. Always you."

He moves the hair from my face and I can see him smirking at me. "I forgot what a little minx you can be. It's so fucking hot."

I don't say anything, instead pushing my ass back against him in an attempt to gain some friction. I can feel him there, the tip pressing at my entrance but he holds himself steady – just out of reach.

"Please." I beg once again, but I know exactly what he's looking for. "Please fuck me."

"That's better, Princess."

In one fluid motion, he slams inside of me. The moan I let out mixes with the sigh of relief that comes from him. He pulls out then pushes back in again, letting me feel all of him.

"Tell me how you want it." He demands.

"You know how. You've always known."

"Ah ah." He tsks. "I want to hear you say it."

"Hard." I cave.

His hips snap forward as he plows into me. "Like that?"

"Harder."

The small laugh that comes from him is maddening, but it's quickly wiped from my mind as he wraps my hair around his hand and pulls my head back. He bends forward and kisses me, wet and messy but every bit exhilarating. When he backs away, I whine at the loss of contact before he uses the hold on me as leverage and starts pounding into me. He's so deep I can feel him in my stomach. The pressure is already starting to build inside.

"You feel so incredible." He groans out. "Fucking hell, I swear you were made just for me."

"Only you."

The hand he has on my hip wraps around me and moves down to my clit, putting just enough pressure on it to turn me into putty. "Yeah? Show me. Cum all over my cock, Princess. Make me yours."

As those words come from his mouth, I couldn't deny him if I tried. The orgasm practically rips me in half as he fucks me harshly through it. His teeth sink into my shoulder and my legs collapse.

"Colton!" I scream out as I'm pushed to levels of ecstasy I forgot existed.

"That's right, baby. You're mine. This," He uses his whole hand to grip my sex as he's still thrusting inside of me, "is all fucking *mine*."

His pace grows quicker and becomes sloppy as he chases his own high. He pulls me close and wraps his hand around my throat, slipping his tongue into my mouth just before he explodes. He fills me completely, pumping his hot cum deep inside – no fucks given about the scare we had three weeks ago.

"You are magical." He murmurs with his lips against my skin. "I don't know how I've ever lived without you."

I smile mindlessly as he pulls out and we collapse onto the bed. His arm is draped across my body in a comforting way that makes it so I could fall asleep easily. Just as I let my eyes begin to droop closed, my phone starts ringing on the floor.

"Ignore it." Colton mumbles, as exhausted as I am.

A few seconds later, the ringing stops – only to start again. The two of us groan and he releases his hold on me so

I can get up. Without even looking at who it is, I hit answer and bring it to my ear.

"Hello?"

"McKenna, thank fuck." Ivy panics. "We have a problem."

Sitting on the edge of the bed, I run my fingers through my tangled hair, working the knots out. "What's going on?"

"I just ran into Parker at the store."

At the sound of my fiancé's name, my heart starts to race. Even Colton, who can hear her from where he lies behind me, sits upright. If Parker saw Ivy, then he knows that I'm not *with* Ivy. Shit, this is bad. *Really* bad.

"Did he see you?! What did you say?!"

"I told him that you and I were at dinner but your mom needed your help with something wedding related."

My eyes roll instantly. "Ivy, my mom isn't *dealing* with anything wedding related. That's all Tatum."

"You think I don't know that? But if I told him Tatum needed you, he would have went to Maverick's, and she can't necessarily lie for you in front of him."

"Okay, okay. You're right, good thinking." I release a breath but then realize we're not out of the woods yet. "Wait, so where is Parker now?"

"On his way to your parents' house."

Colton and I don't hesitate for a second before jumping up and throwing our clothes on. I hit the speaker button and toss the phone onto the bed as I pull my bra back on and clip it behind my back.

"What store were you at?"

"Crackerjacks."

"Okay, if we hurry, we may make it there in time." I slide my shorts up my legs and then throw my shirt over my head. "Thanks Iv. I'll text you later."

"Good luck!"

She hangs up the phone just as I grab it. Colton and I climb off the boat and run as fast as we can back up the

237

docks. As soon as we get in his car, I realize I've never been so glad for the v8 engine. He rips out of the parking lot and speeds down the road, gripping my hand with the one that isn't on the steering wheel. I appreciate the comfort, but I can't manage to look away from the window.

If we get to my parents' house and Parker is already there, everything is going to come out. The choice I've been dreading making, may end up being made for me and there will be nothing I can say about it. I'm sure it would only be a matter of time before Maverick finds out why my engagement ended in a chaotic mess of arguments and broken hearts. This isn't how I wanted this to go. This isn't how I wanted any of this. I finally had everything back in order, and then I went and made a mess of it all. *What have I done?*

Colton drifts the car around turns, pressing the pedal to the floor as we fly down the street. If I wasn't so terrified, this drive would be incredible. The potential for excitement is huge, but my head just isn't there.

We pull up in front of the house and I don't see Parker's truck, but what if he's already been here and realized I wasn't? No, he would have called me – I hope. Regardless, I need to get in there to find out. I give Colton's hand a squeeze before jumping out of the car and running down the long driveway. As soon as I get in the house and shut the door behind me, my mom comes out from the kitchen.

"McKenna? Is everything alright?"

I nod, trying to think of how I'm going to explain this. "I-I…" My hands run over my face. Fuck, this is a disaster. "I messed up, Mom."

"Whatever it is, you can talk to me." She comes closer and runs her hand down my arm.

I pull myself from the door and go into the living room. My feet start to pace across the floor as I try to figure out the right words. The second I go to open my mouth, there's a knock at the door. My breath hitches as she goes and opens it to find Parker standing there. He greets her as he steps in, then his eyes land on me.

"There you are. I saw Ivy, she said I could find you here."

I nod half-heartedly. "I thought you were studying."

"I was, but I needed something to drink and realized we were all out of anything but water. I ran to the market to stock up." He looks me up and down before his eyebrows furrow. "Why is your shirt inside out?"

Looking down at myself, I notice he's right. *Shit.* My mouth opens and closes like a fish. I can practically feel the way both our hearts are about to shatter. There's no getting out of this now.

"I, uhm," I start, but my mom quickly cuts me off.

"I made her switch it around. With what we were dealing with, a stain could ruin it, and it looks too good on her for that."

Parker smiles at my mom and then at me. "That it does." He comes closer and kisses my forehead. "Well, I just wanted to make sure everything was alright. I'm going home to unload the groceries. I'll see you in a bit?"

"Yeah, I'll be there soon." I stare down at the ground, not able to look at anyone.

As soon as I hear him say goodbye to my mother and shut the door behind him, I exhale. My whole body falls onto the couch and my heart rate finally starts to slow. That was way too close. Everything could have gone up in flames. It's a miracle that it didn't. I really need to make a decision, and fast.

"Have either of you told Maverick?" My mom's voice startles me. In my relief, I had forgotten she was even there. My eyes meet hers and it hits me. *She knows.*

"Mom, I can explain."

She raises one hand to stop me. "No need. You're a grown woman, McKenna, and Colton is a grown man. Both of you are old enough to make your own choices. I just hope you know what you're doing."

I wish I could tell her that I do, that I have a handle on all of this, but I don't. Every time I think I'm getting close to being sure of what I want, something happens that throws all my logic into a blender and turns my brain to mush. The bottom line is, I'm greedy and I don't want to lose either one of them.

20

COLTON

AFTER COMING RIDICULOUSLY CLOSE TO GETTING caught last week, I fully expected McKenna to disappear again. So, imagine my surprise when I woke up the following morning to a text from her. It was a simple message letting me know that she was thinking about me, but it made my whole day brighter.

I could tell by the way she was that night, that I don't have her nearly as convinced about us as I had thought. The panic of potentially losing Parker was all over her face, making it impossible to ignore. If I want her to take us seriously, I need to step my game up. Otherwise, I'll lose her to him and there will be no one to blame but myself. *Story of my life.*

With Ivy being my own personal little spy, she lets me know that Parker is going to be in Boston late tonight. Something about an exam tomorrow morning that he needs to be fully prepared for. I use the opportunity to my advantage and have her deliver the dress I picked out to McKenna with a note on top that reads *"You deserve to be treated like the princess you are. Be ready by five."*

It's time I show her how hard I'm willing to fight.

I PULL UP TO McKenna's house. It's ironic, really, because I remember designing the place. The client who hired me was an older couple who wanted a spacious and open floor plan. I knew when I was sketching it out, that it was the kind of place Mac would love. Even being away for four years, she never really left my mind. She was there in just about everything I did. And being best friends with her brother was like having my biggest mistake flaunted in front of my face every day.

Like a proper gentleman, I grab the bouquet of flowers from the passenger seat and walk up the steps. As soon as I ring the bell, she opens the door and the breath is sucked right out of my lungs. The dress she's wearing is one Ivy helped me choose. It's a black, satin material that goes down to just above her knees. She left her hair natural, which is my absolute favorite. The silky smooth lengths flow down her back and curl at the ends. I take in every inch of her, realizing I'm one lucky son of a bitch.

"You look stunning."

She smiles at my words and then takes the flower from my hands, thanking me softly. I follow her through the house and into the kitchen. It's weird being here, knowing this is the space she shares with Parker. What I wouldn't give to spend every possible moment with her. Does he even know how good he has it? Well, obviously not. If he did, he would've chosen to spend the summer with her rather than get an early start on med school. That still blows my mind. How could he stand being anywhere that isn't right by her side?

McKenna fills a vase with water and puts the flowers inside before placing it in the middle of the kitchen island. I'm a little surprised by her willingness to showcase them. To be honest, I assumed they would be hidden away in the guest room or somewhere else Parker wouldn't look. Hell, a part of me even wondered if she would give them to Ivy, but she doesn't. She puts them somewhere she will see them every day until they wither. Is it unreasonable to be jealous of an inanimate object?

"So, where are we going?" She questions, as if I'll actually tell her.

"Now Princess, don't you know better than to ask that?"

"Maybe, but it was worth a shot."

The innocence on her face makes me chuckle as we leave the house. I hold the car door open for her and she slips inside. Seriously, I've never regretted a choice so much as I do picking *that* dress. It'll be a miracle if I can make it through dinner without needing to pull her into the nearest bathroom. I can already feel myself hardening in my pants.

I get in the car and start driving towards the restaurant, a low key place outside of town where she doesn't have to worry about us being seen. It overlooks the water and has all of her favorite foods on the menu – I checked. It may be one of those places that doesn't list the prices on the menu because they're so high, but she's more than worth it. I'd pay all the money in the world if it meant having her by my side.

"So, how has your week been?"

She reaches over and grabs my hand, obviously grateful for such a simple inquisition. "It's been great. I'm working on the lesson plans for the upcoming school year. It's so exciting."

The way she lights up as she talks about teaching is mesmerizing. I swear, I could sit and listen to her all day. There isn't a single doubt in my mind that she will make an incredible teacher. Her students will love her from the second they walk in the door.

"I'm happy for you, Mac. You're getting everything you've ever wanted."

She smiles and I don't miss the way her hand tightens slightly. "Just about."

A part of me wonders if she's finally starting to make her mind up, and I'm practically bursting at the seems to ask her what she means by that. However, I don't want to do anything that could potentially ruin tonight, so I decide against it.

We spend the rest of the drive talking about the office building I've been overseeing the renovations on. It's a small tech company that's trying to expand and they need to appear more economically friendly. With the way the world is lately, you need to do everything in a certain way so no one strikes against you.

Of course, during the conversation about my work, she once again brings up the house I'm having built. I can tell how eager she is to see it, but it's just not the right time yet. I know I'll be showing it to her one day, no matter how things go between us. I just don't want anything influencing her decision. If I'm the one she picks, I need to know that it was a fair fight.

The restaurant is everything I pictured and more. I tell the hostess I have a reservation for Brooks. She grabs two menus and leads us back to a table that has the most amazing view of the ocean. A lit candle sits on the table between us, making it all that much more romantic.

"How did you find this place?" McKenna asks as she looks around in awe.

"A client of mine recommended it. She's a certified matchmaker."

Her eyebrows raise. "That's a thing?"

"Apparently."

"Huh. I'm surprised she didn't try to hook you up with someone."

I chuckle. "Oh, she did, but I told her I already have my

sights firmly set on someone and there's no changing my mind."

The corners of her mouth raise and she blushes as she looks down at the table. Watching her get flustered like that has always been one of the most endearing things I've ever seen. She opens the menu to look at the choices, then narrows her eyes at it.

"There are no prices. Why are there no prices?"

How did I know she was going to notice that? "Because you don't need to worry about it. Just order whatever you want."

She gives me a knowing look and puts the menu down. "This is one of those super expensive places where the entrées are like $100 a plate, isn't it?"

"McKenna, you're sweet for caring, but seriously – stop thinking about it. I chose this place because it has all of your favorites, and the food is supposed to be delicious. Just focus on having a good time tonight, okay?"

Her hand slides across the table and her fingers interlace with my own. The way my body tingles at her touch should make me feel like less of a man, but it doesn't. There's always been something different about McKenna Taylor. She has the ability to make me feel like I'm flying just with a brush of her hand.

The waiter comes to take our orders and I can't help but notice how his eyes linger on Mac a little too long for my liking. Can't he see that she's on a date? Or does he just not care if she's taken? Shit, listen to me. Talk about being the pot calling the kettle black.

McKenna orders the Chicken Marsala while I go with the Filet Mignon. I also order a bottle of wine for the table, one that came highly recommended throughout almost every review they have. It might be the most expensive wine I've ever bought, but like I said, she's worth it.

"Okay, we're going to play a game." She announces with a

245

glimmer of something in her eyes that I don't recognize. "It's called 'Marry, Fuck, Kill'. I name three people and you say which one you would marry, which you would fuck once, and which you would kill."

"Oh god, alright."

She leans back against the seat and crosses her arms over her chest. "Me, Ivy, Tatum."

"That's easy. Marry you. Fuck you. Kill Tatum. Done."

The way she laughs is something I want burned into my memory for the rest of my life. "That's not how it works!"

I rest my elbows on the table. "Sure it is. I picked which one out of the three for each category."

"No. Only one category per person."

My nose scrunches up in disgust. "You mean I have to pick if I'd rather fuck Ivy or Tatum?"

"Well, it seems like you've already offed Tatum without a second thought, so it looks like you're stuck with Ivy."

"Yeah, okay." I chuckle. "Like you'd *ever* let that one happen. And besides, Rome would probably bury me, even if it is only a game."

The second her eyes widen, I realize what I let slip. Sure enough, she caught it. "Roman likes Ivy?!"

"What? I didn't say that." I try to play it off but judging by the way she looks at me, I know there is no point.

"You didn't have to. You said enough." She takes her phone from her clutch but I instantly reach across to pull it from her hand. "Hey, give me that."

"Nope." I pop the p as I slip it into my pocket. "Tonight is about us, and if you start texting Ivy about something she was *never* supposed to find out, you'll be distracted all night."

McKenna rolls her eyes but then smiles. "I wonder if she likes him, too. We should totally set them up!"

"Like oh my god, and then we could go on double dates and paint each other's nails!" I tease.

She goes to kick me under the table but I react quickly,

wrapping my legs around her ankle and trapping her foot into place. She attempts to pull it away, but I won't let her. Instead, I rub my calf against hers. Her whole body settles and her hand tightens around mine. I'm so turned on that if this place wasn't so classy, I'd probably find a way to finger her under the table.

AFTER WE'RE FINISHED EATING, we walk back out to my car hand in hand – gushing about how incredible the food was. Not only do I plan on coming back again, but I'll be sending a thank you gift to the woman who recommended this place. The food, the atmosphere, the mood – it all went better than I could have imagined.

"Thank you for tonight. It was perfect." McKenna tells me as I pull out of the parking lot.

I smile and glance over at her. "We're not finished yet, Princess."

"We're not?"

I shake my head but don't say anything else on the matter as I drive to our next destination. It's not far, but on our way there, she sings along with the radio. Her voice has always been music to my ears, even though she won't let many people hear her. I remember when we were younger, I used to hear her singing in her room. I'd stop by the door and listen without her knowing. Maverick thought I was doing it because it was funny, but he couldn't have been more wrong.

Over the years, I've learned that the way McKenna acts when there is music playing, can tell you a lot about the mood she's in. If she isn't at least mouthing the lyrics or letting her body move to the beat, something is wrong. She sings along when she's happy, and sways to the song when she's simply content. The times when she looks like she's not even listening to it, are when there's a lot plaguing her mind.

The club we arrive at is one that neither of us have been to before, but I've never heard a bad thing about it. The last time I got to dance with her wasn't anywhere near long enough, so I'm rectifying that. I park the car and the two of us climb out, showing the bouncer our IDs before making our way inside. It's a gorgeous place, with the bars lit up in neon lights and DJ on a platform high in front of the dance floor.

I place a hand on McKenna's lower back as I lead us through the crowded place and over to the bar. Already knowing they have her wine, because I had a supply of it sent here last week, I order her a glass and get myself a beer. When I hand her the drink and she takes a sip, her eyes light up.

"They carry this here?!"

I shrug. "Sure. You could say that."

Her eyes narrow on me. "What did you do?"

"I made a phone call to the manager and insisted he give the stuff a shot. When he brushed me off, I offered to pay for the first shipment."

"That's an expensive glass of wine." She murmurs over the rim of the glass.

The corners of my mouth raise. "I'd pay all the money in the world to keep that smile on your face."

For the umpteenth time tonight, she blushes. I swear, I could spend every day of my life putting that pink tint in her cheeks and never tire of seeing it. Knowing I have that affect on her gives me all that much hope for us. Maybe one day we won't have to sneak around. I'll be able to take her to places in town for lunch, bring her flowers at work, hold her in front of her family – all things that seem so insignificant but would mean everything to me.

The two of us talk some more as we enjoy a couple of drinks. I make sure to pace myself, knowing I need to drive home, but McKenna doesn't. By the time she finishes her third glass of wine, I can tell she's starting to feel it. She grabs my hand and drags me onto the dance floor. Her body molds against mine like it was made for it. I wrap my arm around her and hold her close. *Yeah, I could get used to this.*

Songs change as the two of us move together, but it's as if no one else is in the room. The only person that matters to either of us is each other. She looks up at me through her lashes and it's like someone hit me in the chest with a battering ram. Staring into her eyes, I know with absolute certainty – there will never be anyone for me but her.

A little while later, we grab another round of drinks and stand at one of the high top tables near the bar. As much as I don't want to leave her here alone, the urge to piss becomes too much to ignore. She insists I go, telling me she'll stay to watch our drinks and hold the table.

Moving as quickly as possible, I do my business, wash my hands, and head back out. As soon as my eyes land on McKenna, I see red. There's a man standing beside her, clearly unable to recognize the level of disinterest gracing her perfect face. I push through the crowd with more force than necessary, desperate to get to her before this douchebag can say anything else.

"Hey babe." I greet her as I put my hand on her lower back. She instantly relaxes at the sound of my voice.

"Hey."

The asshole standing way too close for my liking looks me up and down before scoffing. "Really? You're with this tool? Honey, I can show you a *much* better time."

Mac shakes her head and leans into my touch, trying to put some distance between her and him. "I'm okay. Thank you though."

Leave it to McKenna to still try to be polite while this guy is practically salivating over her. I really should have thought it through before I had her wear that dress. She looks breathtaking in anything, but the way the material accents her every curve – it could easily bring any man to his knees, myself included.

"Come on, baby." The dumbass with a death wish continues, reaching forward and grabbing her hand. "Leave with me. Let me show you what you're missing."

That's it. I can't watch this anymore. I move so that I'm standing in between them, my back to McKenna. I'm shielding her like a body guard as I grab his wrist and forcefully remove his hold on her. Now that I'm standing this close to him, I can smell the alcohol in his breath. *He's drunk.*

"Listen man, she's not interested. There are plenty of women here. How about you go find someone who is."

He runs his eyes over my body, obviously sizing me up. "Who the fuck are you to decide what she wants?"

"Her boyfriend, and I'm not opposed to doing whatever it takes to keep her safe from guys like you."

Looking as if he's given up, he turns around and takes a step away. I relax my shoulders and wait for him to leave but at the last minute he spins back and lands a right hook directly to my cheek bone. The hit catches me off guard, but as soon as I realize what happened, I strike. Using all of my body weight, I tackle him to the ground. The sound of McKenna screaming behind me barely even registers. I land punch after punch to his face, watching as blood spews from his mouth.

"Don't you *ever* fucking look her way again!"

Finally, the sound of Mac begging me to stop echoes through my brain. I'm distracted for only half a second before the mother fucker manages to buck me off of him. He gets up, shoving McKenna out of his way as he runs toward the exit. The suddenness of the attack throws her off balance and she doesn't have a chance to steady herself. Instead, she flies backwards and slams her head on the metal railing. It's as if it happens in slow motion and my every fear becomes a horrifying reality.

"Shit, McKenna!" I scurry to my feet and rush to her side. "Are you okay?"

"M-my head." She groans, pulling her hand away to find it covered in blood. The force in which she hit the bar must have cracked her head open. "I'm bleeding?"

I grab a wad of napkins from the table and hold them firmly to her head. "It's okay, baby. It's going to be okay."

McKenna looks like she's starting to float in and out of consciousness as I take out my phone and dial 9-1-1. Everyone is standing around staring at us, but no one is doing anything. Even the bartender watches on from his perch without even the slightest offer to help. By the third ring, I hang up. Screw waiting, she needs to get to the hospital *now*.

I pick her up in my arms and bolt towards the door. The crowd parts like Moses with the Red Sea as I run through them and outside. As soon as I get to my car, I manage to pull the keys from my pocket and unlock the door. McKenna slumps in the passenger seat, groaning as I buckle her. Once I'm done, I rush around to the driver's side and jump in.

The drive to the hospital is a panicked one, but somehow I manage to formulate a logical thought.

"Hey Siri. Call Ivy Williams."

The phone starts to ring through the speakers of the car, and within seconds, she answers the phone.

"Colton? Is everything okay?"

"No. There…" I take a deep breath to try and compose myself. "There was a fight. McKenna got caught in the crossfire. She's hurt."

Ivy gasps. "What the fuck do you mean she's hurt?"

"It's bad, Iv. She cracked her head open and she keeps passing out. I'm rushing her to the hospital now."

"Shit. Okay, be careful. The last thing you need is to get in an accident." I can hear the sound of keys jingling in the background. "Text me what hospital and I'll meet you there."

We hang up the phone just as I pull up to the emergency room. If I had obeyed any traffic laws, it probably would have taken a little longer. I run around to her side of the car, yelling that I need some help. She slumps in my arms as I lift her and carry her inside. Two nurses run over to me with a stretcher.

"What happened?"

I lay her down on it and follow them as they push her into a trauma room. "We were at a club. Some asshole shoved her and she hit her head on the railing."

Within seconds, a doctor comes in and starts to evaluate her. "She's got a head lac with a skull fracture. Run a CT to check for any intracranial hemorrhage." He glances at me for a second. "Sir, I'm going to need you to wait outside."

"I'm not going anywhere."

He shakes his head as he focuses on McKenna. "Your girlfriend is in good hands, but you need to let us do our job. Someone will come update you as soon as possible."

I don't want to leave, but if that's what it takes for her to get the care she needs, I'll do it. With one last kiss to her forehead, I reluctantly turn around and head for the waiting room.

IVY ARRIVES AT THE hospital much sooner than I thought she would. As soon as I see the wispy blonde hair, I relax. However, when her eyes meet mine, I begin to fear for my life. She marches toward me with a fury I've never seen on her before.

"What the fuck, Colton?! A bar fight? Are you fucking kidding me?!"

I stand up and raise my hands defensively. "It wasn't my fault. Some asshat was hitting on her and when I told him to back off, he wouldn't. He swung first."

"And that's supposed to make it okay?!" The more she talks, the higher her voice gets. "You're not a goddamn idiot. You know better than this shit. For God Sakes, you're not a 21 year old kid anymore!"

Sitting back down, I run my hands over my head. "I know. Fuck, okay? I know. It's just, when I saw him looking at her like a piece of meat, something came over me. I wanted to rip his head clean off his neck."

"Yeah, well, you're lucky the club didn't call the cops." She runs her fingers through her hair. "If you can't handle seeing someone flirt with her, how are you going to be if she ends up going through with the wedding? Are you going to beat Parker's ass, too?"

At the mention of her fiancé, my blood runs ice cold. "Shit, you didn't call him, did you?!"

She looks at me as if I've grown an extra eye in the middle of my forehead. "Of course, I did. What did you expect? That she'd go home with a few staples in her head and no one would ask what happened?"

"I-is he coming here?!"

"He's in love with her. What the hell do you think?"

I groan. "Fuck! How did all of this go to such shit?! Everything was perfect until that fuckwit had to go and ruin it."

She gives me a sympathetic look. "I'm sorry I yelled. I know you didn't mean for any of this to happen. But, you should probably get out of here."

"What?" I recoil. "No, I can't. I have to make sure she's okay."

"I will let you know as soon as I hear something, but you have to go. Parker *cannot* see you here."

Every part of me wants to stay. Tell Ivy to go fuck herself and refuse to leave. However, I know she's right. If he gets here and sees me, he'll start asking questions. McKenna will be forced to make a decision before she's ready and that may not go in my favor. So, as much as it kills me, I swallow down the lump in my throat and agree to leave.

MCKENNA

I wake to the beeping of a heart monitor. As I try to open my eyes, a shooting pain radiates throughout my head. I groan and my hand goes to my hair, only to find it disgustingly matted down with what must be dried blood. *Shit, the bar, the fight, Colton.* The memory of what happened runs through my mind like a movie reel.

"Mac?" A familiar voice catches my attention. "Are you alright?"

"Hurts." It's not everything I want to say, but it's enough.

The light in the room flicks off and I'm finally able to open my eyes. Ivy is standing at my bedside, but Colton is nowhere to be found. I blink as I look around, taking in my surroundings. When I look back up at my best friend, it's like she can read my thoughts.

"I sent him home. I had to call Parker and I didn't think you'd want him to find Colton here with you."

A huge part of me wishes she didn't do that, but deep down, I know she's right. Still, I need to talk to him – let him know I'm alright. I look over and find my phone on the table beside me. When I go to reach for it though, Ivy stops me.

"You can't keep doing this, Mac. Sneaking around with Colton and living with Parker."

My eyebrows furrow. "Uh, do you not remember whose idea this was in the first place?"

She crosses her arms over her chest. "Yeah, I know, but that was when I thought you were only doing it to help make a decision. It's been almost two months and you're yet to do that." I go to cut her off but she raises one finger. "If you want to be with Colton, by all means, be with him. But if you still plan on marrying Parker, you need to stop all this. It's time to decide. You can't have them both."

21

MCKENNA

FOR THE PAST FEW DAYS, IVY'S WORDS HAVE PLAYED on repeat throughout my mind. I know she's right. I'd be an idiot not to acknowledge that. It shouldn't have taken a blow to the head and three staples in order for me to see it. I've been playing a dangerous game of relationship roulette. The fight Colton got into the other night showed me a side of him I haven't seen in years. His brawling tendencies aren't new to me. He was known to get in quite a few fights during high school and the beginning of college. There just haven't been many I've seen first-hand – and I've *never* been hurt in the process.

None of what happened was intentional. I know Colton well enough to know how badly he feels about it. And even if I didn't, the 15 voicemails, 27 text messages, and box of chocolate covered strawberries sent to my house were enough to tell me. A huge part of me would love to go to him – tell him everything is going to be okay and hold him close to assure him of it – but I can't. I have *way* too much to think about.

I throw myself backward on Tatum and Maverick's couch, groaning to myself as I try to figure out what the hell I'm going to do. The only reason I came here is because I know Colton and Maverick are both at work. Usually I'd go to Ivy's, but lately she's been looking at me like the choice should be obvious. She likes Parker, don't get me wrong, but she firmly believes that if I was meant to be with him, that Colton wouldn't have ever been an option in my mind. She might be right, but having feelings for someone else doesn't mean my feelings for Parker don't exist.

Taking one of the throw pillows, I put it over my face and scream. I've never been pulled in so many different directions before. It's absolutely infuriating. Maybe I'd be better off choosing no one. I could be single, become a nun. Yeah, right. As if *that* would ever happen.

"You're adorable when you're frustrated." Tatum quips.

I pull the pillow from my face and throw it at her, hitting my target. "Tell me what to do."

"Why? So that you can blame me forever if I choose wrong? Nope. No thank you. Not going to happen."

My bottom lip juts out in a pout. "Some friend you are."

She shrugs. "Sorry babe. I tried telling you what to do when this whole mess started. You didn't listen to me."

It's not like she's wrong – she isn't. However, there's not a single part of me that regrets getting involved with Colton this summer. He's wild, and spontaneous, and makes me feel alive in a way I haven't felt in years. It's exhilarating as hell. But Parker... Parker is my safe space. He's the one that I know will always be there to listen, or even just to hold me when I don't really want to talk. My head says to choose Parker, but my heart isn't hearing it. It's too busy beating for Colton.

"That's it. I'm joining the monastery."

Tatum snorts. "They wouldn't take you."

"Why the fuck not?!"

She looks at me knowingly. "Well, for one, you have the mouth of a sailor." I chuckle softly and flip her off. "Besides, with the way you and Colton have been going at it lately, you wouldn't last a week."

"Yeah, you're probably right."

"I know I am, and that's not even including the times you've had sex with Parker. Getting it from two different men – is it wrong that I'm kinda jealous?"

I look down and fiddle with the pillow in my lap. "Uh, I'm- I'm not."

"Come again?"

Gritting my teeth together, I take a deep breath. "I haven't had sex with Parker. Not in the last couple months anyway."

Her jaw is practically on the floor as she stares at me. "He hasn't tried?"

"No, he has. I've just always been able to get out of it. I've faked more headaches than I'd like to admit."

She smirks. "Well in that case, I think you've already made your choice."

To my relief, nothing else is said on the topic. However, that doesn't stop my head from spinning over the whole thing. Ivy was right, I need to choose. Stringing them along isn't fair, and if I don't decide soon, it could all go up in flames. I may even end up losing them both.

I WAKE TO A light kiss on my forehead. My eyes open to find Colton standing in front of me. I must've fallen asleep on the couch while Tatum and I watched *Mean Girls*. There's just something refreshing about watching someone else's drama. I sit up and rub my eyes with the back of my hand.

"Where's Tatum?"

He sits down beside me. "Her and Maverick went to pick up dinner. She said to let you sleep."

My eyebrows furrow. "You listen so well."

"Yeah." He snickers. "Could you blame me though?

You've been avoiding me again for nearly a week. Then I come home to find you on my couch."

"Maverick's couch."

"McKenna." His authoritative tone tells me I'm not going to get out of discussing this. "Why haven't you answered me? I've been worried about you."

I sigh. "I'm sorry. I've had a lot on my mind and an almost constant headache. Plus, I've really needed to get my lesson plans done."

"So, you're not running away from me?"

"No." *Not yet, at least.*

For the first time since this conversation started, he smiles. His arm wraps around my waist and he pulls me into his side. I go willingly, basking in the comfort his hold brings. He places a kiss on the top of my head, and then moves my hair out of the way.

"How is it?"

I shrug. "I get the staples taken out on Wednesday."

"Do you want me to come with you?"

It's an enticing offer, and a large part of me wants to take him up on it. Having Colton there would definitely ease my anxiety about getting metal pulled from my skull. However, the doctor taking them out is the same one who put them in – while Parker sat at my bedside

"Thank you, but it's okay. Ivy already took off work to bring me."

"Alright, baby." He presses another kiss into my hair, then moves me away so he can stand.

"Where are you going?"

"I promised Avery I would pick her up from school and take her to lunch." He puts his hand out. "You're welcome to join us."

Running my fingers through my hair, I smile sadly. "I would, but I can't."

My answer doesn't seem to surprise him. "Will I at least see you tomorrow night?"

"What's tomorrow night?"

He looks at me like I've forgotten something important. "The annual bonfire on the beach."

Okay, so maybe I *did*. For Maverick's 18th birthday, he wanted to have a massive bonfire. He even went through all the trouble of getting the town to grant him approval to have it on the beach. The turnout was so big that it ended up becoming an annual thing. Now, there are food trucks that come, and a local DJ volunteers to provide music for the event. It may not be for his birthday anymore, but it's still *his* event. It's one thing my brother is really proud of and I've missed it for the last four years. There is *no way* he's going to let me miss it again, not that I'd even want to.

"Yeah. I'll be there."

He grins then bends down, caressing my face and pressing his lips to mine. It's soft and sweet, with no underlying intentions. When he pulls away, the level of emotion in his eyes is overwhelming.

"Text me, okay? It's like living in my own personal hell when you don't."

I nod, and with one last kiss, he leaves. My body flops back down onto the couch, burrowing under the blanket he must have covered me with while I was sleeping. *Why can't my life be simple?* I wish the choice was as easy as Ivy thinks it is. Maybe she's right. Maybe I'm just making this harder than it needs to be.

THE FRONT DOOR OPENS as I'm in the middle of putting on mascara. I don't need to look to know who it is. No more than five seconds later, Ivy's voice booms through the foyer.

"Mac?"

"In here!" I shout back.

She comes around the corner and leans against the doorway to the bathroom. I can see her reflection in the mirror. She's wearing a pair of shorts and a gray crop top, with her blonde hair straightened to perfection. I've always wondered why she didn't become a model. She's gorgeous.

"Is that waterproof?"

I smile. "Of course, it is. I know my brother. The chance of getting hit with a water balloon is high, no matter how much he promises there won't be any."

"Smart girl." She chuckles.

The summer before I left for school, I made the mistake of wearing non-waterproof make up. I was absolutely mortified when I ended up looking like a raccoon only two hours into the bonfire. No amount of Tatum's make up wipes could save my face that night.

The jeans I'm wearing cling to my hips in all the right places, and my halter top hangs perfectly around my neck. I make sure to wear a hair-tie on my wrist, just in case my hair becomes a ratty mess. Once I deem myself ready to go, I slip my phone into my back pocket and we head out.

It's only a mile away, so Ivy and I decide to walk. That way, neither of us need to be the designated driver. There is nothing better than drinking a beer next to a fire on the beach.

"So, Colton will be there." She says, as if I didn't already know.

"Yup."

"Is Parker coming?"

I wince. "God, I hope not. He's in Boston right now."

Her eyebrows furrow. "It's Saturday night."

"I know. He has a study session with a group from one of his classes." She hums, but doesn't say anything. "What?"

"Nothing."

I nudge her with my elbow. "It's not nothing. Spill."

She shrugs. "I just think he's been having an awful lot of *study sessions* lately."

What she's insinuating is clear, but I can't seem to bring myself to believe Parker would do that. He's never been the kind of person to go behind my back. And even if he was, could I really be mad? I mean, I've spent the last couple months having an affair with my ex. That doesn't exactly scream victim.

"See? That. That right there." Ivy points at my face. "Whatever the hell is going through your head right now should be enough to tell you who you should choose."

I roll my eyes playfully. "I don't know what you're talking about."

"Mhm." She waves me off. "Take the jump, McKenna. Just take the jump."

The rest of the walk is relatively quiet, giving me way too much time to be in my own head. I'd be lying if I said I haven't missed Colton every second that I'm away from him, but I'd also be lying if I said I won't miss Parker if I leave him. I feel like no matter what I decide, I lose. I just have to determine which loss I can live with.

As soon as the beach comes into view, the air gets sucked from my lungs. Colton is already there, looking like sex on legs. He's throwing a football back and forth with Maverick. Sweat glistens across his torso, making his already perfect body look even more magical. I've never been more grateful for the heat and his lack of wearing a shirt.

"And you pretend you don't know what you want." Ivy murmurs.

I lightly smack her arm with the back of my hand, then continue to walk towards Tatum and Roman. Ivy follows. As soon as Colton sees me, he bites his lip to conceal his smile. His muscles flex a little more than necessary as he throws the ball back to Maverick.

"Look who finally decided to join us." Roman quips. I try not to laugh at the way his eyes widen when he sees Ivy. *How have I never noticed this before?*

I hug Tatum hello, then give one to Rome. "Well, I was told I didn't have a choice."

"Because you don't." My brother comes up and wraps his arms around me. "It's been too long since you've come to one of these."

Nodding, I look around and try my best not to let my gaze linger on Colton for too long. "This is crazy, Mav."

"It's the biggest event of the year now." He nudges me. "You'd know that if you had come home for a summer, or at all."

Leave it to Maverick to consistently bring that up. "Yeah, yeah." I wave him off. "Oh, is that a taco truck?! I'm starving."

I grab Ivy's and with a discreet smile at Colton, we leave the gang behind and go get some food. If I'm going to handle being around Colton with his shirt off and *not* being able to touch him, I need a clear head. Just the sight of him takes all my thoughts and jumbles them up.

THE ENERGY ACROSS THE beach is electric. Everyone is in a great mood as they listen to music and catch up with old friends. Still, no matter how many people from my past come up to say hello, I can't seem to take my eyes off Colton. He's standing with Maverick, Roman, and a couple other guys from their graduating class, laughing about something and looking like he just stepped off a Calvin Klein photoshoot. *God, he's flawless.*

"You know, I've seen you look at Parker plenty of times." My mother remarks, making me wonder how long she's been sitting next to me. "And I have *never* seen you look at him the way you look at Colton."

"Mom." I whine.

She raises her hands in surrender. "I'm not judging. I'm just trying to understand why you're still engaged to someone who *isn't* him."

"It's complicated."

"It doesn't have to be."

I run my fingers through my hair and give her a defeated look. "There's so much that you don't know."

She gives me one of her comforting smiles. "You mean, how you two were a thing before you left for school?"

My jaw drops. "How did you…"

"I'm not blind, McKenna. I've always known."

"Why didn't you say anything?"

She shrugs. "It wasn't any of my business. You were happy, and I figured if there was something to tell, you'd come to me."

My eyes widen. "Does Maverick know?!"

"Oh, god no." She scoffs. "He's oblivious to everyone and everything that isn't Tatum."

I may argue that she's wrong if I hadn't seen how little he noticed at his birthday dinner. I swear, Colton could have told me every sexual thought he had about me, and Maverick wouldn't have realized a thing. Still, even the idea that he could find out makes me sick to my stomach. He'd hate me for stealing his best friend, and he'd probably kill Colton for as much as *thinking* about me that way. Maybe staying with Parker would be best for everyone.

"It doesn't matter." I murmur.

"If that were true, you wouldn't have strayed from Parker in the first place." When I don't say anything, she continues. "Look, McKenna, I might not know much about what you two have going on, but I do know he's a great guy, and that he looks at you like you hung the moon." She stands. "Don't let the fear of upsetting someone keep you from what you truly want."

"Well, if it isn't my two favorite women." The familiar voice has my heart racing in an instant. I turn my head to see Colton walking toward us.

My mom laughs. "I don't think your mother would be too happy to hear that." She gives him a loving hug, and I don't miss the way she speaks lowly as she pulls away. "You need to tell her."

It's clear her words were only meant for him, but my curiosity gets the better of me as she walks away and Colton takes the seat beside me. "Tell who what?"

He looks like he's hiding something behind those oceanic eyes of his, but instead of explaining, he shakes his head. "It's nothing. How's your evening? Are you enjoying yourself?"

I nod. "Definitely. It's crazy how big this thing has gotten over the years. I still remember hearing you and Maverick plan the first one."

Dusting the sand off his knees, he snickers. "Nah, this was all Mav. I was just the best friend who always got roped into his crazy ideas."

"He's had some wild ones, hasn't he? Like the time that he made you and Roman go with him to try and find elephant ear leaves and girls who would fan you with them."

He throws his head back and groans while laughing. "Don't remind me. That was the day I got a milkshake poured over my head."

"Classic." I tease. "That should happen more often."

Colton glares playfully. "You'd like that, wouldn't you?"

The corners of my mouth raise into a smirk. "I mean, I can think of better ways to cover you in chocolate."

His breath hitches and his pupils widen, showing his arousal. "Fuck, Mac. You can't just say things like that."

"And if I do anyway?"

"I'm sure I can find somewhere around here to sneak you away to."

There are so many things that turn me on about the concept of us running off to fool around. I've been craving the feeling of his hands on my skin for a week now, and since the second I got here, my core has been aching.

I survey the area before looking back at him. "Think your car would be safe enough?"

"Don't fuck with me, Princess." He growls.

Giving him a wink, I get up and start walking toward the parking lot. After five steps, I turn around to see he's still sitting in place. "Are you coming?"

He gets up and follows me without another word. The two of us are all laugher and smiles as we make our way to his car, which thankfully, has tinted windows. Colton reaches over to tickle my side, causing me to jump out of his reach, giggling like a school girl. If there weren't hundreds of people able to see us right now, I'd leap into his arms and have him carry me the rest of the way while I kiss his neck.

"Keep your hands to yourself, Brooks." I tease.

"Yes, Brooks. Please keep your hands to yourself."

The British accent has me stopping dead in my tracks. My head whips over to see Parker standing no more than twenty feet in front of me. I swallow hard as I try to gauge his expression – stoic.

"P-Parker, hey." I try to gain control of my breathing. "I didn't know you were coming."

He grins. If he has any idea of what's been going on between Colton and I, he doesn't show it as he walks toward me and wraps his arms around my waist. "I wanted to surprise you. Were you leaving?"

Out of the corner of my eye, I can see Colton looking just as uncomfortable as I feel. Still, he comes to my rescue when the words get caught in my throat. "No. McKenna was just coming with me to get something out of my car, but you two go enjoy the party. I can get it."

"Are you sure?" My eyes are begging to know if he's okay.

He nods. "Of course. Parker has never been to one of these. Go show him around."

With that, Colton runs his fingers through his hair and continues his trek to the parking lot. I glance up at my fiancé, only to find him smiling down at me. I should be happy he's here, but the feeling I get as I look at him does little to ease the stabbing pain in my chest from seeing the hurt expression on Colton's face.

This is not the time, McKenna. Not right now.

My subconscious is right. I shake the thought from my head and plaster on the best smile I can manage. "Come on. I'm sure everyone will be happy you're here."

———————

LONG AFTER THE SUN has set, the DJ announces last song and the crowd starts to clear out. Instead of going with them, Maverick, myself, and our closest friends all head toward the fire. Since the second year this event became big, we've made it a tradition to stay later. With Roman being on the fire department, they leave him in charge of one of the trucks and allow us to keep the fire going as long as we want.

"It isn't over?" Parker questions, confused.

Roman snorts. "No way. This is when the party starts! Isn't that right, Mackey?"

"Oh god." I groan. "Don't call me that."

Colton and Maverick both chuckle, but only Colton speaks. "Shit, I remember that! It was like a good three months you demanded everyone call you Mackey!"

"Okay, I was like twelve. I hardly think you can hold that against me now."

Ivy laughs from beside me. "Maybe not, but remember

the first time we got drunk? You and I started thinking of what our stripper names would be if we didn't get into college. What was yours? Mc-"

I slap my hand over her mouth as fast as possible, letting out a sigh of relief when the rest comes out muffled and inaudible. The last thing these guys need is something else to pick on me for. Maverick having a lifetime worth of memories is bad enough. He does *not* need more.

"Oh, come on!" Colton whines. "I wanted to hear that!"

I give him a lighthearted glare, but I know it's never going to deter him. He'll get it out of me eventually, but it won't be in front of everyone else. "Not a chance."

"You were going to become a dancer if you didn't get into university?" Parker questions, his voice laced with concern for my moral standards.

I shake my head. "No. It was only a joke."

He exhales. "Oh good. If my mother found out her future daughter-in-law considered taking her clothes off for money, she'd have a coronary."

Ivy, Tatum, and I all cringe at the mention of where our relationship is currently heading. Thankfully, Parker doesn't notice. Just as my eyes meet Colton's, Maverick interrupts the awkward situation.

"Who's coming with me to get the cooler?"

Colton jolts up. "I will."

I swallow down the lump in my throat at the way he's jumping at the opportunity to get some distance. In my heart, I know it's not *me* he's trying to get away from, but Parker being here *with me*. I can't say I blame him. If he was here with another girl, I don't think I would've shown up at all.

After a few drinks, I start to feel the alcohol coursing through my veins – providing the perfect buzz to let loose a bit. I've missed nights like this, ones spent around the fire with those most important to me. They were always my favorite.

Colton takes out his guitar and starts strumming random cords. As soon as the sound meets her ears, Ivy stands and grabs my hand. She pulls me away from Parker and into the empty space, a little too close to the fire.

"Colton, play something we can dance to!" She demands.

He starts to play a tune I don't recognize. Ivy and I sway to the melody and soon, Tatum joins us. We spin around, laughing and letting our bodies move to the beat. It's probably the furthest thing from attractive, but none of us care.

Suddenly, the song changes to one that sends chills through my entire body, making the hair on my arms stand straight up. *From the Ground Up*. My eyes find Colton's and he doesn't look away from me as he continues to strum the tune with utmost perfection. The look on his face is so intense and full of adoration. It takes everything in me not to throw myself into his lap right now.

"McKenna." Ivy whisper-shouts, grabbing my hand to snap me from my stupor. *Shit, Parker. Maverick!*

I look to my brother first only to find him completely immersed in a conversation with Roman. Then, I dance in a way that causes me to spin around so I can catch a glimpse of Parker. To my relief, he's looking down at his phone. *Phew, that was a close call.*

I RUSH INTO THE house, peeling the drenched fabric of my sweatshirt from my body. Just as we were about to start playing one of those stupid games you only play when you're drunk, the skies opened and rain started to pour down on us. It put out the large bonfire entirely on its own, so we all grabbed what we could and booked it for the parking lot. None of us even got the chance to say goodbye.

Walking over to the sink, I ring my hair out. What I need right now is to get out of these wet clothes and into a hot shower. Just as I'm about to head upstairs, Parker comes in the kitchen and tosses his keys onto the counter.

"So, tell me something." He requests.

I pull my hair into bun as thunder cracks loudly outside. "What's up?"

"How long has something been going on between you and Colton?"

And just like that, I'm stone cold sober.

22

MCKENNA

THE STORM OUTSIDE DOESN'T EVEN BEGIN TO compare to the one brewing inside this house. I stare blank faced at Parker, silently debating between complete denial and telling him everything. He holds my gaze and doesn't move an inch. I can tell by the expression on his face, it's not a matter of *if* he knows, it's *what*. There's no getting out of this. I'm caught.

"I can explain." I try, but him and I both know that's not true. Nothing I say can justify my actions.

His eyebrows raise as he walks around the island and stands directly in front of me. "By all means, please."

The ways I could tell this story are endless. I don't even know where to start, so I go with the beginning. "Do you remember our first date? We were sitting at dinner and you could tell I was guarded."

"I asked who had made you that way." He finishes for me.

I nod. "It was Colton…"

It's been three days. Three torturous, long, excruciating days since my brother's best friend stole my first kiss, and my heart right along with it. Since that night, I haven't been able to focus at all. The feeling of his kiss still lingers on my lips, like he branded me with them and claimed me for himself. Ivy tells me I need to get a grip – that it was just one kiss. Well, tell that to the part of me that has been in love with him since I was old enough to know what love is.

Maybe I wouldn't be driving myself crazy if I was able to talk to him about it. The idea of asking him what the kiss meant, or if it meant anything at all, is the most nerve wracking thing I've ever faced in my life, but I know it needs to be done. However, that requires seeing him, which I haven't – at all. He seems to be avoiding this house like the plague, which should be my answer but it's not one I'm willing to accept.

I'm washing the dishes with Ivy on speaker phone, going through the events of the other night for the billionth time.

"But he kissed me, Iv. And not in a way that seemed accidental. He kissed me like he needed it, like he wasn't going to live another second if he didn't get his lips on mine."

"So you've said." She murmurs, lacking any enthusiasm at all.

"And now I haven't seen him since. The next morning, he was gone. Literally, just gone. He usually stays for breakfast. I tried to get information from Maverick without seeming suspicious, but all he said was that Colton had to go home early in the morning. What if something bad happened?"

"Or what if he realized he made a mistake?"

"Ouch." I know she means well, but that stung.

She sighs. "I'm sorry. I don't mean to be harsh, but you have to look at the bigger picture. When's the last time he's gone more than a day without being at your house? If that kiss meant something, wouldn't he have come to you already?"

"Maybe he didn't know what to say." Colton's voice from behind me sounds.

I spin around so fast it almost gives me whiplash. My heart practically breaks through my chest when I see him standing there. There's a hint of a smugness on his face, telling me he heard enough of

274

my conversation to know I've been driving myself, and my best friend for that matter, absolutely insane.

"Is that Colton?!" Ivy asks, her tone suddenly louder.

"I'll call you back."

"Wait! Leave it on speaker! I want to-"

Without a second thought, my hand swipes my phone into the soapy water filled sink and Ivy's inquisitive mind goes with it. Colton's eyes widen and he snickers as he looks behind me.

"You just destroyed your phone."

I hold back my wince. I know my mom might kill me for it later, but she'll buy another one. I'll just tell her it was an accident. That I was holding it to my ear with my shoulder and it slipped. Yeah, that'll work.

"M-Maverick isn't home." Really, McKenna? That's what you come up with?! Pathetic.

He smiles nervously. "I know. I came to talk to you."

"Oh." I run my fingers through my hair, only to realize my hand is covered in suds. Wonderful.

Colton chuckles and takes a step toward me. "You've got a little…"

He grabs the dish rag from beside me and wipes the bubbles from my forehead. Then, he takes each of my hands and cleans them as well. He's so close that I can smell his cologne. It's infiltrating my senses and making it nearly impossible to concentrate. If it meant he'd keep touching me like this, I'd dive into that sink head first.

"Thanks." I say softly as he steps back.

"No problem."

An uncomfortable silence fills the room, making me wish I could run away and keep the hope that him and I might have a future together alive. The way he's refusing to make eye contact with me right now, tells me that hope is about to die a very painful death. It's my fault, really. I should have known better than to fall for my brother's unattainable best friend. What's that thing my mother always says? Better to rip the band aid off? Well, I guess we should get this over with.

"You kissed me." I declare with as much confidence as I can manage.

He bites his lip and nods, still looking at the ground. "I did."

"And now you're here to tell me that it can't happen again."

He exhales. "Ivy was right. That kiss was a mistake."

If I thought hearing my best friend say it hurt, hearing it come from his mouth is a whole different kind of blow. I do my best to hold back the tears, but my voice waivers anyway. "Okay, cool. You did what you came here to do. You can go now."

"McKenna."

"No. Really, it's fine. I'm fine. I'll, uh, see you later."

I go to slip past him but he stops me with a gentle grasp on my wrist. As I look up at him, a tear escapes from my eye and slides down my cheek. Colton catches it with his thumb, wiping it from my face. There's something I don't recognize in his expression. Something that makes my every nerve ending come alive and want to obey anything that comes from his mouth.

"Maverick would kill me." He whispers.

Of course my over-protective, over-invasive, asshole of a brother is what's keeping me from getting what I want. Even the thought of it makes me want to scream. Why does he have any influence in what I do?

"I'm not a little girl anymore, Colton."

A humorless laugh emits from the back of his throat. "Oh, trust me, Princess. I know." His one hand moves from my wrist to the small of my back, and he uses it to pull me closer – making it so my body is pressed against his own. I stare up at him, eyes full of wonder, and he sighs when he finds his resolve. "I'm going to hell."

Without another word, his lips meet mine for the second time and it's absolutely invigorating. As soon as I gasp, he slips his tongue into my mouth, making me his and his alone. Every single thing in my mind is instantly replaced with all thoughts of him. I may not make it out of this unscathed, but I'll bask in this feeling for as long as I can.

PARKER AND I STAY seated on the couch across from each other, neither of us saying a word. I spent the last hour telling him everything – from the fling Colton and I had before college, to the way we ended, all the way to how it started again. Seeing the pain etched across his face as he listened to me admit to cheating on him, threatened to rip my heart to shreds. I never intended to hurt him, or maybe I never intended for him to find out. All I know is that it's all come out in the wash, and now I have to see where we go from here.

"Are you in love with him?" He asks. I open my mouth to speak, but he shakes his head. "Wait, don't answer that."

Leaning forward, he rests his elbows on his knees. His hands cover his face and make it hard for me to gauge his expression. A part of me wonders if I should go try to comfort him but I don't know how that would be accepted, so I stay where I'm at.

"I'm sorry."

He scoffs. "Yeah, you've said that already."

The weather outside has since let up, but the mood in this room is still just as dark. It's two o'clock in the morning, and yet I've never been so wide awake. My phone still lies where I left it on the counter – all texts remaining unanswered. When I woke up this morning, I never imagined *this* is how tonight would go. *How could such a great day, have such a shitty ending?*

"Okay." Parker announces with a new-found certainty.

My eyebrows furrow in confusion. "Okay?"

He nods. "Okay. We can get through this."

"We can?!"

His eyes meet mine for the first time in over an hour, and narrow as they study me. "Is that not what you want?"

"I- I…"

Is it? I've hit a fork in the road, the time and place where I need to decide, and all I want to do is set up camp right here and stay forever – in this limbo where I can have them both. As selfish as it may be, I can't picture my life without either one of them.

Parker stands and comes closer, filling the space beside me and pulling my hand into his. "McKenna, I meant it when I said I want to spend the rest of my life with you, and as much as your infidelity hurts, it doesn't change anything. However, I only want that if you want it, too. Please don't marry me if your heart isn't fully in it."

"You're not leaving me?" My bewildered state is evident. I thought for sure he would be gone the second an admission came from my lips.

He shakes his head. "I love you, McKenna, and I can love you through this – but only if you want me to. It'll take a lot of work to get back to where we were, but I'm willing to do that because I want you. You just have to decide if that's what *you* want."

This is it. This is where I have the opportunity to make a decision and make it known, but still, I freeze. In the battle between Parker and Colton, head and heart, I come up blank. It's like my whole body malfunctions and can't formulate a single rational thought.

"Do you need the answer now, or can I think about it?"

I can tell by his face that he was hoping I'd jump into his arms and thank him for staying, but that isn't going to happen right now. Reluctantly, he nods and releases my hand from his hold. The two of us stand and I head to the bedroom, taking a duffle bag from my closet and starting to fill it with some clothes. If I'm really going to think this through, I can't do it here.

Just as I'm zipping the bag closed, Parker comes into the room. His tear stained cheeks send a jolt of pain through my heart. He places a kiss to my forehead and I do my best to stay strong.

"Come back to me." He whispers.

With that, he steps back and lets me leave. It isn't until I'm outside waiting for my Uber that I allow myself to cry, to feel the pain of everything in full force, and to start the process of finally making a choice.

I WAKE IN THE morning to the sound of someone knocking lightly on my bedroom door. As soon as my eyes open, my mom steps inside. Her face holds nothing but love as she comes over and places a cup of tea on my nightstand.

"Are you okay? You were a bit inconsolable when you got here last night."

I sit up and pull the warm mug into my hands. "I don't know. I think so?"

"Do you want to talk about it?"

If she wasn't one of the most comforting people I know, I may have turned down that offer. Instead, I move out of the way and gesture for her to take a seat on my bed.

"Parker found out about Colton and I."

"Oh, McKenna." She pulls me into her arms and I go willingly. "So, what happens now?"

I shrug. "He said he wants to make it work."

"And I take it you said no? I mean, judging by the fact that you slept here last night."

"I told him I need time to think, and I do. I can't see him every day and make that kind of decision. He'll just try to do things to sway me, and I need to make sure this is what I want."

She nods, agreeing with me. "Well, you know you're welcome to stay as long as you'd like. And I'm here, if you need someone to talk to or even just someone to listen."

"Thanks Mom, for everything."

She smiles and then excuses herself, leaving me alone to ponder my thoughts.

THE FIRST DAY IS spent wallowing in self-pity. I only come out of my room to pee or get something to eat – not that I have much of an appetite. I dodge the few incoming calls from Parker and Colton, and only responding to texts with one word answers that make it clear I'm not up for talking. The second day, I force myself to get up and shower. The brownie crumbs found in my hair are enough to tell me that I need to get a grip. Life is moving on, and if I don't go with it, it'll leave me behind.

I blow dry my hair just enough to make it look presentable and throw on a pair of leggings with a tank top. A few months ago, a few days even, I would've been mortified at the idea of going out in public looking like a bum. Today, I really couldn't care less. I grab the keys to my mom's car, tell her I'll be back in a bit, and head out the door.

Listening to the GPS on my phone, I follow the directions until I reach my destination. The sound of hammers pounding on nails echoes through the air. I kill the engine and step out of the car. As soon as I enter the building, I see Colton leaning over a blueprint with Roman at his side. They're clearly immersed in conversation, and it takes a minute before anyone notices me.

"You lost, darlin?" A man in a hard hat asks, looking at me like I'm just what the doctor ordered.

Colton picks his head up and glares at the man. "Back off, Flynn. That one's taken."

He takes one step back and raises his hands in surrender. "And here I thought you were trying to be a monk or some shit. You been keeping this little beauty locked away in an ivory tower somewhere?"

"No, but maybe I should. That's not the worst idea." Colton comes closer and takes me into his arms. "Everything okay?"

I shake my head slightly. "Can we go somewhere and talk?"

"Yeah, of course." With one last nod at Roman, he leads me outside and away from all the noise. "What's going on?"

"Parker knows."

He looks a little confused. "Parker knows what?"

"Everything."

His eyes widen. "Everything, everything?" I nod. "Wow, okay. I wasn't expecting that. Are you alright? He didn't hurt you, did he? Was he civil about the whole thing?" He takes a deep breath but doesn't give me a chance to say anything. "Do you have somewhere to stay? If you don't, my house is still being built, but we can get an apartment in the meantime."

"Colton."

"Yeah, I know. You're right. We need to tell everyone first. Oh! Did you tell Tatum to cancel the wedding?! I guess that needs to come first."

"Colton!" My tone cuts off his rant and he stops to face me. The look on my face must say it all, because his mouth opens and closes as his expression darkens.

"Oh my god." He takes a step away from me. "You're still with him."

"I told him I need time to think."

Outrage takes over his features. "Time to think?! You've had *months* to think, and you still don't know?!"

Tears build in my eyes, once again. It feels like all I've done lately is cry. "It's not that simple!"

"It is, McKenna! You either want to be with me, or you want to be with him!" He scoffs and shakes his head as he retreats slowly. "You know what? Take all the fucking time you want." He doesn't even give me a second glance as he turns around and disappears back into the building, leaving me a sobbing mess. *I guess old habits die hard.*

I **SPEND THE WEEK** hidden away from the world. Texts from Parker filter in daily, asking how my day is and telling me he misses me. Colton, however, hasn't said anything since our argument on Monday. I can't say that I blame him. He got so excited, only to have it ripped away from him as quickly as it came. Talking to me is probably the last thing he wants right now.

"McKenna!" My mother calls. "You have a visitor!"

My eyebrows furrow as my heart starts to race. I know Parker would never show up unannounced. He respects my boundaries too much for that. There's only one person I can think of that could be at the door. I clamber off my bed and make my way toward the stairs. As I see who it is, however, I can't help but feel disappointed.

"Rome?"

He gives me one of his friendly smiles and waves. My mother stands with her back to him, looking at me with her eyebrows raised – as if she's wondering what the hell I'm up to.

"Mom, no. Whatever you think is happening between Roman and I, is wrong."

When he realizes what I mean, he chokes on his own saliva and starts coughing profusely. "Oh god. No, Mrs. Taylor, that's not why I'm here."

My mom chuckles. "I'm just messing with you. And Roman, I've told you, call me Marissa."

"My mother raised me better than that, ma'am."

"Well, I don't see her here."

I laugh at their antics and slip out the door, gesturing for Roman to follow me. He does, and the two of us sit on the porch steps. "So, what makes me so special for you to come visit me on your birthday?"

He grins widely. His birthday is, and always has been, his

favorite holiday. I already texted him this morning and wrote on his facebook, but it wouldn't surprise me if he was going around collecting verbal 'happy birthday's as well.

"What? I can't come see my favorite 'best friend's little sister' without needing a reason?"

I smirk. "I'm going to tell Avery you said that."

"Don't you dare. That little shit may only be sixteen, but she's dangerous." When I give him a teasing look and pretend to take out my phone to text her, he stops me. "Okay, you win. I have an ulterior motive."

"Which is?"

"I'm worried about you, and I'm tired of seeing Colton mope around job sites like someone shot his puppy."

"Kicked his puppy." I correct.

"What?"

"The term is *kicked* his puppy. Shot his puppy sounds morbid."

He groans. "Tomayto, tomahto."

I chuckle softly. "Okay, I'm sorry."

"Brat." His shoulder bumps my own. "So, how are you? And don't give me that generic 'I'm fine' answer, because you and I both know that's a crock of shit."

I never thought I'd be having this conversation with Roman of all people. Ivy and Tatum have been trying to talk to me all week with no success. Perhaps a fresh perspective is exactly what I need.

"I don't know." I confess. "Having to choose between my fiancé and my childhood crush isn't easy. I love them both and Colton doesn't seem to understand that. He thinks it's all black and white. Him or Parker."

He nods, listening to me until I'm done. "And you're still undecided?"

"Yeah." I sigh. "Sometimes I wake up almost positive that I want to be with Colton, other times the fear of losing Parker is so intense I can't breathe."

"Well, what about the thought of being *with* Parker?"

"What do you mean?"

He shrugs. "You said you've thought about being with Colton, and you've thought about losing Parker. What about the thought of being with Parker and losing Colton? How does that make you feel?" When I stay quiet, he continues. "Personally, I think you already made your choice. You just don't know it yet."

My eyebrows furrow, wondering where he's going with this. "I have?"

"Yup." His tone is full of confidence is determination. "Think about it. What was your reaction when Parker said he wasn't leaving you?"

"I was shocked."

"And why's that?"

I fiddle with the hem of my shirt. "Because I was almost positive he was going to leave me."

He nods again. "So then, why'd you tell him?"

"He figured it out."

"Maybe, but you didn't have to admit it. If you were so sure he was going to leave, and you didn't want that, you could have denied it. You could've stopped everything going on with Colton and focused all your attention on your engagement. He couldn't prove anything, which is why he asked you in the first place."

The revelation hits me like a slap in the face. "Oh my god. I was hoping he'd leave."

Roman's smile widens. "There you go! I knew you didn't get through NYU just on your good looks." I roll my eyes but can't fight off my grin. He stands. "So, you ready to go?"

"Go where?"

"To my surprise party."

A bark of laughter leaves my mouth as I get up and follow Roman to his Jeep. "I didn't know you knew about that."

Personally, I wasn't going to go because I didn't think Colton wanted to see me.

"Please." He scoffs. "I figured it out weeks ago. Your brother is a *horrible* liar. I just hope he got a cake."

I smirk. "Why? So, you can wish for a certain blonde on your birthday candles?"

Roman's jaw drops, and as he puts the car in drive, he shakes his head. "Fucking Brooks."

THE PARTY IS A lot bigger than I thought it would be. I don't even recognize half the people here. Then again, this is a party for Roman and he's always had a lot of friends.

We walk through the back gate and onto the patio. As soon as people notice our arrival, shouts of 'surprise' fill the large yard. However, the second my eyes find what they were looking for, my heart feels like it was ripped for my chest. Colton is standing next to my brother with a girl hanging on his arm, but it's not just any girl.

It's Olivia, *his ex-girlfriend.*

23

COLTON

I STAND ON THE LADDER, TRYING NOT TO FALL AS I hang the decorations. It's bad enough that I have to *attend* this party, let alone help set up for it. Don't get me wrong, Rome is one of my best friends, but I'm just not in a celebrating mood.

The shaking beneath me pulls my attention away from the banner and down to the ground. I narrow my eyes at Tatum, who seems to be too engrossed in her phone to actually do her job.

"The fuck, Tate? Hold the ladder before I fall off the damn thing!"

She rolls her eyes, but pockets her phone to grip the base again. "I see you're still in a lovely mood. Would it kill you to not be such an asshole?"

"It would, actually."

For a minute, I think she's going to keep her mouth shut for once, but just as I finish placing the last piece of tape, she proves me wrong.

"I don't understand why you don't just go talk to her."

I groan, climbing down the ladder and walking away.

"This again?! Don't you ever get tired of sticking yourself in everyone else's damn business?"

"Nope. Especially not when I see the two of you miserable when you don't have to be."

Her words, mixed with the frustration of this whole situation, stop me in my tracks. I turn around to face her.

"Please. She's in her perfect house, with her perfect fiancé, planning her perfect wedding. I'm sure she's *anything* but miserable. It's time to face the facts. She's never going to leave him."

Tatum's eyes narrow. "Oh my god. Have you not talked to her at all?!"

"Not since Monday." I go to leave again but she grabs my arm.

"Colton, McKenna has been staying at her parents' house for the past week."

My stomach drops and time stands completely still. "What?" I shake my head. "But she told me. She *told me* her and Parker didn't split up."

"They didn't, not yet anyway, but she hasn't been staying with him since Saturday night. Actually, I'm pretty sure she hasn't even *seen him* since then."

Fuck. So this entire time, I've been pissed at her, beating myself up thinking she ended up choosing him, and she hasn't. This whole week she's been halfway to being mine, and I've been nothing but a prick. I screamed at her on Monday. She came to tell me, and I actually yelled at her. I should have let her talk.

"Shit, Tate. What if I screwed this all up?!" I start to pace back and forth. "I need to go find her."

"Yeah, that might be a good place to start." She answers sarcastically.

Just as I'm about to grab my keys, Maverick comes through the back gate. He had gone to pick up the keg from the liquor store. However, it's not him that makes my jaw drop – it's who's *with* him.

Olivia Benson, also known as the girl I dated for two years in college. We met at a party during freshman year and we got along well enough. What she doesn't know, however, is that I started dating her to try and keep my attention off McKenna. My best friend's fifteen-year-old sister was so far off limits that even looking her direction would've been grounds for murder. I needed a distraction, and Olivia was a pretty good one – until she wasn't.

"Look who I found!" Mav announces with way too much enthusiasm. Tatum chokes on air behind me as Olivia comes closer.

"Colton! It's been ages." She wraps her arms around me and I breathe through my mouth to avoid gagging from the overwhelming gust of perfume. When she pulls away, she turns her attention to Tatum. "And I see the golden couple is still going strong."

"Liv, hey." She graciously hugs her back, mouthing 'what the fuck' at me when Olivia can't see.

If someone asked me what I expected for the day, the idea of my best friend bringing my ex-girlfriend back from the liquor store wouldn't have even been on my radar. I haven't seen her since we broke up five years ago – a break up that was far from civil, mind you.

"Mav? A minute?" I nod toward the side of the yard.

He smirks. "Sure. You can help me get the keg from the car."

I follow him out to the driveway, doing my best to bite my tongue until I know we're out of earshot. Finally, the coast is clear.

"Okay, are you out of your mind? I mean really. Have you lost brain cells recently?! Why the hell would you bring her here?!"

Maverick chuckles. "Why not? I've seen the way you've been lately. You need to get laid."

"And you thought Liv would be the answer to that?!"

He shrugs. "Well, no. I was originally going to hire you a hooker, but then I saw her at the store and thought 'eh, close enough'. Come on man, she's always wanted you. It's not even like getting her in bed would take any effort."

I take a deep breath, forcing myself to think before I speak. If I don't, I may end up spilling everything. Such a big part of me wants to scream in his face that I *have* gotten laid recently, and that the only girl I want in my bed is McKenna. But this is not the time, nor the place, for that kind of conversation. Especially not when the fate of her and I is so unknown.

"Look, I appreciate your concern for my sex life, but please – worry about your own dick." I tell him, putting the keg down behind the tiki bar.

As I'm walking away, Maverick calls after me. "My dick is doing just fine. My woman takes care of me!" He laughs as the words leave his mouth.

"Nice." Tatum deadpans from the back door. "Real nice."

Olivia giggles as she stands by the pool. *What did I ever see in her?* I slip inside and pull Tatum with me. The second the door shuts behind us, I slam my fist down on the counter.

"Your boyfriend has lost it."

She puts her hands up. "Hey, he was *your* best friend before he was *my* boyfriend. I will not take responsibility for his crazy."

"Fair enough." I grab a beer from the fridge and pop it open. "What the hell am I going to do? I need to find McKenna, and I can't do that with Mav forcing Olivia down my throat." My eyes widen. "Oh god, Roman's party. She can't find Olivia here. She can't."

"Okay, relax. Mac isn't coming to the party."

"She's not?"

"No. She told me she didn't want to put you in an awkward place, so you don't need to worry about that. Stay at the party for a couple of hours, satisfy Maverick's weird need to involve himself in your sex life by talking to Liv, and then go get your girl."

Everything she's saying makes sense. I just hope I have the patience for it. "Okay." I nod. "Okay, yeah, I can do that. It's only a couple hours."

FOR THE 20TH TIME since she got here, I pry Olivia's talon-like nails from my arm. This girl has serious boundary issues, even more so than I remember. Just like every time before this, she loosens her grip, but keeps her hands on me. It's as if she's trying to announce her claim on me to every other woman here. Too bad for her, there isn't a single part of me that doesn't already belong to someone else.

"I cannot believe the two of you managed to work things out." Leigh, another blast from college's past, says to Olivia and me.

Nearly choking on my beer, I shake my head. "Oh, we're not back together."

Liv winces but then plasters a fake smile across her face. "Not yet, anyway. We just reunited today, but who knows what will happen."

I do. Getting back with Olivia is not, and never will be, an option. If I didn't think it would make Maverick suspicious as hell, I would've kicked her out the second she showed her face. There is nothing I want less than to be anywhere near this chick. I just need to wait for Rome to get here, then I'll be able to go find McKenna – the only one who matters.

"Brooks!" Maverick shouts from where he stands behind the bar. "You need another?"

Glancing down at my cup, I notice it's almost gone. I nod

and down the rest of it. Mav brings me another full cup. I thank him and then quickly guzzle half. If I'm going to deal with another ten minutes of Olivia, I'll need a lot more beer.

"If I didn't know any better, I'd think you're trying to get drunk." She teases and then brings her lips to my ear. "And I know how handsy you get when you're wasted."

Her words almost make me throw up in my mouth. I don't miss the way Maverick chuckles next to me. *Fucking asshole*. He knows damn well how relieved I was when her and I broke up. She was never meant to be more than a little fun in the sack. His thought process is obvious though. She's basically a guaranteed lay, but I'd rather fuck a cactus.

I'm just about to pull out my phone to text Rome when the word 'surprise' starts to echo throughout the backyard. *Thank fuck. Now I can get out of here*. I turn my head towards the noise but as soon as I do, the smile falls from my face. There, standing next to Rome, is McKenna – looking at me with nothing but hurt in her eyes.

Shit.

I can see her tears forming from here. She turns around and runs inside. Without a second thought, I pull Olivia off me and follow. Just before I get to the door, Roman steps in front of me.

"What the fuck are you doing with Olivia?!"

Rolling my eyes, I gesture toward Maverick. "Ask shithead over there. Now excuse me, I have a mess to clean up."

The second I enter the kitchen, I find McKenna pacing back and forth. Her gaze meets mine and it's like everything goes a few shades darker. Seeing her tear-stained cheeks breaks my heart.

"Mac, listen to me. It's not what you think."

A dry laugh emits from her mouth. "No? So, you aren't at a party with your ex-girlfriend hanging all over you?"

"Nothing. Happened. I was waiting for Rome to get here

so I could come find you. Why didn't you tell me you've been staying at your parents' place?"

She crosses her arms over her chest. "You didn't give me a chance. Now I see why."

"Oh stop. It's not like that." I reach out to touch her but she backs away. Groaning, I grit my teeth together. "Maverick saw her when he went to get the keg and brought her back here."

"Why would he do that?"

I shake my head. "It doesn't matter."

"*Why*, Colton?!"

My eyes stare down at the floor. I know I'm not going to get away with not answering the question.

"Because he thinks I need to get laid." It comes out as a mumble but I know she heard me by the pained noise that comes from her. "Mac, you have to believe me. I never wanted her here."

She keeps her eyes on the ceiling, trying to blink away the tears and refusing to look at me. "It's never going to change."

"What's not?"

"This! Us!" Her face is practically beet red. "I'm never going to be anything more than your dirty little secret."

The pain in my chest is excruciating as I hear what she's saying. "That's not true. McKenna, don't do this. You're so much more than that."

"Am I? Because Maverick brings home a girl for you and instead of telling him about us, or making her leave, you decide to indulge him by letting her think she has a chance with you!"

I throw my hands in the air. "I didn't think you wanted me to tell him!"

She scoffs. "It would have been better than *that*!" Stopping for a second, she takes a breath. "Everything is exactly like it was four years ago, and I won't put myself through that again."

293

Words won't formulate and my body won't move as she walks back outside – leaving me the same way I once left her, broken and alone. This can't be happening. I need her too much to let this be the end of us. There *can't* be an end to us.

A newfound level of determination builds inside of me as I head out the door. McKenna is only ten feet away, talking to Tatum about something with her back to me. I swallow down the lump in my throat, but just as I'm about to go to her, Olivia grabs my hand.

"There you are. I've been looking for you." She presses herself up against me. "I'm getting kinda bored. What do you say we go up to your room and make up for lost time?"

I peel her off me, pushing her away with both my hands on her shoulders. "I can't."

She giggles like she's still the same flirty nineteen-year-old. "Of course, you can."

"I'm dating someone." I try to step around her but she doesn't let me. My patience is hanging by a very thin, single thread.

"No, you're not." Her hand finds her hip and she looks so sure of herself. "Maverick said you're single. I think he would know if you had a girlfriend."

"He doesn't know."

She snorts. "Why not? Why wouldn't you tell your *best friend* who you're dating?"

Like the crack of a whip, my self-control snaps. "Because I'm dating McKenna!"

My voice is loud enough to be heard over anything that could provide cover to my words. Everyone goes completely silent, telling me they all heard what I said. Still, I only have eyes for one person. McKenna spins around to face me, her eyes the widest I've ever seen them.

"What are you doing?" Her voice is practically a whisper.

I smirk as I walk toward her, placing my hand on her face

as soon as I'm close enough. "What I should have done four years ago."

My lips meet hers in a heated kiss that breathes the life into me. For the first time, I'm letting the whole world see what she means to me, and I couldn't be happier. As our mouths move against one another's, everyone around us seems to fade away. It's just her and I, the only thing that matters.

I break the kiss and pull back, feeling like the weight of the world has been lifted from my shoulders. Her eyes blink open slowly and still, all I see is her – until a fist pummeling into the side of my face forces my attention away.

***

MCKENNA

Every ounce of anxiety dissipates as Colton holds me with such a gentle touch. However, it's quickly replaced tenfold when I see him get hit. His head is moved by the impact and he immediately grasps his cheek.

"Maverick!" Tatum shrieks.

Colton stretches out his jaw, then turns to glare at my brother. "What the fuck?!"

"*What the fuck* is right! You've been banging my sister?!" He lunges again, punching Colton directly in the nose.

"Stop it!" I scream, but it only makes Mav glare at me.

"Stay out of this!"

Colton cracks his neck and pinches his nose. "Don't speak to her that way."

Maverick chuckles evilly. "Oh, that's really fucking rich. How long has this been going on?!"

"Mav."

"How long?!"

Colton's eyes meet mine and I swallow, hard. His eyes soften before focusing back on Maverick.

"Since your birthday, but we had a thing before she left for NYU."

Suddenly, Maverick turns a scary shade of red and trembles with anger. He throws himself at Colton, tackling him down onto the ground and punching him once again. It's clear Colton is only trying to protect himself, but he manages to get a few hits in as well. Tatum holds me close as we scream for them to stop. Finally, Roman comes over – dropping his cup and grabbing Maverick. He pulls him off Colton and in the struggle to calm him down, they both go flying into the pool. Rome keeps his hold on Mav as the two of them emerge from the water.

"Get the fuck off me!"

"Why?! So, you can go hit your best friend some more?! Not a fucking chance."

Maverick glares at Colton from the pool as he picks himself up off the ground. "You lying sack of shit. Pack your things and get the fuck out of my house!"

Colton spits the blood in his mouth out onto the patio. "Gladly."

My chest physically hurts from watching two of the most important men in my life go at each other like animals. As soon as Maverick gets out of the pool, I slam my fists against his chest.

"What the fuck is wrong with you?! Are you fucking crazy?!" I yell in his face, but it's no use. There is no getting through to him. I turn around and head into the house.

Going straight up the stairs, I find Colton in his room – shoving as much as he can into a large duffel bag. He's actively bleeding from his forehead and wipes it with his shirt every time it starts to drip into his eye.

"Are you okay?"

It's a stupid question, one I shouldn't have asked, but I don't know what else to say. He shakes his head but doesn't answer. I go into the bathroom to get a washcloth and run it under some warm water. When I get back into the bedroom, I grab his shoulders and force him to sit down. Reluctantly, he stays put.

"Ow." He hisses as I start to clean the wound. Thankfully, it doesn't need stitches, but it looks like painful.

"I cannot believe he did this."

He snorts. "I can. You're his sister. He just wants to keep you safe."

I roll my eyes. "Yeah, well, fighting you isn't the way to do that."

"He loves you."

And I love you. The words are on the tip of my tongue, but just as I'm about to say them, the door opens. Tatum stands there, panting heavily with her clothes wet. She must have been trying to calm my brother down, and failed.

"Mac, we need you downstairs."

The sound of Maverick breaking things radiates into the room. I look to Colton and he nods.

"Go. I have a couple things left to grab."

I give him a sad smile and kiss him once more before leaving the room. I follow Tatum down the stairs to where Maverick stands in the middle of the living room. The coffee table is flipped and the lamp lies shattered on the floor. As soon as I get down there, he focuses all his anger on me.

"What the fuck were you doing up there?! Consoling your little fuck-boy?!"

"Okay, stop!" I shout, allowing myself to get in his face. He may be stupid and angry, but he would never lay a hand on me. "Stop throwing a temper tantrum like a child! That's your *best friend*. You just fought your best fucking friend!"

He scoffs and shakes his head. "*That* is not my best friend.

A best friend wouldn't go behind my back like he did. He's a fucking liar and I'm done with him!"

"You don't mean that."

"The fuck I don't. He went behind my back and fucked my baby sister, and then lied about it for *years*! I don't ever want to see his deceitful ass face again. He's dead to me, and if you have anything to do with him, so are you!"

His words cause me to recoil slightly. "Maverick."

"Don't *Maverick* me. You've been cheating on your fiancé for months with the closest person to me!"

At the worst possible time, Colton comes down the stairs and stops at the bottom. Maverick glares at him but with Roman only an arm's length away, he doesn't move. Colton doesn't even look at him, instead focusing all his attention on me.

"Are you coming?"

I take a step in his direction when my brother speaks again. "If you leave with him, you're no better than dad – and we both know how my relationship with him is."

He's trying to hurt me, and he hits his target dead on. Before my dad's cheating came to light, him and Maverick were as close as can be. They did everything together – fishing, working on cars, even talking about girls. Afterward, however, things were never the same again. It's been over four years, and Mav still can't stand being in a room with him for longer than a couple of hours. Is that really what he thinks? That I'm just like dad? Even the idea makes me sick to my stomach.

My movements halt and I realize now the choice is no longer Parker or Colton, it's *Maverick* or Colton. I can either have my boyfriend or my brother, but not both. Mav might be an asshole right now, but the man knows how to hold a grudge. I'm not sure I can handle a life without my brother.

"McKenna?" Colton's voice is soft but I can't look at him

as I shake my head and take a step back. "That's great. Just *fucking* great."

After a few footsteps, the sound of the front door slamming shut causes me to jump. He's gone. He left. We're over. The dread that washes over me is the same as what I felt that night I broke into pieces. Sobs rack over my entire body as I wrap my arms around myself.

"You made the right choice, Squid." Maverick goes to hug me.

I step away and glare at him. "Don't!"

The engine from Colton's car roars outside and his tires squeal when he rips out of the driveway. The only thing I can do is throw myself into Tatum's arms, breaking down as she catches me. All the pain I was trying to avoid, I feel it anyway. This time might even be worse.

24

MCKENNA

How many times in your life are you really sure of what you want? At eighteen years old, I never thought I would be, but lying here with Colton, I've never been so sure of anything. I want him, bad. I don't think there was ever a time where I didn't, but I never allowed myself to think too far into it. Now, even the idea of him pushing himself inside of me has me squirming in anticipated ecstasy.

"Colton?" I whisper. His thumb rubs gently over my hip, telling me he's listening. "I want you."

The movement stops and his eyes snap open. "As in…"

"I want…" I stop and take a deep breath. If I'm going to be mature enough to do it, I have to be mature enough to say it. "I want you to fuck me."

He studies my face, looking for any indication of being unsure. "Have you ever…" I shake my head. "And you want that with me? You trust me enough for that?"

"I trust you with my life."

His lips part in a smile and then seal over my own. The kiss isn't rushed or heated, it's patient – like he's making sure to savor every moment of this. I can feel him hardening in his jeans as he pulls me into him. It's not the first time he's gotten turned on around me, but it's the first time I get have it stretching me open. Colton's big, though it's not like I have much to compare to. He's thick enough for my jaw to hurt after blowing him for a few minutes, and there isn't a chance in hell of him fitting entirely in my mouth. Imagining how the pain will feel is a bit intimidating, but there isn't anything that could deter me now.

"Do you have a condom?" I murmur against his mouth.

He breaks the kiss and shakes his head. "I didn't think I'd need one. You caught me a little off guard here, Princess." I'm just about to pull my shirt back down when he perks up. "Give me one second."

Colton gets up and heads out into the hallway. No one is home. My parents are at some work party, and Maverick is at his girlfriend's for the night. We have the house to ourselves, but the idea of him being anywhere but my room still makes me nervous. If we got caught…

He comes back in and pulls me from my anxious thoughts. The condom he holds up and the grin on his face, make me laugh. He comes closer and tosses it down on the nightstand, then climbs back onto the bed.

"You just stole that from Maverick's room, didn't you?"

"Yup." He answers, popping the p.

I chuckle. "He would kill you if he found out why you took one."

His shoulders shrug. "There isn't anything about this that he wouldn't kill me for." He moves his lips to my neck and kisses softly. "Now, enough talking about your brother."

I moan, breathless, as his hand slides under my waistband and grazes my clit. My hips arch up in search of his touch. I need it. I need him.

Colton removes my clothes the same way he kisses me, slowly and delicately, like too strong of a touch may break me. My hands shake as I unbutton his jeans. He takes them into his own and presses light a light kiss to one palm.

"Relax, baby." He whispers.

The term of endearment causes butterflies to come to life in my belly. He slides his pants and boxers down his legs, leaving us both naked at last. I watch as he rips the condom open with his teeth and

302

slips it over his cock. Just as I feel him at my entrance, he lifts my chin and forces me to look at him.

"You're so beautiful, McKenna."

I jolt awake and sit up instantly, tears soaking my cheeks. My hand covers my mouth in an attempt to mask the sobs, but it's no use. I can already hear Parker stirring beside me. The hand he places on my back is meant to be comforting but it only makes things worse.

"Are you alright?" He questions tiredly.

"Fine." I tell him, but the crack in my voice gives me away.

He sighs. "It was only a dream, love. Go back to sleep."

A pain shoots through my chest and I find it hard to breathe. It wasn't just a dream – it was a memory.

I'M SITTING ON MY couch, wrapped in the softest blanket I could find. It's the only thing that brings me any sense of comfort lately. After the fight between Colton and Maverick, I waited another three days before I finally went back to my house. My mom was starting to get worried and I didn't want to go into the details of everything that happened. The truth of the matter is, we all seemed to lose everything that day.

Parker had called and asked if we could get together and talk. He's still hurt, obviously so, but he told me that he partially blames himself. He feels like if he hadn't been so busy with med school, I wouldn't have felt the need to stray. If I'm honest, I think it would have happened anyway, but the point is moot. I agreed to come home, and for the last week since I've been back, he's been trying to be more attentive.

I'd be lying if I said I'm not still dealing with the pain of losing Colton. When the house is empty, which thankfully is often, I spend my days watching Netflix and crying over a tub of ice cream. It may not be the healthiest thing, but it's all I can manage lately. Quitting that man cold turkey is the hardest thing I've ever done, and now I've had to do it twice.

The front door opens and before I know it, Tatum and Ivy are standing in between me and the TV, blocking my view. They both have determined looks on their faces that make me dread whatever is about to come from their mouths.

"Get up." Ivy demands.

I cringe. "I'd really rather not."

"I don't care what you'd *rather* do. We're going out to lunch, so get up."

I can't necessarily blame them ambushing me. I *have* been dodging all calls and texts for the past week and a half. It's clear they decided on good cop and bad cop before coming in, because as Ivy yells at me to get dressed, Tatum rubs my back and whispers that it'll be good for me.

"I'm not hungry." I grumble as I pull the shirt Ivy picked out over my head.

She shrugs. "That's fine. You can watch us eat."

"Sounds like a *blast*."

It takes longer than I'd like to admit to brush all the knots out of my hair. Self-care hasn't exactly been my top priority as of late. Still, once I'm done, the three of us climb into Tatum's car and head for the restaurant. They opt for a little place on the water, 7th Wave. Years ago, it used to be my favorite. However, now the only thing I can think of is how you can just barely see the gap in the trees and the stone ledge of mine and Colton's secret spot. I don't think I'll ever be able to handle going up there again. My heart will never mend enough for that.

As the waitress comes around, we all order drinks. Tatum and Ivy opt for water, but I ask for a glass of wine. Ivy narrows her eyes at me but waits until the three of us are alone again before saying anything.

"If you're going to drink, you need to eat something."

I scoff and focus on Tatum. "When did she become such a hard-ass?"

Tatum laughs but Ivy doesn't lighten up. "McKenna."

"Alright, alright." I cave. "I promise I'll eat something, Mom."

Despite the level of sass and sarcasm that drips from my tone, Ivy seems satisfied by my vow. I open the menu and look for the smallest thing I can find. I said I'd eat *something*. I didn't say it would be filling.

"So, I came up with this new recipe at work the other day. It's so good. I took-"

"Is that what we're gonna do?" I cut her off. "Act like everything is completely normal and hasn't gone to shit?" My attention goes to Tatum. "Have you heard anything from Colton? Is he okay?"

"I don't think this is a safe topic to talk about." Ivy intrudes, but I give her a dirty look.

"Then go somewhere else. I want to know."

She looks at Tate and then sighs, nodding. Tatum seems to understand and smiles sadly at me. "I haven't spoken to him much. Last I heard, he's staying at a motel for now."

I hum. "But he's safe? He's alive?"

"Yeah."

"That's good. And Maverick? Is he still furious?"

Something in her face twitches, telling me it's been more than difficult to handle my brother lately. "He is, but I've been working on him. I think I'll get him to come around soon, at least enough to have a civil conversation with Colton. They need to clear the air."

"They do. I never meant for all this to happen. I didn't think it would go so wrong."

Ivy puts down her phone and looks at me. "Okay, fine.

You want to talk about this, we'll talk about it. You seriously chose Parker?! After everything, you chose *Parker*?!"

I take a deep breath. I knew this question was bound to be asked at one point. Both of them were convinced I was going to end up with Colton. Hell, I thought the same thing. I know I could lie, tell them that I realized Parker is the one for me, but if I can't be honest with my best friends, my life will become a lonely place.

"I didn't." I confess. "Roman came to my house before the party and made me realize that Colton was the one I wanted. I came to the party to tell him, but when I got there, he was with Olivia."

"Olivia?!" Ivy gasps then turns to Tatum. "What the fuck was *Olivia* doing there?!"

"Maverick invited her. He thought Colton needed to get laid so he would stop being such a prick."

Ivy rolls her eyes and shakes her head. "Okay, but I thought Mav threatening you was the reason you didn't leave with Colton."

"It was." I take a sip of my wine and lean back in my seat. "At first, anyway. But then I kept thinking about how Colton was letting her hang all over him to make my brother believe his plan was working. It was *that* important to him to hide us from Maverick, and it made me think about what he was doing the first time we were together. I mean, I always assumed there were other girls, but seeing him with her just confirmed it for me I guess."

Tatum cringes. "Actually, that part may be my fault."

"What do you mean?"

"Well, he wanted to go find you as soon as I told him you'd been staying at your parents' house. I guess he realized he made a mistake not talking to you. But then, Mav came back with Olivia and he was stuck. If he tried to leave, she would have insisted on going with him. I told him to please

Maverick for a couple hours by talking to Liv, and then sneak out after Roman showed up."

Her explanation provides a little bit of relief, knowing it wasn't all his idea, but still – he let it go too far. "You told him to *talk* to her, not make it look like they were together. I mean, he can't handle seeing me in the same *room* as Parker. Can you imagine the fit he would throw if he saw his hands on me?"

They both snicker. "Point made." Ivy says. "But if you chose Colton, how did you end up back with Parker? If you're only staying with him because you don't want to be alone, is that really fair?"

"I was going to end things with him. I swear, I was, but when we met at the restaurant, I felt warm again." I shrug. "He loves me and all he wants is to make me happy. With him, I never need to worry about other women, pissed off brothers, or even getting my heart broken again. Everything's so simple and easy."

Tatum makes a face but doesn't say anything. Ivy, however, forgets how to filter herself. "So that's it?! You're going to marry Parker just because you're too afraid to take a risk?! Mac, you *love* Colton. You have for as long as I can remember."

I keep my eyes trained on the tablecloth in front of me. "Sometimes, the love of your life isn't what's best for you after all."

COLTON

The sound of pounding on the door pulls me from my drunken slumber. I pull the pillow over my head, but it's no use. I'd like to tell whoever it is to fuck off, but it could be the housekeeper and my mother taught me manners. When the banging doesn't stop, I get up and walk over to the door.

"I'm coming, I'm coming." I open it only to find Rome standing there. "Oh, it's just you."

Attempting to shut the door in his face, he shoves his boot in the way and forces himself into the room. "Not today, asshole."

He walks over to the window and pulls the blinds open. The amount of light that fills the room causes a shooting pain to ricochet in my head. I wince and use my arm to shield my eyes.

"Do you mind?!"

"No." He snaps back. "What the fuck are you doing, Colton? Do you really think this is what McKenna wants for you?!"

"Don't! You don't get to say her name to me! No one does!"

Two weeks ago, when I stood there vulnerable as hell and waiting for her to come with me, I finally felt what she did four years ago. A part of me knew the only reason she stayed was because of Maverick, but it didn't make the pain any less excruciating. When faced with the same decision I was, *Maverick or our relationship*, she chose Maverick. I couldn't necessarily blame her for it. After all, I had done the same thing.

I stayed on the boat that night, hoping she'd come find me, but she never showed. The next morning, I stopped at the liquor store and then checked into the motel. Thanks to my good friend Jack Daniels, it didn't take long to numb the pain. Thoughts of her still plagued my mind, but the emptiness in my chest ached a little less. I don't know how she got through feeling like this while staying sober. If I ever talk to her again, I'm sure that's something I'll ask.

I've had a few people check on me, like Tatum and Rome.

Even Ivy has called a couple times, but the only thing I have from the person who matters is a text message.

I'm sorry.

She sent it two days after everything was shot to hell. I didn't know what to say, and still don't, so I never answered. Any time I've asked Tatum how she is, she dodges the question. That could mean one of two things – she's just as broken as I am, or she's back with Parker. I don't have the balls to ask which it is.

"You've got to get back to work." Rome tells me. "Two weeks is long enough to wallow in self-pity. You have clients, and a business to run."

I roll my eyes and grab the bottle of Jack from the mini-fridge. "You can't fucking tell me what to do. I'm your boss!"

He gets up, ripping the bottle from my hands. "I'm your right-hand man, douchebag. Unless you want to ruin everything that you've worked so hard to build, you need to get your ass back to work, *sober*."

"Fuck off. I could fire you."

He goes to say something, but then looks down at his phone. His expression changes. "Take a shower and get dressed. You smell like a distillery."

I could fight him on it, tell him to get the fuck out and not come back, but my words would just be wasted breaths. I know that if I push him too far, he'll pick me up and throw me into the shower, clothes on and all. So, instead of making things harder on myself, I grumble a final 'screw you' and head to the bathroom.

SITTING IN HIS JEEP, I carefully watch every turn he makes. Apparently, I'm not allowed to know where we're going, but if this fucker pulls up to an AA meeting, I'll deck him right in the face. I'm not an alcoholic. I'm just using the liquid gold to make everything hurt a little less. My tension eases slightly when we pass the church. I know from living here most of my life that they host meetings in the basement on the weekends. However, as we pull up to the familiar house, my stomach churns.

"What the fuck are we doing here?!"

He doesn't answer me as he shuts off the car and climbs out. Reluctantly, and because I'm given much choice, I follow. We climb the steps of the house I've lived in for the past six months and step inside. The sound of the football game can be heard from the door. Tatum has been known to watch the sport occasionally, but only Maverick tunes in to the preseason games.

Sure enough, we walk into the living room to find Mav sitting on the couch. He nods a silent hello at Rome but doesn't even look my way. Not going to lie, his lack of acknowledgment of my presence stings. Him and I have been best friends for the last fifteen years. I never thought anything would get in between us, but I guess I was wrong.

"Sit." Rome tells me in his authoritative voice. I flip him off but do what he says anyway. "I'm going to be in the other room so you two dumbasses don't kill each other."

He walks out, leaving Maverick and I alone. The tension in here is so thick I could choke on it. I run my hands over my face, still trying to rid myself of this hangover.

"You look like shit." Mav tells me.

I roll my eyes. "Thanks asshole. You don't look much better."

"I do." He chuckles. "Rome said you haven't been at work in a while." I grunt. "And that you've practically been drinking yourself to death."

"What the fuck is this, an intervention?!"

310

"No, fucker, but you're better than this shit. What the hell are you doing with your life?!"

A dry laugh emits from the back of my throat. "Don't you get it?! *My life* lost its significance the second you threatened the *best thing in it* into leaving me."

His eyes widen at my admission. "McKenna?"

The name alone shoots daggers straight through my heart. "No, the pope. Yes, McKenna, dickwad."

"I don't get it. You could have almost any girl you want. Why the hell did you have to pick her?! She's my little sister!"

"You think I don't realize that?!" I run my fingers through my hair. "I tried for *years* to get over it. To convince myself it was only because she was the forbidden fruit, that it was just a phase – but none of it ever worked. The more I saw her, the more I needed her attention. Just being in the same room as her helped feed the monster inside me for a little while. Then one day, it didn't."

He nods, focusing down at his lap. "Don't think I haven't put two and two together. You said you two had a thing before she moved to New York. She wouldn't come anywhere near this town for years after she left, and never once asked how you were doing. She had asked about Tatum, and Roman, and our parents, but always avoided the topic of you. You hurt her, didn't you?"

"Yes." I confess, thankful that Rome is nearby. "The day before she left, she told me she wanted more. She wanted to tell everyone about our relationship and try to make the long-distance thing work."

His eyebrows raise. "And you turned her down?"

"I was a chicken shit. I was too afraid of what you would think and to lose you as a friend. Hell, maybe I even feared for my life a little bit." I tell him, reliving the biggest mistake of my life. "By the time I realized my mistake, it was too late. She was gone."

He looks like he's running it all through his mind before he looks up and groans at the ceiling. "I'll be honest, I don't like it. Don't get me wrong, you're a great guy, but she's my baby sister, man. You've known her since she was seven and you're practically my brother. Isn't that almost like incest?"

Well, that's a gross thought, but not at all accurate. I shake my head. "She may be your sister, but she's my everything."

"Y-you're in love with her, aren't you?"

He knows that word isn't something I take lightly. When I dated Olivia, she said it to me for most of the time we were together, and I never once said it back. I haven't used that word to or about anyone – not that they know of anyway. Therefore, the heaviness of my answer is not lost on me.

"Yeah, I am. I have been for a long time."

Grabbing the throw pillow from beside him, he throws it at me. "God damn it, Brooks. Now I feel like an asshole. I thought you two were just fooling around. She's had a thing for you since we were kids and I thought you were taking advantage of that. But if this is serious…"

My eyes land on the large binder lying open on the coffee table. Tatum usually hides it when I'm around, so she must not have known I'd be coming here. As I glance at it, I see that she just made a call about catering yesterday. *She's still planning the wedding. There's still a wedding.*

"No." My knuckle knocks twice against the table. "She made her choice. She's his now."

25

MCKENNA

THE CLASSROOM IS LINED WITH ALL THE BRIGHTEST colors. My students' names are written perfectly on desk mats. Even all my supplies are organized to a fault. To say I'm nervous about my first day would be an understatement. I've been imagining this for years and I need it to go flawlessly. *Something in my life needs to be how I pictured it.*

I watch the minutes tick by as I await the arrival of the tiny humans I get the pleasure of teaching this year. I'd met them all a week ago during orientation. Each one of them is so sweet and eager to learn. The amount of fun we're going to have this year is immeasurable.

A knock on the door startles me. I place a hand on my heart and turn to see who it is. Principal Jackson enters the room with a shy smile, holding a vase of flowers.

"I'm sorry. I didn't mean to scare you."

I shake my head. "No, you're fine. I was zoned out. What have you got there?"

"*These* were delivered for you."

He places the vase on my desk and I catch a glimpse of the card.

Good luck on your first day. I love you. – Parker

The bouquet is beautiful, with white and pink roses, baby's breath fillers, and vibrant green leaves. It's everything I should love, but it only makes me think of the ones Colton sent me the morning of my interview. *Calla lilies, my favorite.*

"From your boyfriend?" Principal Jackson asks.

"Fiancé." I smile. "We're getting married at the end of this month."

His eyebrows raise. "Wow, that's fantastic. Congratulations!"

"Thank you."

Tatum has been losing her mind with all the planning. I cannot count the number of times she's yelled at me for not only making her do this on such short notice, but having her slow down for a couple of weeks. According to her, every minute is vital. A part of me considered using that as an excuse to postpone the wedding, but I couldn't bring myself to tell Parker that I don't want to marry him this fall - especially not when I know Tatum *can* get it done.

"Are you going to need time off for the honeymoon? I'd like to know in advance if I need a substitute."

"Oh, no." I chuckle. "That won't be necessary. Parker is a med student. I'm lucky he found enough time to have a wedding, let alone go on a honeymoon."

He nods in understanding. "Well, it looks like it's time to go get the kids from the gym. How about we walk down there together?"

Getting up from my desk, the two of us leave the room and head toward the boisterous sound children playing. *Here goes nothing.*

THE DAY GOES ACCORDING to plan, and I cannot seem

to keep the smile from my face. All my students are incredible little kids. They were shy at first, but once we started to play a few 'break the ice' games, they warmed right up. I can already tell this year is going to be amazing.

I pack up and make my way to the exit, waving goodbye to other members of the faculty as I pass. When I get into my new car - something Parker bought me when we both decided a Vespa isn't cold weather friendly - I realize who the first person I want to tell about my day is.

Ever since I got the flowers from Parker this morning, I haven't been able to get Colton off my mind. He's the most supportive person I know, and I can picture him now – smiling brightly as he listens to me ramble about how much I love my students already.

It's been too long since I've seen him. Since I've heard his voice, since I've touched his skin. Tatum mentioned that he moved back in after a couple weeks. I was glad to hear that him and Maverick worked it out. The last thing I want is for them to lose each other; they're too close for that.

I haven't been able to bring myself to go to my brother's house since the day of Roman's party. Even when Colton wasn't there, I knew every inch of that place would remind me of him. And since he moved back in, I've stayed away to avoid seeing him. Judging by the way he's been absent from family dinners, he's doing the same.

PARKER GETS HOME A few hours after I do. I'm cooking sausage and peppers for dinner when he comes up behind me and wraps his arms around my waist. I smile as he places a light kiss to my cheek.

"Hello, love." He greets me.

"Hi. You hungry?"

"Starved. How was your first day?"

"It was better than I could have imagined. The kids are so smart and kind. I couldn't have asked for better students." Putting the lid back on the pan, I turn to lean on the counter, only to find him staring down at his phone. "Are you even listening?" He doesn't answer. "Parker?!"

"Huh? Oh, yeah, that's great."

I roll my eyes, unsure of why I even bother. Med school has always seemed to take priority over me. It's something I should be used to by now and for the most part, I am. Since I moved back a month ago, him and I have worked to get back to where we were before my affair. For the first two weeks, I had his undivided attention. However, when I finally started to *want* him around me again, he went back to focusing on school. I guess that's what I get – my karma for cheating on the person I promised to spend forever with.

My phone ringing on the counter is the only thing that pulls Parker from whatever he was doing. I glance over to see Maverick's name on the screen.

"Who is it?" He questions accusingly.

I exhale, frustrated but understanding of his paranoia. "My brother."

It took a little while after the fight for things between Maverick and I to be okay. Despite not leaving with Colton in order to not lose my brother, I couldn't bring myself to talk to him. Not only did he physically attack Colton, but he said some really hurtful things to me. It wasn't until I started to feel a little more stable that I saw him at our parents' house for dinner. We ended up agreeing to let bygones be bygones. I had lied and hidden things from him, and he had reacted badly to finding out about it.

I answer the phone and put it to my ear. "Hey Mav. What's up?"

"How much do you love me?"

"Depends. What do you want?"

He hesitates for a minute. "I'm trying to get everyone

together for a night out on Saturday. It's *really* important to me that you be there."

Everyone. The word sticks out like a flashing neon sign in my mind. Could I handle seeing *him* again? I know there is no chance in hell that Parker will let me go without him. The mere thought of me being within 100 feet of Colton enrages him. Still, I know Maverick wouldn't be asking if it wasn't a big deal.

I sigh. "What time and where?"

He excitedly gives me the name of a fancy place in Boston and tells me to get there around six o'clock on Saturday. After thanking me repeatedly, we say goodbye and get off the phone. *Well, this should be interesting.*

COLTON

I'm putting the final sketches of a blueprint I've been working on. It's a two-story house meant to replicate the one my client grew up in as a child. A little weird, in my opinion, but I can understand the sentimental value. As I pick up my stylus from the tablet, a knock sounds on my door.

"Mr. Brooks?" My sister teases as she addresses me. "There's a Mr. Stanford here to see you."

Avery was complaining about wanting money for things. While I was more than willing to just write her a check, our mother told me it wouldn't help in teaching her the value of a dollar. So instead, I hired her as my part-time secretary. She may be making more than the average sixteen-year-old, but what can I say? I've always had a soft spot for that little girl.

"Did he say what he wanted?" She shakes her head. "Strange. Okay, send him in."

Landon Stanford is a former client of mine. Not only did I design his last two houses, but I've also redone his office. He probably has another idea in mind, or his wife is once again growing tired of their perfect home. Every time she watches something on HGTV, she ends up going on this tyrant about building a new house. It doesn't end until he gives in to whatever she wants. Not that it matters much to him – they have more money than God.

"Ah, if it isn't my favorite architect." He greets with a too friendly smile as he comes into the room.

I stand up from my desk and shake his hand. "Landon. To what do I owe this pleasure?"

He chuckles. "See, that's what I like about you, Brooks. Straight and to the point, 100% of the time."

"No better way to be." I glance at the clock. "Besides, I have somewhere to go soon. You caught me just before I was leaving."

"I better make this fast then." He sits down across from me and rests his ankle on the opposite knee. "Cora and I are moving to Los Angeles. She's decided that we've outgrown it here and I'm inclined to agree."

My eyes widen. "Wow, that's quite a move. Although, I'm not sure what it has to do with me."

"Well, for one, I'd like for you to design our house there as well as oversee the construction. I don't know anyone out there enough to trust them with it." I go to respond when he holds up one finger. "Secondly, I've purchased a very large piece of land right outside of the city. My plan is to build a development on it."

"And you'd like me to design the plans for the houses." I finish for him.

He grins. "Precisely."

Standing, I push my chair in. "While I'm honored you're considering me-"

"I'm not just considering you, son." He interrupts.

318

"You're the only one I'm willing to work with on this. So, before you turn me down, take a few days to think on it. There's no rush."

After working with this man so many times, I know he's not one who gets turned down often. Still, I have way too much on my mind right now to add this to the pile. I nod, letting him know that I'll consider the offer, and the two of us leave my office.

I PULL UP TO the club in my overpriced suit. If Maverick and Tatum weren't the closest people to me, there's no way I'd be here right now. I've already been given the heads up by Tate that Parker will be here with McKenna – unsurprisingly enough. From what I've heard lately, he's been keeping her on a tight leash since she decided to work on things. I really wish I knew what she sees in him. Maybe then it would be a little easier to come to terms with the fact that she's not mine.

The valet waves me toward them but I choose to park my car myself. Not only do I not trust any of these people to drive my overpowered baby, but I also need another minute to breathe before I go inside. Roman already texted me, letting me know that McKenna is there. She's less than 500 feet away, and Christ, my body knows it.

It took two weeks before I could stand to think her name, longer until I could hear it spoken without zoning out into a depressed state of nothingness. Maverick has jokingly told me to man up more times than I'd like to admit. Realistically, I've been in love with McKenna Taylor for years. It's going to take a bit longer than a month to get over it.

Giving my name to the bouncer, he pulls back the rope and lets me through. It's not like any club I've ever been to. The music that's playing is less 'bump and grind' and more classy instrumentals. All the men are dressed in suits, and the women in dresses. It's clearly an expensive place, not that I expected any less with what Maverick has planned for tonight.

I grab a beer from the bar and then go to stand along the railing, overlooking the dance floor. As if my eyes are drawn to her, they immediately find McKenna in the crowd. She's spinning around with a smile on her face that says she doesn't have a single worry in the world. She looks so carefree and happy that I almost forget how to breathe. Seeing her again makes me feel a way I haven't in weeks.

"Might want to wipe that drool off your chin before someone notices." Maverick teases, suddenly appearing next to me.

I scoff playfully. "Have your nerves made you piss yourself yet?"

"Ha-ha. No, asshole. I've got this in the bag."

"You sure? She could turn you down again." When the smile drops right off his face, I smirk. "I'm kidding. She loves you. Not sure why, but she does."

He takes a sip of his beer and then turns to lean against the railing, facing me. "Probably for the same reason Mac loves you."

I should've known he would bring this up. If there is one thing Maverick is incapable of, it's minding his own damn business. Him and Tatum really are two peas in a pod.

"Don't go there, man. Not tonight."

He nods in defeat but still makes sure to have the last word. "All I'm saying is you could fight for her. I mean, you waited years for a chance to get her back. Giving up now just seems like a waste."

With one last shrug, he walks away and leaves me to ponder my thoughts. What if he's right? McKenna being the one for me has been the only sure thing in my life since I was a kid. Breaking her heart was a mistake that I beat myself up over endlessly. For us to end like this, to end at all, feels like everything we went through was for nothing.

Parker comes out of nowhere and takes McKenna into his arms. When her eyes meet his, she smiles even brighter. She clings to him like she used to do with me, only, she's happier. The ring she always remembered to take off glistens in the chandelier lighting, a blatant reminder of what's bound to be the worst day of my life, only a couple weeks away. As much as I wish Maverick was right, he's not.

I'M STANDING WITH TATUM and Roman, laughing at Rome's inability to keep his attention off Ivy. I don't understand why he doesn't just make a move. She's sweet, gorgeous, and single – the perfect trifecta. Still, he stays away and watches her from a distance.

"You know, I could find out if she's interested." Tatum suggests.

He turns to glare at her. "Absolutely not. You start asking questions like that and she's going to figure it out. It's bad enough this dipshit told McKenna."

I chuckle. "It slipped! Besides, that was over a month ago and she hasn't said anything."

"Who hasn't said anything about what?" Ivy steps up with a newly made drink in her hands.

Rome's eyes go wide as I choke on my beer. Tatum laughs. "No one has said anything about how handsome Roman looks all dressed up."

"Oh." She checks him out from head to toe, somehow missing that he's practically squirming under her gaze. "Yeah, you clean up nice Rome."

"T-thanks."

Her eyes narrow at his stutter, but just as she's about to

say something, a voice that has my heart on overdrive interrupts.

"There you are! Ivy, you can't just leave me with no heads up. I probably looked like a weirdo dancing out there all on my own!"

McKenna is so busy yelling at her best friend that she doesn't even notice my presence. All eyes are on me, except for hers, trying to gauge my reaction. I do my best to keep my face neutral, but my skin is crawling. I shove my one free hand into my pocket to avoid reaching out to touch her.

"Are you even listening to me?!" Finally, Mac follows Ivy's line of sight until she lands on me – finding me already staring back at her. She swallows hard. "Colton."

All the times my name has rolled off her tongue play in my mind, each one sounding better than the last. This one, however, is different. This one sounds pained, and trust me when I say I know the feeling.

"McKenna. How've you been?"

"Good." She tells me, but I can see in her eyes that she's lying. "How's everything with you?"

Over the 15 years that I've known this girl, she's always been honest with me. Yet, here we are, exchanging forced pleasantries and lying about something as simple as how life is. The reality of the situation hits me straight in the gut. I can't do this. Not with her.

"Excuse me." I tell her with the best polite smile I can manage.

No one tries to stop me as I walk away and head for the bathroom. Immediately going to the sink, I cup water into my hands and splash it onto my face. *I'm here for Maverick. Tonight is important for Maverick.* I take a calming breath, but am quickly right back where I started when a stall door opens and Parker steps out of it. His reflection in the mirror comes closer as he chooses the sink right beside mine.

"Mr. Brooks." He spits my name out like a disease.

"Look, Parker, I really don't want any trouble."

He laughs humorlessly. "Maybe you should have thought about that before you shagged my fiancée." Turning off the water and grabbing a towel to dry his hands, he looks straight at me. "How do you live with yourself, knowing the one person who thought she would always love you, doesn't anymore? Must make you feel like quite the failure."

"Do *not* speak to me about McKenna. She may be marrying you, but I will *always* mean more to her than you do." I growl.

"See, that's where you're wrong, mate. You think I haven't heard her and Ivy talking about you? About how she'll never truly be able to trust you? That's what happens when you destroy a girl. Little pieces get lost in the mess of it all, and no matter how impeccably you put her back together, she'll never be the way she once was – and she'll *never* look at you the way she once did."

"You don't know anything about the way she looks at me."

He throws his head back in evil laughter. The sound of it makes me want to sucker punch him in the stomach. "I don't need to, because I can give her what you never could – safety, trust, and security. You see, if she were to be with you, she would always wonder when the next argument is going to happen or if that day will be the day she gets her heart broken again. She will never feel secure in a relationship with you. With me, however, she doesn't have to worry about any of that. I can give her the love and future she's always dreamed of having."

My blood is boiling as I clench my fists. "Yeah? Well, have fun spending your days knowing what you have with your wife, will never even begin to compare to what she had with me."

Placing the towel back down onto the counter, he looks like he's about to walk away but stops. "Face it, Brooks. I'm the better man for her. Surely you know this, or you wouldn't be getting so angry. And if you love her the way I think you do, you'll leave her alone and let her be happy."

He pushes past me with his shoulder and exits the room, allowing everything he just said to sink in.

IF I THOUGHT SEEING McKenna with Parker was hard before, it's fucking unbearable now. He makes sure to have one hand on her at all times, giving me snide glances that show he's only doing it to rub in that he can and I can't. I try to keep all my attention on the conversation I'm having with Roman, but even he sees that I'm struggling.

"I could spill a drink on him." He suggests. "That suit looks expensive enough to at least piss him off a little."

I chuckle but shake my head. "Thanks man, but that's alright. I don't want to ruin this night for Mav."

His eyes narrow. "I thought he just wanted to pretend to be rich snobs for the night. What does he have planned?"

The sound of Maverick trying to get all our attention meets our ears. "You're about to find out."

I watch as my best friend holds a glass of champagne in his hand and looks like he's going to vomit. "I have something I'd like to say." He looks to me for reassurance and I give him a curt nod. Then, he focuses on his girlfriend. "Tatum, for as long as I've known you, I have loved you. We've spent the past eight years together and still, it isn't nearly enough. You're my best friend, sorry Brooks..." We all laugh as I feign being hurt. "... you're my favorite person, and you're the only one I can see myself spending the rest of my life with." Tears start pouring down Tatum's face as Maverick places his champagne on the table and gets down on one knee. "I'm going to ask you this again, and I'm not taking no for an answer this time. Tatum Elizabeth Blakley, will you marry me?"

The question is barely out of his mouth before she nods and mumbles a watery yes. All the women are crying and even Roman is blinking away a tear as Maverick pulls the ring from the box and slips it onto her finger. *God, I want that.*

My gaze finds McKenna, though I instantly wish it hadn't. I catch sight of her just in time for Parker to dip her back and press his lips to hers. My stomach churns with jealousy. When they break the kiss, however, it gets worse. Because there, right in front of my eyes, I can see it. The happiness etched across her face is pure, untainted, and without any bit of hesitation. *Parker was right, he's the better man for her.*

The revelation is too much. It feels like the room is closing in on me and the air is too thick to breathe. Before I can look away, McKenna's eyes meet mine. The smile is wiped from her face by what I can only assume is the pain she sees all over my own. Let's face it, that girl can read me like an open book. Even if I attempted to mask it, she'd know. I have to get out of here.

I congratulate Maverick and Tatum, giving them each a hug and teasing Tatum about how I'm stuck with her for life now. In a silent exchange, Mav can see that I need to leave and takes no offense by my exit.

"See you at home?"

I nod. "Take your time. I'll be alright."

Pushing through the crowd of people, I finally get out the front door. The fresh air only provides a small amount of relief from the ache in my chest. The further I get from here, *from her*, the better. I'm halfway to my car when a familiar voice calls my name.

"Colton, wait."

I don't stop walking. "Go back inside, McKenna."

"Colton!"

"I said go back inside!" I spin around to face her. "Go back in there with your future husband and live the life I could never give you."

Her eyebrows furrow. "What are you talking about?"

"Nothing." I turn and continue to my car. "It doesn't matter anymore."

None of it does.

26

MCKENNA

The room is decorated beautifully with balloons and lace that match the theme of my engagement party. A large banner hangs over the breathtaking view of the water. *"Congratulations Future Mrs. Hall."* The name on the sign matches the one of my sash. When Tatum does something, she really goes all out.

I'm talking to my grandmother about how I'm all grown up when two unexpected guests come through the door. *Avery and Mrs. Brooks.* It's not that their presence is unwanted, I just didn't think they'd be here. I excuse myself from my grandmother and go over to say hello.

"McKenna!" Avery greets me. It's crazy to see how big she's gotten. The last time I saw her, she was twelve.

"Hey, Av. Wow, look at you!"

"Me?!" She gives me a once over. "You look amazing! My brother is an idiot for not snatching you up when he had the chance."

I tense at the mention of Colton but mask it quickly. "And Mrs. Brooks, it's great to see you again."

"You too, dear. Congratulations on getting married." She

gives me a warm smile. "I hope he knows what a lucky man he is."

"Thank you. I hope so, too."

After a few minutes, Ivy comes over and pulls me away. As much as I love Colton's family, I'm glad for the distraction. There are too many people here for me to be zoning out thinking of what it would be like if things were different – if the sash read *Future Mrs. Brooks*.

THE DAY IS FILLED with games and tons of people asking me things like if we're going to start a family right away and if we plan on moving to England. Apparently, marrying a British man means immediately leaving the country and getting knocked up. When Ivy saw me roll my eyes at the question for the fifth time, she implemented a new game – no saying England, baby, bride, groom, or wedding.

By the time the party is over, I'm exhausted. I've opened more presents and thanked more people than should be allowed in a four-hour period. I step out onto the back porch to get some fresh air and look at the water. Nothing makes sense to me. I should be in a better mood today. In one week, I'll be getting married. This is supposed to be a happy time, so why am I just...not?

"Mind if I join you?" Mrs. Brooks asks hesitantly.

I glance back at her and smile. "Not at all." She comes to stand next to me and the two of us admire the view. "Did you have a nice time?"

"Oh, it was lovely. Tatum is very good at her job."

"She is." I agree.

The sound of the water and seagulls fills the silence before she finally speaks again. "I have something to give you but I don't want it to make you feel uncomfortable in any way. I just wouldn't feel right keeping it from you."

"Okay?"

She opens her purse and takes out a tattered envelope. "The morning you left for New York, Colton had rushed out of the house only to come back less than a half hour later. He had this in his hand. Maybe it was wrong of me to keep it, but I know that if you weren't already gone when he got there, this would've gotten to you."

Written on the front is my name in Colton's handwriting. The revelation of everything is making my heart hurt. "He came after me?"

She nods. "When he came home, he wouldn't speak to me, or to anyone for that matter. He crumbled up the letter and threw it in the trash."

"Well, thank you, for saving it and for giving it to me."

"Of course, dear."

She places a hand on my arm and squeezes lightly before heading back inside. Immediately, I open the envelope and pull out the letter.

McKenna,

By the time you're reading this, you're probably already on your way to NYU and I'm most likely off moping somewhere, missing you. This past summer has been the best time of my life, and that's all because it had you in it. I know after our talk yesterday you probably think that you meant nothing more to me than a good time. Hell, you had those suspicions the whole time – but I want you to know that you're wrong. There has never been anyone but you, not for a long time. What we have between us is something I can't even begin to explain, and I don't want to lose it. You were right when you said that we could make this work. I don't see a reason why we can't. So your brother will be mad, and may even kill me in my sleep, but who cares? The truth is, you're worth the risk. What I'm trying to say is that if you still want me, and you want to try an actual, legitimate, public knowledge relationship, then I want that too because I love you, McKenna. There's never been a day where I haven't.

See you soon (I hope),
Colton

My vision is blurry from the tears welling up in my eyes. There are a million things going through my mind right now, but the main thought is crystal clear. *I need to see him.* Running inside, there's no one around but Avery. Since the altercation we had at the club, I know he won't answer if I text him, but his sister on the other hand…

"Av, I need to borrow your phone."

She narrows her eyes at me. "Uh, why? Yours is right in your hand."

"Please." I beg. "I'll do anything. I just need two minutes."

Reluctantly, she hands over her phone and I immediately open a text with Colton.

Avery: Where are you?

It only takes a few seconds before he's typing.

Colton: The docks. Why? Everything okay?

That's all I need to know. I toss the device back at Avery and thank her as I book it outside. In the distance, I can see the tops of the masts. I take off my heels and start sprinting towards the boats. By the time I get there, I have no idea what I'm going to say – only that I need to say *something*.

I turn onto the ramp and run down towards the slip.

Jumping onto the boat, I can hear Colton's voice from the cabin.

"What the hell?" He comes up the steps and his eyes meet mine. "Mac? What are you doing here?"

"Why didn't you tell me?!" I hold up the letter that's clenched tightly in my hand. "All this time, and you never told me."

His eyes widen when he realizes what it is. "Where did you get that?"

"It doesn't matter! What matters is I didn't get it from you!" I throw it onto the ground in front of him and let my shoulders sag in defeat. "You came after me."

"I did."

"What kind of coward goes after someone and then doesn't have the balls to tell them?!"

"Coward?!" He seethes. "Maybe if you had waited and not gotten engaged to the first man that came along, I would've had the chance to tell you!"

"I *waited* for you to get your head out of your ass for two years! Two *fucking* years, Colton! You never said a damn word!"

He throws his hands in the air and takes a step toward me. "How could I when you had blocked me in every possible way?! You made it pretty fucking clear that you moved on and I was *not* welcome in your world anymore!"

"You left! I put my heart on the line for you. I told you what I wanted, I put myself out there, and you walked out the door."

He scoffs and looks down at the ground. "A mistake I'll regret for the rest of my life, believe me."

My anger is doused by his honesty. "You loved me."

"I did."

"Did?" I'd be lying if I said I wasn't disappointed.

"Do." He corrects. "But it doesn't matter anymore."

"Why do you keep saying that?! It matters and you know it."

He runs his fingers through his hair frustratedly. "Why, McKenna? Why does it matter?"

"B-because. Because I... I..." My brain is working but my mouth just won't cooperate. "It just does!"

"It doesn't. If it did, you'd be able to say what's going through your mind right now."

Shaking his head, he goes to walk away. My body shifts into ultimate panic mode as I see that I'm losing him, again.

"Colton?!" I shout in desperation. When he stops and turns around, our eyes meet. Suddenly, the most truthful words I've ever said flow from my mouth with ease. "I love you."

He closes the distance between us in just a few steps, slipping his hand around the back of my neck and pulling my mouth to his. I don't hesitate to kiss him back. Our tongues collide and tangle together. As he grips my waist, my entire body responds to his touch. It's like feeling it for the first time all over again.

"Inside, now." He murmurs against my lips. "Before every bit of my restraint snaps and I fuck you right here."

I don't need to be told twice. Grabbing his hand, I lead the way down into the cabin. Just as he closes and locks the door, I use the belt loop of his jeans to pull him toward me. He gazes at me with such want and need that it almost knocks the wind out of me. There's no denying what's about to happen.

Taking the hem of his shirt in my hands, I peel the fabric from his muscled body. Once it's free for me to admire, I run my hands down his chest, onto his abs, then to his waistband. I look up at him through my lashes and pull my bottom lip between my teeth – that's all it takes. He growls and takes a step forward, pressing himself up against me.

"I need you to say it, McKenna."

It takes a couple seconds to figure out what he means. Then, it hits me. *He wants consent, and fuck that's sexy.*

"Make love to me, Colton."

He whimpers as the final piece of him stops resisting and crashes into me, pushing us back through the cabin and into the bedroom. I'm lifted up and placed on the bed before he pulls my dress off. His one hand cups my face while the other unclips my bra. As soon as it slips down my arms, he moves his attention to my breasts. Taking one nipple into his mouth, he teases the other between his thumb and index finger. I throw my head back and release a pleasured moan.

I lay back as he starts kissing down my stomach, all the way to right above my panties. He pulls them to the side, teasingly blowing over my sex. I squirm at the sensation, but just when I'm about to chastise him, he lunges forward and sucks on my clit. Two fingers slip inside of me and he crooks them to rub the bundle of nerves inside. It feels so good that I swear I see stars. My hands grip the bed sheets as the pressure starts to build in my core. Judging by the way he speeds up, I know he can feel it too. If I make it through this orgasm alive, it'll be a miracle.

I arch my hips, grinding myself against his mouth. It's so intense, how he devours me like I'm his favorite meal. My body craves his touch in a way that no other man can satisfy, and now that I have it again, I don't think I'll ever be able to stop.

Our eyes lock and he lets out a moan, sending me over the edge and into euphoric oblivion. My whole body shakes as he rides me through my high. Before I've even come down, I can hear him removing his belt. He slips his arms under me and lifts me up, pinning me to the door. When I feel myself stretch around him, I'm sure I'm going to combust.

He lowers me down onto his thick length, only to lift me back up again. Finding his rhythm takes a minute, but once he does, there's no holding back. He attaches his lips to my neck as he pounds into me, rattling the door with every thrust.

"Tell me again."

I know it's not consent he's looking for, because we're well past that. I quiver as I figure it out. "I love you, Colton." My voice is breathy. "I love you."

"Fuck, I love you, too."

To read it in a letter was one thing, but to hear it come from his mouth is something entirely different. Tears spring to my eyes as I listen to him repeat the words that I've been dying to hear for so long.

"I love you so damn much, McKenna."

His motions start to get sloppy and before I know it, he's emptying himself inside of me while I explode around him. My body sags against his. How he manages to keep us upright is beyond me. I'm in a state of sexed out bliss as he carries me over to the bed and gently lays me down. I roll over to snuggle into his side, sighing in relief when he wraps his arm around me.

"My Colton." I mumble tiredly.

He chuckles. "All yours, Princess. That's never changed."

COLTON

The two of us are lying in bed, still naked from when we ripped each other's clothes off earlier, when McKenna's phone starts to vibrate next to us. Parker's name flashes across the screen. Without any hesitation, she hits ignore. I should be happy with her obvious choice to be with me instead, but as she turns her head to look at me, I see it – the stress and fear written all over her face.

"She will never feel secure in a relationship with you." The irritating British voice repeats inside my head. *"If you love her the way I think you do, you'll leave her alone and let her be happy."*

As much as it kills me to admit it, maybe the trust fund brat is right. The way she looked at him the night of Maverick's engagement – she was happy, there's no denying that. There wasn't any hesitation or confusion. She was free to just *be*. If she hadn't gotten ahold of that letter, which I can only assume was the handiwork of my mother, would she still have come back to me after all? I could spend hours convincing myself that she would, but the truth is I'm not sure – and reading a letter from four years ago isn't enough of a reason to throw everything good for her to hell.

"So, where do we go from here?" She asks, lightly rubbing her knuckle in between the ridges of my abs.

I take a deep breath, knowing the answer is going to hurt both of us like hell. "Now, you go and marry Parker."

"W-what?! But... But we just... You said..."

"I know what I said, and I meant it with everything I am, but that doesn't change anything."

She scoffs. "The hell it doesn't! Why are you doing this? If you love me, why are you sending me away?"

I sit up to face her but I can't let my eyes meet hers. If I see the pain in them, I'll cave. "He's the better man for you, Mac. There's no denying that."

"Isn't that for me to decide?!"

"Maybe, if I thought you'd make the right choice, but I know if given the option, you'd pick me. You *can't* pick me."

A choked sob is muffled by her hand as she covers her mouth. "Oh, I get it. You just wanted one last fuck. One last time to remember me by, right?! You never actually wanted me. You never wanted *this*."

"That's not true and you know it."

"Do I?! Because I'm starting to believe I don't know anything about you anymore." She picks her dress up off the

335

floor and throws it on. "I can't believe I let you do this to me, *again*." After grabbing her phone, she rushes out the door.

"McKenna!" I try but it's no use.

She's long gone before I even make it onto the dock.

LATER THAT NIGHT, I'M lying in my bed, replaying the events of today in my head. God, when she showed up looking like a perfect mix between completely enamored and royally pissed, I was knocked off my axis. I had no idea my mother even kept that letter, let alone planned to give it to her. I would lecture her about the importance of not meddling in other people's lives, but I know it would just be a waste of breath. Her intentions were good, her timing was just a little off.

When I got home, Tatum didn't even let me make it to the stairs before she pushed me up against the wall and kneed me in the balls. Then, after I caught my breath enough to explain, she did it again. According to her, there's a fine line between being chivalrous and being an idiot. Still, there's nothing she could say that would change my mind. McKenna is better off with Parker, and while I wish things were different, they're not – which is what brings me to my current dilemma.

I stare at my phone, my finger hovering over Landon Stanford's name. For the past three hours, I've been debating on whether or not to call. The job offer in Los Angeles is a great opportunity for me. I could have Roman running the show here – he's more than qualified – and I'd be leading a new project out in California. However, what's really making me consider taking it, is McKenna. By getting out of this small town, I'd finally be able to give her what she needs – freedom.

Facing the facts, I know that if I stay here, her and I will never fully be over. There's always going to be that drunken night where we fall into bed together, or those fleeting looks across crowded parties. The constant battle between Parker and I in her head will never end, and that's no way to live. She deserves to have her dreams come true. She deserves the perfect marriage with the beautiful children and the white picket fence. *She deserves to be happy.*

I press call and put the phone to my ear. It only takes a couple rings for him to answer, and I can tell by his tone, he's thrilled to hear from me.

"Mr. Brooks, I was expecting to have to call you."

I swallow down the lump in my throat. "Well, what can I say? You're a very hard man to say no to. So, tell me more about this job in LA."

27

MCKENNA

I SIT ON THE EDGE OF MY BED, REREADING THE letter for what's probably the millionth time in the last week. No matter how much it hurts, I can't seem to stop. How did we go from what's written on this paper, to where we are now? This isn't how things are supposed to be. This *isn't* how my life was supposed to go.

My bedroom door opens and in one swift movement, I shove the letter back into my nightstand and kick the drawer closed. Thankfully, it's just Ivy – who rolls her eyes and shakes her head. *Yeah, I'm busted.*

"Reading that thing *again*?!"

I shrug. "I just don't get it."

She sits on my bed next to me and gives me a sympathetic look. "If you're so hung up on this, why are you still getting married?"

Ah, the infamous question – why. There are a million things I could tell her, but I can predict her response to every single one. I love Parker; *but you love Colton more.* I see a future with Parker; *if that were true, you wouldn't be imagining a future with Colton.* Parker loves me; *so does Colton.* The list goes on and on, but one thing remains the same. If Colton really

339

meant what he said, he wouldn't have pushed me away under the pretenses of it being what's best for me.

I come to a conclusion and stand up. "You're right, it's stupid. I'm over it."

"Okay, that's *not* what I meant."

"Well, in the words of the infuriating Colton Brooks, it doesn't matter anymore. Now, where did you say my dress for this dinner is? I need to start getting ready."

And just like that, I vow to leave this conversation and all thoughts of *him* where they belong – in the past.

***

THE WHITE LACE FABRIC clings to my body, making me glad I got so tan over the summer. Its cocktail-like length goes down to just above my knees. It's probably a little more revealing than Parker's mother would prefer, judging by the looks she keeps giving me, but I like it. Besides, it's only the rehearsal dinner. It's not like my wedding dress is this short.

"Everything alright?" Parker asks with a caring hand on my lower back.

I smile up at him. "Couldn't be better."

We haven't seen each other for most of the day. His mom flew in and insisted they go to lunch together – without me. I've only met the woman on a few occasions, mostly when she would come and try to talk Parker into going back to England. However, each time was never very pleasant. It's not that she doesn't like me, it's just that she would rather see her son with a woman of the same wealth, same social status, and preferably British. Any reason for him to stay in America is her undoing. Thoughts of Colton's mother start to flow through my mind, but I instantly push them out. *Leave it in the past.*

The restaurant Parker rented out for the event is fancier than I would have preferred but gorgeous all the same. I find my comfort zone by sticking near Ivy, Tatum, Maverick, and Rome. He who shall not be named was invited, but politely declined; much to my fiancé's satisfaction. Still, it's probably for the best. Tonight is about Parker and I, and the marriage we're about to embark on.

Marriage, wow. It's a word with such strength that I never fully took into account. In two days, I will be standing in front of God and everyone we love, and promise to spend the rest of my life with him. That thought alone makes me both excited and uneasy. I embrace the former and ignore the rest. It's just your typical cold feet – nothing to be alarmed about.

JUST BEFORE DINNER IS served, I start to feel the pressure under my future mother-in-law's harsh glare, so I go outside to get some fresh air and a minute away. Maverick is already out there, holding his phone in his hand and looking like someone just told him some of the worst news of his life. His face is pale and if I didn't know any better, I'd think he's about to cry.

"Are you okay?" I question hesitantly.

He snorts and shakes his head. "Define okay. Everything as I once knew it is gone. In a couple days, my whole life is going to be different and there isn't a damn thing I can do about it."

"Uh, what are you talking about?"

"This!" He snaps, shoving his phone into my face. "Congratulations, you did it. You pushed my best friend right out of my life."

My heart drops as I grab the device and read over the text message.

Colton: Hey Mav. I just wanted to give you a heads up that there are boxes in the hallway. I ended up taking

that job in LA. It's a really great opportunity for me and I would be an idiot to pass it up. My flight is on Sunday.

"He's leaving, McKenna, *for good*."

Leaving? He can't leave. What the hell is he thinking?! His whole life is here. His friends, his family, his business, everyone who loves him – me. We're all here and he's just going to walk away from all that?!

I sigh and run my hands over my face, careful not to smudge my makeup. Is this why he told me to marry Parker, because he wanted to take a job in California? The potential truth of that hits me right in the stomach. *A job is more important to him than I am.* Anger courses through me.

"I hope you realize you did this." My brother accuses.

I scoff. "*I* did this?! No, you don't get to do that. *He* doesn't get to do that! Don't you get it?! I chose him, twice! Hell, three goddamn times if you include before college. I keep choosing him, over and over and over, and for what?! So he can give some excuse as to why we can't be together and then move away to start a new life without me?! No, fuck that. I won't accept it. If he wants to be a coward, that's on him, but I *will not* take responsibility for it." I take the envelope from my purse and shove it into Maverick's chest. "I was going to give him this myself, but I don't even want to see his face. You can do it."

Turning around, I storm back inside, feeling worse than I did when I went out there. Colton is leaving. He's not going to be everywhere I turn anymore. And I'm stuck here – with everything that will always remind me of him. What a sick joke this turned out to be.

I sit down between Parker and Ivy, both of which watch me with concerned eyes. I give Ivy an 'I'll explain later' look and smile at Parker. I can do this. I can push the mentally crippling thoughts aside for a couple more hours. I'm not going to let him ruin another night for me. He's done enough of that lately.

My brother avoids my gaze as he comes back in and sits down beside Tatum. When he whispers something in her ear, her eyes widen. A silent conversation goes on between them and Roman before Tatum looks at me. Her expression says everything I don't need to hear – not right now. I shake it off and mouth 'later' at her. To my relief, she nods.

"If I could have everyone's attention, please." Parker says as he stands up with his glass. "I'd just like to make a toast to my beautiful bride. McKenna, I cannot tell you how lucky I am to be able to call you my wife in just 48 short hours. You are the brightest light on my darkest days and I love you dearly."

I blush as we all take a sip of champagne, but I don't miss the heavy stone sitting in my stomach.

THE BAR IS LOUD, but my thoughts are louder. As soon as the rehearsal dinner was over, Ivy and Tatum informed me they were taking me out for my bachelorette party. It was a welcome surprise, being as the last thing I need right now is to sit in a room with Parker and his parents. My 'I'm so happy to be marrying your son' act may not be all that convincing tonight.

Ivy smiles at something behind me, but before I can turn around, two hands cover my eyes.

"Guess who?" A voice says into my ear.

In an instant, my whole mood lightens and I spin around to find Julia standing there. "Oh my god! You're here! You're actually here!"

She chuckles. "Of course, I am. Couldn't miss the wedding of the century, could I?"

When my smile falters, it doesn't go without being

noticed. After all, we spent four years in the same cramped space. I don't think there is much I could do that she wouldn't pick up on. My every expression, every nervous habit, every thought process – she knows it like the back of her hand.

"Okay, spill." She says as she takes up the seat next to me.

"Spill what?"

"Don't give me that. I can see it all over your face, something's up." Julia looks at Ivy and Tatum who are being unusally quiet right now. "Oh my god, did he cheat on you?! Do I have to kick some English ass?!"

I look down at the table. "If you're going to hit anyone for cheating, it'd have to be me."

Her jaw drops. "McKenna Rae Taylor, you little minx." As if the lightbulb finally comes on, she gasps. "Don't tell me it was with-"

"If you say his name, there's a good chance *she'll* be the one hitting *you*." Tatum cuts her off, still rubbing the place where I punched her in the arm after she wouldn't stop talking about the bomb he dropped on Maverick tonight.

Julia moves back an inch playfully. "Alright, tell me everything."

And that's exactly what I do. We spend the next hour going over all of it – how he came onto me while helping me move, the kiss in my childhood bedroom, the almost-sex in a stingy bathroom. Ivy gets a death glare from Tatum when I mention that it was her idea for me to see things through with Colton, but Julia seems to be on her side.

"Eh, if I had known how it would turn out, I probably wouldn't have given the same advice." Ivy explains when Jules goes to give her a high five.

"Oh god, what happened?"

That's when the story takes a turn for the worst. I tell her about Roman's party and my eventual humiliation when I slept with him again after my bridal shower – only for him to send me back to Parker in the end. By the time I'm done explaining everything, or at least enough for her to understand the whole affair, I'm a mess of emotions; hurt, confused, nostalgic, exhausted.

"You need to talk to him." Julia announces.

My eyebrows furrow. "Parker?"

"Colton."

I shake my head. "I can't do that. For one, I don't even know what to say to him. And two, Parker would be so pissed. He'd prefer we just forget this summer all together."

"Yeah, well, in a perfect world, that could happen. Unfortunately, this isn't a perfect world. You need to get your feelings in order and your thoughts in line before you walk down that aisle. Otherwise, you'll just end up another statistic in the 'divorced in under a year' category."

Ivy beams from the other side of the table. "I like her."

Julia chuckles but becomes serious as she places her hand over mine. "I'm serious, Mac. You may not be able to have them both, but if you lose Colton from your life entirely, you're going to end up resenting Parker for it – and that's no way to start a marriage."

I feel like I want to scream, tell her she's wrong, and lock myself away from the world, but I know she's not. When Maverick showed me that text and I found out Colton is moving across the country, I wanted to throw up. Then, I wanted to take all my anger out on everyone around me. On Parker, for keeping me from choosing Colton months ago. On my brother, for stopping me from leaving with Colton the day of Rome's party. On Colton himself, for pushing me away after we finally made a breakthrough. However, I couldn't do any of that, not because I was at my rehearsal dinner, but because I'm more hurt than angry. It's four years later, and once again, I'm in pieces over a boy I've loved since I was seven.

"Okay." I all but whisper. "I'll try talking to him tomorrow."

Tatum crosses her arms and pouts. "Oh sure, she can say his name and get through to you, but I say it and I get punched."

The three of us laugh at her while Ivy slides Tatum's glass of wine into the center of the table. Just as I'm about to go get another drink, my phone starts ringing on the table. *Avery Brooks.*

"Uh oh." Tatum says drunkenly. "Someone's in trouble."

I roll my eyes and answer it. "Hello?"

"McKenna!" She slurs. "How are you?"

"Avery? Are you drunk?"

"No." The one word is interrupted by a hiccup. "Okay, maybe a little. I need your help. My friend wants to drive me back to her house, but she's drunk too. Can you come get me?"

"Yeah, of course. Send me the address. I'll be right there."

"Thank you."

"And Av?"

"Yeah?"

"I'm glad you called me."

We hang up the phone and I grab my wallet from the table. "We have to go pick up Avery. She's drunk at a party and needs a ride."

I look to Ivy who happens to be designated driver for tonight and she nods. The four of us close out our tab and climb into the car. I give Ivy the address. She puts it into her GPS and heads toward the house. In the meantime, I take out my phone text Colton.

McKenna: I may be the last person you want to talk to right now, but you need to meet me at the boat. It's about your sister. P.S – Plan on sleeping there tonight, and bring an extra pair of sweats.

It takes a few minutes, but just as we're pulling up to Avery sitting on the curb, a response comes through.

Colton: On my way.

I open the door and she climbs in, sandwiched between me and Julia in the backseat. She looks around at us, confused.

"Did it really take *all of you* to come get me?" She looks over my outfit and it hits her. "Oh! This was your 'I'm getting married so let's be sloppy' party, wasn't it?!"

Trying not to laugh at her choice of words, I tell Ivy to head to the docks. She gives me a look but does it anyway as Avery continues.

"I'd say I'm sorry for interrupting, but I'm not."

I snort. "Wow, Av. Tell me how you really feel."

She sinks down into the seat. "I would, but I'm drunk and mad at you. He's leaving, and it's all your fault."

"Avery." Ivy tries but I wave her off.

"It's fine. She's allowed to be mad."

"Yeah! I'm allowed to be mad."

For only being sixteen, she's drunk off her ass – probably due to her very low alcohol tolerance. Still, I've known this girl since she was a toddler. If she wants to be angry with me, that's her right. Besides, I probably deserve it.

We pull into the parking lot in front of the docks and find Colton leaning on the hood of his car. As soon as Avery sees him, she turns to glare at me.

"You told him?!"

"I had to." I explain. "If your parents see you drunk, you'd be grounded for the next year. You're going to sleep on his boat tonight."

"His boat?!" Ivy and Tatum both ask in unison.

Avery groans. "You mean the sex boat he got for the two of you? Gross."

I can feel three pairs of eyes staring at me, but I don't have time for this tonight. My main concern right now is getting Avery into bed before she vomits. I climb out of the car and help her out behind me.

"Should we wait for you?" Ivy asks.

Looking at Colton, I shake my head. "No. I've got some things to take care of here. I can walk home."

Ivy gives me a warm smile but then raises her eyebrows. "He bought a boat for you?"

I shut the back door and take a step away from the car. "I'm not getting into this with you now."

"Mhm." She teases. "Call me if you need anything."

"I will."

Watching as they drive away, I take a deep breath and then start walking towards Colton and Avery. I can tell by her face that he's lecturing her about the dangers of drinking so much. As soon as I'm close enough, I stop him.

"You're wasting your breath. She's not going to remember any of this tomorrow." I look down at what's in his hand. "Are those the clothes I asked for?"

He nods and hands them to me. "I thought they were for you."

There are so many questions those words bring, but right now is not the time for them. I put one arm around Avery and guide her down the dock, holding her steady so she doesn't fall into the water. Colton helps me get her onto the boat and I bring her down into the cabin. I'm not sure if she's starting to fall asleep or about to puke as she sways.

"Here, put these on." I hand her the sweatpants.

Thankfully, she does what I ask. Once I'm done helping her get changed, I open the door to allow Colton inside. The two of us get her tucked into bed and she falls asleep within seconds. I watch as he lovingly kisses her forehead and whispers that they're going to have a long talk tomorrow.

With Avery under control, Colton and I leave her to rest.

He follows me up the stairs and out of the cabin. As soon as he closes the door behind us, he sighs frustratedly.

"I can't believe she drank that much. It's so unlike her."

I shrug. "She just found out her favorite person in the world is moving almost 3,000 miles away. I can't say I blame her."

He winces slightly. "Y-you know?"

"Yeah." I focus on anything but him to keep from getting emotional. "Maverick told me. Everyone thinks it's my fault."

"Your fault?!" Even the idea of it seems to outrage him. "Why would they think it's your fault?"

"Isn't it?"

With the knuckle of his index finger, he lifts my chin until I'm looking right at him. The amount of sincerity in his eyes is overwhelming and I need to remind myself to breathe. He slides his hand down my arm but our gazes stay locked.

"Believe me when I say that you are not *to blame* for anything."

"But-"

He shakes his head. "Not for anything, Princess. It hurts to leave you, to leave everyone but especially you. This is just something I need to do."

I force myself to look away in fear of doing something I may regret. "This place isn't going to be the same without you."

"Maybe not at first, but soon, you'll forget all about me."

A wet laugh leaves my mouth as I wipe a stray tear from my cheek. "That will never happen. How could it when this whole place is filled with memories of you, of us?"

He sighs and turns to lean against the railing with me. "You'll be busy. Your students will keep you distracted at work, and being a wife will keep you occupied at home. Eventually, you and Parker will start a family and you'll have so many great things to look forward to. That's all I've ever wanted for you, to have everything you've ever dreamed of."

My heart is breaking as I listen to him, knowing this is likely the last time I'll see him for a while. Doesn't he realize that all I've ever dreamt of is him? For Christ sake, I've been dreaming of him since I was a child. Colton and I playing on the swings. Colton and I getting ice cream. Colton and I kissing. Colton and I getting married. Colton and I having a family. It's always been him, and now he's leaving. And me? I'm getting married to someone who *isn't* him.

I love Parker, and I know our future together is so bright. He'll always do whatever it takes to make me happy. He'll be there to listen when I need him to, and give me space when I don't want anyone around. He's the ideal fiancé and I know he'll make the perfect husband. Who knows, maybe Colton is right – but I doubt it. They say you never forget your first love, and I agree. He's burned into my memory like a permanent brand. There will never be a way to rid myself of him. My four years away are enough proof of that.

"Well, for what it's worth, I hope LA is everything you're looking for." I exhale and wipe the tears from my face. "I should get going though. Parker is probably going to get worried if I'm not home soon."

He smiles but it doesn't reach his eyes. "Right, of course. I'm glad we could clear the air before I left."

"Me too."

The two of us walk in silence back up the dock until we're on solid ground. He opens his arms for a hug and I go willingly, allowing myself one last time of being wrapped in his hold and breathing in his intoxicating scent. It goes on for what feels like forever, neither one of us wanting to let go. Finally, we separate.

"Have a good flight."

He nods. "Enjoy your wedding."

I turn away from him and take a few steps when something hits me. "Colton." I spin back around. "Remember when you asked me what my biggest regret is?"

"Yeah?"

"I can't remember our last kiss." I shrug in defeat. "That's my biggest regret. That I didn't commit it to memory so I could save it for a rainy day."

He bites his lip and at first, I think he's just not going to answer, but when I go to leave again, his voice hits my ears.

"You were half asleep. We had just made love on the boat and I asked you if you wanted anything to drink. You beckoned me toward you like you were going to whisper it in my ear or something, but instead, you put your hands on my cheeks and you kissed me."

I can feel him behind me, and his fingers skim lightly from my shoulder down to my elbow. I slowly turn to face him. He's already looking down at me, searching my eyes for something unbeknownst to me.

"Refresh my memory?" I whisper.

He smirks, putting a hand on each cheek and bringing his lips to mine. My breath hitches at how gentle it is, until I grab the collar of his sweatshirt and pull him closer. He laces his fingers into my hair and brings his other hand to my back. It's intense, and electrifying, and unlike any kiss before it. My heart hurts when it all sinks in. *This is goodbye.*

28

COLTON

I slip the key into the lock and open the door. Of course this house would be finished the day before everything changes. Stepping inside, I look around – perfection. It's exactly how I designed it; exactly how *she* explained it.

"When did you know that you wanted to be an architect?" McKenna asks with her head in my lap. She's always so curious and I swear it's going to be my undoing.

I run my fingers through her hair, feeling it's silky softness. "I was eight. My parents got me legos for my birthday and I spent the whole day building a model of my dream house. I guess I had a knack for it, even at such a young age."

Her smile brightens. "That's amazing, to be so sure of what you want that early. Do you think you'll ever build the life size version?"

"God, no. My mom showed me pictures. I put the bathroom on the front porch."

She laughs along with me. "You have to have some kind of ideal house in mind though, don't you?"

"Yeah, I guess." I tell her. "But I think I'll incorporate a little bit of it in every house I design. There are too many ideas in my head for just one place." She hums in understanding. "What about you? You ever think about your dream house?"

Taking her bottom lip between her teeth, I will myself not to get turned on. Finally, her eyes meet mine and she nods. "A piece of property up high but still overlooking the water, with no other houses in sight. An open floor plan throughout most of the downstairs, with floor to ceiling windows across the whole back wall, so you can always admire the view."

"That sounds nice. What else would it have?"

"A fireplace in white stone with a light gray granite hearth and mantle. The kitchen would be all white and there would be a wine fridge built in as one of the appliances. The whole outside would have a wrap around porch, and in the one corner would be a swing where I could sit and look out at the water – the perfect place to read."

"And bedrooms?"

"Four. All of them would be upstairs. A guest room, the master, and two for our future kids." She stops for a second. I don't miss her slip up, but she keeps going before I can delve too deep in the idea of us raising a family together. "The master would of course have a balcony, so that I could wake up in the morning and go out there to welcome the day."

If I'm being honest, I could sit here and listen to her for hours, but imagining a future together? I'm not willing to torture myself that much. One day, she'll grow up and realize she deserves so much better than me. She'll find someone else and I'll stand in the audience next to her family, watching her father give her away to someone who isn't me. I'm not delusional enough to think I'm the lucky bastard that will get to grow old with her. Even so, one day I'm going to build her that dream house.

For the rest of the summer after that conversation, we always managed to go back to the topic. She would throw out little details here and there, and I secretly wrote down every single one – not that I needed to. There isn't much McKenna has told me that I've ever forgotten. Each memory I have with her is too sacred to let it slip my mind.

I sit down at the table and take a deep breath before putting my pen to paper.

Dear McKenna,

Congratulations on getting married. I always knew you would find someone who'd make you as happy as you deserve. I hope your future together is everything you've ever imagined it would be. Thank you for being there for me when I needed you, and for giving me a chance to say goodbye properly. You are, have been, and always will be my favorite memory. Maybe one day I'll come to visit, and you and I will be able to talk like we once did, when things weren't so complicated. You'll tell me about how perfect your life is, and I'll hang on every word, because that's all I've ever wanted – for you to have true happiness. I'm so glad you found someone to give you that.

Enclosed in this envelope is my gift to you. I've already had my lawyer transfer the deed into your name. If you have any questions, his card is in there too. Please don't try to tell me it's too much, or that you can't accept it. This place was yours from the start. It's only right that I leave it to you.

I hope you achieve everything you want in life. I've been so lucky to have known you.

I love you.

I sign my name and slip the letter into the envelope with the deed and the keys. Admiring the breathtaking view once more, the swing catches my eye. I can picture it already – McKenna rocking back and forth with a little girl in her lap, reading her a story. It's almost painful to picture, knowing I won't be a part of it.

─────────

THAT NIGHT, I'M CARRYING my suitcase out to my car when Maverick pulls in the driveway. He eyes me with disdain before sighing and giving me a manly hug. I know he's not happy about me leaving, but he understands why I feel like I need to.

"You're not going to become one of those stuck-up California guys, are you?"

I laugh. "Not a chance. And if I do, I'm sure you'll come kick my ass for it."

"You better believe it." He leans against my car and eyes the envelope on the seat. "What's that?"

"Oh." I reach in and pull it out. "I need you to give this to your sister for me, but wait until after the wedding."

He takes it from me and, despite my protests, opens it. As soon as he sees the deed, his eyes widen. "Is this…?"

I nod. "You can see it when she does, but you have to promise me you'll give that to her."

"Any chance of you giving it to her yourself?" He asks hopefully.

I shake my head. "You know I can't do that. Saying goodbye to her last night was hard enough. I can't do it again. Besides, I don't want to ruin her wedding day."

He reluctantly places the envelope in his car, but takes out a smaller one when he does. "Apparently, you two think alike. This is from her."

It's a white, card-like envelope with my name written across the front. A part of me considers opening it now, but I don't need Maverick watching me as I do. I slip it under the visor in my car and remind myself to open it when I get to the airport. Roman will be coming to pick up my beloved

GTO after the wedding, and he'll be shipping it to California for me in a couple weeks. Unfortunately, I just don't know if it would survive a full drive across the country.

"Alright, let's go have a drink for your last night in town." Maverick suggests.

I consider turning him down, but I know it would be a lost cause. I'll tell him no, and he'll tell me I have no choice in the matter. Better to save us both some time and energy, and just agree to go.

"HERE'S TO YOU, BROOKS. May you be just as much of an overachiever in LA as you were here." Maverick toasts.

As soon as we got here, Tatum, Roman, and Ivy were all waiting for us – a makeshift going away party of sorts. We spend the night drinking and reminiscing on the good times. Of course, Maverick has enough embarrassing memories to last a lifetime, and the more he drinks, the more he shares. By the end of the night, Ivy and Tatum know more about me than I had ever wanted.

When it hits midnight, we all decide it's time to go. I have a flight to catch in the morning, and they have a wedding to attend. We head out to the parking lot and I start to say goodbye.

Ivy is first. I give her a hug and chuckle when she whispers 'you two are idiots' into my ear. I don't even bother denying it. After the summer we put that girl through, she deserves a medal.

Roman is next, and significantly harder considering he's been at my side every day for the last three years. I make sure to tell him to make his move on Ivy already, because if he doesn't, someone else will. The last thing I want is for him to be in the same predicament I am.

After giving Rome a hug, I climb into the car with

Maverick and Tatum. The whole ride back to the house is quiet and it isn't until we get inside that Tatum starts to cry.

"Tate." I murmur.

She rolls her teary eyes and slaps my chest. "Shut up."

I pull her into my arms and kiss her head. This girl may be a royal pain in my ass at times, but she's one of my best friends. At times, she was the only one who could talk some sense into me, especially when it came to McKenna. I don't know what I'm going to do without her constant nagging.

"You know I'm just a seven-hour flight away. I'll even buy your ticket."

She sniffles. "I'm going to hold you to that."

"I hope you do."

As we let break apart, she goes into her room and leaves Maverick and I alone. He needs to leave bright and early tomorrow, so I know this is going to be the last time I'm seeing him for a while. If I thought saying goodbye to everyone else was hard, nothing beats this – except McKenna.

"You better come back to be my best man." He orders.

I chuckle. "Wouldn't miss it for the world."

"No chance of talking you out of this, is there?"

"Afraid not, man."

He thinks for a moment, then sighs. "I'm going to be girly for a minute and you're not going to give me any shit for it." I laugh but let him continue. "You're going to text me every day, and you're going to call me every night. No exceptions."

"Are we going to exchange pretty bracelets, too?" I can't resist and tease him anyway.

"Don't tempt me, asshole."

We embrace for a minute and try to hide that we're both crying. Refusing to say the word goodbye, we nod instead and go into our separate bedrooms. As soon as the door shuts behind me, the emotions take over. *Well, here goes nothing.*

I END UP GETTING a late start and get stuck in traffic on my way to the airport. Thankfully, I left with plenty of time to spare before my flight leaves. As I ease the car up further, the sun peaks through the trees and shines right into my eyes. I pull down the visor, causing the envelope from McKenna to fall in my lap. *I may as well open this now. Nothing better to do.*

Breaking the seal, I open the flap and pull out the picture that was tucked inside. It's a familiar one of Maverick, McKenna, and I on the beach. I can still remember the day Ivy took it like it was yesterday. We were so happy and didn't have a care in the world. The picture looks a little worn, like she's been carrying it around in her pocket. There's even a crease down the middle where it was folded. I flip it over and see her handwriting on the back.

Thank you for always being my happy place.

Her happy place. I turn it back to the front and look at her face – it's the same smile I'd go through hell and back to put on her face. My mind flashes to all the time I've seen that smile since then – the picnic on the beach; while we sailed across the ocean in the boat named after her; when I handed her a glass of her favorite wine at the club. All this time I've been too blind to see it. *I'm* what makes her happy. I spin the car around, illegally crossing the grass median, and press the gas pedal to the floor. I really hope I'm not too late.

MCKENNA

I stand in the mirror, looking at myself in the dress I've always imagined. It's been altered to fit me perfectly, accenting all the right places. My makeup is professionally done and my hair is curled to look like something out of a magazine. The veil sits neatly on top of my head and flows down my back. It's all exactly how I pictured it. *Well, almost.*

"Are you ready to go?" Ivy asks.

I nod, and follow her and Tatum out to the limo where my mother is waiting for us. Just before I climb in, a plane in the sky catches my attention. Thoughts of Colton fill my head, reminding me of how he's leaving today. I take a deep breath and shake the thoughts away. Tomorrow, I'll let myself be sad. Today, I get married.

The ride to the venue is filled with champagne toasts and happy smiles. Even Ivy seems to have gotten over her doubts about me going through with the wedding. We pose for pictures and gush over how pretty we look – no matter how vain it may be.

As we get inside, I smile at my brother who's been patiently waiting for us to arrive. His breath hitches as he looks me over. "You look beautiful, McKenna."

"Thank you."

When all the planning started, I asked Maverick to walk me down the aisle. However, standing here and getting ready to make one of the most important commitments of my life, something feels missing.

"Can you do me a favor?" I ask him hesitantly, not knowing how he will react to my request.

His brows furrow. "Anything. What do you need?"

"Go get dad for me."

My words seem to shock everyone within hearing distance, but he agrees and walks through the doors – the same doors that have my future husband right on the other side of them. I swallow down the lump in my throat as my brother comes back with our dad at his side.

"What's wrong, sweetheart? Is everything okay?"

There was such a long time where I resented him for what he did to our mom, but after this summer, I've never understood it more. Cheating was wrong of him, but it doesn't mean that he didn't love her. There could be a countless number of reasons why he did it, but all that matters, is what he did after. My mom was able to forgive him, why can't I? If we're ever going to make amends and get back to the family we once were, a step needs to be made.

I nod, looking to my brother and then back to him. "I'd like for both of you to walk me down the aisle, if that's okay."

He gasps and his eyes well with tears. "Are you sure?"

"Yes." My eyes meet Maverick's and he grins, understanding exactly where I'm coming from. "Absolutely."

Tatum comes back into the room and tells us that once the music starts playing, we'll begin. I do my best to compose my emotions. Just as the sound of the piano comes from the other room, the front doors burst open. Ivy squeals and I whirl around to see Colton standing here, breathing heavily.

"What are you doing here?! I thought you were getting on a plane today."

"I am." He pants. "Unless you can give me a reason to stay."

"Colton…" I say unsurely, but he cuts me off.

"No, just hear me out." He steps toward me. "I have made more than my fair share of mistakes when it comes to you. I've been reckless, and I've hurt you, and I thought I ruined any chance we had together, but what if I didn't? For the last two weeks, I've been convincing myself that you're better off with him. God knows he's the better man for you. He's the one you *should* choose, but I'm standing here anyway, asking you to pick me. I may not be the better man, but if you give me the chance, I will spend every single day proving that I can be deserving of you. Be with me, Princess.

Grow old with me, because he may be able to make you happy, but he will never love you like I do."

The music goes quiet as I stand there, gaping at him and willing myself to say something, anything.

"I don't want to hurt you." I tell him.

"Then don't."

The familiarity in the words is not lost on me. My heart is pounding inside my chest as the room stays quiet. It's all too much, too fast. I take a deep breath when behind me, the door opens and my fiancé's British accent fills the room.

"McKenna? Is everything alright?"

I look at Parker and then back at Colton – speechless as they both wait for an answer.

EPILOGUE

MCKENNA

FIVE YEARS LATER

I WAKE UP TO THE FEELING OF A TINY HUMAN jumping on my bed. Peeking my eyes open, I see Tanner, my three-year-old son, excitedly staring down at me. I reach up and grab him, wrapping him tightly in my arms as he giggles happily.

"Wake up, Mommy."

I groan and pretend to still be asleep. "Mmm. Cuddle with my teddy."

"I'm not a teddy, I'm Tanner!"

"Tanner teddy." I grumble, trying not to smile as he peels my eyelids open.

"You have to wake up, Mommy. Grandma's downstairs and she says you need to get out of bed or you lazy."

I sigh and rub my hand over my eyes. "Okay, okay. I'm up."

Throwing on a pair of my favorite sweats, I scoop up my son and carry him down the stairs. My mom is sitting at the table, reading the newspaper with two cups of coffee – one for me and one for her. I put Tanner down and tell him to go play with Grandpa, smiling as he runs over to my dad.

"Good morning, honey." My mother greets me.

"Morning." I murmur, mentally thanking her for the caffeine dose. Who knew children could be so tiresome?

She hands me the newspaper turned to the front page. "Have you seen this?"

I look down at the marriage announcement that covers most of the page. My ex's face is front and center with his new bride. I knew it was coming, having heard from Tatum that they were planning their wedding. I honestly thought it would sting, seeing him married to someone else, but looking at this picture, it only assures me that I made the right choice all those years ago. He's content and in a good place. That's all I ever wanted.

"I'm happy for him." I smile.

Taking the coffee mug in my hands, I walk out the back door and over to the swing. The ring on my finger glistens in the sunlight, matching the one on the man next to me. I lay my head on his shoulder as we watch our son run around with my dad.

"Thank you." I tell him.

"For what?"

"Never giving up on us, no matter how hard things got."

He rests his head on top of mine and reaches over to hold my hand. "Of course, Princess."

I smile at the infamous nickname that never seems to go away, not that I ever want it to. It's a part of us, of our story. And everything that has to do with us, is everything I cherish.

"I love you, McKenna."

"I love you too, Colton. There's never been a day where I haven't."

Thank you so much for reading Returning to Rockport.

I hope you enjoyed reading McKenna and Colton's story as much as I enjoyed writing it. If you could take the time to leave a review, I would greatly appreciate it. This book is something that I put a lot of time, effort, and emotion into, and one that I'm especially proud of. While it may be controversial, it's a real life situation that people go through.

Keep a lookout for the spin offs titled Wrapped in Ivy (staring Ivy and Roman) & Taylor Made (a prequel staring Maverick and Tatum) - both coming in 2020.

Sign up for my newsletter to get exclusive content and updates on new releases and giveaways. Also, like my facebook page and join my reader group to stay up to date on everything I have coming out soon.

Thank you so much for reading my books and supporting my writing. You are all incredible.

♥ ✌ Kels

www.kelseyclayton.com

Books By

KELSEY CLAYTON

The Sleepless November Saga

Sleepless November

Endless December

Seamless Forever

Awakened in September

Standalones

Returning to Rockport

Made in the USA
Las Vegas, NV
02 March 2021

18876443R00219